Three Trapped Tigers

the text of this book is printed
on 100% recycled paper

Three Trapped Tigers

G. CABRERA INFANTE

Translated from the Cuban by
DONALD GARDNER *and* SUZANNE JILL LEVINE
in collaboration with the author

HARPER COLOPHON BOOKS
Harper & Row, Publishers
New York, Hagerstown, San Francisco, London

For Miriam,
to whom this book owes a lot
more than it seems

A hardcover edition of this book is published by Harper & Row, Publishers, Inc.
Assistance for the translation of this volume was given by the Center for Inter-American Relations.
The book was first published in Spain under the title *Tres Tristes Tigres*.

First HARPER COLOPHON edition published 1978

ISBN: 0-06-090636-7

Designed by Lydia Link

78 79 80 81 82 10 9 8 7 6 5 4 3 2 1

". . . And she tried to fancy what the flame of a candle looks like after the candle is blown out."

LEWIS CARROLL

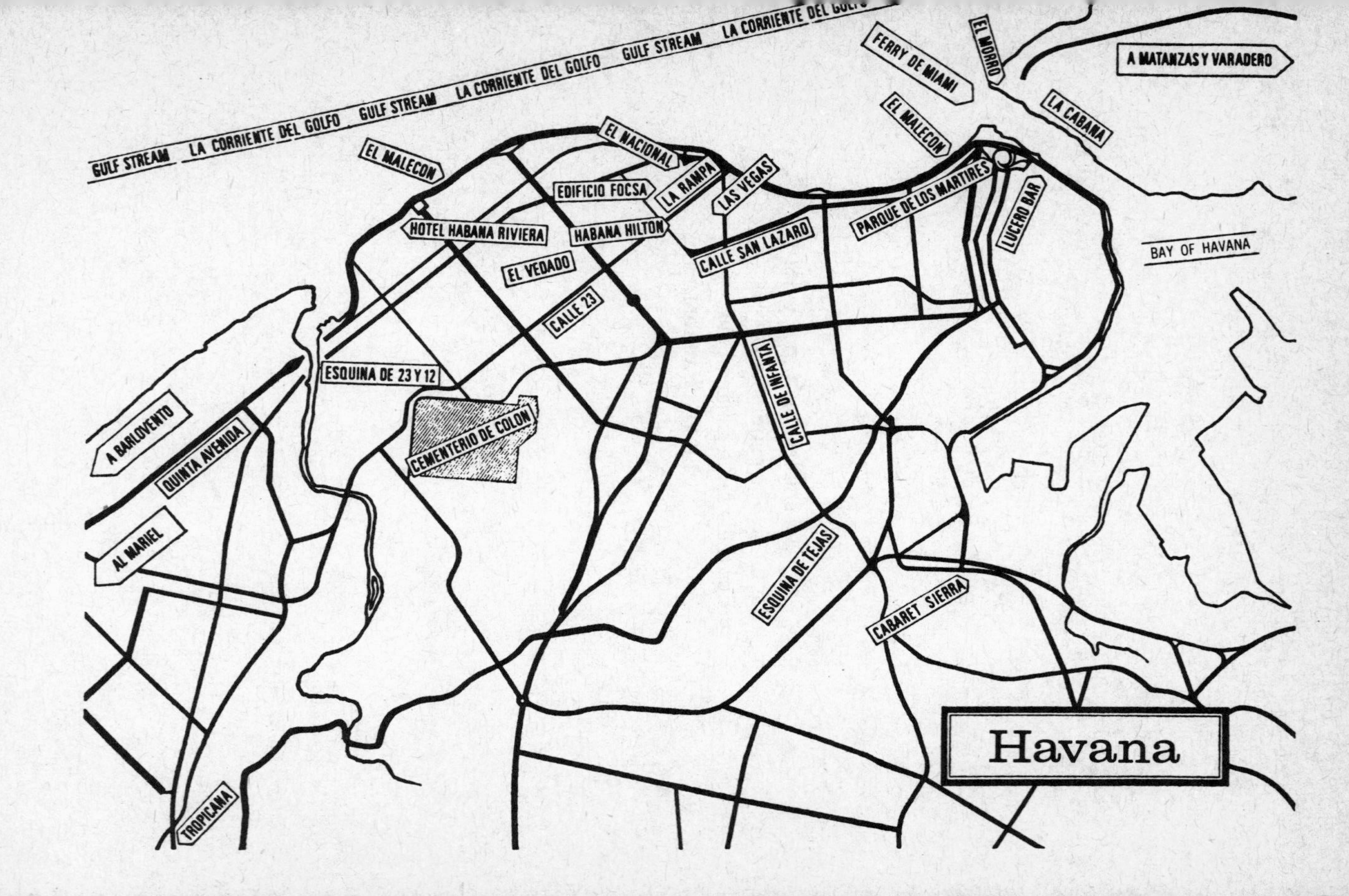
Havana
A MATANZAS Y VARADERO
BAY OF HAVANA
LA CABANA
EL MORRO
LUCERO BAR
FERRY DE MIAMI
EL MALECON
PARQUE DE LOS MARTIRES
CABARET SIERRA
ESQUINA DE TEJAS
CALLE DE INFANTA
LAS VEGAS
CALLE SAN LAZARO
LA RAMPA
EL NACIONAL
EDIFICIO FOCSA
HABANA HILTON
CALLE 23
EL VEDADO
HOTEL HABANA RIVIERA
CEMENTERIO DE COLON
EL MALECON
ESQUINA DE 23 Y 12
QUINTA AVENIDA
A BARLOVENTO
AL MARIEL
TROPICANA
GULF STREAM
LA CORRIENTE DEL GOLFO
GULF STREAM
LA CORRIENTE DEL GOLFO
GULF STREAM
LA CORRIENTE DEL GOLFO

PROLOGUE

Showtime! *Señoras y señores.* Ladies and gentlemen. And a very good evening to you all, ladies and gentlemen. *Muy buenas noches, damas y caballeros.* Tropicana! the MOST fabulous nightclub in the WORLD—*el cabaret* MAS *fabuloso del mundo*—presents—*presenta*—its latest show—*su nuevo espectáculo*—where performers of Continental fame will take you all to the wonderful world of supernatural beauty of the Tropics—*al mundo maravilloso y extraordinario y hermoso:* The Tropic in the Tropicana! *El Trópico en Tropicana!* In the marvelous production of our Rodney the Great—*el gran Roderico Neyra*—entitled *Me voy pal Brasil*—that means "Going to Brazil." . . . *Brazuil terra dye nostra felichidade.* That was Brezill for you, ladies and gentlemen, in Brassilian! *El Brasil brasileiro, damas y caballeros que me escucháis esta noche.* That is my very, very particular version of it! *Es decir, mi versión del Brazil de Carmen Miranda y de Joe Carioca*—Brasil, the land of Carmen Miranda and Joe Carioca. But—*Pero*—Brazil, dear public assembled here in this coliseum of pleasure and gaiety and happiness! *Brasil una vez más y siempre*—Brazil once and for always, eternal Brazil, honorable and dear visitors to our Romance Forum of song and dance and love by candlelight!! Ouh, ouh, ouh! ooh! la! la! My apologies! . . . *Público amable, amable público, pueblo de Cuba, la tierra* MAS *hermosa que ojos humanos vieran, como dijo el Descubridor Colón* (*eso es, el colón de las carabelas—ho ho ho!*) . . . *Pueblo, público, queridos concurrentes, perdonen un momento mientras me dirijo a la selecta concurrencia que colma todas y cada unas de las localidades de este emporio del amor y la vida risueña. Quiero hablarles, si la amabilidad proverbial del Respetable cubano me lo permite, a los caballerosos y radiantes turistas que visitan nuestra tierra*—to our ENORMOUS American audience of glamorous and distinguished tourists who are visiting the land of the gay senyoritas and brave caballerros. . . . For your exclusive pleasure, ladies and gentlemen, our Good Neighbors, you that are now in Cuba, the most beautiful land human eyes have ever seen, as Christofry Callumbus, the *Dis*coverer, said once, you, hap-py visitors, are, once and for all, welcome. WelcoME to Cuba! All of you . . . be WELLcome! *Bienvenidos!* as we say in our romantic language, the language of colonizadors and toreros (bullfighters) and very, very, but verry (I know what I say) beautiful duennas. I know that you are here to sunbathe and seabathe and sweatbathe—ha ha ha! . . . My excuses, thousand of apologies for You-There that are freezing in this cold of the rich that sometimes is the chill of our coolness and the sneeze of our colds: the Air-Conditioned, I mean. For you as for everyone here, it's time to get warm and our coming show will do that for you. In fact, to many of you it will mean heat! And I mean, with my apologies to the very, verry old-fashioned ladies in the audience, I mean Heat. And when, laydies and gentlemen, I mean heat—is HEAT! *Estimable, muy estimado, estimadísimo público, ahora para ustedes una traducción literaria. Decía yo a mis amigos americanos, a los buenos vecinos del Norte que nos visitan, les decía, damas y caballeros, caballeros y damas, señoras y señoritas y . . . señoritos, que de todo tenemos esta noche . . . Le decía a la amable concurrencia norteña que pronto, muy pronto, en unos segundos, esa cortina de plata y lamé dorado que distingue el escenario prestigioso de Tropicana—el cabaret más lujoso del mundo!—les decía que el frío invernal bajo techo de esta noche de verano tropical, hielo del trópico bajo los arcos de cristal de Tropicana, se derretirá muy pronto con el calor y la pimienta de nuestro primer gran show de la noche. Calor y sabor!* Back to you, *amigos!* I was telling them that the cold winter under the roof of this night of tropical summer, ice of the tropics under the crystal arcades of the Tropicana . . . (Are you with me? DEE-VAHN!)—this cold of the rich of our air-conditioned will very soon melt in the heat and the spicy piquant of our first great show of the evening, salt & pepper, when this curtain of silver and gold lamé rises. But first, with the excuses of my kind audience, I would like to welcome some old friends to this palace of happiness. . . . Ladies and gentlemen, tonight we are honored by one famous and lovely and talented guest . . . *la bella, gloriosa, famosa estrella del cine, madmuasel Martín Carol! Luces, luces! Miss Carol, tendría la amabilidad . . . ? Gracias, muchas gracias, señorita Carol!* As they say in your language, Merdsi Bocú! (Asyouhaveseenmydearaudienceitisthevisitofthe-greatstarofthescreenthebeautifulglamorousMartínCarol!) Less beautiful but as rich and as famous is our very good friend and frequent guest of Tropicana, the wealthy and healthy (he is an early riser) Mr. William Campbell, the notorious soup-fortune heir and world champion of indoor golf and indoor tennis (and other not so mentionable indoor sports—ha ha ha!). William Campbell, our favorite playboy! Lights (Thank you, Mr. Campbell), lights, lights! Thanks so much, Mr. Campbell! Thank you very much! (*Amableypacientepúblicocubanoes Mister Campbell elfamosomillonario herederodeunafortunaensopas.*) Is also with us tonight the Great Emperor of the Shyners, His Excellency Mr. Lincoln Lee Uggu. Mr. Lincoln Lee? Mr. Lee Uggu? (*Es el señor* Lincoln Lee Uggu, *emperador de los Shyners, paciente público.*) Thank YOU, Mr. Uggu. Ladies and gentlemen, with your kind permission . . . Cubans, countrymen, it is now time for us to give a warm hand to our clientele in the courtyard, who have welcomed with the proverbial generosity and typical courtesy of the Criollos, so typically ours, typically Cuban as these palm trees which you see at the end of the salon and these *guayaberas* (with a black tie, eh?) which is the typical dress of the elegant *habanero,* with that typical hospitality as always—our typitality, ho ho ho!—you have allowed *us* to present to *you* first our international clientele. Now, as is only fitting, it is the turn of the more familiar spectators of our social, political and cultural life. I will pass on to the triumphant and serious youth and the invincible and juvenile Cold Age! I pass on to the most delightful and enchanting audience in the Universe-WORLD! Lights, please? Thank you! That's better. I want to extend a hand to the enchanting jeune-fille, as our society columnists say, Miss Vivian Smith-Corona Alvarez de Real, who is celebrating tonight her fifteenth birthday and has chosen to spend it with the always glorious showcase of the nightclub under the stars, tonight under its canopy of glass because of the rain and bad weather. May all her desires be fulfilled, fifteen golden springtimes, ah! which for ourselves have long ago passed. Though we can console ourselves saying we are only fifteen years old—but twice over. Our heartimost congratulations, Vivian. Happy, happy birthday! Let's all sing the happy birthday to Vivian. *Todos juntos!* All together! Happy birthday to you, happy birthday to you, happy birthday, dear Vivian, happy birthday to you! Now let's show a little spirit there and all of you sing it, altogether, I don't want to see one of you staying silent, together with Vivian's mother and father, Mr. and Mrs. Smith-Corona Alvarez de Real, whom you can see surrounding their precious and adorable offspring! Come on, put your hearts into it! *Todos juntos ahora!* All together now! Happy birthday to you, happy birthday to you, happy birthday, dear Vivian, happpyyy-birthdaaayyy tooo-yyyoouuuuuu! That's the way it's done! *Así se hace!* Very good! Now to more serious things. *También tenemos el honor de tener entre nuestra selectísima concurrencia al coronel Cipriano Suarez Dámera, M.M., M.N., R. y P. . . . pundonoroso militar y correcto caballero, acompañado, como siempre, por su bella y gentil esposa, Arabella Longoria de Suárez Dámera*—It's none other than Colonel Damera, an exemplary soldier and perfect gentleman, and his beautiful, gracious and elegant wife, Arabella Damera. *Una buena noche feliz para usted, Coronel, en compañía de su esposa*—A very pleasant and happy evening to the colonel and his missus. *Veo por allí, en esa mesa, si ahí mismo, junto a la pista*—by the side of the Silvery Moon!—*al senador y publicista doctor Viriato Solaún, concurrencia frecuente al interior de este domo del placer*—Dr. Viriato Solaún, a frequent visitor to the innards of this pleasure dome, the *Tropicana!* I see the senator and publisher is keeping good company as always. *Paso a la cultura!* And now from the world of culture we have someone who truly adorns our evenings at the Tropicana, the beautiful elegant and sophisticated poetess Minerva Eros, a reciter of the utmost dramatic perfection and with a refined and exquisite voice: the verses she speaks rhyme with velvet and are sweet and caressing. *La elegante y sotifiscada poetisa.* MINERVA EROS! Lights! Lights! LIGHTS! (*Coño!*) Just a minute, *amigo,* please, it's the ladies' turn now. But—hold it!—if it isn't our great Great Photographer of the Stars! *Sí, el Gran Fotógrafo de las Estrellas!* Not a great astronomer but our friend, the Official Photographer of Cuban Beauties. *El Gran Códac!* Let's greet him as he deserves. *Un aplauso!* A round of applause for the Great Códac. And now finally we have Minerva, Minerva Eros for you, dear audience. *Aplausos, aplausos!* A round of applause. That's right. I want to announce to you that starting next month, Minerva will adorn the last show—every night!—at Tropicana! with her classical manner and her sculptor's figure plus her voice, which is the voice of culture itself. Until then, I give you Minerva! *Tomen Minerva!* And all the best! No, thank *you,* Minerva, who but you is the muse of our tables? *La musa de las mesas!* And now—*señoras y señores*—ladies and gentlemen—*públicoquesabeloquesbueno*—discriminatory public, without translation—*sin traducción* . . . Without words but with your admiration and your applause . . . Without words but with music and happiness and joy . . . To you all! Our first great show of the evening—*El primer Gran Show de la noche* in *Tropicana!* Curtains up! *Arriba el telón!*

BEGINNERS

But what we *never* told anyone was that we too used to play with each other's things under the truck. We did tell everything else and all the people of the town heard about it and came and asked us questions and wanted to know all about it. Mommy was proud too and whenever people came to our house on a visit, she'd invite them in for coffee, and when coffee was served they drank it in one gulp and then put the cup, very gently, as carefully as possible on the table as if the cup was made of eggshells and then they all looked at me smiling but pretending not to know anything at all. Afterward they always asked me the same question all sweet and innocent: *"Come over here, little girl. Tell me what you were up to under the truck."* I said nothing and then Mommy would stand in front of me and put her hand under my chin and say, "Tell them what you saw, child. Just like you told me, don't be shy." I wasn't shy or anything, but I wouldn't say a thing unless Aurelita was there and so they always went to look for Aurelita and she came with her mommy and both of us told it all together and as well as we could. We knew we were the center of attraction in the neighborhood, the whole town, the neighborhood first and the whole town later on. So that when we went out for our Sunday walk in the park, all nice and proper, looking neither left nor right, not stopping for anyone, we knew everyone was staring at us and that when we went by they'd whisper and give us funny looks and so forth.

All that week Mommy put on my new dress and I went out to look for Aurelita (who was also putting on a new dress) and we strolled up and down main street till sundown. And the whole town ran to their doors to see us go by and sometimes someone called us from a house and we told the whole story again.

By the end of the week everybody had heard it and they no longer called us or asked us anything. That's when Aurelita and I began making things up. Each time we added more details to the story and we came very close to saying what we'd really done but Aurelita and me, we *always* stopped just short and so we never let on that she and I were playing with each other's things while we watched what was going on. When Ciana Cabrera and her daughter finally moved to Pueblo Nuevo, they gave up asking and then Aurelita and I caught on and before you could say Jack Rabbit we were in Pueblo Nuevo telling everybody. Every time we invented something I was quite willing to cross my heart and swear to die it was true, because I could no longer tell truth from lies. In Pueblo Nuevo it was different, it was mostly the men who asked us and they always stood in the store on the outskirts with their elbows on the counter and cigars in their mouths, winking as if they knew the story by heart, but they always seemed keen to hear and asked us to tell them all about it, as if it was news to them, saying in a very low voice, "*Come over here, girls,*" and they made us come just a little closer though we were close enough and then they said, "Now tell us just what you were up to under that truck." The funniest thing was that every time I heard the question I thought they were really asking something else, like what were we *really* up to under the truck, and more than once it almost slipped out. But we always told the story, me and Aurelita, and we never, never let on that we were also playing with each other's things under the truck.

What happened was that Aurelita and I went to the movies on Thursdays, because it was ladies' day though it was actually night, but we didn't go to the movies after all. Mommy gave me a nickel and Aurelita came to pick me up early and we made as if we were going to the movies every Thursday, because on Thursday children only had to pay five cents. In the theater they always showed love movies with Jorge Negrete and Carlos Gardel and so on, and we soon got bored and left and went to the park and started doing it. Sometimes they showed funny movies and that made us laugh, but the other kind, as soon as they started singing and kissing we got up and left and hid under the tobacco truck. When the tobacco truck wasn't there we hid in the long grass in the vacant lot. It was more difficult to see from there, but when the truck wasn't there they did a lot more things. Petra's boyfriend, Petra that's Ciana's daughter, would come every Thursday. I mean he came on Thursdays and also on Sundays. On Sundays they would go into the park but on Thursdays we made as if we were going to the movies and went to look through the open door instead. Petra's mother also stayed in the house but at the far end of it and as the floor was made of wood it creaked loudly when she was coming and then she'd get up and return to sitting in her own seat and she'd come and talk or look through the window and gaze up and down the street or she would look at the sky or make believe she was looking at the sky or at the street and then she'd go back in and stay there. But between the time Petra's mother went into the house and when she came to the sitting room to talk or look out the window, they made full use of the place, and as for us, we got a front-row view, as they always left the door open to make everything look innocent.

It always began the same way. She would be sitting in her rocking chair and he'd be in his, like this, side by side, and she'd always be wearing a hoop skirt but in her customary half-mourning, and sitting in the rocking chair good as gold, talking or making as if she was talking. Then, when the old lady was safe inside, she'd turn her head and then he took out his thing and she began to touch it, to run her hand over it, and then fondling it, she would look out to see if the old woman was coming or not, then she got up from the rocking chair, picked up her skirts and sat in his lap and she began moving and he began rocking and all of a sudden she jumped up and sat down in her chair and he simply crossed his leg, like this, so that the old lady wouldn't notice anything, and the old lady would go to the window and look at the street innocent-like or look at the sky or make believe she was and go back in again and they'd start necking again. They spent the whole night like this, she touching his thing and him handling her and then she got down and put her head between his legs and stayed there for a while and then suddenly she sat up and it was because her mother was coming again and she would come and peer out of the window or else he would put on an act and talk to the old woman and laugh and all and she, Petra, would laugh too and talk in a high voice and the old woman would go to the window again and then back in once more and this time she would stay a long time, saying her prayers or something like that because she was very religious and always said prayers, especially since her husband died. Then they'd take up where they left off and began really making it and as we could see it all from our hiding place so we took full advantage of it too.

The scandal began the day though it was night that we were almost killed by the truck. The driver started it up without realizing we were underneath and we were within an inch of being crushed by the rear wheels but we began to scream and scream again and everyone rushed out to see what was going on. I think the driver didn't know we were under the truck but sometimes I think sure the driver knew and was probably the only one who did. The fact is everyone rushed out and the driver stood there shouting at us and Petra shouted at us and so did Petra's boyfriend and Petra's mother, Ciana, she didn't shout at us, but she told us she was going to tell my mother and Aurelita's mother as well, and it was then that we decided that if she, Ciana Cabrera, was going to tell, we were going to tell too. She told, so we told too. I was positive Mommy was going to spank me but when I told her everything she cracked up laughing and said it was about time Petra made it. It seemed she meant Petra was quite old and that she and her boyfriend had been going together for about ten years, and it was about time, so everyone said. But what my mother really said was, "Well, looks like Petra made up her mind to get married behind the church after all." I know this didn't mean Petra got married in another part of the church, at the back of it, but that it meant something else but I knew quite well that I wasn't supposed to say it (just as I couldn't say what we were doing under the truck) so I asked Mommy, "Mommy, how can you get married behind the back of the church? With no priest?" and Mommy nearly split her sides laughing. "Yes, love, just like that: without the priest," and she almost choked herself to death. Then she went and called the neighbors.

This was how Aurelita and I began to tell the story of what had happened and whenever someone arrived at the house all he had to do was to say good evening or good morning or good afternoon (by this time Mommy had stopped serving coffee) and then ask, *"Come here, children. What were you up to under the truck?"* And we told the story again and again and again till we came within an inch of telling what we were *really* doing under the truck. But then Ciana Cabrera and Petra her daughter moved to Pueblo Nuevo, which isn't really either *nuevo* nor a *pueblo* but a shanty town at the other end of our town where people live in houses with dirt floors and thatched roofs, and as the neighbors left off asking us to tell them the story, Aurelita and I decided to go to Pueblo Nuevo every day when school was out, so that they'd ask us, *"Come here, girls. Tell us what you were up to under the truck."*

It was in Pueblo Nuevo that we learned that Petra's boyfriend had never come back to the town on Thursdays or on Sundays either and that afterward he only came back on Sundays just to take a walk in the park and we knew that Petra didn't go out at all as her mother kept the door locked all day and as she wasn't speaking to anyone in Pueblo Nuevo they no longer had any dealings with anyone, not like before when they had always been paying calls on people and vice versa.

Havana April 22 1953

My dear Estelvina,

I am hoping that this letter finds you and yours well. As for us here neither good or bad. Estelvina your letter was a wonderful surprise. You don't know what a thrill it is to get a letter from you after such a long time that you haven't written to us. Now I understand that you was right to be standoffish and strict with us after everything that has happened though in fact it was hardly our fault if Gloria your daughter ran away from home and came to shelter here in Havana. Don't forget she pulled a fast one on us too, telling us like she did youd sent her here to study and she even showed us a letter which she said you had written yourself and in this letter you said that youd sent her here so she could study and get herself a decent job and we were stupid enough to believe it because we read it and didn't give it another thought. So we let her sleep here and you know what that means without being told because we all live in one room so you can imagine theres not much room left.

Now youre asking after her and you say she hasnt written you for over eihgt months now, so I have to tell you that its also been a long time that we haven't heard a thing from her either, not so much as a word. I don't know if where you are living now which as Gilberto says is where you may lose your own shadow, you can get Bohemia the magasine. If Basilio doesnt bring one with him when he next goes to town Ill send you a copy myself which is ours but you can consider yours and so youll know what your daughter has been getting upto. It seem she's been working as a girl model which is not in the least as decent as it sounds. I don't know if you happen to know that she beggan working hear a cupla weeks after she arrived in Havana city and that she got a job as baby sister taking care of children in a private address on El Vedado a classy district here in Havana though not Havana proper. The thing is when we asked her were she was studying she told us she had no intention of studying anymore, those were her words and whats more she told us she wasnt going to spend four or five years in the prime of her life killing herself working days and studing nights and never go out and enjoy herself only to end up working like a dog in some office or other and get as much money as a dogflea, thats what she said and further more she added that if she had any studying to do she'll be doing it from now on at the School of Hard Knox, her very words.

I swear to God Estel I felt like slapping her face twice, she said it with such nerve and effrontery and put on so many airs when she was speaking she sounded like an old hore though she cant be more than sixteen your own daughter. Thank God Gilberto was there to stop me by saying to me right in front of her after all she was no daughter of mine and I had enough to do minding my own business and let the rest of the world take care of itself. Your daughter, you know what she said? Thats exactly what I think myself, she said to us and then just to me youd better follow your husband's advice she said and then she left. She didn't come back to my house for about two weeks or so at least and when she came back next she came back very properly and modestly dressed and asking for me to forgive her on account of her past behavior towards me and she said she had given up baby sistering and that now she was working in a beauty parlor and as she was making much more money there it suited her better, so she was moving into a boarding house close to work.

I swear to you Estel that I was even pleased to hear it and I swear by all thats sacred on earth and the All Mighty Estel that I remember when we was children and played in the yard at the sugar mill and went to school together and all the good times we had and you know what a silly woman and how emotional I am I burst into tears at the slightest which I did then so much so Gilberto had to put an end to it by getting mad at me and saying I was crying for cryings sake, which it simply isn't tru. So we quareled over it and werent speaking to each other for about a week or so and to top it off it was just then your letter came, which Im telling you because you were always like a sister to me, that close. It hurted me very deep and made me cry so much I had to hid myself like a criminal though it was only tears. Well I suppose that evrythings bygones even bygones can be bygones as Gilberto says, so I gotten over that little upset bynow. But I can swear to you by the Blessed Virgin Mary that we didn't know a thing about all this bussines and that this daughter of your who dont look like a daughter of your at all could pull the wool over the eyes of God Himself if she only had the chance to go to heaven.

The thing is she came by here a little while ago and I just had to scold her. You I said to her are not behaving yourself like a daughter of my old friend Estelvina I said to her my oldest friend Estelvina is a decent and honest woman and I said it twice so as to rub it in and you girl could take a lesson or two from your mother my oldest friend Estelvina Garcés. And I told her how there werent two women like you in the whole wild world and that you would die of shame if you ever knew what she's up to and then she would know what its like to live without a mother just like you and me who had to grow up mother less and like orphans and right there your daughter bust into tears and I was so upset to see her like that I gave her all sort of friendly advice to cheer her up, but youll never guess what she did next. Just before leaving and after she was quite and calmed for a little while and had stopped sobbing all together I even maid her a cup of coffee and she drank it. Well she goes and stand in the door way with one hand on the door and a very pretty handbag in the other hand and from over there she says to me as cool as the morning, almost dying of laughter rather, she says to me, youre miss pronouncing it. The what I asked her? And she answers youve got one ess too many. Its E Telvina not Ess Telvina and she closed the door in my face before I had time to put her in her place. Believe me this daughter of yours who you spent so much trouble over Estel has turned out a bad egg and I havent even told you the half of what she really is believe me or youd think she's a rotten egg.

I just finished doing the dishes and Gilbertos gone back to work, so now I can carry on with this letter I began this morning. As I was saying this daughter of your's turned out a right good for nothing hear in Havana which is a very dangeroused city for young peeple from the Country without any experience on life whatso ever. Harsenio Qué live here now and met her and he told us she was working in the beauty parlor of Radiocentro which is this tall sky scraper about twelve floors high where they have the radio station CMQ and a theater and cafes and restaurants even a chinese one, and God knows what. Gloria hadn't been here for ages and then one day she comes and without so much as a formal Hello she sits down and askes for a glass of Polar beer just like am telling you. Lissen girlie, I said to her real mad, you think we keep a bar here or something. We dont stock beer, we dont even have an icebox, besides Gilberto doesnt drink because he has a liver. You know what that daughter of yours said to me? Well then let Gilberto go and buy me a beer, Ill drink it myself and youll be able to see how I gone up in the world. I didnt know what she meant I swear. Gone up I said, how gone up? Then she said go and bye a newspaper and youll see what I mean.

Poor Gilberto went out not to buy the newspaper but to borrow one from Genaro whose an old aquantance, a cigar roller who lives nexdoor, himself a negro but a very decent person so he lent him his newspaper. No sooner had Gilberto brought it back she snatched it from his hands, opened it and handed it back to us open, and would you beleive she was in el Mundo, your daughter was, advertising Polar beer! There she was almost nakid waring one of those things they call here a bequeenis I dont expect you to know about them, nothing more than two strips of cloth one up here and one down there which look more like a womans headscarf and hand kerchief over the hips and breasts only with nothing but nothing else not even to cover the naval. She was standing dressed with no dress next to would you beleive a polar bear. Not only that but putting her arm around the animal and all that. The advertisement said in big letters Beauty and the bear enjoy life with Polar beer and then under neath there was a small lettering which seemed like something indecent and it isnt yet it was because if you look at it long enough you see that the words are like a hand and the letters are fingers and they go all around her nakid body and where it says dig it's like a middle finger this word going into your daughter Gloria Pérez, who of course is no longer either Gloria nor Pérez or any thing like that any more.

She is called Cuba Venegas now which is a name for good saleman ship so she told me herself, however dont ask me what shes selling. Your daughter Cuba Venegas also poses for other commercial products and among these other products she poses for Pepsy which is a beverage and theres one advertisement which says If You Want to Take Cuba Take Pepsy first and then quite clear Then Take Her. What with one thing and another shes becoming quite famous I must admit and making lots and lots of money because she came here in one of those big automobiles which don't have a roof or anything on top and she invited us to come down to the street and look at her convertible, that's how she called the automobile. I didnt go down because this street is always full of people and I was dressed in my working clothes which I always wear during the day but Gilberto whose just like a boy and has always been crazy about automobiles poor soul he went down and told me it was fantastic. He also told me there was a man driving it, I asked Gilberto who he was and he said he didnt know, he was not introduced and I asked him how he looked and he said he couldn't tell, that he couldn't for the light of him say if he was dark or blond or black or white or if he had a nose or a sweet potato on his face and that he knew he was a man because he wore a mustache and that though their are women who have mustaches they don't have drooping handlebar mustaches, which was the kind of mustache the man driving the car was waring.

Your daughter Cuba Venegas, excuse me Estel but I have to laugh, she came here sevrall times and evry time she was better dressed than the time before. One time she arrived and came in and she had a boy with her, ever such a pretty boy, very young and quiet delicate and who was always licking his lips with his tongue and wetting them and he wore some kind of peek aboo hair doo, his long blond hair hanging loose in waves down to his cute face and covering one of his blue blue eyes, and he was carrying a little straw case that your daughter said was hers. But he didn't sit down as if he was afraid he would get his little white pants dirty on my poor furniture I swear they were made of white satin or something. Your daughter was very well dressed and she looked so fancy and elegant in her crispy new dress. She told me then she was now a star to let, something like that, that she was working for the radio and television and she also told me she was making a mint of money. But when I asked her if she was sending you any she said of course she had sent some for Christmas but that she had to spend so much on shoes and clothes and make up and so on and soforth and not only that but now on a personal manager as well, meaning the boy as she pointed to him standing there so stiff holding the straw case for her. How do you like that, your daughter with a personal manager, whatever that is. Then she told me she hoped I would watch her on the television shows and she said lots of other things, mainly a lot of garbage I don't remember now. Another time she came waring a very smart silk gown silk or something like it and she told me they were doing a picture storey on her and she came with a photographer a fellow with green eye glasses for the sun and a face like a toad and a mustache which looked as though it had been just pencilled in, though he was not the same as the other man who came the other time because the other one had a drooping walrus mustache. He took many pictures here in my house and your daughter who used to be called Gloria told me the photographer wanted to put a storey about her in Carteles which is another magazine here in Havana with the story of her life, that's what she told me and they stayed here taking pictures the whole afternoon. I'm quite sure this photographer is a real disreputable character who spent the afternoon not only taking pictures of your daughter but handling her, giving her nasty wet kisses in every corner of the room and I nearly threw him out because if theres one thing I dont like its disorder in my house. When she left he told me he would send me copies of the pictures as a present, me who was working myself to the bone doing the washing of the week in the court yard all the time. I'm still waiting for them. Gilberto brought the magazine and all you see of the house is the worst part of it which is that hidious court yard and the water faucets and the outhouses, all that part of the house which are not supposed to be seen but you can smell quite clearly. Well thats in the back ground and your daughter is in the for ground making pretty faces and poses, and under neath the writing is quiet disgusting with all kind of double meanings. The only good thing about it being mainly that we dont appear in the pictures.

The last time I saw your daughter was about six months ago I hardly knew her any longer let alone what her name could be by now, she came here one evening with a pretty blonde girlfriend and the two of them were wereing men's pants though tighter than I have ever seen, tight every where but tighter in the wrong places if you know what I mean, and they were smoking cigarettes, a kind of cigarette that smells very rich and sweet, like candies but cigarettes, American I beleive. I made coffee for them and they stayed here for a bit and sat down and I almost felt happy because she looked so pretty, your daughter. Its tru she was wearing too much makeup and lipstick and eyeshado but all the same she looked really lovely. She and her friend talked under their sweet breath and whispered together so much it must have been something nasty about us but I swear to you I didn't care at all though it wasn't nice, and then they lighted their cigarettes one from the other or with the two cigarettes in the mouth of one of them and then passed it on to the other and then they said such things I didn't understand them hardly and then they giggled together and laughed loudly and even went into the court yard and laughed at the neighbors as they linked arms and said so many things to each other like my sister and dear dearest friend, well you know, things like that. When they finally left they went away hand in hand and they were almost choking with laughter as if it was all such a terrific joke which nobody but them could understand. Out of politeness I went down with them as far as the door of the building and say goodby to them and they both waved goodby to me from the auto which was without its roof top but with no man driving it so they drove off with a lot of noise and dying but reelly dying of laughter. That was the last time your daughter who used to be called Gloria Pérez and is now called Cuba Venegas or something or other was here.

What with all this fuss and bother I almost forgot to tell you I lost my last hope of having a child of my own about a year ago. It looked very promising but to no avail and now I have given up this illusion all together because already I am almost middle aged and am about to withdraw. Nothing new as far as you can see Estel except that we are getting old and a little while longer we will be getting much older and ready to be gone for ever. Write to me soon please and dont forget your friend who always have fond thoughts of you and never forget how at school when we were little girls every body always mistook us for sisters.

With much affection
Delia Doce

P.S. Gilberto says to send his best, also to your spouse.

I let her go on and on and on and on just so she could get to an end and when she got tired of shootin off her big mouth and kinda breathless I told her but dahling you got it all wrong (those very words, yeah) youre an ole bag, I said, you know about life O.K., but you dont know nothin about living, but nothin dear, believe you me, thats what I said, what I really want is to go out and have me a ball, I said, cos Im not going to shut myself up like a mummy in a tomb like they say the Farouks and all those ancient people lived, so lemme ask you what do you take me for, dearie, a fassil? well I swear to God Im not goin to sit around here all cooped up and not go dancin in the streets, come on now honey, you must be jokin if you think I will: I rather be a virgin again, and then she said, she spoke like this, reachin her hand out like she was stopping a bus or somethin, Im tellin ya, she said, ya can go where the heck ya like, its all the same to me for aint gonna stop ya: Im not ya mother, but you lissen to me cause Im tellin you somethin not for today but for tomorrow, she said, puttin her tiny black hand all creased up and wrinkled over those fat nigger liverlips of hers, screaming fewchur right in my ear so loud she almost bust my drums, so I told her what it is madam (yeah, madam I said cause I can talk nicely if I have to) is that you dont know how to live for the moment cause thats somethin reel difficult and youre a little bit over ninety yousself to see what I mean, if you see what I mean, and she came back at me in that funny peculiar accent she has: you, you can go where ya damn well pleese, damnyou, I doan give the smallest goddam damn what ya do with ya life and with what ya got between your legs cause thats your business and I aint got no ticket in that sweetcake, so ya can get the heck outa here when ya like, and the sooner the better, so she told me and so I told her: lissen, lady, I said, youse sure got somethin mixedup here: who gave you the idea when I said ballin I meant makin it with men and all that, theres nothing to it and theres nothin wrong bout dancin neither, so she said to me O.K., O.K., one *last* word, Im not keeping ya here in chains and wearin a chastisy belt so ya can go where ya damn well please but she got me so mad almost blastin my head off with her yellin insults after me I had to tell her somethin to make her stop so I told her, all Im sayin is you only got one life, so you might as well live it dearie and you gotta know howta, like its a science somethin ya gotta learn, if you know what I mean, and she went after me and said saying, lissen lissen theres ya music and ya dancin and all that chachachá so ya can go where you like right now and have your damn ball but lissen now lissen to what Im saying cause I aint sayin it nomore, you go but you doan come back, youre not comin back here nomore, not in this house youre not cause if ya do come back ya gonna find the door wont open that nice and eesy and thats cause Ise gonna lock it from inside cause Ise gonna have a police lock put on it and if youse plannin to stay in the hallway Ill put the super onto ya, you hear, so now you know, thats how its gonna be, but just as Im bluein my cool I can hear the music all rite comin up the street with its varoom boom, varoom broom, boom boom varoom, with its onetwothree time percussion and its shake rattle and roll rhythm and as Im beginning to rock it up so much I barely can stop I gotta give it to her one more time, but honeychile youre reelly a case: just cool it, woman, or go get yousself some tranquilizers and what she did, the old witch, she says nothin but nothin more than—well, I rather not tell what she said but what she did was to turn her back on me the old bag so Im intitled now to do the same on her and so I pick up my stylish stole and my bitchy bag and I take one mean step, yeah, then two mean steps, yeah yeah, then one step more, yeah, and then I'm already at the door but instead of leavin I turn around suddenly like Beddy Davis in Now Voyeur and I say to her, lissen *you* carefully because Im gonna tell you somethin and you might learn a thin or two: youse only leave once and so you might as well live it to the hill while it lasts for when I die the carnival is gonna stop meanin its gonna die with me and the music will die and all the happiness will die too and so will life die, see what I mean, bein alive means bein alive here and now and this here chick, Magalena Crus, aint gonna bother herself nomore with the other side cause you dont see nothin there and you dont hear nothin neither from overthere and its nothin for it just happens that when the ball finishes its like finished, but esackly! and so she turns around reel dignifiant so I can see her black profile in the door frame and from there she says to me, you know somethin, girl, you dancin dotters are reel mean. The devils avocado, thats what you are, she said and thats all she ever said.

My brother and I had discovered a new way of getting into the movie house, patent pending. We were no longer able to get into the Esmeralda the way we used to because we were too big: we used to get in by keeping the attendant talking or pretending to fight with each other or calling the attendant for help so one of us could slip past and then the other would go and ask permission to go in and look for his missing brother and give him an urgent message from his mother and this way we would both succeed in getting through—but this was no longer possible. Now we got in through the Santa Fe trail. First of all we'd collect all the used paper bags we could and then we'd sell them at a cent for every ten at the fruit stand on Calle Bernaza (where the owner had told me once he'd give me twenty-five centavos for every hundred paper bags and when, still dazzled by the discovery I'd just made—a gold mine; an idiot, a man who couldn't even count up to ten; an unprospected vein to exploit—I went back with twenty paper bags at full speed, caught up by the momentum of my own gold rush, and demanded my five centavos and all I got for my pains was a smile, then a laugh, then a guffaw, then he said, "Do ya think Im outa my mind," and concluded to my utter confusion, "Don't come bothering me with your bags again, you jerk!" for the first time in my life I knew I'd been conned twice over), and if the day went badly for bag-hunting, we would see how many old newspapers we could collect, we would go round the whole neighborhood asking for them or we would look wherever we could and then we would go with our precious cargo to the fish store, where newspapers were worth less than paper bags. (I never tried to make a tip running errands because I would do those for free: they were so poor on the *solar* and already Lesbia Lamont, the kindhearted fifteen-year-old whore and spendthrift, Max Urquiola, our friendly neighborhoodlum, and Lala, the generous, old, almost venerable widow of the triple hero: aviator, colonel and politician—they were all personae, so you shouldn't disdain as poor characterization this kind of writing coming from an epic cure—they had all moved or gone away or died: we had lost them together with the innocence of childhood when we could accept a tip without blushing: now we were growing up and we knew already what it meant to sell a favor—it's easier to sell used paper bags, old newspapers or . . .)

Our last and best resort was books: my father's or his uncle's or his great-uncle's: we sold off the family's literary inheritance. First there was a collection—or rather a row—of dreadful plays by Carlos Montenegro, which he had given my father so as to get money (from my father) and fame (for himself) and publicity (for the book), which was called The Hounds of the Radiziwills. Nobody would ever read it: what's more, nobody had ever read it, because the books sat there in their original uncut virginity. There was also another present from the same author but a different book, Six Months with the Loyalist Shock Troops. Both collections took the Santa Fe trail, as immaculate as the conception: we sold them by the pound in weight not in money—because all we got for them was fifty centavos: booksellers have never had any respect for literature. Other books followed, illustrious but not illustrated (they didn't say much to us), via the same secret passage. Sometimes they went (taken along by my brother and myself: merchandise doesn't go to the market of its own free will) in bundles of five by five, sometimes ten by ten, or three by seven or four by two. (I will spare the reader any cries of protest, explosions of anger or Damoclean threats from my father; I will not spare you any obscenities: the fact is I never heard him utter any. I will also pass over my mother's weak but very effective arguments, which, goodness knows how, succeeded in neutralizing my father's love for that library which every day became more like the memory of a library: the shelves lying empty, the piles of books tilting too far over to left or right, missing the intimate touch of their fellow volumes sacrificed on the altars of the cinema . . . because it should be emphasized that every book that was given the final solution of the secondhand bookshop—and what a ghetto this was for secondhand bookshops: how many of them there were to beguile the passerby on the trail . . . to Santa Fe—was transmuted from literary lead into a silver screen, the titles that memory imagined it could still conjure up but which a close acquaintance denied, were proof that the Fox had entered the bookyard. What image could be more fabulous: would it be better to say the MGM Lion and the Unicorny?)

On my way on the trail to Santa Fe

(1st variation:
I'm on my way
Yes on my way
on the trail to Santa Fe)

(2nd variation:
I'm on my on my on my way
on the trail to Santa Fe)

(3rd variation:
I'm a goin'
I'm a goin' on my way
I'm a goin'
(*I'm a gayin' on my woe*)
on the trail/the trail/the trail/the trail
to Saaaantaaaaaaaa Feeeeeeeeeeeeeeeeee)

This tune (together with its Goldwyn Variations) was sung with the appropriate music, which is the malady of the Santa Fe Trail—only we didn't know that at the time. Where could we have got it from, me and my brother? Without a shadow of doubt from a film—from a Western.

That day, that Thursday (films cost less on Thursday) I am talking about, we had already completed the first stage of the journey to Santa Fe (because Santa Fe, as the reader will have guessed already, was Arcadia, the glory and panacea of all the sorrows of adolescence: the movies), and before my father returned from work we had taken a bath, selected the program—or to be more precise selected the movie house, the Verdun, which in spite of bearing the name of a battle was very peaceable, popular and cool with its iron roof and its tin plating, which opened onto the hot night with all kinds of whirrings and whinings and which it was never possible to close quickly enough on rainy days (nights, rather): it felt good there, in the gallery facing the screen, especially if the second-balcony front row was free (which we nicknamed paradise: a place for princes, the equal of the royal box of other times, other spectacles) and directly under the stars: it was almost better even than my memory of it—and we were climbing the stairs when we encountered none other than Tiny Tina, who was, like so many of our neighbors, not so much a person as a personality. But, sad to say, Tiny Tina (a misshapen, toothless and dirty old dwarf with an insatiable appetite for sex) was also a bird of ill omen. "So you're going to the movies?" I think that was what she said. My brother and I answered in the affirmative, without stopping on our way down the suddenly dirty, twisting staircase. "Have a good time, boys," she said, the poor old midget, as she climbed the stairs with some difficulty. We didn't stop to say thank you: the only thing to do was to knock on wood, cross our fingers and keep our eyes open for oncoming cars.

We continued on our way to the cinema. As we crossed Central Park it was already getting dark. We went through the Centro Gallego colonnade to take a look at the photos of Spanish *bailaoras* and maybe a rumba dancer in tights. Then we followed the sidewalk of the Louvre, where the people who come here to talk every night were already beginning to show up and the regular coffee drinkers, in the café on the corner, and we stopped at the newsstand, drawn like so many moths by the colored covers of the American magazines, and we fluttered around and around without buying or touching anything. The sidewalk of the Louvre seems endless: now we are passing another café with more people and a group of men who have stopped in front of the huge oil portraits of the candidates for mayor, or councillor, or for the senate, looking like so many nominees for an Oscar, if you could believe the artist who had painted them larger than life—and touched them up considerably. Now we are at the shooting gallery with six flippers and a mechanical punching bag. Target shots are heard over the ring of the pinball tables and just over the cussing of the cheater who made a tilt. The last bit is to knock out the tattered punching-bag machine—whose mechanism would certainly be punch-drunk in a short time. Someone (the boy who operates the flicker, the sailor of the shooting gallery, the Negro at the punching bag) hits the bull's-eye. We move on and fall prey to the aroma of *fritas* and hamburgers and steak sandwiches you can buy at the hot-dog stand. We haven't eaten, nor are we going to eat. Who would think of eating when the road is so long and patience so short—or was the reverse more true—and when in Santa Fe we would find adventure, freedom and dreams fulfilled? A few more steps take us across three streets—a piece of Prado, Neptuno and San Miguel—in this crumbling, noisy, malodorous, brilliantly colored, densely peopled triangle of crossroads where one day in the future La Engañadora herself would pass, deceitful and lascivious, walking sweet and gentle with all the harmony of a cha-cha step. We reach one of the stages of the trail, the Rialto. Tonight they are showing *The Razor's Edge*, but (we suspected) wasn't this title a little bit metaphysical? We decided it was, only we said so in different words. Better to wait till next week or the next section of the library, and have the good fortune to see *The Short Happy Life of Francis Macomber*. The title is very long and complicated and there's this woman in it, the one who looks so much like Hedy Lamarr, to spoil our pleasure. But, and a big but, there are lions and safaris and big-game hunters: all Africa will be there, which is the same as saying the heart of Santa Fe. *Vendremos*.

We go on immersed in the noise of the city and at this point also in the smell of fruit (mammee, mangoes, custard apples naturally: that sinister fruit, green like a chameleon on the outside and gray like gray matter inside, with pulp like a brain disease, black dots of seeds enveloped in their viscous skins, but such a fragrant fruit is found only on the tree of knowledge, with the aroma of the hanging gardens of Babylon and the savor of ambrosia, whatever that may be) and the smell of milk shakes, of melon and tamarind juices and coconut milk, and in the mixture another smell, shoe polish and cobbler's last, coming from the heel bar right next to the corner which is the stage where we would change horses, Los Parados, a name which means that the customers never sit down but implies an obscenity, though it actually is the place where for five centavos (for a collection of *Nueva Generación* magazine, rather) we will be able to buy two coffee sodas, before entering on the desert, with all its perils and hazards. Death Valley!

Hitting the dusty trail again. Now, right in front of us, we have the temptation of the Alcazar, where they always show good movies. But last week they had a singer there who made such a noise she could be heard in the street—although the film, *Battleground,* was, would you believe it, a war movie. It's not her fault, but the live performers' union that's forcing these shows on moviegoers. Farther on, very close to Santa Fe, is the Majestic, with such good programs, double, triple and even quadruple features, though they're often not suitable for children and we must beg the usher to let us in or buy him a coffee first only to find out that (after all) it was only sick people and a woman (and a very skinny one at that) taking a bubble bath plus a young couple eloping by night and then there is a storm and next they take shelter in an old barn and the next morning she is in labor. All crap, really.

Suddenly order is thrown into chaos. People start running, someone crashes into my shoulder, a woman is screaming and hides behind a car and my brother pulls and pulls at me by the hand, by my arm, by my shirt, as if in a persistent dream, shouting, "Silvestre look out they'll kill you!" and I feel myself being propelled toward a place which I discover later is a *fonda* or Chinese restaurant and tumble under a table, where there is already a couple sharing the precarious refuge of a wood-and-straw chair and a palm tree in a pot and I hear my brother's voice calling me from the ground asking whether I'm wounded or not and it's then I hear shots far off/very close and I get up (to escape? to run farther into the restaurant? to face the danger? no, only to have a peep) and I look out through the door and already the street is deserted and half a block away or at the end of the street or just a few yards away (I don't remember) I see a fat old mulatto (to this day I don't know how I knew he was a mulatto) stretched out on the ground, gripping another man's legs, who in his turn is trying to shake him off with his feet again and again and as he can see no other way of getting rid of him he fires at his head twice in succession and I can't hear the shots, I can only see a spark followed by a white red and green orange flash coming from the hand of the man who is standing on his feet and lighting up the face of the dead—because there is no doubt that he's dead—mulatto now and the man loosens one of his thighs from his grip, then the other, and then he starts running, firing his pistol in the air, not to frighten anybody, nor to cut a passage for himself, but to announce his victory, I think, like a cock crowing in the pit after the kill, or like Tarzan of the Jungle, and the street fills again with people and they start screaming and calling for help or the police and the women begin weeping and howling and someone says very softly, *"They've killed him!"* as though the dead man had been a celebrity and not just a carcass stretched out in the street—no: just now four men are lifting it and carrying it off to disappear around the corner, in a car, maybe, into the night for sure. My brother returns from somewhere and stands there looking dazed. I tell him, "If you could see yourself in the mirror now." He answers, "If *you* could see yourself!" . . .

We go on to the movies. On the corner there is a black pool of blood under the street light and a crowd has gathered around it, staring and making comments. I can't for the life of me remember the name of the film we were going to see, which nothing would have stopped us from seeing, which we did see.

That you, Livia? It's me—Beba. Beba who? Beba *Longoria*, that's who! The one and only, yes! How are ya, darlin? Oh, I'm so pleased to hear it. Me? Couldn't be fitter. A custard apple a day keep the bugger morticians away, you know. No, not so long ago, darling. But anyhow that's how my twelveo'clockinthemorningtoneofvoice sound. You just do what you can when you pleases and all the rest is for the birds. *You* know what I'm like. I'm always been only half awake anyhow. All lazybones and high cheekbones. So now that I can take advantage of my vintage years, I do. Sure, darling, still in bed. As my granny used to say, the only place to drink coconut milk is right under the coconut tree. So, to give you a mint phrase, you should lie down and rest right there where you get tired. Yeh, same as ever. What should I change for? Or rather, who for? Not a girl like I, in any case. Lissen, Livia, hold on a minute willya, don't hang up I won't be a minute. What was I saying? Oh no, nothing of the kind, it's just I left my Chanel Number Five with the top off. Where was I? Well, *darling*, it's *all* the same to me. Completely immaterial. No, darling, I *swear*, it wasn't *that* important. Well, if I'm getting it right you were asking me if I'd just got up and I told you, I think, the same as always or something or other, wasn't it, just like I used to tell you when we were living together in that crappy boardinghouse. Just my midmorning slogan. Roger? Yeah, that comes from him. Natchurly it all come from him nowadays, that's the way the fortune cookie crumbles, darling. You *know* what he's like. Yeh, he imitates *him* in everything, but in *every*thing. Well, cepting that. At least, I *think* so. They all talk like that, funny. But let me finish with this *obstruct* conversational piece, as my old man would say, by beginning telling you the story I was gonna tell you when I phoned. What I called you for, rather. You know they're making my man Cipree a member of the club. But, darling, the *only* club on earth, the Yatch Club. Well, no, the Yatch or Yat is strickly for nonmembers, darling, we members call it simply the Club. How dya like that? Well, darling, to tellya the truth and nothing but, they simply couldn't of done otherwise. *The* general shot the works and threatened two ministers, no names mentioned, who are founder members, that they were going to be shot for real if they didn't comply. So they just don't have any choice but to let him, *us*, in. Simple as that. Well, that's not *that* simple. I think we gotta get married in church now. You know, that's the trend. But it's gonna be a gas anyway, what with the wedding gown and all, so I've already been seeing to the true so or whatever way you say it. What dya think of that? Me a bride after being Cipriano's *querida* or kept woman as my granny loved to hate to say, balling in sin as long as I can remember, to start doing it same as always but with the bishop's blessing this time. Ain't it wild? Specially now I'm on my way to matchurity . . . Of course I'm *not!* Over *thirty*? I'm not even twenty-five yet, but that's like an old bag nowadays, darling. And the same to you. I'm only kidding but I'm not kidding you about the bride bit and the white lace and all. Yeh, white but with some polka dots thrown in for good measure. Well, we're in society now, baby, and it's about this I called you. Last night the old bugger took me to the Tropicana to celebrate. No, you dumb blonde. Tropic not Toprick. What a filthy mind you got, darling, under all that platinum-blond hair! *Whew!* Well, anyway, we went to the *Tropicana* and had a simply incredible marvelous time there under the star-studded glass rooftop. But marvel-ous like you would say. Well, you know what Cipriano's like. Wha-what, what was that? Don't be silly, sweetie, it sure make *me* laugh too. But he get in a rage with me cos I cain't stop laughing. Anyway, he say it's a name that's brought him his share of luck. Acksolutely. If *the* general can call himself Fulgencio and his brotherissimo Hermenegildo, why shouldn't he be called Cipriano, the poor darling? Hein? He couldn't be better off. In the top aichilongs as he says. I don't know if you've heard but they given him a concession in the market La Lisa. Well, darling, not *a* stall, of course, the market *intotal,* as he say. Yes, about a month ago. That's what we were celebrating really, as well as this thing with the club. Thanks a million, darling. Well, no, the service station will be looked after by his kid brother, Deogracias. Well, the name means thank God but he certainly didn't have to thank anybody for it. You're telling me! Off her rocker, the poor old lady. Completely out of her mind, baptizing her sons with such names. That's not christening but name-calling. You ain't heard nothing yet, honey. There's another brother called Berenice and another who died like two hundred years ago who was called Metodio and another who was living in darkest Oriente, still is if I'm not wrong and he's not gone, because he's a gourmet. . . . Well, you know, one of those people who don't want to have anything to do with the family or anybody else, not even with women, mind you! . . . Yes? Yes . . . Well, gourmet, hermet, it's all the same to me. The thing is he lives in a *bohío,* palm-leaf roof and dirt floor and all that filth somewhere in the jungle and he's called Dio Gene Leerso or something like that. . . . Where? Moa or Toa or Baracoa, where they're all from, in the heart of the bush or rough or whatever it's called. Well, darling, as a matter of fag I'm not acksolutely certain but he used to know *the* general in an outpost in that fart east cos they entered the army together and became officers . . . yeh, from sargents to kernels in two weeks and all that crap. . . . Same thing I tell him but he says he's quite satisfied being just a kernel and I should look at Genovevo and Gómez-Gómez and right after he begin reciting me all those names of deposed C-in-C's as he says just to shut my fucking mouth. What's good for the goose, etc. Well, he say that what's best for yourself is not to be noticed very much or not at all so you can keep your hands free to go catchascatchcaning here and there and everywhere. That's what he say. No, sweetiepie, nothing doing. They tried to send him on garrison overthere but he managed to get away from that too. My old fucker is a *vivo*, very bright and on the ball all the time. He went straight to the horse's mouth which amount to saying to *the* general hisself and told him his talents, meaning his wits, were needed on the general stuff what with his knowledge of military strategy and the history of trench warfare he was best needed in the HQ's or whatever plus so many other unpronounceable namethings he drove me crazy with. So they left him right there where he is and quite quiet. No, that's cool for now but could flare up any minute, you know how it is. You probably know about Kernel Curbelo already. At least what they say about him. Well, number one, about the way he took all the moneys for vitchels and all that, so that's no mean bonus. Number two . . . But what about the gorillas? the gor-il-las, darling, what else? Well, guerrillas, gorillas: it's all the same to me. Not King Kong, you dumbbell! You know perfeckly well what I mean: Natcherly, yes, certainly, but of course I mean *them!* Yes! Anyway, that's all very rough and tough and besides he know I'm not going to live in the bush, not for all the china in China. I don't wanna have anything to do with mosquitoes or gnats and ticks and bush ulcers. Well, yes, in Santiago but as far as I'm concerned, darling, the jungle begin on the other bank of the Almendares. Well, that's one reason we're not moving, what with all the houses they've offered Cipriano in the Cuntryclub and the Biltmor cartier and all those places. You know, he's always following my scent close behind. That's right, you just said it: he's mad about me. Crazy he is. *Give* 'em? *Me*? I didn't give him anything that's not in the book. Nothing but nothing of the kind. You know perfeckly well I wouldn't have anything to do with that kinda thing. I wouldn't waste my time on any filters—I don't even smoke filtertips, now you mention it. I know you don't mean the Big C, you big cunt! I know what you mean. But lemme tell you I make no them bones about it. I prefer to akcentchuate the positive. So you give 'im what you got plus experience. It balances out perfeckly: the more you got of one thing the less of another. It's all in the mind, darling. Everything is on the mind. Not only everything that exist but everything that's existed or is going to. Everything's on the mind first. But anyways, something I must of had about me because he's very much stuck, sticking like long hairs on a rainy day. A torch? Darling, it's a *bonfire* he's carrying! Yeh, that he is, fifty if he's a day. God forbid! Lissen, don't even tell me about strokes or love-strokes or whatever you call it or any kind of heart sickness. I get very but *very* upset. But, darling, didn't you ever hear what happened to John Garfeel? No, that's right, the film actor. Garfeldt, yes. Same man. He died on his wife on the couch. Bed or couch or bedcouch, it's the same thing, sweetie. And you know what happened to a friend of a girl friend of mine? More or less the same thing, yes. This girl *killed* a fellow she was going with. She just pulled her cunt on him right there in the hotel on 11th and 24th streets. C'mon, baby, don't pretend to be so innocent! The *posada* yes, but exackly! The night hotel near the river on your way to Miramar. Yeah, that's the one. Of course I know it. You're trying to tell me you don't? Who're you kidding? Good, that's better. Never try to con a cunt, kiddo. Well, as I was saying, this girl friend of my girl friend went thataway but when she's in there and at it next thing she knows her man's going from swinger to stiff before you can say cock and then he's lying dead right there on the bed. *On* the bed, darling! How d'you like that for a postcoitem? At two o'clock in the morning! It gives me the creeps just to tell it. But not her. You know what she did? She just got up cool as hell, got dressed very calmly, made herself up and all, then got him dressed, calls the manager and tells the guy to bring his car—*not* the manager's, you jerk, but the dead man's car—and they both put him in the car, quiet as possible so as not to alarm the clientell, that's the manager, and not to create any fuss with the police, this girl friend of my girl friend cos she's a society girl and the dead man is, *was*, a big shot. Well, to make a tall tale short, they both put him in the car and she starts it up—Yeh, right you are! That's why I'm learning to drive myself—and she drives off to the first-aid hospital and say the person in question as they say in the papers has died of a cardiac infaction while driving his car and no foul play is suspected. How does that catch you? *The* perfect murder, darling! You don't even need an alibi or being on the other side of town at the time of the murder because you're right there with the stiff and you're his next of skin. Yes, yes, of course, natchurly, I'll be very careful, don'tcha worry.

. . . No, no complaints about that. On the contrary, Mary, he leaves me alone a lot because he know he can't keep me on a short rein. And between you and I, darling, in the strickest confidence of course, I believe he likes it, perhaps a little tiny weeny bit but he likes *it,* if you know what I mean. Yes, love, they're all like that at his age. An old ledger . . . well, lecher, ledger—it's all the same to me. D.O.M.s. Yes yes. Acksolutely. So let 'em stop the carnival, after I've had my ball, of course. You can't take it with you. Or you can take it but then again you can't, not *it.* Fine, find another word for it if you want but please don't Frenchkiss and tell. You just keep it to yousself. . . . Well, about that, whenever you feel like it, darling. I don't need to tell you that this house is not a house, it's *my* house and you're more than welcome to it. Also I'll invite you to the club any day now, just to scare the fucking hell out of all those socialits. . . . Lits, lights, it's all the same to me. Well, catch you later, darling. I'm just going to take a bath and wash my hair because I'm going to the hairdresser's. No, he's no lady but a Frenchie queenie. So I should be saying I'm going to che lay coffure instead. Right? He's very young and very cute and very very good. He works miracles with my hair. Wait till you see it. Okey-dokey, darling, I'll see you sooner than soon. Bye for now. Or like my man say, over and out.

Incredible! A math lesson was what it was. I stood stock still looking at the wall. Not at the wall but at a lithograph behind—behind the man, not behind the wall: I am Supermouse more than Superman. It was a romantic drawing in which some capricious sharks (and therefore buggers, Códac would say) were surrounding a raft running adrift, with two or three daring young men on board who were so well-built and handsome they looked more like male models than castaways, all of them leaning over languidly to port. I thought the sharks in the print were sissy sardines compared to this shark of everyday life who was seeking out my eyes without blushing or embarrassment, no doubt assuming it would be me who would do the blushing. I remember I looked from the picture to the desk, from the teas of roubles (or is it the sea of troubles?) which ended in distant waves on the Malecón—because, at the back, yes, I know, it seems incredible, in the background of the gravure the gray Havana of the nineteenth century could be seen—I leaped onto the firm or black land of his negative answer, passed from the engraved wavy gray to the billiard-cloth green of the desk pad, to the aggressive-looking paper knife—a long tusk with a gold-plated gun for handle—to the burnished brown humidor with its rococo monogram, perhaps designed by the same artist of fish and fairies, to the black leather baroque writing case with its gold stitching, and my eyes traveled trembling all the way up his charcoal-gray Italian silk tie (my pupils stopping in disbelief at the enormous cipollina pearl he wore as a tie pin under the exactly triangular knot, outlining on my reluctant retina the perfectly drawn neck of his shirt, made to measure in Mieres) to discover his head—hard work he would have been for the guillotine, this eighteenth-century shark: he didn't *have* a neck—unexpectedly, like those Hokusai-like full moons which rise in the summer astonishingly orange so at first one thinks it's a globe lamp then the moon and ends up convinced it's a suddenly lit street light before finally settling for certain that it is in fact the moon of the Caribees and not a ripe tropical fruit, invisibly suspended so as to hang up Newton. His well-groomed, plump, almost shiny face was on the edge of a smile while his blue European eyes stared at me with that frank open gaze which converted him almost at once from a penniless immigrant into a tycoon, and his mouth, his thin bloodless lips, his expensive teeth, his tongue which had long used the familiar form *tú* with all the delicacies of the kitchen moved in unison to ask me softly: "Do you see?" smiling so that his lampion head disappeared but the grin lingered on.

I was going to tell him that not only was I able to draw the numbers, I was also able to add them up, but it wasn't my mouth that opened but the door which had etavirP (or is it etariP?) painted on its glass panel. Ten—no, five, perhaps three minutes earlier I had also been outside in the hall which I'd come to now because there was nothing left for me to do in there but say good-bye not see you soon and to exit closing the door silently behind me.

Then earlier, I had imagined he wouldn't see me, that was what I was thinking at the moment when Yosi or Yossi or Jossie told me, "Señor Solaún will see you, in a minute, Ribot." "Citizen Maximilian Robespierre Ribot," I said to Jossie or Yossi or Yosi, but she wasn't listening. That's the story of my life: not a few cartridges have I wasted in a good many salvos. I could have told her as I had done on other occasions when I was equally little listened to or even heard, Giambattista Bodoni Ribotto or William Caslon Rybot or Silvio Griffo di Bologna. I was no longer the printer of genius or the famous popular musician

(Sergio Krupa or Chanopozo Ribó) but a notorious revolutionary, a villain about to stalk through the palace seeking revenge. Overlapping over my public parts and private fantasies her voice—servile to her superiors, superior when talking to me—asked me, "What did you say?" But by now I was thinking that the Lord of Solaún was going to admit me to his castle and grant me a private audience, although he knew I was going to ask him for a raise, if only because of what happened yesterday. So I answered, "Nothing."

It had been more than a month since I'd tried to get the Guild of Printers to give me a raise appropriate to my job, but nothing had come of it, and this was exactly what I might have expected of the union for graphic arts, because I wasn't a worker. I wasn't an artist either or even an artisan. I was a *professional* (should I write it in capitals and have it printed in Stymie Bold typeface?) and I found myself a refugee in no-man's-land, in this black hole of malformation: neither artist nor technician nor artisan nor worker nor scientist nor *lumpenproletariat* nor prostitute: a hybrid, a half-caste, an abortion, a *parturiunt montes* (as you would say, Silvestre, speaking Latin with a Cuban accent) *nascetur ridiculus mus*. A *copy* writer, come on! Now, today, actually for a week, I had decided upon the personal approach, which means sailing minus a rudder through hostile or indifferent seas, like the messenger bottle from a shipwreck. Because I, on my heterosexual raft, was also running adrift.

Then came the flying-trapeze act. Since yesterday morning I had seen a swarthy man, his clothes dirty and full of patches, in the outside waiting room. He didn't smoke or talk with the others who were waiting, nor did he carry a briefcase or portfolio or vademecum. Could he be an exotic anarchist, a desperate latter-day reader of Bakunin with his bomb a fortiori, a domestic regicide? I asked myself this triple question three times. I saw him when I came in the morning, he was there at lunchtime, I came back to find him in the afternoon. In the evening when I was leaving, he got up, all six feet of him, and we left together. At that moment Senator Solaún turned up, feudal lord, administrator, ruler from birth, all in one little, plump man. Agilely he leaped from his Cadillac, dressed in 100-

percent-white drill, his custom-made Panama hat tilting over his bald head. Distant rolling of drums. A voice announcing, "Ladies and gentlemen, Senator Solaún is now ascending the staircase! No net, ladies and gentlemen! No net! Silence, please! The slightest noise could cost the *capitaliste* his life!" The visitor and I both saw him at exactly the same moment but I'm certain we weren't thinking the same thought. The man hunched his shoulders, lowered his head and, without looking at the Great Solaúni, climbed back up the monumental stairs, almost made a gesture of stretching out his hand, or rather made the absence of such gesture, in a metaphysical petition: the beggar's operation.

—Señor Solaún, the man said in a voice which wouldn't have been heard if it hadn't been for the silence of that star-crossed moment to which we were both, he and I, mute witnesses. Solaún looked him up and down and I realized then that one doesn't need to be taller than the other man to look him up and down. The distant drums ceased to roll and in their stead was a roar: it wasn't the noise of lions, but of Solaún speaking.

—But, my good man, how *dare* you! Stopping me on the staircase!

No more words were needed, because the visitor, the suppli-cant, the professional beggar or all of those men disappeared and in the place they had occupied all there was was a poor hunched-up tall man, who had been made a fool of, reduced finally to derision. I wondered if I should laugh or applaud or make remonstrances, but I didn't do any of these things because I was watching the scene in total fascination. Or was it fear? Solaún noticed me and said to the man:

—Go and speak to my secretary, and he continued on his way up the staircase. But this time he was a man like anybody else climbing an ordinary staircase in the normal way.

It was I and not the intruder on the stairs who followed his advice and now Yossie or rather Josefa Martínez was lowering the drawbridge and I was crossing the feudal moat with the peasant awkwardness of the Surveyor admitted to the Castle for the first time.

—Please come in, Viceregent Solaún said, with all the aside-ness one can muster when some transaction of vital importance is being undertaken at the same time: signing a check for the wife so she can go shopping, saying one last word to your *querida* on the phone, lighting that Churchill (he was so rich he could afford the luxury, metaphorically speaking, of setting fire to a British prime minister every hour on the hour) cigar with its afterlunch aroma.

—What can I do for you, young man?

I looked at him and was on the verge of saying: Sort my whole life out and my death as well, perhaps. What I actually said was:

—The thing is, you know, actually, I have a problem. . . .

—*Sí, sí.*

—I'm not making very much money.

—What! But we gave you a raise only six months ago!

—Yes, that's true. That was when I got married, but . . .

—*Sí, sí.*

It was the same as if he'd said: Don't say another word, but he knew how to arrange those two words or rather that single word repeated so skillfully that I yielded.

—The thing is we are, my wife that is, she is expecting . . .

—*Sí, sí.* A son.

I should have corrected him: Or a daughter, possibly even a hermaphrodite. But it was he who spoke first:

—These are big words. Have you thought about it seriously?

The truth was I hadn't thought about it, neither for better nor worse, I just hadn't thought about it! Children—you don't think about them, you don't even feel about them, nor do they seem to come. They come, that's all. They're almost like errata. Oh, I made a slip of a son in this Evanol layout! I'd make it an interruptus lay only.

—Think? I suppose I didn't think about it.

—Ah, Ribot, about children you really have to think.

Fucking *e una cosa mentale,* Leonardo said. Tell you what, the next time I sit at my table, I'll prop my chin on my hand, like Nobel in all the portraits of him, and pin a notice on the door: DO NOT DISTURB. I AM DESIGNING A BEAUTIFUL EIGHT-POUND BABY.

—You're right, I said servilely,—you have to design, I mean think about it.

The moment had come when the master could make a conciliatory gesture toward this sylvan serf.

—Let's see, he said. —What can I do for you?

For a minute I said nothing. I hadn't expected my petition to be an answer. I had come to make requests, all of which I had rehearsed beforehand. What can the land baron do for Badsin the Sailor? That was all I could think of at the moment. Meet me on shore? Throw me a life saver? Lose me over the horizon? I decided to make the request which came easiest. Or was it the most difficult?

—I was wondering, if it's possible, if you could do me the favor of giving me a rise, I mean a raise. Only if it's possible, of course.

I had used exactly the right grammatical construction to convey to the keeper of the castle the idea of respect and hierarchy and necessary distance. All of which predisposed him to charity, both public and private. But he didn't reply. At least, not immediately. This is the secret of great men. Of little great men too. They know the value and price of everything, including words. And silence, like musicians. And gestures. Like actors or Buddhists. Solaún, as if he were performing a religious ceremony, drew his pigskin eyeglass case out of the inside pocket of his jacket and slowly and with great deliberation took out his bifocals. He put them on ceremoniously. He stared at me, he stared at the blank sheet (or should I say he stared at the sheet blankly?) he had on his desk pad, then calmly took a perfectly useless pen from an unnecessary inkwell, because pen and ink were, like the engraving, the tobacco box, the letter case, the paper knife and the pearl, purely for ornament. He proceeded at this moment to create a silence. I should have been able to hear all the noises of the Creation but in fact all I heard was the *Om* of the air-conditioner, the pen tattooing its path over the sheet of paper and his Aeolian belly playing reveille in the afternoon. The sphinxter spoke.

—How much do you make?

—Twenty-five a week.

Another silence ensued, which seemed to me to be forever. This time it was the turn of Pandora's box of smells. But there was hardly anything to follow the scent except for the faint odor of Guerlain drops in the blue handkerchief that rose like a sartorial horizon a little way off the coast of his lapel pocket. I think it was then, through a connection of metaphors, that I began gazing attentively at the masterwork of etching which wedded cartography and pederasty. His actual hand, already perfectly done (before this tonsorial adjective my hands were the barely conceived fetus of a hand and the hand of that anonymous artist who had so perfectly engraved that scene of the romantic tragedy which would one day become allegory, the hand which had since returned to dust and oblivion, was the nonidea of a hand, according to the concept of a hand a manicure has)—his hand was clutching the pen as if it were a bare bodkin. If this hadn't been the beginning of fiat looks and the start of my marine reflections, I would have heard the sounds of the written abacus, because just like Vincent, I have an ear for painting. In fact, if I were modest I would have been the composer of *Pictures at an Exhibition* and not Moussorgsky. A visibly sonorous movement robbed me of these illusions and allusions worthy of (or copied from) *Bustrófedon.*

Viriato Solaún y Zulueta, Senator for life of the Republic, man of affairs, honorary president of the Centro Basco and of the Rotary Club, founding member of the Havana Yacht & Country Club, leading shareholder of Paperimport and managing director of Solaz Publications, Co. Ltd., who together with his sons, daughters and sons-in-law, grandchildren, nephews and great-nephews took up an entire page in the Social Register of Havana (illustrated), spoke again and at last, alas:

—Twenty-five a week? Goodness me, Ribot, but that works out to be a hundred pesos a month!

Before I knocked I looked at my nails: all of them were embellished with a black crescent of grime. I went back down the steps for the second time. The first time was because I'd seen that my shoes were caked with mud and I'd gone down to clean them in the street. It had been a bad idea after all. The heel of the left shoe had almost come off and I'd had to mend it by banging it on the sidewalk like a maniac. The two parts refused to stay together and of course an old woman walking her dog had to stop and watch me from across the street. "I am Cuba's answer to Fred Astaire," I yelled, but she acted as if she hadn't heard me: it was her dog that answered, barking like one more lunatic in that quiet street. Now I was hunting on the ground for a twig and when I'd found one I carefully cleaned my nails with it. I went back slowly up the marble steps, studying the sedulous symmetry of the garden and gaping at the white stone facade of the building. On reaching the top, I thought it might be better to return another day, but my hand was already on the knocker and, in any case, would I be able to return? Even today I hardly had the strength for it.

I knocked once, meaning to give the knocker a discreet tap, but it slipped from my hand and sounded like a gunshot: it was a heavy chunk of bronze. Nobody came. Thinking it would be better if I went away, I knocked again, twice this time and more softly. I heard a sound like footsteps but it was some time before anyone came to the door. A man in uniform opened it.

—What's the matter? he asked as though letting me know that I had already knocked three times too often. He used the familiar form of the pronoun but his tone was certainly more contemptuous than loving—*tú*?

I began rummaging in my pockets for the piece of paper I had brought with me. I couldn't find it. I pulled out a bus ticket and the address of Edelmiro Sanjuán, professor of diction and phonetics, and the last letter my mother had sent me, all crumpled up and without its envelope. Where could I have put that damned paper? The man was waiting and he looked more capable of slamming the door in my face than of being patient. Finally I found it and gave it to him. He took it with an antiseptic gesture. He thought this would be the end of it. I told him whom it was for and that I expected an answer.

—Wait *here*, he said and closed the door. I examined the knocker carefully. It was the amputated paw of a bronze lion which grasped a bronze ball in its huge bronze claws. I heard some children playing in another part of the building, shouting names at each other. A bird was whistling and cackling *tiatira tiatira* to itself in the trees of the park. It wasn't hot, but it looked as though it would rain in the evening. The door opened again.

—Come in, the man said reluctantly.

The first thing I noticed when I went in was a delicious smell of cooking. Perhaps they will invite me to lunch, I thought. For more than three days I had had nothing but coffee with milk and an occasional piece of bread dipped in oil. I saw a young man opposite me (he was to one side of me as I entered, but I turned around), tired-looking with ruffled hair and hollow eyes. He was badly dressed, his shirt was filthy and his loosely knotted tie hung free of his collar, which had no button or clasp. He needed a shave and a limp unkempt mustache drooped round the corners of his mouth. I raised my hand to shake his, bowing slightly at the same time, and he followed suit. I saw he was smiling and sensed that I was smiling too: we both got the message at the same time: it was a mirror.

The fellow (whoever he was: butler, secretary, bodyguard?)

was still waiting for me at the end of the corridor. He seemed impatient or perhaps bored.

—He says you can sit down, he said, pointing to a door on the left, the only way out of the dark hallway where I could just make out the vases of artificial flowers, comfortable armchairs, a table with magazines. The open door gave a glimpse of another room which was brightly lit and welcoming. (From the dark hallway it gave the impression of being luminous.) I went in. I saw the light was streaming from the windows: two wide-open bay windows. There was a hooded buff wicker chair, an easy chair in dark brown leather, a Viennese rocking chair, and also a desk of inlaid wood and a spinet, I think, or baroque piano. There were a number of pictures in heavy frames on the walls. I couldn't see what they were portraying or what colors they were because too much light shone from the varnish and concealed them. I think there were other pieces of furniture and before I sat down with the distinct impression I had entered the house of an antique collector three things happened simultaneously or one on top of the other. I heard a sharp vibrating sound followed by a very loud slap, I heard a shot and I saw something like the hand and arm of a man in uniform closing the door.

I sat down thinking that there was someone calling from outside and when I settled in my chair (I noticed that I was utterly exhausted, to the point of nausea) I saw the angel. It was a statue of biscuit or some other unglazed porcelain, on a pedestal of the same material—or of plaster. It was a mighty angel wrapped in a cloud with a rainbow over his head. He had a little book open in his hand, his right foot was set on the sea, and his left foot on the earth, and he lifted up his right hand toward heaven. What attracted my attention particularly was the little almond-colored book which looked like marzipan, almost edible. I felt so hungry (I only had one small cup of coffee on the street that morning) that I would have eaten the book if the angel had offered it to me. I decided to forget it.

I would have forgotten it anyway, because the door opened and a girl appeared, a very young woman who looked at me without any surprise. She was drenched from head to foot: water poured from her black hair and over her face, her arms and her legs. Her cheekbones were high and wide and her square chin was dimpled at the tip. With her large fleshy mouth, her broad high-bridged nose and great black eyes with still darker lashes and brows she would have been beautiful. But her forehead was too high, convex and masculine: perhaps because her wet hair clung to her skull. She stuck out her tongue to sip the water or in her effort to fasten the upper part of her yellow bikini. One of the straps had slipped and she supported the bra with her armpit only, holding her left hand behind her. Medium height, with full-fleshed thighs arching in front, she was very suntanned, although her skin could never have been pale. She looked at me again, her mouth almost touching her chest, as if trying to hold onto an imaginary elusive towel with her chin.

—You seen Gay Breel? she asked and without waiting for an answer she turned around and went away, leaving the door open. I saw she had finally unstrapped the top half of her bikini. Her long tanned shoulders glowed alongside a fluid furrow of flesh which glided down her waist to disappear into her sudden monokini. I got up and closed the door. As I was closing it I heard another loud knock, another shot.

The door opened again before I sat down. I half thought that it was another unexpected visitor, but, no, I decided finally: it was him. In his hand he was holding my note. He looked at me, or rather, because I was standing between the open windows, he *tried* to look at me. He lifted the piece of paper instead of greeting me.

—Th-this is y-yours. It was neither a statement nor a question, but it wasn't the monotonous voice that disturbed me, nor his stutter (unexpected: I had expected a different voice, maybe more virile or authoritative: so many stories had been told about him and they all sounded like legends or tall tales), nor the fact that he walked toward me raising the paper like a questioning finger, nor that he didn't use the familiar *tú* when he spoke to me (everyone else did in this house), nor that his manner was insolent: the thing that made my blood run cold was that in his left hand he was holding a large black pistol. He walked toward me and I thought of stretching out my hand to shake his, but which one should I shake? Then he went to the window and closed it, shutting out the voices of the children, the cackling song of the bird and the amber light: he was banning the evening. Then he sat down opposite me. He noticed that I was too fascinated by the weapon in his hand to look at him.

—T-t-target practice, he said, without bothering to elaborate. He wasn't either young or old: he was aged. I had never seen him in the flesh: only a passing glimpse of him on television, eating hot dogs one after another to advertise a brand of sausages. That had been a long time ago and now he was a celebrity, a tycoon, a political leader. He really must have eaten the hot dogs because he was fat, indecently so, in his white flannel pullover, sky-blue trunks and fashionable dark-blue espadrilles. His horn-rimmed eyeglasses hung loosely between bushy eyebrows and untidy mustache (an "English" mustache, the papers called it), and his hair was more curly and less black than on television. He looked like Groucho Marx but it was obvious that he had some Negro blood in him. "*Un ruso,*" someone had told me, "a Russian mulatto." His eyes became small and greedy as he looked at me, craftily.

—So you're María's son, he said abruptly.

—So they tell me, I answered, smiling. He didn't smile back.

—You want something.

—Yes, I said. —I want some advice.

—What? It was his first question. Instead of an answer a torrent of music gushed out of my mouth: violent, rhythmic, nonstop. It was rock 'n' roll being played in some part of the house. Under my chair, perhaps? He didn't stop to discover the source of the sound: he knew better. He leaped up and rushed toward the door, opening it with his right hand (I wondered what he could have done with the piece of paper), waving the pistol in his other hand and yelling above that music that poured through the door and drove all the air up against the far end of the room:

—Maga!

The music continued, undulating and barbaric.

—Maga!

Between the hot electric guitars, the moans of the saxophones in heat and the screams of some Spanish version of Elvis Presley, I thought I could make out a human voice.

—Magalena, you cunt!

The music was turned down and remained only as a discreet backing to that sweet innocent voice.

—What did you say, Peepo?

As soon as she said Peepo I knew he wasn't her father.

—That noise, he said.

—What noise?

—The music.

—What about the music? Don't you like it?

—Sure, honey, but not so loud, *ti prego.*

—I just turned it down, she said, no more than a voice in some part of the house.

—Good, he said and closed the door.

He went back to his seat and stared at me again. This time I saw that there was something odd about the way he looked at me. Not so much odd as furtive. I tried to bring him back to the point where the subject had changed from biographical notes to music criticism.

—Well, that's how it is! I need some advice.

—What kind of advice? he said, lowering his voice again and speaking monotonously.

—I don't know. Frankly, I don't know what to do. With my life. I can't carry on any longer in my home town. There's no future for anyone there.

—So what are you going to do?

—That's what I want to find out. I hoped you'd be able to help me. I'd like to study.

He didn't reflect long on the idea.

—Where? There are schools everywhere. What do you want to study?

—Theater.

—You want to be an actor?

—No, I want to write for the theater, for TV.

TV—that's how I said it. I swung like a pendulum between hunger and the ridiculous.

—But you know what it involves, this kind of life. It's rotten through and through. It wouldn't do for a country boy like you.

—You might not think so but I've seen a lot. I've written a lot too.

I should have told him that the lots I had seen were those

which passed by my window on the bus from my home town to Havana and that Havana was as far as I could go. Also that I had written a book of sonnets and some stories, so far unpublished. But I couldn't go on: my hunger wouldn't let me. I had borne with it well until now, had forgotten it in the heat of the day, which became more stifling every minute in that closed room. I looked at the angel again and my hunger increased. If only the book of marzipan had really been edible, if it had been made of *millefeuilles*, layers instead of leaves. I stared my angel in the face. He seemed to be offering me his open book. Then I turned to my interviewer and I thought I saw the aura of a smile about him. Does hunger radiate saintliness?

—O-of c-course, he said and I was surprised that he stammered over the two words. He had talked all this time without doing so. He was speaking to me in the familiar form. He had used the *tú* before, but I only noticed it now because the tone of his voice had changed.

—Yes. Didn't you see my note? It was written in blank verse.

In actual fact he hadn't seen or heard anything.

—What do you think? He was asking me a direct question at last.

—What of? I thought vaguely that he must have been talking about the poem.

He smiled for the first time.

—Of her.

—Who?

—Magalena.

He was asking me about the girl who had been blasting off rocks 'n' rolls from upstairs, the one who had been bathing in the swimming pool in the patio and who had been looking for someone called Gabriel, probably the man in uniform. I was on the point of asking him if she was his daughter, out of malice, but he didn't give me time.

—Not bad, is she?

I didn't know what to say and answered as simply as possible.

—No.

—You like her?

—Me?

Who else could he have meant? But I had to say something.

That was what I said, I'm ashamed to admit.

—You, of course. As for me, I like her very much, naturally.

—I don't know. I didn't see her very well, hardly at all.

—But she was here talking to you.

—No, she opened the door, looked in, asked for someone called Gabriel and went out again without closing the door. And I added something, to die laughing, which is better than dying of hunger:—She was drenched in water, but he took it seriously.

—Yes, and she left water all over the room and the staircase and upstairs as well.

He seemed to sink into a meditation on hydraulics but, suddenly, surfaced, to his favorite subject.

—Well, do you or don't you like her?

—Perhaps, yes, I said timidly. I'm from the country. He got up. Something was bothering him.

—O.K., let's get on with it. What is it you w-wanted?

—Someone to give me a start in life. Was I dramatizing?—I feel cooped up. I can't go on any longer, in the town I mean. I haven't any money left now, here, in the city, whole days spent with nothing more than a cup of coffee. If nobody helps me there's nothing left for me but to kill myself. I can't go home again.

—Your name is Antonio.

I thought it was a question.

—No, Arsenio.

—No, I'm saying that your real name is Anthony, that you are Saint Anthony.

—I don't understand. Why?

—You'll soon understand. You want a start in life.

—Yes, I said.

—Good, I'm going to give you one, he said, raising his pistol and leveling it at me. He fired from a distance of less than two yards. I felt a blow in my chest, a violent jolt in my shoulder and a savage kick in the pit of my stomach. Then I heard the three shots, which sounded like someone banging on the door. My body went limp and I fell forward, already blinded, my head hitting hard the hard shoulder, the mouth of a well instantly dug in the floor. I fell into.

I HEARD HER SING

I knew La Estrella when she was only Estrella Rodríguez, a poor drunk incredibly fat Negro maid, long before she became famous and even longer before she died, when none of those who knew her well had the vaguest idea she was capable of killing herself but then of course nobody would have been sorry if she did.

I am a press photographer and my work at that time involved taking shots of singers and people of the *farándula,* which means not only show business but limelights and night life as well. So I spent all my time in cabarets, nightclubs, strip joints, bars, *barras, boîtes,* dives, saloons, *cantinas, cuevas, caves* or caves. And I spent my time off there too. My job took me right through the night and into dawn and often the whole morning. But sometimes, when I had nothing to do after work at three or four in the morning I would make my way to El Sierra or Las Vegas or El Nacional, the nightclub I mean not the hotel, to talk to a friend who's the emcee there or look at the chorus flesh or listen to the singers but also to poison my lungs with smoke and stale air and alcohol fumes and be blinded forever by the darkness. That's how I used to live and love that life and there was nobody or nothing that could change me because time passed so fast by my time that the days were only the waiting room of evening and evenings became as short as appointments and the years turned into a thin picture spread, and I went on my way, which means preferring nights to evenings, choosing night instead of day, living by night and squeezing my night, I mean my life, into a glass with ice or into a negative or into memory.

One of those nights I arrived at Las Vegas and I met up with all those people who like me had nobody who could change them and suddenly a voice came up to me from the darkness and said, *Fotógrafo,* pull up a seat please. Let me buy you a drink, and it was no longer just a voice but none other than Vítor Perla. Vítor has a magazine entirely devoted to half-naked girls or naked half-girls and captions like: A model with a future in sight—or rather two! Or: The persuasive arguments of Sonia Somethin, or: The Cuban BB says it's Brigitte who is her look-alike, and so on and so forth, so much so that I don't know where the hell they get their ideas from, they must have a shit factory in their heads to be able to talk like that about a girl or girls who only yesterday were or was probably just a *manejadora,* that is half maid and half baby-sitter, and now is half mermaid and half baby doll, or a part-time waitress who is now a full-time temptress, or who only yesterday worked in the garment center in Calle Muralla and who today is hustling her way to the top with all she's got. (Fuck, here I am, already talking like those people.) But for some mysterious reason (and if I were a gossip columnist I would spell it my$terious) Vítor had fallen into the deep, which was why it surprised me to find him in shallow waters and such spirits. I'm lying, of course. The first thing that surprised me was that he wasn't in the clink. So I told myself, He's loaded with shit but still manages to keep afloat: that's grace under morass, and I said it to him too but what I really said was, You keep afloat like good Spanish cork, and he burst out laughing. You're right, he said, but it's loaded cork! Confidentially, I must have a bit of lead somewhere inside—I'm keeling over. And so we began talking and he told me many things confidentially, he told me all his troubles, confidentially, and many other things, always confidentially, but I'm not going to repeat them because I'm a photographer not a press gossip, as I've said. Besides, Perla's problems are his own and if he solves them so much the better and if not it's curtains for Vítor. Anyway, I was fed up listening to his troubles and the way he twisted his face right and twitched his mouth left and as I had no wish to look at such ugly curly lips I changed the subject and we started talking about nicer things, namely women, and suddenly he said, Let me introduce you to Irena, and out of nowhere he produced the cutest little blonde, a doll who'd have looked like Marilyn Monroe if the Jívaros had abducted her and cut her down to size, not just shrinking her head but all the rest—and I mean *all* the rest, tits and all. So he hauled her by the arm like fishing her up from the sea of darkness and he said to me or rather to her, Irena, I want you to meet the best photographer in the world, only he didn't say the world but *el mundo*, meaning that I work for *El Mundo*, and the cutest little blonde, this incredible shrinking version of Marilyn Monroe smiled eagerly, turning up her lips and flashing her teeth like she was raising her skirt to show her thighs and her teeth gleaming in the darkness were the prettiest thing I've ever seen: perfectly even, well-formed and sensual like a row of thighs, and we started talking and every so often she would show off her teeth without blushing and I liked them so much that after a while I was meaning to ask her to let me touch her teeth or at least fondle her gums, and we were sitting at the table talking when Vítor called the waiter with this Cuban sucking sound we use to call waiters that is exactly like an inverted kiss and the drinks came as if by themselves but actually via an invisible waiter, his swarthy face and dirty hands lost in the darkness, and we started drinking and talking some more and in next to no time I'd very delicately as if I hadn't meant to place my foot on top of hers and I swear I almost didn't notice it myself, her foot was so tiny, but she smiled when I said sorry and I knew instantly that she noticed it and in the next next to no time I was holding her hand, which by now she couldn't help noticing that I meant it but I lost one fucking hour looking for it because her hand disappeared into my hand, playing hide and seek in between my yellow fingers that are permanently smeared with these hypo spots I pretend are nicotine stains, after Charles Boyer, naturally, and now already after I had finally found her hand I started caressing it without saying excuse me or anything because I was calling her Irenita, the name was just her size, and in next to next to no time we were kissing and all that, and when I happened to look around, Vítor had already got up to leave, tactful as ever, very discreetly, and so there we were on our own for a long time alone touching each other, feeling each other up, oblivious to everybody and everything, even to the show, which was over now anyway, to the orchestra playing a dance rhythm, to the people who were dancing in and out of the dark and getting tired of dancing, to the musicians packing up their instruments across the dance hall and into the dark, going home, and not noticing the fact that we were left alone there, very deep in the darkness now, no longer in the misty shadows as Cuba Venegas sings but in the deep darkness now, in darkness fifty, a hundred, a hundred and fifty fathoms under the edge of light swimming in darkness, in the lower depths, wet kissing, wet all over, wet in the dark and wet, forgotten, kissing and kissing and kissing all night long, oblivious to ourselves, bodiless except for mouths and tongues and teeth reflected in a wet mirror, two mouths and two tongues and four rows of teeth and gums occasionally, lost in saliva of kisses, silent now, keeping silent silently kissing, moist all over, dribbling, smelling of saliva, not noticing, tongues skin-diving in mouths, our lips swollen, kissing humidly each other, kissing, kissing before countdown and after blastoff, in orbit, man, out of this world, lost. Suddenly we were leaving the cabaret. It was then that I saw her for the first time.

She was an enormous mulatto, fat-fat, with arms like thighs, with thighs like tree trunks propping up the water tank that was her body. I told Irenita, I asked Irenita, I said, who's the fat one? because the fat woman seemed to dominate the *chowcito* —and fuck! now I must explain what the *chowcito* is. (The *chowcito* was the group of people who got together to get lost in the bar and hang around the jukebox after the last show was out to do their own *descarga*, this Afro-Cuban jam session which they so completely and utterly lost themselves in that once they went down they simply never knew it was daylight somewhere up there and that the rest of the world's already working or going to work right now, all the world except this world of people who plunged into the night and swam into any rock pool large enough to sustain night life, no matter if it's artificial, in this underwater of the frogmen of the night.) So there she was in the center of the *chowcito,* this enormous fat woman dressed in a very cheap dress made of caramel-colored cotton, dirty caramel confused fused with the fudge judged with her chocolate skin wearing an old pair of even cheaper sandals, holding a glass in her hand, keeping time to the music, moving her fat hips, moving all her fat body in a monstrously beautiful way, not obscene but sexual and lovely as she swayed to the rhythm, crooning beautifully, scat-singing the song between her plump purple lips, wiggling to the rhythm, shaking her glass in rhythm, rhythmically, beautifully, artistically now and the total effect was of a beauty so different, so horrible, so new, so unique and terrifying that I bitterly regretted I didn't have my camera along to catch alive this elephant who danced ballet, that hippopotamus toe-dancing, a building moved by music, and I said to Irenita, before asking what her name was, as I was on the point of asking what her name was, interrupting myself as I was asking what her name was, to say, She's the savage beauty of life, without Irenita hearing me, naturally, not that she would have understood if she had heard me, I said, I asked her, I said to her, to Irenita, Tell me, *tú,* who is it? And she said to me in a very nasty tone of voice, she said, She's the singing galapagos, the only turtle who sings boleros, and she laughed and Vítor slipped up beside me from the side of darkness just then to whisper in my ear, Careful, that's Moby Dick's kid sister, the Black Whale, and as I was getting high on being high I was able to grab Vítor by his sharkskin sleeve and tell him, You're a faggot, you're full of shit, you're a shitlicking bigot, you're a snot Gallego, a racist cunt and asshole: that's what you are, you hear me? *un culo,* and he said to me, calmly, I'll let it pass because you're my guest and you're drunk, that's all he said and then he plunged, like someone slipping behind curtains, into darkness. And I drew up closer and asked her who she was and she said to me, La Estrella, and I thought she meant the star so I said, No, no, I want to know your name, and she said, La Estrella, I am *La* Estrella, sonny boy, and she let go a deep baritone laugh or whatever you call the woman voice that corresponds to basso but sounds like baritone—cuntralto or something like that—and she smiled and said, My name is Estrella, Estrella Rodríguez if you want to know, Estrella Rodríguez Martínez Vidal y Ruiz, *para servirle,* your humble servant, she said and I said to myself, She's black, black, black utterly and finally eternally black and we began talking and I thought what a boring country this would be if Friar Bartolomé de las Casas had never lived and I said to him wherever he is, I bless you, padre, for having brought nigrahs from Africa as slaves to ease the slavery of the Injuns, who were dying off anyhow what with the mass suicides and the massacres, and I said to him, I repeated, I said, Bless you, padre, for having founded this country, and after making the sign of the cross with my right hand I grabbed La Estrella with my left hand and I said to her, I love you. La Estrella, I love *you!* and she laughed bucketloads and said to me, You're plastered, *por mi madre,* you're completely plastered! and I protested, saying to her, I said, No I'm not, I'm ferpectly so ber, and she interrupted me to say, You're drunk like an old cunt, she said and I said to her, But you're a lady and ladies don't say cunt, and she said to me, I'm not a lady, I'm an *artista* and youse drunk *coño* and I said to her, I said, You are La Estrella, and she said, And youse drunk, and I said to her, All right, drunk as a bottle, I said to her, I said, I'm full of quote methylated spirits unquote but I'm not drunk, and I asked her, Are bottles drunk? and she said, *No, qué va!* and she laughed and I said, So please consider me a bottle, and she laughed again. But above everything, I said to her, consider me in love with you, La Estrella, I'm bottle-full of love for you. I like the Estrella better than I love the estrus, also called heat or rut, and she laughed again in bucketloads, lurching back and forward with laughter and finally slapping one of her infinite thighs with one of her never-ending hands so hard and loud the slap bounced back off the wall as if outside the cabaret and across the bay and in La Cabaña fortress they had just fired the nine-o'clock-sharp salvo like they do every evening at five past nine, and when the report or its echo ceased fire she asked me, she said to me, she said, You love me? and I said, Uh-huh but she went on, Kinkily? and I said, Kinkily, passionately, maddeningly, meaninglessly, foreverly but she cut me short, No, no, I meant, you love me with my kink, kinky hair and all, and she lifted a hand to her head meaning, grabbing more than meaning her fuzzy hair with her full-fat fingers, and I said to her, *Every* bit and piece of you—and suddenly she looked like the happiest whale in the whole world. It was then that I made my great, one and only, impossible proposition. I came closer to her to whisper in her ear and I said to her, I said, La Estrella, I want to make you a dishonorable proposal, that's what I said, La Estrella, let's do it, let's have a drink together, and she said to me, De-light-ed! she said, gulping down the one she had in her hand and already chachachaing to the counter and saying to the bartender, Hey, Beefpie, make it mind, and I asked her, What's mind and she answered, Not mind, baby, mind you I said mine, m-i-n-e, make it mine and mine is La Estrella's drink: no one can have what she has, not open to the public, see what I mean. Make it mine then, and she started laughing again in bucketfuls so that her enormous breasts began shaking like the fenders of a Mack truck when the engine revs up.

At that moment I felt my arm gripped by a little hand and there was Irenita. You gonna stay all night with La Gorda here? she asked, and as I didn't answer she asked me again, You gonna stay with Fatso, and I told her, *Sí,* nothing else, all I said was yes, and she didn't say anything but dug her nails into my hand and then Estrella started laughing in bucketloads, and putting on a very superior air, she was so sure of herself, and she took hold of my hand and said, Leave her alone, this little hot pussy can do better on a zinc roof, and to Irenita she said, Sit on your own stool, little girl, and stay where you belong if you don't mind, and everybody started laughing, including Irenita, who laughed because she couldn't do anything else, and showing the two gaps in her molars just behind her eyeteeth when she laughed, she exited into daylight.

The *chowcito* always put on a show after the other show had finished and now there was a rumba dancer dancing to the jukebox and as a waiter was passing she stopped and said, Poppy, turn up the lights and let's rock, and the waiter went off and pulled out the plug and had to pull it out again and then a third time, but as the music stopped every time he switched off the jukebox, the dancer remained in the air and made a couple of long delicate steps, her whole body trembling, and she stretched out a leg sepia one moment, then earth-brown, then chocolate, tobacco, sugar-colored, black, cinnamon now, now coffee, now white coffee, now honey, glittering with sweat, slick and taut through dancing, now in that moment letting her skirt ride up over her round polished sepia cinnamon tobacco coffee and honey-colored knee, over her long, broad, full, elastic, perfect thighs, and she tossed her head backward, forward, to one side, to the other, left and right, back again, always back, back till it struck her nape, her low-cut, gleaming Havana-colored shoulders, back and forward again, moving her hands, her arms, her shoulders, the skin on them incredibly erotic, incredibly sensual: always incredible, moving them around over her bosom, leaning forward, over her full hard breasts, obviously unstrapped and obviously erect, the nipples, obviously nutritious, her tits: the rumba dancer with absolutely nothing on underneath, Olivia, she was called, still is called in Brazil, unrivaled, with no strings attached, loose, free now, with the face of a terribly perverted little girl, yet innocent, inventing for the first time movement, the dance, the rumba at that moment in front of my eyes: all of my eyes and here I am without my fucking camera, and La Estrella behind me watching everything and saying, You dig it, you dig it, and she got up off her seat as though it was a throne and went toward the jukebox while the girl was still dancing, and went to the switch, saying, Enough's enough, and turned it off, almost tearing it out in a rage, and her mouth looked like it was frothing with obscenities, and she said, That's all, folks! Dancin's over. Now we'll have *real* music! And without any music, I mean without orchestra or accompaniment from radio record or tape, she started singing a new, unknown song, that welled up from her breast, from her two enormous udders, from her barrel of a belly: from that monstrous body of hers, and I hardly thought at all of the story of the whale that sang in the opera, because what she was putting into the song was something other than false, saccharine, sentimental or feigned emotion and there was nothing syrupy or corny, no fake *feeling* or commercial sentimentality about it, it was genuine soul and her voice welled up, sweet, mellow, liquid, with a touch of oil now, a colloidal voice that flowed the whole length of her body like the plasma of her voice and all at once I was overwhelmed by it. It was a long time since anything had so moved me and I began laughing at the top of my voice, because

I had just recognized the song, laughing at myself, till my sides ached with belly laughs because it was "Noche de Ronda" and I thought talking to Agustín Lara, Agustín, Agustín, you've never invented a thing, you've not ever invented a thing, you've never composed anything, for now this woman is inventing your song: when morning comes you can pick it up and copy it and put your name and copyright on it again: "Noche de Ronda" is being born tonight. *Esta noche redonda!*

La Estrella went on singing. She seemed inexhaustible. Once they asked her to sing "La Pachanga" and she stood there with one foot in front of the other, the successive rollers of her arms crossed over the tidal wave of her hips, beating time with her sandal on the floor, a sandal that was like a motorboat going under the ocean of rollers that were her leagues of legs, beating time, making the speedboat resound repeatedly against the ground, pushing her sweaty face forward, a face like the muzzle of a wild hog, a hairless boar, her mustaches dripping with sweat, pushing forward all the brute ugliness of her face, her eyes smaller now, more malignant, more mysterious under her eyebrows that didn't exist except as a couple of folds of fat like a visor on which were sketched in an even darker chocolate the lines of her eye makeup, the whole of her face pushed forward ahead of her infinite body, and she answered, La Estrella only sings boleros, she said, and she added, Sweet songs, with real feeling, from my heart to my mouth and from my lips to your ear, baby, just so you don't get me wrong, and she began singing "Nosotros," composing the untimely dead Pedrito Junco's melody all over again, turning his sniveling little *canción* into something real, into a pulsating song, full of genuine nostalgia. La Estrella went on singing, she sang till eight in the morning, without having any notion that it was eight until the waiters started to clear everything away and one of them, the cashier, said, Excuse me, family, and he really meant it, family, he didn't say the word for the sake of saying it, saying family and really meaning something quite different from family, but family was what he meant, really, and he said: *Familia,* we have to close. But a little earlier, just before this happened, a guitarist, a good guitarist, a skinny emaciated fellow, a simple and dignified mulatto, who never had any work because he was very modest and natural and goodhearted, but a great guitarist, who knew how to draw strange melodies out of any fashionable song no matter how cheap and commercial it was, who knew how to fish real emotion out of the bottom of his guitar, who could draw the guts out of any song, any melody, any rhythm between the strings, a fellow who had a wooden leg and wore a gardenia in his buttonhole, whom we always called affectionately, jokingly, Niño Nené after all the Niños who sang flamencos, Niño Sabicas or Niño de Utrera or Niño de Parma, so this one we called Niño Nené, which is like saying Baby Papoose, and he said, he asked, Let me accompany you in a bolero, Estrella, and La Estrella answered him getting on her high horse, lifting her hand to her breasts and giving her enormous boobs two or three blows, No, Niñito, no, she said, La Estrella always sings alone: she has more than enough music herself. It was then that she sang "Mala Noche," making her parody of Cuba Venegas which has since become famous, and we all died laughing and then she sang "Noche y Día" and it was after that that the cashier asked us *familia* to leave. And as the night had already come to an end, the *noche* already *día,* we did so.

La Estrella asked me to take her home. She told me to wait a minute while she went to look for something and what she did was to pick up a package and when we went outside to get into my car, which is one of those tiny English sports cars, she was hardly able to get herself in comfortably, putting all her three hundred pounds weight in a seat which was hardly able to take more than one of her thighs, and then she told me, leaving the package in between us, It's a pair of shoes they gave me, and I gave her a sharp look and saw that she was as poor as hell, and so we drove off. She lived with some married actors, or rather with an actor called Alex Bayer. Alex Bayer isn't his real name, but Alberto Pérez or Juan García or Something Similar, but he took the name of Alex Bayer, because Alex is a name that these people always use and the Bayer he took from the drug company who make pain-killers, and the thing is they don't call him that, Bayer I mean, these people, the people who hang out in the dive at the Radiocentro, for example, his friends don't call him Alex Bayer the way he pronounced it A-leks Báy-er when he was finishing a program, signing it off with the cast calling themselves out, but they called him as they still do call him, they called him Alex Aspirin, Alex Bufferin, Alex Anacin and any other pain-killer that happens to be fashionable, and as everybody knew he was a faggot, very often they called him Alex Evanol. Not that he hides it, being queer, just the opposite, for he lived quite openly with a doctor, in his house as though they'd been officially married and they went everywhere together, to every little place together, and it was in his house that La Estrella lived, she was his cook and sleep-in maid, and she cooked their little meals and made their little bed and got their little baths ready, little etceteras. Pathetic. So if she sang it was because she liked it, she sang for the pleasure of it, because she loved doing it, in Las Vegas and in the Bar Celeste or in the Café Nico or any of the other bars or clubs around La Rampa. And so it was that I was driving her in my car, feeling very much the showoff for the same reasons but the reverse that other people would have been embarrassed or awkward or simply uncomfortable to have that enormous Negress sitting beside them in the car, showing her off, showing myself off in the morning with everybody crowding around, people going to work, working, looking for work, walking, catching the bus, filling the roads, flooding the whole district: avenues, streets, back streets, alleyways, a constant buzzing of people between the buildings like hungry hummingbirds. I drove her right up to their house, where she worked, she La Estrella, who lived there as cook, as maid, as servant to this very special marriage. We arrived.

It was a quiet little street in El Vedado, where the rich people were still asleep, still dreaming and snoring, and I was taking my foot off the clutch, putting the car into neutral, watching the nervous needles as they returned to the point of dead rest, seeing the weary reflection of my face in the glass of the dials as if the morning had made it old, beaten by the night, when I felt her hand on my thigh: she put her 5 *chorizos* 5, five sausages, on my thigh, almost like five salamis garnishing a ham on my thigh, she put her hand on my thigh and I was amused that it covered the whole of my thigh and I thought, Beauty and the Beast, and thinking of beauty and the beast I smiled and it was then that she said to me, Come on up, I'm on my own, she said, Alex and his bedside doctor, she said to me and laughed that laugh of hers that seemed capable of raising the whole neighborhood from sleep or nightmares or from death itself, They aren't here, she said: They went away to the beach for the weekend, Let's go on up so we can be alone, she said to me. I saw nothing in this, no allusion to anything, nothing to nothing, but all the same I said to her, No, I've got to go, I said. I have to work, I've got to sleep, and she said nothing, all she said was, *Adiós*, and she got out of the car, or rather she began the operation of getting herself out of the car and half an hour later, as I was dozing off from a quick nap, I heard her say, from the sidewalk now, putting her other foot on the sidewalk (as she bent threateningly over the little car to pick up her package of shoes, one of the shoes fell out and they weren't woman's shoes, but an old pair of boy's shoes, and she picked them up again), she said to me, You see, I've got a son, not as an excuse, nor as an explanation, but simply as information, she said to me, He's *retardado,* you know, but I love him all the more, she said and then she left.

First session

you're going to laugh. No, you're not going to laugh. You never laugh. You don't laugh, you don't cry, you don't say anything. All you do is sit there and listen. You know what my husband says? That you're Oedipus and I'm the sphinx, but that I don't ask you anything because I'm no longer interested in the answers. Now all I say is, Listen or I'll eat you up, and I talk and talk and talk and talk. I tell you everything. I even tell you things I don't know. Because I'm the sphinx that's had its bellyful of secrets. That's what my husband says. He's so cultured, my husband, so clever, so intelligent. The only thing wrong with him is that I'm here and he's there, wherever that is, and I'm talking and you're listening and when he gets home he sits down and reads or eats or listens to music in his room, the one he calls his studio, or he says to me, Get dressed, we're going to the movies, and I get up and get dressed and we go out, and since he's the one who does the driving he still doesn't say a thing, all he does is shake his head or grunt yes or no to anything I ask him.

Did you know my husband's a writer? Yes, of course you know, you know everything. But what you don't know is that my husband wrote a story about you. No, you didn't know. It's very clever, this story. It's the story of a psychiatrist who makes a fortune, not because his patients are millionaires but because whenever they tell him a dream he goes and plays the numbers. If someone tells him he dreamed he saw a turtle in a pond, he goes and calls his bookie and tells him, Pancho, five on number 6. If someone else tells him he saw a horse in his dreams, he phones him and says, Pancho, ten pesos on number 1. If someone else tells him he dreamed of a bull that had fallen into the water and that the water was full of prawns, he goes and phones Pancho and says, Give me five pesos on number 16 and five on number 30, just for coincidence. And this psychiatrist in the story, he always comes up with the winner because his patients always dream the number which is going to come up and one day he hits the jackpot and retires and lives happily ever after solving crossword puzzles in his home which is a palace shaped like a couch. How do you like it? Funny, eh? But you aren't laughing. Sometimes I think it's you who are the sphinx. My husband's the same, he hardly ever laughs. He makes people laugh with the stories he writes and his column in the magazine, but he doesn't laugh himself, at least not very often.

Did you know I've also got a story about a psychiatrist? No, you wouldn't know, because I've never written it down, because this is a story I've never told anyone except my husband. It was something that happened to me the first time I thought of going to a psychiatrist. Or was it the second time? It wasn't the first time. Yes it was, it was the first time. I had two appointments with him. This psychiatrist played background music during his sessions. Just imagine, background music. I remember it was always the ending of a piece and then a moment passed and you could tell what it was because they started playing it over again. It was like a piano roll. That's the word, roll, isn't it? The session began and there I was listening to the music while I was waiting my turn and then when it was my turn the music continued and it was still playing when I went away and it was already dark and this receptionist with bad teeth he had disguised as a nurse smiled good-bye at me but she didn't say good-bye, she said, See ya soon, quite sure I'd come back the next day I had an appointment, and all the time this damn music was rolling around nonstop. Sometimes there were Argentine tangos, again and again, or international rumbas. Or background music that *really* came from way back because you didn't know where it came from, I mean not what part of the house it came from, but what part of the *world*. I'd already been there twice to listen to the Muzak and to hear that doctor with his face like an alligator in glasses asking me questions! and asking and asking. And the things he asked me. What a knack for asking embarrassing questions! You'll excuse me for saying so, but I think he was quite the opposite of my husband's psychiatrist, I mean the psychiatrist in my husband's story: this psychiatrist I'm telling you about, after he had finished with me he had to go not out to play the numbers but in to play with himself. I have a real dirty mouth, I know. That's what my husband says. But that psychiatrist, he had an even more dirty *mind*. The first day I was there he gave me a notebook so I could write down everything that crossed my mind. I had to show it to him later. It was *la escuelita* all over again. I took the notebook around with me, and jotted down everything that crossed my mind, not what happened but what I was thinking of everything that happened, everything I thought or what I thought I thought, and then he read it, ever so calmly, and he read it once and then he read it again and while he was reading he pinched his lips, his upper lip, plucking the penciled mustache he had above it and he nodded his head back and forth. When he finished he said, Perfect, and he didn't say another word. My third appointment, he came and sat right next to me on the couch, against my legs. I sat up very quickly and he said, Don't be afraid, he said. Consider me another Freud, he said. Freud, I said, *another* Freud, I said to myself, another *fraud* is what you are, Dr. Fraud. But I didn't say anything, I only sat there with my legs very close together and my hands on my knees. I didn't look right or left, but straight ahead along the floor, and so we stayed like that for a moment, until I felt the man get up and come and sit almost on top of me, by my side, but so close to me it felt as though he was sitting on my lap. That's what it felt like, I swear. I closed my eyes and got up, but I wasn't able to get up right and then I did something stupid. I sat down again on the couch, but a little farther away, and the man moved next to me again and I moved away again and sat a little farther along the couch and he moved up against me again. So we went the whole length of the couch and neither of us said a word. The end of the couch felt like a cliff and it took me as much effort to stay seated there as if I had really been on the edge of an abyss. Then I got up and managed to find my voice, very squeaky, like an old woman's, and I said to the man, Doctor, I'm very sorry but your couch comes to an end here, and I got up and rushed out.

My husband died of laughter when I told him and he said to me that it would make a great story, that's what he told me. But whenever I felt like I feel now, he began talking me into seeing a psychiatrist, so much so that he made me go to another one. This psychiatrist belonged to the school of reflexes. Pavlovian, that's what he called himself. Also he belonged to the hypnotic school. Induced hypnotherapy, he called it. The way he looked at me, he could have been Rudolph Valentino. He stood there looking at me for something like a month. He didn't make me write things down in a notebook nor did he sit beside me on the couch nor did he show me the inkstains or anything. Finally after about a month and a half, he suddenly said to me out of the blue, What you need is a man like me. He was as sure of himself as if he had been a political candidate. It was almost as if he was saying, Havana needs a mayor like me. I told my husband, and you know what he said to me? You should write a book, he said, and you could call it Couch, Ouch! A funny guy, my husband. But he's the one who's always sending me to a psychiatrist.

Are you an analyst, doctor? That's what it's called, analyst, right? I'm asking you because I don't see a couch or an easy chair by the wall or anything like that and I know you're not a reflexologist. At least you don't look at me like a Pavlovian. Ah, now you're smiling! No, I mean it, doctor, I really mean it: you know, doctor, this time I've come to you of my own will.

I HEARD HER SING

Ah Fellove they were playing your "Mango Mangüé" on the radio and the music and the speed and the night enveloped us as though they wanted to protect us or vacuum-pack us and she was riding beside me, singing, humming that rhythmic melody of yours I think and she wasn't she, I mean she wasn't La Estrella but Magalena or Irenita or Mirtila I think she was and in any case she wasn't she because I'm quite clear about the difference between a whale and a sardine or a gold fish and possibly it was Irenita because she really was a demoiselle kept in the fish tank of the night. Could her name be Gary Baldi? No, she looks damn selfish and in any case fishes' teeth can be seen sticking out of a little mouth not the great whale's maw of La Estrella which had room for a whole ocean of life, but: what the hell is one stripe more to a tiger? I picked this blond stripe up in Pigal when I was on my way to Las Vegas, late at night or early in the morning, and she was standing alone under the street light outside El Pigal and she shouted at me as I was slamming my brakes on, Stop your chariot, Ben Hurry, and I drew up to the curb and she said, Where you going pretty thing? and I said Las Vegas and she said couldn't I take her a little further, where I said and she said, South of the border, Where? and she said, Across Esquina de Texas, Texas she said not Tejas corner and it was this that decided me to let her in, aside from the things I could see now that she was in the car and the street lights hit her enormous boobs bobbing up and down under her blouse, and I said, Is that for real, and she didn't answer, just opened her shirt, because what she was wearing was a man's shirt not a blouse and she unbuttoned it and she let her breasts, no: her tits, no: her udders hang loose: her enormous white round pointed boobs that were sometimes pink sometimes blue sometimes gray, and they began to look forever rosy under the lights of the streets we were passing and I didn't know whether to look to the side or the front and then I started worrying that someone would see us, that the police would stop us, because although it was twelve o'clock or two in the morning there were people everywhere in the street and I crossed Infanta doing sixty and at the seafood stand there were people eating shellfish and there are eyes like flashlights, eyesight tracking at the speed of light and sights more accurate than Marey's gun because I heard people shouting, Melons for the market! and I put my foot down on the accelerator and with my engine going at full throttle crossed Infanta and Carlos Tercero and suddenly the Esquina de Tejas disappeared behind Jesús del Monte and in Aguadulce I took the wrong turn and missed a number 10 bus by perhaps a couple of seconds and we arrived at El Sierra which was where this girl now very coolly buttoning up her shirt in front of the cabaret wanted to go and I say, O.K., Irenita and reach out a hand toward one of the melons which never made it to their market because they still had to be picked and be carried there, and she says to me, My name isn't Irenita, it's Raquelita, but don't call me Raquelita, call me Manolito el Toro because that's what my friends call me and that's what I am, a bull! and she removed my hand and got out, I'm thinking of having myself rechristened. Legally I mean, she said and started crossing the street toward the entrance of the cabaret where there was this pinup of a beautiful chick waiting for her and they held each other's hands and kissed on the mouth and began talking in whispers at the entrance under the neon sign which flashed on and off red and black and I could see them and I couldn't and I could and I couldn't and I could and I got fed up and up and out of the car and crossed the street and joined them and I said, Manolito and she didn't let me finish my sentence but said, And this one you see here is my gal Joe, pointing to her friend who looked at me with a very solemn face, but I said, Delighted to meet you Joe and she smiled and I went on, Manolito, I said, I'll make it a round trip for the same price and she said nothing doing and as I didn't want to go back into the Sierra because I hadn't the slightest desire to meet up with that mulatto Eribó or with El Beny the singer or with Cué who would begin with their music discussions which belong in the library, all of them talking at once about music as if it were the race question, arguing in unison that if two black keys are worth one white, and about mixed bars and all that, then jumping from black keys to black magic and voodoo and *santería* and then telling stories about ghosts not in haunted houses at midnight but in front of a radio announcer's mike in the early morning or at midday in a rehearsal and they talk of that piano in Radioprogreso which has played by itself since Moisés Simons, the composer of "Peanut Vendor," died and things like that which would keep me awake at night if I had to go to bed alone. So I turned around and went back to my car but not before I had said good-bye to Joe and Manolito, saying, naughty of me, Good-bye *girls!* and off I went almost at a run.

I went to Las Vegas and arrived at the coffee stand and met up with Laserie and said to him, Hi, Rolando, how're things and he said, How're you, *mulato* and so we began chatting and then I told him I was going to take some pics of him here one of these nights when he was having a cup of coffee, because Rolando really looks good, a real singer, a real Cuban, a real regal *habanero* with his white drill suit, very neat and dandy from the white tan shoes to the white straw hat, dressed as only Negroes know how to dress, drinking his coffee very careful making sure not to spill a drop and stain his spotless suit, with his body tilted back and his mouth on the rim of the cup and the cup in one hand and the other hand under it resting on the bar drinking the coffee sip by sip, and I said good-bye to Rolando, See you soon, I said and he said, Whenever you feel up to it, *mulato,* and I'm just about to go into the club when you'll never guess whom I see in the door. None other than Alex Bayer who comes up to me and shakes my hand and says, I've been expecting you, in that very fine very educated very polished accent of his and I say, Who, me, and he says, Yes, you, and I say, Do you want me to take some shots of you and he says, No, I want to talk with you, and I say, Whenever you want, but isn't it a bit late now thinking he might or might not be trying to pick a fight, you never know with these people, like when José Mujica was in Havana he was walking along the Prado with an actress on each arm or a couple of singers or just two girls, and a fellow who was sitting on a bench shouted at them, Hi girls, and Mujica, very serious, very much the Mexican movie star, in pitch, as though he had been singing, went over to the bench and asked the fellow, 'Xcuse me, what did you say and he said, What you heard, miss, and Mujica, who was a really big man (or is, if he's still alive, though people tend to shrink as they get older) picked him up and held him over his head and threw him down on the street, not on the street but onto the grass borders between the Prado and the street, and went on his way as naturally and easily and unrivaled as though he were singing "Perfidia," Mexican accent and all, and I don't know if Alex was thinking what I was thinking or was thinking what Mujica was thinking or if he was thinking what he himself was thinking, all I know is that he laughed, he smiled and said, Let's go and I said, Let's sit at the bar and he shook his head, No, what I have to talk to you about it's better that I say it outside and I said, Better still, let's sit in my car then and he said, No, let's take a walk and I said, All right and we went off down along P Street and as we were walking he said, Night is made for walking in Havana, isn't it, and I nodded and then said, Yes, if it's cool, Yes, he said, if it's cool it's nice for walking. I do it very often, it's the best tonic there is for body and soul, and I felt like shitting on his soul thinking that all this faggot wanted to do was to walk around with me and pretend he was a philosopher. Peripathetic.

As we were walking along we saw the Cripple with the Gardenias coming out of the dark opposite, with his crutch and his tray of gardenias and his good evening said so politely and with such courtesy it seemed almost impossible he could be so sincere and crossing another street I heard the harsh, nasal and relentless voice of Juan Charrasqueado the Sing-Singing Charro singing the single verse of the lottery which he always sings and repeats a thousand times, Buy your number and buy your number and buy your number and buy your number and buy, meaning they should throw money into his sweaty sombrero as he forcibly passed it around, creating an atmosphere of mock obsession which is poignant because everyone knows he's incurably mad. I read the sign above the Restaurant Humboldt Club and thought of La Estrella who always ate there and I wondered what the illustrious baron who had discovered Cuba would say if he knew he is best remembered here as the name of a cheap restaurant, a dingy bar and a street famous for an infamous political massacre and also for a notorious brothel specializing in living pictures, featuring Superman! and Fernando's Hideaway and Bar San Juan and Club Tikoa and The Fox and the Crow and the Eden Rock where one night a black woman made the mistake of going down the flight of stairs to the door, in there to eat, and they threw her out with an excuse that was an exclusion and she began to shout LitelrocLitelrocLitelroc because Faubus was in the news and she started a great uproar down there, and La Gruta where all the eyes are phosphorescent because the creatures who inhabit this bar and club and bedroom are fish from the lower depths and Pigalle or Pigale or Pigal, it's called all these ways, and the Wakamba Self-Service and Marakas with its menu in English and its bilingual menu outside and its neon Chinese sign to confuse Confucius, and the Cibeles and the Colmao and the Hotel Flamingo and the Flamingo Club and on passing down N Street and 25th I saw under the lamppost outside in the street four old men playing dominoes in shirtsleeves and I smiled and even laughed and Alex asks me what I'm laughing about and I say, Oh nothing and he says I know he says. Do you? I asked and he says yes he says, At the poetry of this group portrait and I think, Fuck, an aesthete. But what I tell him is that he hasn't told me what he wanted to tell me and he says he doesn't know how to begin and I say that's very easy, begin at the beginning or at the end and he says, Easy for you because you're a journalist and I say, I'm not a journalist, I'm a photographer, Albeit a press photographer, he says and I say, Hélas yes I am and he says, Well, I'll begin in the middle and I say, Fine and he says, I take it you don't really know La Estrella and you go about telling lies about her and about us. Never mind that, I know what the truth is and I'm going to tell you, and I am not offended or anything and I see that he isn't offended or anything, so I say, Fine, shoot.

Second session

There were three bathhouses, one next to the other, and I went into the last one, which had an open terrace, with a wooden floor and against one of the walls there were a number of easy chairs with people sitting in them taking in the fresh air and talking and sleeping. I asked for someone, I don't remember who, and they told me to look for him on the beach. I climbed up to the path, where the sun was really hot. The road was dazzling white and the grass looked burnt. The beach was way back to the left and I continued walking and came to a quiet beach, where the waves rolled all the way in and returned to the sea and came in again very gently. There was a dog playing on the beach, but then I think he stopped playing, because he was running the whole length of the shore and he dipped his mouth in the water and I saw that smoke was coming out of it. Not out of the sea but out of the dog: smoke was coming out of his muzzle and his ribs and his tail looked like a torch. Now there was a very poor wooden house to the right and the sky which until a moment ago had been that of a mild winter's day was gray now and there was one cloud, only one but very large, very swollen and very white, and there was a wind and I can't remember whether or not it was raining. I saw two more dogs running toward the first one, with smoke coming out of them, and they also plunged into the sea. I think they disappeared. When I reached the corner of the house, the other corner, the one that was farthest away, I saw two or three dogs trotting around and around a bonfire and dipping their muzzles in it and trying to get something out of the fire. One after another they burned themselves and they ran toward the sea which was now much farther off. I came closer and saw that there was another dog in the fire, right in it, burnt up, an enormous dog, in the middle of the fire with his paws sticking up, all swollen, and some parts of him, the paws, were charred and he had no tail or ears, they must have turned to ashes.

I stood there gazing at the dog watching him slowly burn and I think that I decided to go into the house, through the door which led to the square where they were burning the dog (because there was a square and the dog had been burned on a pile of sand), to let anybody who was there know. I knocked and nobody answered and then I pushed the door open. Inside, staring at the door, was another dog, an enormous one, almost the size of a calf, his face covered with hair and his ears pointed and a filthy gray color. He was really scary! I think his eyes were red or perhaps they were blazing because the room or house was very dark. When I opened the door he got up and snarled and leaped at me. I was on the verge of screaming when I realized he had passed to one side of me and had pushed the door open with his body. I saw him run toward the monument where the other dog was burning and without showing a scrap of fear he plunged into the flames and ate the burnt dog. I remember him standing there with a piece of scorched meat in his mouth. He went on eating the dog and picking him up in his muzzle and the dog that had been burnt was almost as big as he was and I say almost because the other dog was missing those parts of him that had been lost in the fire. The live dog lifted the dead dog above the fire, carried him without any difficulty and returned with him to the house, without any part of the burnt dog touching the ground. They must have gone past me, because I hadn't moved from the door, but I didn't even hear them going by.

I HEARD HER SING

You are being *so* unfair! Alex said and I was about to protest when he said, No, let me speak and afterward you'll know that you really are being unfair, and I let him talk, I let him go on talking in that voice which was so rounded, so beautiful, so well-manicured, which pronounced all the *s*'s and all the *d*'s and in which all the *r*'s were *r*'s and I began to understand as he was talking just why he was so famous as an actor on the radio and why he got thousands of letters from women every week and I understood why he rejected their proposals and I also understood why he took such pleasure in making conversation, in telling stories, in talking: he was a Narcissus-cum-Echo who let his & her words fall into the pool of conversation and then listened to himself rapturously in the ripples of sound she made. Was it his voice that made him a faggot? Or the reverse? Or is it that in every actor there's an actress struggling to get out? Oh, well, asking questions is not my line.

What you are saying is not exactly true, he said. We, he said (and that we was all he conceded on his beautiful arrangement), we are not Estrella's masters, *La* Estrella as you call her. In actual fact we are more like Polyphemus's sheep. (A beauty, ain't it? But you'd have to hear him say it to get the full flavor.) She does what she likes in *our* house. She's not a servant or anything like that, but an uninvited guest: she arrived one day six months ago because we invited her one night when we heard her sing in the Bar Celeste: *I* invited her but just to have a drink with us. She overstayed, then she stayed over to sleep and she slept all day and when night fell she went away without saying a word. But the following morning she was knocking at the door. She went directly upstairs and lay down in the room we had given her the night before, my painting studio which, incidentally, I *traded* with her for the servant's room on the roof after *she* gave notice to *our* servant, who, poor soul, had been with us for years and years, taking advantage of the fact that we were away on holiday. Instead, she brought a cook into the house, a little Negro boy who obeyed her in everything and whom she went out with every night. Do you see what I mean? He used to carry her *neceser* for her, which at that time might be an old commando handbag or even a shopping bag with the label of El Encanto store still on. Then they would do the town at night and return in the wee hours of the morn. That was until we dismissed him. This happened, of course, much later. A week after that night she spent here as our guest she told us the story of her invalid son and taking advantage of the fact that we felt sorry for her—only for half a mo', let me tell you—she asked us if we could take her into our house, though as it was she could hardly ask us to allow her to stay, as she had already been staying with us a week. We *took* her in, as she called it, and after a few days she asked us if she could borrow a key. "So as not to disturb you," she told us. She gave it back the following day, it's true, but she didn't disturb us anymore, because she didn't knock on the door anymore. You know why? Because she had surreptitiously had another key made, her own of course.

I take it you were moved by the story of her idiot son, as we were. Well, I'm telling you, that's not true either: there is no son nor moron nor monster. It's her husband who has a daughter, a girl about twelve and perfectly normal. He had to send her to the country because she made life impossible for her. She is married, there's no doubt about it, to this man who owns a hot-dog stand on the beach at Marianao. He's a poor man whom she blackmails and when she visits him in his shop it's to rob him of hot dogs, eggs, soft or hard-boiled, stuffed potatoes, the lot, which she eats in her room. I should mention by the way that she eats enough food for an army and that *we* have to buy all this food—and she's still hungry afterward. That's why she's so huge! She's as big as a hippo and like a hippo she's also amphibian. She takes a bath three times a day: when she arrives in the morning, in the afternoon when she wakes up to have her breakfast and in the evening before she goes out. To no avail, mind you, because you wouldn't *believe* how she sweats! She drips water as if she were in a permanent state of high fever. So she spends her life in the water: sweating and drinking water and taking baths. And she's always singing: she sings when she's getting ready to go out. She never stops singing! In the morning, when she comes in, we know she's arrived before she starts singing, because she holds onto the railings to climb the steps and you know what they're like, those marble steps and wrought-iron balusters of old Havana. So she climbs the stairs and as she climbs them she clings to the banister and the whole balustrade trembles and resounds right through the house and when the iron is loudly ringing against the marble she starts singing. We have had a thousand and one problems with the neighbors below, but nobody can say anything to her because she doesn't listen to reason. "They're jealous," she says, "real jealous. You'll see how they'll worship me when I'm famous." Because she has this obsession about being famous: and we too are obsessed with her becoming famous: we're crazy for her to become famous so she'll finally take her music or rather her voice—because she insists that you don't need musical backing to sing and that she carries her own accompanist inside her—her voice, then, someplace else.

When she's not singing she's snoring and when she's not snoring she floods the house with her perfume—Cologne 1800, can you imagine! although *I* shouldn't be talking *so* badly about my number-one backer—she sprays it all over, she showers herself with it and she's such a huge woman! Besides, she sprays herself with talcum like she sprays herself with perfume. That, plus the way she pours water all over herself and the way she eats, my dear, it's not human, believe you me, it's not human. Believe me! *Croyez-moi! Créeme!* (And this is one of the few Cubans who pronounce the second *e* of the verb *creer*.) Talcum for heaven's sake! Have you seen the folds of flesh, of fat on her neck? Then take a look next time and you'll see that in every crease there is a crust of talcum. To top it off—listen to this, I beg you—she's obsessed with the imperfections of her body and she spends the whole day pouring scents and perfumes and deodorants over herself and plucking out hairs from her eyebrows down to her feet. I swear I'm not exaggerating. One day we returned home unexpectedly and we found her walking up and down naked in her birthday suit all over the house and, alas, we got a very good view of her! Nothing but rollers of human flesh and not a *single* hair on her whole body. Believe me, this Estrella of yours is one of nature's true freaks! More than that, she's a cosmic case. Her one weakness, the only human thing about her, is her feet, not their shape, but because they hurt her, yes, she's flatfooted, and how she complains. It's the only thing she complains about. There are times when her feet really hurt. She just puts them palms up, legs perched high on any chair, and she lies on the floor complaining, complaining, complaining. Almost to the point when you begin to begin to feel sorry, almost pity for her, but that's when she gets up and starts shouting up and down the house, shouting at the poor neighbors, "But Ise gonna be famous! Ise gonna be famous! *Famous*, you fuckers!" You know who her enemies are aside from the invisible neighbors? (A) Old men, because she's only interested in young men and she falls in love with adolescent boys like a bitch in heat. (B) The impresarios who'll exploit her when she's famous. (C) People who will call her a nigger or allude to her black color behind her back. (D) *Dose* who'll make signs in front of her that she won't understand or who'll laugh without saying what they're laughing at or who'll use some private code or other which she'll have no means of deciphering. But the biggest unseen enemy is death. She's frightened to death that she'll die before she is, as she says, discovered. I know what you're going to say before you'll agree with me: that she's pathetic. Yes, she's pathetic, but, my dear, it's one thing being pathetic in a tragedy, and another being pathetic in a comedy. The latter is simply intolerable.

Have I forgotten anything? Oh, yes, to tell you that I prefer freedom to justice. You don't have to believe the truth. Go on being unfair to us. Love *La* Estrella. But, *please*, help her to be famous, see that she makes it big, rescue us from her. We will adore her like a saint, mystically. That is to say, in the ecstasy of her memory.

SESERIBO

Ekué was sacred and lived in a sacred river. One day Sikán came to the river. The name Sikán perhaps meant curious woman once or just woman. Sikán, just like a woman, was not only curious but indiscreet. But are the curious ever discreet?

Sikán came to the river and heard the sacred sound which only a few men of Efó were permitted to hear. Sikán listened and listened—and then talked. She went and told her father, who didn't believe her because Sikán was the fibber of Efí. Sikán returned to the river and listened again and this time she also saw. She saw Ekué and heard Ekué and told all about Ekué. So that her father would believe her she pursued Ekué with her gourd (which she used to drink water with) and she caught up with Ekué, who wasn't made for running. Sikán brought Ekué back to the village in her gourd of drinking water. Her father believed her now.

When the few men of Efó (their names must not be repeated) came to the river to talk to Ekué they didn't find him. The trees told them that he had been chased and followed, that Sikán had caught him and taken him to Efí in the gourd of water. This was a crime. But to let Ekué talk without stopping up the ears of profane listeners and to tell his secrets and to be a woman (but who else could have done such a thing?), this was more than a crime. It was sacrilege.

Sikán paid with her skin for her blasphemy. She was skinned alive and died. Ekué died too, some say of shame at letting himself be caught by a woman or of mortification when traveling in the gourd. Others say he died of suffocation in the pursuit—he certainly wasn't made for running. But his secret was not lost nor the custom of reunion nor the happiness of knowing that he existed. With his skin they clad the *ekué* that speaks now in the rites for initiates and is magic. The skin of Sikán the Indiscreet was used to dress another drum, which has neither nails nor ties and which has no voice, because she is still suffering the punishment for not holding her tongue. She wears four plumes with the four oldest powers at her four corners. As she is a woman she has to be beautifully adorned, with flowers and necklaces and cowries. But over her drumhead she wears the tongue of a cock as a sign of eternal silence. Nobody touches it and it is unable to talk by itself. It is secret and taboo and it is called *seseribó.*

Rite of Sikán and Ekué
(Essential mystery of Afro-Cuban magic)

I

On Fridays we don't have a show, so we can take the night off, and that Friday seemed the perfect day to be at the opening night of the summer dance hall at the Sierra. So it was the perfect night for taking a ride up there to hear Beny Moré singing. Besides, Cuba Venegas was making her debut that night and I just *had* to be there. You know it's me who discovered Cuba, not Christopher Columbus. I heard her the first time at the time when I was just starting to hear again and at that time I was hearing music wherever I went, so my ear was in perfect pitch. I'd given up music for advertising, but I made very little money in that agency which was more like a regency and as there was a whole load of new cabarets and nightclubs opening up I brushed up my *tumbadora* (a *tumba* is not a tomb, a joke I repeat like a ritual and every time I say it I remember Innasio: Innasio is Ignacio Piñeiro, who wrote that immortal rumba about a rejected lover who seeks revenge by composing this epitaph on his sweetheart's tomb—you got to hear Innasio himself singing it—which is the lyrics of a rumba: *"Don't weep for her, gravedigger / Don't weep, please / She's not my wife, she's a whore / You dig, gravedigger? / If you do, don't weep!"*) and began practicing my drums nonstop and in one week I was making them sing smooth and sweet and suave, so much so I went to see Barreto and told him, "Guillermo, I want to make a comeback," joking of course.

Anyways, Barreto found me work in the second band at the Capri, the one they have playing between two shows, for people to dance to or to trample themselves to death to but in rhythm or to tread on corns in six-eight time. Take your pick.

Anyways, I was listening to someone singing through the window and the voice didn't sound at all bad. The song (it was Frank Domíngues' "Images": you've got to know it, it goes like this: *"Like in a dream, quite unexpectedly you came to me . . ."*) and the voice came up from below and then I saw that behind it was a tall mulatto girl with hair like an Indian, going up to the patio to hang out her washing. You've guessed it: it was Cuba, who was called Gloria Pérez at that time and obviously I hadn't been working in an advertising agency just for fun and I got her to change her name to Cuba Venegas because nobody named Gloria Pérez is going to be a halfways decent singer, so that *mulata* who was once Gloria Pérez is now Cuba Venegas (or the other way round) and as she's in Puerto Rico or Venezuela or someplace like that and I'm not going to gossip about her now, I can tell you this in passing.

Cuba made it in a very short time: the time it took her to leave me for my very good friend Códac, who was the in photographer that year, and then she discarded Códac for Piloto & Vera (Piloto first and then Vera), who've written two or three good songs, among them "Sad Meeting," which Cuba made *her* instant creation. Finally she moved in with and/or onto Walter Socarrás (Floren Cassalis said in his column that they were married: I *know* they weren't married, but as Arturo de Córdova would say, *Eso no tiene la menor importancia*), he's the musician-arranger who took her on tour through Latin America and who was conducting from his piano stool in the Sierra that night. (*Eso no tiene la menor importancia* either.) And so it was that I went to the Sierra to hear Cuba Venegas sing, with that very pretty voice of hers and her lovely face (Cubita Bella, they call her for a joke) and her tremendous stage presence, and to wait for her to see me and make eyes at me and dedicate to me her song "Stop Him on Site," just for fun.

II

So there I was in the Sierra drinking at the bar no less and chatting with Beny. Let me tell you about Beny. Beny is Beny Moré and to talk about him is the same as talking about music, so let me tell you about music. Remembering Beny made me remember a common past, that is music: a *danzón* titled "Isora" in which the *tumbadora* repeats a double beat of the double bass filling the bar and beating the most accomplished dancer, who has to put up with or dive under the swaying mean measure of the rhythm. Chapottín repeats this tricky beat in a record that did the rounds in '53, the offbeat riffs of "Cienfuegos," which is like a *guaguancó* turned into a *son* where the bass fiddle plays a dominant role. Once I asked old Chapo how the hell he did it and he told me it was (long life to the long fingers of Sabino Peñalver) by improvising the choruses when they were cutting the record. Only this way was a circle of happy music made out of the rigid square of Cuban rhythms. I was talking about this with Barreto in Radioprogreso one day after a recording session where he was on drums and I was playing my *tumba* and from time to time I happened to cut across him. Barreto told me you had to break the mandatory two-two/four-four beat of Cuban rhythms, and I told him about Beny who, in his songs, made fun of that four-to-the-bar prison for squares, making the melody glide over the rhythm, forcing the band to follow him in his flight and making it supple as a saxophone, as a legato trumpet, as if he were conducting a rubber band. I remember when I was playing in his *banda gigante*, standing in for the drummer, who was not only my friend but who had also asked me to take his place as he wanted the night off to go *dancing!* It was one hell of a job playing behind Beny, turning his back to the band, singing and making faces at the audience, sending the melody soaring over the heads of our earthbound instruments and their dragging feet and then all of a sudden to see him turn and ask you to throw a bomb at precisely the metronomic moment, right on the spot. *Ese Beny!*

All at once Beny gives me a slap on the shoulder and says, "Hey, Charlie, that nymphet from your school? She doesn't look your class!" I didn't know what he was talking about and as you never know what Beny is talking about I never paid him much attention except when he's making music but then he's not talking about singing now. However I turned and looked around. Do you know who I saw? I saw a girl, almost too young for consent, about sixteen, staring hard at me. It's always dark both inside and outside the Sierra, but I was able to see her from the bar though she was on the other side, outside, on the patio, and looking at me through a dark glass panel. She was staring at me all right and real hard, there was no doubt about it. Besides I could see she was smiling at me now, so I smiled back and then I left Beny 'xcuse me a moment and went up to her table. At first I didn't recognize her because she was very tanned and she had her hair down and looked all woman. She was wearing a white dress, almost up to the neck in front, but cut very low down the back. Very, very low, so I could see the whole of her back and a very pretty back it was too. She smiled at me again and said, "Don't you recognize me?" It was then I recognized her: it was Vivian Smith-Corona and you don't need me to tell you the meaning of that double-barreled name. She introduced me to her friends: Havana Yacht Club types, or Vedado Tennis, or Casino Español. It was a grand table. Not just because it was the size of three tables put together, but because there were several millions sitting in those wrought-iron chairs branding asses that were prominent both physically and socially. Nobody took much notice of me and Vivian playing the part of a demi-chaperone, so she was able to talk to me for a while, me standing and she sitting and as nobody stood me a seat, I said:

—Let's go outside, meaning the street, where there are many people talking and breathing in the warm dirty fumes of the buses when it's too hot to stay indoors.

—I can't, she said. —I'm chaperoning tonight.

I didn't know what to do and I hovered over the social gathering uncertain whether to go or stay.

—Why don't we see each other later? she said, speaking between her teeth.

I didn't know what exactly she meant by later.

—Later on, she said. —After they've taken me home. Mummy and Daddy are away at the ranch. Come up and see me.

III

Vivian lived in the Focsa building on the twenty-seventh floor, but it wasn't there, not so high up, that I met her for the first time. It was more like a basement where I met her. She came to the Capri one night with Arsenio Cué and my friend Silvestre. I only knew of Cué by name and at a distance at that, but Silvestre was my classmate at high school, until the fourth year when I left to study drawing at San Alejandro Academy, imagining at the time that my real name was Raphael or Michelangelo or Leonardo and that Bernard Berenson would be putting on a volume off my pantings—living under the influence of Bustrófedon. Cué introduced me to his fiancée or girl friend first, a tall slender girl with hardly any breasts but very good-looking and you could see she knew it. He introduced me to Vivian and finally he introduced them to me. Very sophisticated he was—and a regular ham. He introduced us in English and to show he was a contemporary of the UN building he started talking in French to his sweetheart or fuckiancée or whatever she was. I was expecting him to switch to German or Russian or Italian on the slightest provocation, but he didn't. He went on talking French or English or both languages at once. We local lads were making plenty of noise and the show was under way, but Cué spoke his English-cum-French above the music and the singer's voice and above the din of dining and drinking and dealing that you get in cabarets. They were both deeply absorbed in showing they could speak French and kiss at the same time. Silvestre was watching the show (or rather the chorus girls in the show, freaks all legs and breasts) as though he was seeing it for the first time in his life, neglecting this real beauty at his side for ersatz flesh and roboobs. (Big B. again.) As I knew those dancing cheeks and chicks as well as Vesalius knew his anatomy and as I'm as tough as a Lawrence in this Arabia Deserta of sex, I stayed in my oasis, gazing at Vivian, who was sitting opposite me. She was looking at the show but, like a proper young lady, sat so as not to turn her back on me and as she saw I was staring at her (she *had* to see it because I was almost touching her fully clothed flesh with tactile eyes) she turned around to talk to me.

—What did you say your name was? I didn't catch it.

—That always happens.

—Yes, introductions are like condolences, social whispers.

I was going to contradict her and say that this always happens to me *only,* but I liked her intelligence and more than that, her voice, which was soft and caressing and agreeably low.

—José Pérez is my name, but my friends call me Vincent.

She didn't understand but gave me an odd look. So much so that I felt embarrassed. I explained it was a joke, that I was parodying a parody, that it came from a speech by Vincent van Douglas in *Lust for Life.* She said she hadn't seen it and asked me if it was good and I answered that the painting was great but the picture was lousy, that Kirk van Gugh! painted while he was crying and vice versa and that Anthony Gauquinn was a bouncer in the Saloon de Refusés but anyways she must have the second opinion of my friend Silvestre, a thorough professional (no joke intended). Finally I told her my name, the real one.

—A very nice name, she said. I didn't pursue the matter.

Arsenio Cué must have been listening all the time because he freed himself from one of those eight arms of his fiancée who looked like a squid with bones and said:

—*Pourquoi ne te maries tu?*

Vivian laughed, but it was an automatic laugh, a loud smile from a TV commercial, a mocking grimace.

—Arsen, his fiancée said.

I looked at Arsenio Cué who was insisting.

—*Mais oui. Pourquoi non?*

Vivian stopped smiling. Arsenio was drunk and went on using not only his voice but his index finger now. So much so that Silvestre left off looking at the show, though only for a moment.

—Arsen, his fiancée said crossly.

—*Pourquoi, alors?*

He was pissed off. There was a persistent note of annoyance in his voice as though I'd been talking to his fiancée and not to Vivian.

—Arson, she was shouting now. Fiancée not Vivian.

—It's pronounced *Arsen,* I told her.

She looked at me, her blue eyes blazing with fury, unloading all the irritation she felt with Cué on me.

—*Ça alors,* she said to me. —*Chéri, viens. Viens! Embrassez-moi.* This was addressed to Arsenio Cué, presumably.

—Oh, dear, Cué said in English and he forgot us all as he buried himself in those bilingual or trilingual collarbones and ulnas.

—What's the matter with them? I asked. I asked Vivian.

She looked at them and told me:

—Apparently they want to turn Spanish into a dead language.

We both laughed. I was feeling good and now it wasn't just because of her voice. Silvestre turned away from the show again, looked at us very seriously and went back to watching the train of bosoms-cum-limbs which was dollying the conga along a fanciful railroad of music and color and scandal. The number was called "The loco motive of love" and it was set to the tune of "The sea legs."

—*"Let's go to the waterfront, let's get back our sea legs,"* Vivian sang pointedly, touching Cué's fiancée on the arm.

—*Qu'est-ce que c'est?*

—Quit French-kissing and come with me, she said.

—Where to? said Cué's fiancée.

—Yes, where? said Cué.

—To the ladies', *chéris.* Vulgo, jane, Vivian said.

—Wanna wo weewee, Cué said. They got up and as soon as they had left Silvestre turned his attentive shoulders to the show, beating the table with his hand and almost shouting:

—She's bedable.

—What! I said.

—She's an easy lay, Silvestre said.

—Who? Cué said.

—Not your girl, the other one, Vivian. She's a bedable lay.

—Ah! I thought that's who you meant, Cué said and I had never suspected him to be a puritan, but he quickly added, —Because if you meant Sibila (that was the name of Arsenio Cué's fiancée or whatever she was: I'd been trying to remember it all evening) you've got it the wrong way right around, he said, smiling. —I mean you stand correct. She'll go to bed, but with Myselftov, he said, meaning himself, Cué.

—No, Sibila, no, Silvestre said.

—*Sí*, Nobila, *sí*, said Cué.

They were both pissed.

—I say that she will go to bed, Silvestre said for the third time.

—Every night and in her own bedroom, said Cué, lisping out the words.

—Not go to bed to, I mean go to bed *with*, you fucker!

I thought it bedder to come between them.

—O.K., O.K., Charlie, she'll go to bed and then she'll go to bed. But we'd better pretend we're watching the show or they'll shove us out.

—Show us out, you mean, Silvestre said.

—Shove or show, it's all the shame, Cué said.

—No, it's not the same, said I.

—It's not the same, it's a shame, said Silvestre.

—They'll show us out, Cué said, —but you're the one they'll shove out.

—It's true, Silvestre said. —It's true!

—It's true it's true, said Cué and he burst into tears. Silvestre tried to calm him down, but at that very moment Ana Coluton came onto the stage to do her number and he had no intention of missing that exhibition of legs and tits and woman's wit that was capable of suggesting *almost* everything. The show was just coming to tit's end when Vivian and Sibila returned and Cué was bent over the table and crying copiously.

—What's the matter with him? Vivian asked.

—*Qu'est qu'il y a chéri*? said Sibila, fluttering over her tearful fiancé. But it was Silvestre who answered:

—He (meaning me) is afraid they will throw him (meaning Cué) out. Or voice versa.

—Yes, if he goes on making these scenes, Vivian said and

Silvestre shouted over her, —*Ob*scenes, I call them. They'll throw us all out (and he drew an excentric circle with his drunken finger as he was speaking) and as for this fellow (and he directed an erratic arrow with his index finger toward me) they'll fire him, poor fellow, and Silvestre burst into tears too.

Vivian tut-tut-tutted in false chagrin and true amusement and Silvestre gave her a hard look and almost lifted the hand with which he had insisted on Vivian's erotic willingness, but he returned to watching one of the chorus girls pass by en route to the street and the oblivion of the night. Cué cried even louder. When I went back to the band Sibila who was also drunk joined him in his tear-letting and I left the tragicomic scene just as their table floated out into a sea of tears (courtesy of Arsenio Cué & Co.). I arrived on the stage just as they were lowering it into a dance floor.

When I start playing I forget everything else. So there I was beating, scraping, rubbing and swooping and plunging and smashing those drums, crossing, counterpointing them, unisoning them, coming in with the bass fiddle and the piano so I could hardly make out the table of my tearful and timorous and laughing friends, because it was in the dark at the back of the room. I went on playing when all at once I saw that Arsenio Cué was dancing on the floor, no longer crying, with Vivian as amused as ever. I had no idea that she danced so well, so much in swing, just like a Cuban. Cué for his part was being led by her as he smoked a king-size cigarette at the end of a black metallic holder and through his dark glasses he was confronting the world, petulant, pedantic and pathetic. They passed close to me and Vivian smiled at me.

—I like the way you play, *tú*, she said, and the *tú* was like a second smile on top of the first.

They swayed by me a number of times and ended up dancing in my territory. Cué was helplessly drunk and he had taken off his glasses now and was winking at me out of one eye and smiling and then he winked with both eyes, and, I think, he was saying to me, saying in lipspeak, She's bedable, she's bedable. Finally the number came to an end. It was that raveling bolero, "Miénteme." Vivian left the floor first and Cué came up to me and said quite plainly in my ear: —That one really is bedable, and he laughed and pointed at Silvestre, who was slumped over the table, fast asleep, his small Oriental fat body fallen flat like a corpse shrouded in silk: blue against the white tablecloth, his suit looked expensive even from a distance. In the next number Arsenio Cué danced (more or less) with Sibila, who was also drunk and falling all over the place, so that he now seemed by contrast to be dancing better or less badly than before. While I was playing the bongos I noticed that she (Vivian) hadn't taken her eyes off me. I saw her get up. I saw her cross the room and stand near the band.

—I had no idea you played so well, she said when the dance was over.

—Neither good nor bad, I said. —Just well enough to make a living.

—No, you *really* play well. I like it.

She didn't say whether it was the fact that I was playing that she liked or that I played well or that it was me who was playing well. Would she be a music fan? Or a fiend for perfection? Had I given any indication or sign that betrayed my feelings?

—I mean it seriously, she said. —I would like to play like you.

—You don't have to.

She shook her head. Was she friend or fiend? I would soon know.

—Girls who belong in the Yacht Club don't have to play the bongo drums.

—I don't belong in the Yacht Club, she said and left and I didn't know if she had been hurt or hurt herself. Because I went on playing.

I played and played and I saw Arsenio Cué call the waiter and ask for the check and I went on and on and on and I saw him wake up Silvestre and playing I saw the swarthy, skinflint writer get up and begin to go out with Vivian and Sibila supporting his arms and I went on playing as Cué was paying all that money by himself and playing the waiter came back and Cué gave him a tip which must have been a good one judging by the waiter's satisfied face playing and I saw him go away as well and all of them meet up at the door and the doorman opening the crimson curtains and playing they crossed the classy well-lighted gambling saloon and the curtain closed on, behind them playing. They didn't even say so much as bye-bye. But I didn't care because I was playing and I went on playing and I continued to go on playing for a good while longer.

IV

I saw very little of Vivian before that night at the Sierra, but I saw plenty of Arsenio Cué and my friend Silvestre. I don't know why I saw them but I did. One day I was coming out of a rehearsal (I think it was a Saturday afternoon) and I ran into Cué who was walking by himself, on foot surprisingly, along 21st Street. It was very hot that day and although the clouds had piled up toward the south it didn't look as though it was going to rain, but Cué was wearing a raincoat (an *imper*, he called it) and he was holding his cigarette holder and smoking and walking along with that knock-kneed awkward stride of his and puffing the smoke out through his nostrils, both of them, like a double column of gray fumes floating ostentatiously out above his lips. He reminded me of the reluctant dragon. Not so much reluctant as a reticent dragon behind his sempiternal dark glasses and well-pruned mustache.

—This tropical heat is intolerable, he said by way of greeting me.

—You must be drowning, I said, pointing at his trench coat.

—Coat or no coat, clothes or no clothes, I don't know how the hell anybody can stand this climate.

This was his theme song. It was on this note that he began his sound tracts against the tropics, the country, the people, the music, the Negroes, women and underdevelopment. Everything. It was his Third World Man's Theme. That afternoon he told me that Cuba (not Venegas, the other Cuba) was not a fit hangout for man or beast. Nobody should live here except plants, insects and fungi or any other lower forms of life. The squalid fauna that Christopher Columbus found when he landed proved the point. All that remained now were birds and fish and tourists. All of these could leave the island when they wanted. On finishing his diatribe he asked me without changing his tone of voice:

—Do you want to come with me to the Focsa?

—What is to be done? I smiled.

—Nothing. Just to take a stroll around the swimming pool.

I didn't know whether to go. I was tired and my fingers were hurting through the Band-Aid and it was hot. It doesn't make you any cooler going dressed to a swimming pool and stopping on the edge, taking care not to get your clothes wet, just to gaze at the swimmers as if they were fish in a fish tank. I had no wish to go even if the fish were mermaids. I shook my head no.

—Vivian will be there, he said.

The swimming pool in the Focsa building was full, mostly with children. We saw Vivian waving at us from the water. All that could be seen of her was her head without a bathing cap, her hair sticking to her skull, face and neck. She looked like a little girl. But when she got out she wasn't a little girl. She was quite sunburned and there was a taut shine to her shoulders and legs which was very different from the milky white under her black dress the night I met her. Her hair was much more blond also. She asked me for a cigarette and spoke forget-and-forgivingly, letting the bygones be washed away in the alcohol of the night.

—I skindive here every day, morning, afternoon and evening, wet-nursing really, she said, pointing to the pool, which had more kids than water. When I offered her a light she took my hand and lifted it to her cigarette. She had a long fine-boned hand now wrinkled by the water. It was a hand I liked and I liked it still more for holding my hand while she was lighting her cigarette and that she brought it very close to her thick well-formed lips.

—Too windy, she said. Was she talking about my style?

Cué had gone over to the other side of the pool and was talking with a group of young girls who had recognized him. Were they asking him for his autograph? They were all sitting on the edge of the pool, their feet splashing in the water, their legs wet and glistening. No, they were just talking. Vivian and I went to a concrete bench and sat down at a cement table under a metal sunshade. My feet were planted in a square of green tiles pretending to look like grass. I took the tape off my fingers and crumpled it in my pocket. Vivian was watching me doing it and now I looked at her.

—Cué came to see you and ran away.

She gazed at the swimming pool and at Cué and his harem of damp groupies. She didn't need to point him out nor would she have done so even if it was necessary.

—No, he didn't come to see me. He came so they could see him.

—Are you in love with him?

She wasn't surprised by the question, she just burst out laughing.

—With Arsen? She laughed some more. —With that face?

—He's not ugly.

—No, he isn't. In fact there are many girls who consider him pretty. But not as pretty as he thinks he is. Have you seen him without his sunglasses?

—Yes, on the night I met you (was I giving myself away), when I met you all.

—I mean during the day.

—I don't remember.

It was the truth. I think that once or twice I had seen him when he was on television. But I hadn't paid any attention to his eyes. I said that to Vivian.

—I don't mean on television. There he's playing a part and it's different. I mean in the street. Take a good look at him next time he takes his glasses off.

She sipped at her cigarette as though it was an inhalant and let a cloud of smoke loose from her mouth and nostrils. I broke into her aerosol of tar and nicotine.

—He's a famous actor.

Before talking she removed a threadworm of tobacco from her lips by picking it with her fingers and I suddenly realized how in Cuba the men spit out any dirt that clings to their mouth, while the women pluck it off with a fingernail.

—I could *never* love a man who has eyes like that. Still less an actor.

I didn't say a word but I felt uneasy. Was I an actor? I also asked myself how my eyes would look in her eyes. Cué returned before I could answer myself. He looked worried or contented or both things at once.

—Let's go, he said to me, and to Vivian: —It looks like Sibila won't be coming today.

—I don't know about that. And I noticed or wanted to notice that she gave an extra degree of pressure to the cigarette when she stubbed it out on the concrete table. She threw it away into a corner. Then she went back to the pool. —Good-bye, she said to us both and then, gazing into my eyes, only to me:

—Thank you.

—For what?

—For the cigarette and the match and (adding I think without malice, though she paused a minute) for the conversation.

I watched Cué walking off seeing nothing of him but the back of his trench coat. We were leaving the patio when someone started shouting.

—Someone's calling us, I told him. It was a boy who was waving at us from the water. He must have been signaling Cué because I didn't know him. Cué turned around. —It's for you, I said.

The boy was making strange gestures with his arms and head and was shouting Arsenio Quackquackquack. Now I understood. He was imitating a duck, which can also mean a fag in Cuba. I don't know if Cué understood the allusion, but I think he did.

—Come on, he said. —Let's go back to the pool. It's Little Brother. Sibila's, that is.

We went to the edge and Cué shouted to the boy, calling him Tony. He swam toward us.

—What is it?

He was as young as Vivian and Sibila. He clung onto the side of the pool and I saw he had a gold bracelet round one arm, a dog-tag made of gold. Cué spoke to him slowly, picking his phrases.

—You're the one who's a duck. When you were swimming. Now you're a dead duck. He had understood. I laughed. Cué laughed too. The only one who didn't laugh was Tony, who looked at Cué in terror, his face grimacing with pain. I didn't understand why but I soon found out. Cué crushed the fingers of one of his hands with his foot pressing down on it. Tony cried out and thrust his legs against the side of the pool. Cué let him go and Tony shot off backward, swallowing water, trying to swim with his feet, holding his hand to his mouth, almost in tears. Arsenio Cué was laughing now, smiling on the edge of the pool. I was surprised not so much at what had happened as at the fact that he seemed pleased with himself, gloating over his revenge. But when he left he was sweating and he took off his glasses to dry his face. As a concession to the heat and the afternoon and the climate he took off his trench coat too and carried it over his arm.

—Did you see that? he asked.

—Yeh, I said and as I spoke I took the opportunity to have a look at his eyes.

V

I said that this story would have nothing to do with Cuba and now I'm going to have to give myself the lie because there isn't a thing in my life which doesn't have to do with Cuba, Cuba Venegas I mean. The night I've been talking about I had gone to the Sierra with the pretext of hearing Beny Moré, which is a pretty good pretext because Beny is pretty good himself, but in fact I had gone to see Cuba and Cuba ("the most beautiful singer human eyes have heard," as Floren Cassalis said) is for the eyes what Beny is for the ears: when you go to see her you go to see her.

—Come right on in, Cuba said, talking through the mirror in her dressing room. She was putting on her makeup and had thrown a dressing gown over her stage costume. She was prettier than ever with her pouting lips wet and full and red, and the blue shadow around her eyes which made them bigger and blacker and more brilliant, and her hair styled a little like a mulatto version of Veronica Lake and her legs crossed showing through her gown open up to her thighs, taut and dark and smooth, almost edible.

—What's new with Verónica Laguna? I said. She smiled, so as to show off her large round white teeth which were a row of cowries over her pink gums. They were so even and perfect they looked like dentures.

—Ready for Freddy, she said, widening the corner of her eyes with a black pencil.

—What's the matter?

—With me? I'm sick.

I went up to her and held her by the shoulders, without kissing her or anything. But she was very cool and got up and slipped out of the gown and with the gown out of my hands: she didn't so much slip out of my hands as she was taking me off like a piece of clothing.

—Let's go someplace after the show.

—Can't, she said. —I have the curse.

—Only to Las Vegas, I mean.

—The thing is, I think I'm running a temperature.

I went to the door and balanced in the void that came through it, holding onto the edge of the door with my hands. I had to push myself forward with both my arms to go out, when I heard her calling me.

—I'm sorry, love.

I made some kind of gesture with my head. *Sic transit Gloria Pérez.*

I went to meet Vivian at the Focsa building three hours later. As I was going in the doorman already came toward me, but I heard Vivian calling me. She was sitting in the darkness of the lobby, or rather she was sitting on a sofa in the darkness.

—What's the matter?

—It's that Balbina, the servant, was awake when I went up and I came down to tell you to wait for me here.

—What are you laughing at?

—Balbina wasn't awake, but I knocked over a lamp in the dark and woke her up. I was trying not to wake her, and as a result I woke her up completely and that's not the only thing, I also broke a lamp that Mummy was very fond of.

—The matter is there . . .

—Only the form is lost. Hey, what's with these gross comments?

—You forget I'm a bongo player.

—You're an artist.

—Yes, of the drumheads between the legs.

—That's really dirty. It's the sort of thing Balbina would say.

—The *servant,* I said.

—What's wrong with that? It would be worse if I called her a maid.

—Is she a Negro?
—What are you talking about!
—Is she black or isn't she?
—All right, yes.
I didn't say anything.
—No, she's not black. She's Spanish.
—It's always one or the other.
—You're neither one nor the other.
—You just don't know how right you are, sweetie.
—How about coming outside with me and exchanging a few punches?

She was joking of course and then I saw that behind the evening dress she was still a little girl and I remembered the day I had gone to the Focsa to see if I could see her (it was five in the afternoon) with the pretext of having a bite in the pastry shop. I saw her come in in her school uniform, a school for rich girls, and nobody would have thought of her as being more than thirteen or fourteen as she tried to protect her young body with the schoolbooks she held in front of her and standing there almost bending over forward to cover up for the embarrassment of her full breasts.

—Didn't you know my friends call me Bile the Kid? I said and she laughed back but it was slightly forced, not because she didn't think it was funny but because she wasn't used to laughing out loud and at the same time as she wanted to show me she understood the joke and that she appreciated it and that she was really a common pleb herself, she felt her laughter was vulgar because she was taught to believe that well-bred people don't laugh out loud. If all this sounds complicated it's because it is complicated.

I tried another joke:
—Or Billy the Bilious.
—*Basta!* Once you get started there's no knowing when you'll stop.
—Are we going out or not?
—Yes, let's go out. I'm glad I came down, because the doorman wouldn't have let you in.
—How'll we manage it then?

—Wait for me at the corner of Club 21. I'll join you in a few minutes.

One thing I was sure of was that I didn't feel like going out with her anymore. I can't quite say if it was because of the doorman or if it was because I was convinced we wouldn't get anywhere. There was more than one street to cross between me and Vivian. I left the street of metaphor, crossed the street of reality and thought about the street of memory, on that same street of the night I had first met Vivian, and where I had run into Silvestre and Cué, who were returning from seeing Vivian and Sibila back to their homes.

—How's the poor man's Gounod? Cué said, showing off his knowledge of music, of European music. —Did you know that Gounod, yes, the Gounod of the "Ave Maria," was a drummer?

—No, I didn't.

—But you know Gunó, no? Silvestre said. He was drunk and falling all over the place.

—Gunonó? I said. —No, who was Gunonó?

—I didn't say Gunonó, I said Gunó.

Arsenio Cué laughed.

—He's pulling your leg lamely, *mon vieux.* I'll bet you a hundred pesos against a cold cigar butt that this fellow knows who Gounod was. He is something of a tin drummer himself, he said. —Like Gounod, alias Gunó.

I hadn't said anything. Not yet. But I would say it, Cué, *mon vieux.*

—Arsenio, I said and I was about to say Silvestre when I heard a belch behind my back and there was Silvestre almost falling over backward—and Silvestre. The duet.

Were they laughing? Was the duet laughing? I would have blown them apart with a belly laugh, with a smile even. Duets are like that. I know because I'm a musician. There's always a primo and a second fiddle and even in unison they are fragile.

—Silvestre, you know that Cué just laid an egg?

—No kidding? Silvestre said, almost sobering up. —Tell me, tell me.

—I will.

Cué glanced at me. Was he amused?

—Arsenio Monvieux, I've got something very sad to tell you. Gounod never played the drums. The drummer with whom you fuse or confuse him was Hector Berlioz, the author of "Les Valseskyries."

I thought for a minute that Cué wanted to be as drunk as Silvestre and Silvestre as sober as Cué. Or the other way around, as the two of them would say or one or other of the two. If this was the case I happen to know why. Arsenio Cué was in a taxi once and the driver was listening to music on the radio and Silvestre and Cué started discussing whether what they were listening to (it was classical music) was Haydn or Handel, and the driver let them go on talking awhile and then he said:

—Folks, it ain't one nor the other. It's Mozart.

Cué must have betrayed the same surprise in his face then as now.

—How do you know? Cué asked.

—Because the announcer said so.

Cué couldn't let the matter drop.

—Are you, a taxi driver, interested in music?

But the driver had the last word, as usual.

—And you like music, you, a passenger?

Cué didn't know I knew this story a long time before I knew him. Silvestre did, however. It was he who had told me some time ago and now he must have been remembering the incident, and laughing to himself, almost collapsing, doubly intoxicated in body and soul. But Cué was good at getting out of a tight corner. He knew all the stage tricks. He wasn't an actor for nothing. Now he was aping the common Cuban.

—*Mon vieux*, you've just crushed my musical backbone. It's in the drink.

—Tiger's pit, Silvestre said, meaning tiger spit meaning bad rum. Alcohol was turning him into a true disciple of Bustrófedon and instead of a tongue he had tongue twisters.

I saw Cué was looking at me curiously, deliberately. He was conferring with his pard. Top and second bananas. It was burlesque not theater. Oh sweet misery of life.

—Silvestre, I'll lay my pay check against a spent match that I know what *Vincent* is going to say next.

I gave a start. Not because he said Vincent, he could easily have overheard that one.

—I bet I know what you want to know.

I didn't say a thing. I just stared at him.

—Does he know? Silvestre said.

He knew I knew. He's a cunning bastard. I had seen it from the time I first met him. In any case I couldn't help admiring him.

—See low say, Cué said. He seemed to be talking in some fake American accent and Silvestre laughed or snickered to himself before asking moronically:

—Whawhawhat?

—Keep it to yourself, I told Cué.

—Keep what? Silvestre said. —I don't get you.

—Why? I'm not a *ñáñigo*. I'm not even a silent drum.

—Come on, what you mean? Silvestre said.

—We don't *mean* anything, I said. I don't know if I said it rudely. —Just words.

—Quite the reverse, Cué said. —We do mean, words don't.

—Reverse of what? said Silvestre, ritardando.

—Of everything, Cué said.

—What everything? said Silvestre.

I said nothing.

—Silvestre, Cué said, —this fellah (pointing to me) wants to know if it's true or not.

It was a game of cat and mouse. Of mice and cat.

—Is *what* true? said Silvestre. I continued to say nothing. I kept my arms folded mentally and physically.

—If it's true that Vivian is an easy lay or bedable. Or if she isn't. As Trotsky said to Mornard: Take your pick!

—I don't care either way.

—She's an easy lay, Silvestre said, pounding an imaginary table with his fist. —Extremely bedable.

—Oh no, she's not so easy. She's not easy at all, Cué said, sneering at him.

—She is, you fucker, she is, Silvestre said.

—I don't give a fuck either way, I heard myself say wearily.

—Yes you do. And I'll tell you something else. You're getting mixed up with Vivian and she's not a woman. . . .

—She's just a girl, I said.

—What's wrong with that? Silvestre asked. He was almost coherent again.

—No, she isn't just a girl or anything like it, Cué said. He was speaking to me alone now. —That's one thing she ain't. She's a typewriter.

—What you mean? said Silvestre. He was forgetting one of his many maestros, he had drunk so much. —Explain what you mean.

Arsenio Cué, always the actor, looked at Silvestre and then looked at me condescendingly. Finally he spoke:

—Have you ever seen a typewriter in love?

Silvestre seemed to give the matter a moment of thought and then said, —Me, never. I didn't say anything.

—La Smith-Corona is a typewriter. What's in a name? Everything. She's a perfect typewriter. But she's a display typewriter like you see in a window saying please don't touch. She isn't for sale, nobody can buy her, nobody can use her. They are just there to look pretty. Sometimes you don't know if they're for real or just a copy of something real. A dummy typewriter Silvestre would say now if he were capable of saying it.

—I can, of course I can, said Silvestre.

—Let's hear it then.

—A dumb writer.

Cué laughed.

—You're definitely coming on.

Silvestre smiled gratefully.

—Who would fall in love with a typewriter?

—Me, me, Silvestre said.

—In your case that's understandable. But you're not the only one, if you know what I mean, Cué said, looking at me.

Silvestre jettisoned his ballast of laughter and almost keeled over. I didn't say anything. I did nothing except tighten my lips and stare straight into Arsenio Cué's eyes. I think he took a step backward or at least removed his foot. He had stamped on my fingers but he knew that I wasn't Tony. It was Silvestre who spoke, trying to act as peacemaker.

—The point settled, let's go someplace. Do you want to come?

Cué repeated the invitation. It was better that way. I decided that I would also be *sybilized,* as Silvestre would say.

—Where? I said.

—Right here around the corner. To San Michel. To look at the men of wo.

But not as civilized as all that.

—It doesn't appeal to me.

Silvestre seized my arm.

—Come on, don't be silly. With a bit of luck we'll see some of the old familiar faces.

—It's quite likely, Cué said. —You meet all sorts in the night.

—Could be, I said doubtfully. —But it doesn't appeal to me to see the fairies in action.

—Auction is the word, said Silvestre.

—These ones are very gentle, Cué said. —They're followers of Mamma Gandhi. They're passive to a man.

—They don't interest me. Neither passive or active, peaceful or aggressive.

—They call themselves satiaggrahassives.

—Thank you no.

—You don't know who you're missing, said Silvestre.

—This fellahtio here does, Cué said, laughing spitefully.

—No I don't, you cunt! Silvestre said. —I'm going there just for the put-on, that's all.

—What are you going to do then? Cué asked.

I hesitated a moment.

—Mysteriouso as ever.

—I'm going to the Nacional to see some people.

—Some girl. Same boy, said Silvestre. —Don't you ever get bored with seeing Gene Kelly dancing with Cyd Charisse?

Cué laughed. —Oh sweet mystery of love!

Silvestre laughed. They both laughed, then they shook hands. Silvestre went on his way singing, his voice growing fainter, a parody of a song: *"Mister Mystery wants to rule over us / And I just keep on doing what he says / Because I don't want to hear people say / That Mister Mystery wants to rule over us."*

—Ñico Saquito, Arsenio Cué shouted. —Opus Cule de Sax-Kultur 1958.

VI

I didn't go anyplace that night. I stayed where I was standing on the corner under the street light just as I am now. I could have gone to look for a chorus girl after the second show at the Casino Parisien. But that would have meant going on from there to a club and buying drinks, and then going to a hotel and finally waking up in the morning with a tongue like a tombstone, in a strange bed, with a woman who I would hardly be able to recognize because she would have left all her makeup on the sheets and on my body and my mouth, with a knock on the door and a voice off telling me it's time to get up and having to go to the shower by myself and wash and rid myself of the smell of bed and of sex and of sleep, and then wake up that unknown woman, who would speak to me as though we had been married ten years, with the same voice, the same monotonous certainty. Do you love me, sweetie, she'd say, when what she should be doing would be to ask me what my name was, my name which she wouldn't know any more than I would know hers, and so I would say, I love you very much, sweetie.

I was standing there now thinking that playing the bongo drums or the *tumbadora* or just the drums (or Cuban percussion vulgo *timbales* as Cué would say to show how cultivated and brilliant he was and also knowledgeable in sex/folklore) was to be alone, but not to be alone exactly like flying, I thought, I who have never flown in a plane except to Isle of Pines and as a passenger at that, flying, I mean like a pilot, in a plane, seeing the whole countryside flat, one-dimensional beneath one, but knowing that one is enveloped in dimensions and that the machine, the plane, the drums, are the relation which enables one to fly low and see the houses and people or to fly high and see the clouds and to move between the sky and the earth, suspended, without dimension, but in all the dimensions, and there I am swooping and hovering and diving the double drum-plane, counterpointing, stabilizing the beat with my feet, measuring the rhythm in my mind, keeping an eye on those interior *clave* sticks which play all the time, playing like against the *claves* although they're not in the band anyway, counting the silences, my silence while I listen to the sound of the band, doing stunts: banging and twirling and looping the loop first with the left-hand drum, then with the right, then with both, imitating a collision, or a nose-dive, playing possum for the cowbell or the trumpet or the bass fiddle, cutting across then without letting on that I'm off beat, making believe I'm cutting across them, returning to the time, moving in line, straightening up the machine and finally touching down: playing games with the music, playing and drawing music out of that double goatskin nailed to a cube or dice of wood, immortalized kid, its kidding bleat turned into music by its skin between the thighs in form of drumheads the balls of music going with the band staying with it and of course so far away from my solitude and from company and from the world: in music. Flying.

Anyway there I was, standing by myself on the night I left Cué and Silvestre walking to the exhibition of ladybirds in the musical cage of the San Michel, when a convertible passed rapidly and I thought I saw Cuba in it, at the back, with a man who may or may not have been my friend Códac and another couple in front, all of them sitting very close to each other. The car drove on and came to a stop. In the gardens of the Nacional and I thought it wasn't her, that it couldn't be her because Cuba must have been at home, already asleep: Cuba needed some sleep: she had to be in bed early: she didn't feel well: she was *sick,* she said: these were my training thoughts when I heard a car coming up N Street and it was the same convertible that had now halted half a block away, in the dark under the elevated car park, and I heard footsteps coming along the sidewalk and toward the corner and passing behind me and I turned around and there was Cuba with a man I didn't know, and I was very pleased that it wasn't Códac. Of course she saw me there. They all went into the Club 21. I didn't do a thing, I didn't even move.

A short time later Cuba came back to where I was. She didn't say anything. She just put a hand on my shoulder. I removed the shoulder and her hand with it. She remained silent, she didn't even move. I didn't look at her, I looked down the street, and, strangely, I was thinking then that Vivian would be arriving and I wanted Cuba to disappear and I believe I made a pretense of suffering a mental agony as strong as a toothache. Or did I really feel it? Cuba slipped away quickly but then turned around and said to me so softly I could hardly hear her:

—Love, forgive me, do.

It could have been the title of a bolero. Of course I didn't tell her.

—Have you been waiting long? Vivian asked me and I thought it was Cuba speaking, because she had arrived almost at the same moment as Cuba had left and I wondered if they had seen each other.

—No.

—You didn't get tired?

—No, it's O.K., really.

—I was afraid you might have left. I had to wait till Balbina fell asleep.

She hadn't seen anything.

—No, I wasn't bored. I was smoking and thinking.

—About me?

—Yes, about you.

I was lying. I was thinking about a difficult arrangement we were rehearsing in the evening, when Cuba had turned up.

—You're lying.

She seemed flattered. She had changed the dress she had been wearing at the cabaret for the one she was wearing the day I had first met her. She looked much more a woman, but there was nothing pale and ghostly about her as there had been then. Her hair was tied up in a high coil and she had made herself up freshly. She was almost beautiful. I told her so, leaving out the almost, of course.

—Thank you, she said. —What are we going to do? We're not going to stand here all night, are we?

—Where do you want to go?

—I don't know. You decide.

Where should I take her? It was after three. There were many places open, but which of them would be suitable for a girl from a rich family? A mean well-lighted place like El Chori? The beach was a long way off and I would spend my salary getting there in a taxi. A late-night restaurant like the Club 21? She would already be sick of eating in places like that. Besides, Cuba would be there. A carbaret, a nightclub, a bar perhaps?

—How about San Michel?

I remembered Cué and Silvestre, those identical twits. But I thought that by now the frantic locomotive of love that does not dare reveal its name would have reached the terminus, that the hour of the she-wolf had ended and that there would only be a few couples left—perhaps heterosexual.

—That sounds like a good idea. It's not far.

—That's a euphemism, I said and pointed to the club. —The moon isn't far.

There was almost nobody in the San Michel—which Silvestre called a queendom by the sea—and the long corridor, a colony of sodomites earlier in the evening, was deserted. There were only two couples—a man and a woman near the jukebox and two shy well-adjusted queens in a dark corner. I couldn't count the bartender in because I could never tell if he was a fairy or if he pretended to be one to do better business. He doubled up for the waiter.

—What'll you have?

I asked Vivian. A daiquiri for her. O.K., that makes two of us. We had already drunk three daiquiris abreast when a group of people came in making a lot of noise. Vivian whispered under her breath, "Oh my God, not them!"

—What's the matter?

—They're people from the Bilmor.

They were friends of hers, from her club or from her mother's club or her stepfather's and of course they would recognize her and of course they would come to our table and of course there would be introductions and all the rest. By all the rest I mean smiles and knowing looks and two of the women in the party getting up and saying excuse me to all the western world and then going to la toilette. I whiled away the time completing with my index finger the circles of water left by the glasses and making new circles with the moisture I forced to drip from the glasses with my fingertip. Someone showed compassion and put on a record. It was La Estrella singing "Be Careful, It's My Heart." I thought about that enormous, extraordinary, heroic she-mulatto who held the portable black mike in her hand like a sixth finger, singing in the Saint John (all the nightclubs in Havana now have the names of exotic saints: schism or snobbism?) hardly three blocks from where we were, singing from a pedestal raised above the bar, like a new and monstrous dark goddess, as the wooden horse must have been worshiped in Troy, surrounded by fanatics more than by fans, without mus. accomp., disdainful and triumphant, her devotees hovering around her like white moths in the light, blinded by her countenance, seeing nothing but the luminous flow of her voice because what issued from her professional mouth was the song of the sirens and we, every man in her public, we were so many Ulysseses lashed to the mast of the bar enchanted by that voice which the worms would never have for lunch because here it was singing now on the record, a perfect and ectoplasmic facsimile, dimensionless as a specter, as the flight of a plane, as the Spirit of Saint John, the beat of the drums: this is the original voice and a few blocks away there was only its replica because La Estrella is her voice and it was her voice that I heard and I headed for it flying by no instruments, led blindly by that sound flaring up in the night and hearing her voice, seeing it in the dark, suddenly I said, "La Estrella, lead me to harbor, you are my astrolabe, the north of my diamond needle, my Stella Polaris!" and I must have said it out loud, because I heard people laughing at our table and around us and someone was saying, a girl, I think, "Vivian darling, but you've *changed* your name," and I excused myself and got up and went out to the drumhead. I pissed to the tune of "Be Careful, It's My Heart." Demo: *"Be careful, it's my cock / Not a policeman's club / You're holding in my hand."*

VII

When I returned, Vivian was by herself and drinking her third daiquiri in a row and mine was waiting for me in my place, frozen, almost solid. I drank it straight without speaking and as she had finished hers, I ordered two more and we didn't say a word about the people whom I no longer knew whether they'd been there or if I had dreamed or imagined them. But they had been there, because "Be Careful, It's My Heart" was playing for the third time running and I saw the stains of our visitors' glasses on the black formica.

I remember that around us the indirect lighting formed a halo of Vivian's blond hair when I began without saying a word to remove the hairpins from her bun. She gazed into my eyes and she was so close she was squinting. I kissed her or she kissed me, I believe it was she who kissed me, because I remember wondering in my drunkenness where that little girl who was hardly as much as seventeen years old had learned how to kiss. I kissed her again and while I was caressing her shoulders with one hand, I was managing to untie her hair with the other. I opened her zipper and slid my hand right down inside below her waist and she wiggled and twisted, but I don't think I was putting her off at all. She wasn't wearing a bra and that was the first thing that surprised me. We followed the same kiss along and she was biting my lips real hard and saying some nothing or other at the same time. I slid my hand round the side of her back toward her breasts and at last I felt them, small but seeming to bud, to blossom, to develop nipples under my hand. O.K., so maybe I was drunk and just a lousy bongo player, but I can also be an eroticist if I want to. I left my hand where it was, not moving a finger. She was speaking inside my mouth and I felt something salty and thought she had broken my lip. But they were tears.

She slipped away from me and threw back her head and the light fell on her face. It was completely drenched. Some of it was saliva, but the rest was tears.

—Please be good to me, she said.

Then she went on crying and I didn't know what to do. Women who cry always exile me to a state of confusion, and I was drunk which made me even more alien: all the same they alienate me more than the next drink.

—I feel so unhappy, she said.

I thought that she was in love with me and that she knew—she knew *it*—about In Cuba (that's Doña Venegas' wicked name) and I didn't know what to say. Anyway I shut up like a clam. Women who are in love with me ostracize me more than women who cry and more than the next drink. Now as a last banishment she was crying and the waiter came with two extra drinks nobody ordered. I think he wanted to break our clinch. But she went on speaking with the referee there and all. She wasn't exactly a clean fighter, believe me.

—I wish I was dead.

—But what on earth for? I said. —Things aren't at all bad here.

She gazed into my eyes and went on weeping. All the water in the daiquiris was coming out through her eyes.

—I'm sorry, but it's terrible.

—What's terrible?

—*La vida.*

Another good title for a bolero.

—Why?

—You know.

—Why is it terrible?

—Because that's how it is. *Ay!*

I let her go on crying.

—Lend me a handkerchief.

Lend me your tears. I lent her my handkerchief and she dried her tears and the saliva and even blew her nose in it. My only handkerchief. The only one I had for the night, I mean: I have more at home. She didn't give it back. I mean she didn't ever give it back: she must still have it at home or in her handbag. She swallowed the daiquiri in one gulp.

—Forgive me. I'm an idiot.

—You're not an idiot, I said, trying to kiss her. She didn't let me. Instead she pulled up her zipper and straightened her hair.

—I want to tell you something.

—Please do, I said, trying to appear so attentive and understanding and disinterested that I must have looked like the hammiest actor in the world trying to look disinterested and understanding and attentive while speaking to a public that wasn't listening.

—I want to tell you something. Nobody knows about it.

—And nobody else will.

—I want you to swear you'll never tell anyone.

—Of course I won't.

—Above all that you won't tell Arsen.

—I won't tell *any*one. I was sounding now like a drunkard.

—Promise me.

—I promise.

—It's very difficult. But the best thing is to come clean with it. I'm no longer a virgin.

I must have had the same expression as Cué had during the episodes of Haydn, Handel, Mozart & Co., wholesale makers of music and embarrassment.

—It's the truth, she said. I didn't answer.

—I didn't know.

—Nobody does. You and *this* person and myself are the only people who do. He won't tell anyone, of course. But I had to tell it or I would have burst. I had to tell someone and Sibila is my only friend, but she's the last person in the world I'd want to hear about it.

—I won't tell anyone.

She asked me for a cigarette. I gave it to her and put the packet back in my pocket. I didn't feel like smoking. When I offered her a match she hardly brushed my hand, except for the trembling of her hand which communicated itself to mine through clenched and sweaty fingers. Her lips were trembling as well.

—Thanks, she said, blowing the smoke away and without a moment's pause she said, —He is a very mixed-up young boy, very young, very lost and I wanted to give a meaning to his life. How wrong I was!

I didn't know what to say: the surrendering of virginity as an act of altruism left me absolutely speechless. But who was I to discuss the possible avatars of the Salvation Army? After all, I was only a bongo player.

—*Ay,* Vivian Smith, she said. She never used the Corona and it reminded me of Lorca, who always introduced himself as Federico García. But there was no tone of complaint or even self-reproach in her voice. I believe she wanted to assure herself that she was there and that I wasn't spitting in her face, which I didn't do because for me it was also only a dream. Only not the dream I had longed for.

—Do I know him? I asked, trying not to look either too eager or jealous.

She didn't reply at once. I gazed at her steadily and although it seemed there were less lights at the bar, she wasn't crying. But I saw that her eyes were watery. Two tears later she answered.

—You don't know him.

—Are you sure?

I looked her straight in the eyes.

—Oh well, I suppose you do. He was in the swimming pool the day you were there.

I didn't want to, I couldn't believe it!

—Arsenio Cué?

She laughed or tried to laugh or a mixture of both.

—God no! Can you *imagine* Arsen being mixed up for as much as *one* day of his life?

—In that case I don't know him.

—Yes you do. It's Sibila's brother. Tony.

So I did know him after all. But it didn't bother me to know that that cross-eyed driveling shit of a merboy with his crucifix around his neck and identity band on his wrist and all, that this sophomoronic citizen of Miami was Vivian's Number One Mixed Up Boy. What did bother me was the fact that she said *is*. If she had said was, it would have been a passing incident whether it had happened by chance or if it had been forced on her. This could mean one thing only, that she was in love. I saw Tony in another light now, with different eyes. What could she see in his? Eyes, I mean.

—Ah yes, I said. —I think I know who he is.

I was delighted that Cué had stamped on his hand after all. No, more than that, I wished Tony, like me, could have his little soul on the tip of his fingers.

—Please, *por favor*, don't ever tell anyone. Promise me.

—I promise you.

—Thank you, she said and she clasped my hand neither mechanically nor tenderly, nor with any interest. It was just another thing her hand could do expertly: like lifting it to her face to light a cigarette, for instance. —I am sorry, she said, but she didn't say why she was sorry. —I'm truly sorry.

It had to be true. It was the night when all the world felt sorry for me.

—*Eso no tiene la menor importancia!*

I think my voice sounded a little like Arturo de Córdova but also a little like my own.

—But I'm sorry and I feel bad about it, she said, but she didn't say *why* she *had* felt bad about it. Perhaps it was her telling me that made her feel bad. —Could you please get me another drink.

I tried beckoning the waiter with my finger but to succeed I would have had to go out hunting waiters: it is not as easy as you'd imagine: Frank Buck wouldn't have been able to bring a Cuban waiter back alive. When I turned around to look at her she was crying again. She was swallowing her tears as she spoke.

—You really won't tell anyone?

—No, really. Nobody.

—Please. *Nobody,* but nobody, swear.

—I will be quiet as the grave.

"Gravedigger, I plead with you / That for my good you'll sing / Over her grave a requital / Leave her to hell / Let the devil treat her well / Don't cry for her, gravedigger / Don't cry for her! / You just dig." (Chorus)[1]

1 "Requiem Rumba"—Music & lyrics by Ignacio Piñeiro, copyright 1929 (reproduced by kind permission of Musica Ficta, Inc.).

I HEARD HER SING

What do you want? I felt like Barnum and followed Alex Bayer's crooked schemes. It occurred to me that La Estrella had yet to be discovered, a verb invented for Eribó and all those Cuban Curies who spend their lives discovering the properties of radio, television and the silver screen. I told myself that the gold of her voice had to be separated from the muck in which Nature or Providence or whatever it was had enveloped her, that this diamond had to be extracted from the mountain of shit it had been buried in and what I did was to lay on a party, a *motivito* as Rine Leal would say, and it was to Rine that I went to make out as many invitations as possible. As for the rest, I would invite them myself. The rest included Eribó and Silvestre and Bustrófedon and Arsenio Cué and the Emcee who eats shit but I have to invite him because he's the compère at the Tropicana and Eribó would bring Piloto & Vera and Franemilio, who would enjoy the occasion more than anyone because he's a pianist who's very sensitive and besides he's blind, and Rine would bring Juan Blanco who's not a compère but a composer without a sense of humor (this music, not John White alias Johannes Witte or Giovanni Bianco: he's the composer of what Silvestre and Arsenio and Eribó, days when he's a reluctant mulatto, call *serious* music) and I even almost invited Alejo Carpentier and the only person we wouldn't have would be an impresario, because Vítor Perla wouldn't come on my account and Arsenio Cué would refuse even to speak to anyone in broadcasting and there the matter rested. But I could rely on publicity.

I gave the party or whatever it was in my house, in that single large room I had which Rine insisted on calling a studio and people began arriving early and others came who hadn't even been invited, like Gianni Boutade (or whatever his name is) who was French or Italian or from Monaco or all three of them at once and who was the king of *manteca* not because he was an importer of edible fats but because he was the biggest pusher of marijuana in the world and it was he who tried to apostle for Silvestre one night and he took Silvestre to hear La Estrella at Las Vegas some time later when she had become famous everywhere, and who really thought he was her impresario, and with him came Marta Rayo and Ingrid Bergamo and Edith Cavello who I think were the only women who came that evening because I was very careful that neither Irenita or Magalena or Manolito el Toro née Gary Baldi or any other creature from the black lagoon should turn up, whether they were *centauras* (the *centaura* is half woman and half horse and is a mythical beast from the Zoolympus of Havana-by-night and which I cannot or won't describe now) or not or anyone like Lupa Féliz the well-known composer of boleros, who is all horse, and Jesse Fernández came, a Cuban photographer who worked for *Life en Español* and was doing a story on Havana a city open day and night. The only person lacking was La Estrella.

I loaded the cameras (my own) and told Jesse he could use any of them and he chose a Hasselblad I had bought recently and said he wanted to try it out that night and we started comparing the Rollei and the Hassel and went on to talk about the Nikon as compared with the Leica and then we got onto exposure times and Varigam paper which was new in Cuba at that time and all those things photographers talk about and which are the same as long and short skirts and the cut of clothes for women and averages as ranking order for pelota fans and sharps and flats plus pauses and demisemiquavers for Marta and Piloto and Franemilio and Eribó and liver and mushrooms (that is, the nonedible ones: cirrhotic livers, athlete's foot) for Silvestre and Rine: themes for the Boredom Variations, bullets of bullshit to kill time with, talking about today what you can think about tomorrow and *Todo es posponer,* a brilliant epigram Cué had stolen from somewhere or other. Rine meanwhile was pouring the drinks and passing the olives and hors d'oeuvres around. And we were talking and talking and an owl flew past my balcony hooting and Edith Cavello hooted back *Solavaya!* which is an antidote for the bad luck hooting owls always bring when not hooted back at. Then I remembered I had told La Estrella we were going to give the party at eight so that she should turn up at least around half past nine. I looked at my watch and it was ten past ten. I went to the kitchen and said I was going out to buy some ice and Rine looked surprised because he knew there was plenty of ice in the bathtub and I went down to search all the seven seas of the night for this mermaid reincarnated as a sea cow, for a Godzilla that sings when the water is running, for my Nat King Kong.

I searched for her in the Bar Celeste, among the tables of people eating, in Fernando's Hideaway like a blind man without his white cane (because it would have been useless, because not even a white cane could be seen in there), like a real blind man when I came out to the glare of the street on the corner of Humboldt and P, in the Café MiTío with its open terrace where all the drinks are fume-flavored, in the Las Vegas trying to avoid meeting Irenita or any of her species and in the Humboldt bar, and I went to Infanta and San Lazaro really fed up and didn't find her there either but when I returned, I passed the Celeste again and there she was at the back of the room absolutely drunk and alone and carrying on an animated conversation with the wall. She must have forgotten the whole thing because she was dressed as usual, wearing her habit of the Discalced Carmelites but when I appeared at her side she said, How's things Doll Face, come over and join the cause, and she smiled from ear to ear. I looked at her. She was being rude, of course, but she disarmed me by what she said next. I wasn't brave enough, she said, I didn't have the courage: you are too refined and well-bred and respectable for me. I'm just a poor nigger, she said, ordering another drink and gulping down the one she had, the glass a thimble in her hand. I made a sign to the waiter to forget it and sat down. She smiled at me again and began humming something I couldn't understand, but it wasn't a song. Come on, I said, let's go. No no, she said, making it rhyme with yo-yo. Come on, I said, nobody's going to eat you. Me, she asked—it wasn't a question—eat me. Look, she said, raising her head, before any of you so much as touches one curl of my woolly-wig, I'll swallow you whole, she said, tugging hard on her hair dramatically or comically. Come on, I said, the whole of the western world's waiting for you at my house. Waiting for what, she said. Waiting for you to come and sing so they can hear you. Me, she asked, hear me, she asked, and they're in your house, they're in your house, right now, she asked, all I have to do then is to stay right here, because you live next door, don't you, and she began to get up, in the doorway and I'll start singing at the top of my voice and they'll hear me, she said, no, it won't work, and she fell back in her chair which didn't complain because it was no use to any chair, habituated and resigned as they are to being chairs. Yes, I said, it will work, but only if you come to my house because that's where it's all at, and I put on my confidential manner, there's an impresario there and all, and then she raised her head or rather she didn't raise her head, she tilted it on one side and raised one of the thin stripes she had painted over her eyes and looked at me and I swear by John Huston that this was how Movy Dick looked at Gregory Ahab. Had I succeeded in harpooning her?

I swear by my mother and by Daguerre that I thought of loading her onto the freight elevator, but since that's the one the servants use and I knew La Estrella didn't want to be hauled up like a piece of freight or taken for a servant, the two of us took the little elevator facing us which thought twice about going up with its strange cargo, and then ascended the eight floors creaking painfully. We heard music from the corridor and found the door open and the first thing La Estrella heard was the sound of "Cienfuegos," that Montuno tune, and there was Eribó standing in the middle of a group of people endlessly explaining its *montuno* or off-beat choruses and Cué with his cigarette-cum-holder in his mouth walking up and down, approving everything, and Franemilio standing near the door with his hands behind his back, leaning against the wall the way blind people do: knowing more by the tips of their fingers where they are than other people do with their eyes and ears, and La Estrella reacted badly on seeing him and shouted her vintage words pickled in alcohol in my face, Shit, you motherfucker youse been conning me, and I didn't know what she meant and asked her why and she said, Because Fran's here and I know he's come to play the piano and Ise not singing with an accompanist, listen here, Ise not singing, and Franemilio heard her and before I could think let alone say anything, he said, Are you completely off your head? Me with a piano in the house! he said in his soft voice. Come on, Estrella, come on in because here it's you who brings the music, and she smiled and I called for attention everybody and asked them to turn off the record player because La Estrella was here and everybody applauded. See what I mean? I told her, see what I mean? but she wasn't listening to me and was already about to burst into song when Bustrófedon came out of the kitchen carrying a tray of drinks and Edith Cavello behind him with another and La Estrella took a drink as she was passing and said to me, What's she doing here? and Edith heard her and turned around and said, Listen you, it's not me who shouldn't be here. I'm not a freak like you, and La Estrella with the same movement she had made taking the glass threw the drink in Franemilio's face because Edith Cavello for whom the pitch was meant had ducked her head quickly but as she stepped aside she stumbled and tried to cling onto Bustrófedon and grabbed his shirt and he also tripped over, but since he has a great sense of balance and Edith Cavello has a degree in gymnastics neither of them fell over and Bustro made a gesture like a trapeze artiste who has just completed a double somersault without a net and everybody except La Estrella, Franemilio and I applauded. La Estrella because she was apologizing to Franemilio and wiping his face with her skirt, which she had lifted exposing her enormous purple thighs to the warm air of the evening and Franemilio because he couldn't see a thing and I because I was closing the door and asking everybody to turn it down to a dull roar please it was almost twelve and we didn't have permission for the party and the cops would be here any minute. They all shut up. Except La Estrella, who when she had finished apologizing to Franemilio turned to me and asked me, So where's the impresario? and Franemilio without giving me time to make anything up said, He didn't show, because Vítor didn't come and Cué is involved in some private feud with the television people. La Estrella gave me a real mean look, narrowing her eyes till they were as thin as her eyebrows, and said, So youse been conning me after all, and she didn't give me a chance to swear to her by all my fathers and old artificers as far back as Niepce that I didn't know nobody had come, I mean no impresario, and she said, Then you can go fuck yourself, I'm not singing, and she stomped off to the kitchen to pour herself a drink.

I think the feeling was mutual and La Estrella and my guests as well resolved to forget they lived on the same planet, because she stayed all the time in the kitchen eating and drinking and making a lot of noise and Bustrófedon back in the main room inventing tongue twisters and one of the ones I heard was the one of the *tres tristes tigres en un trigal* and the record player was playing "Santa Isabel de las Lajas," sung by Beny Moré, and Eribó was keeping time, beating on my dinner table and on one side of the record player and explaining to Ingrid Bergamo and Edith Cavello that rhythm was a natural thing, like breathing, he said, everybody has rhythm just like everybody in the world has sex and you know there are people who are impotent, men who are impotent, he said, same as there are women who are frigid and nobody denies the existence of sex because of this, he said, nobody can deny the existence of rhythm, what happens is that rhythm is a natural thing like sex, and there are people who are inhibited, he said—that was the word he used—who can't play an instrument or dance or sing in tune while there are other people who don't have this problem and can dance and sing and even play several percussion instruments at once, he said, and it's the same as with sex, impotence and frigidity are unknown among primitive people because they're not embarrassed by sex, nor are they embarrassed, he said, by rhythm and this is why in Africa they have as much sense of rhythm as of sex and, he said, I maintain, he said, that if you give a person a special drug which is not marijuana or anything like that, he said, a drug like mescalin, he said and he repeated the word so everybody should know he knew what he was talking about, or LYSERGIC ACID, and he was shouting now above the music, he will be able to play any percussion instrument, better or worse, the same as someone who is drunk can dance either better or worse. So long as he manages to stay on his feet, I thought and I told myself that that was a whole load of shit and I was thinking this word shit, it was at the exact moment I was thinking this word shit that La Estrella emerged from the kitchen and said, Shit, Beny Moré, you're singing shit, and she entered with *two* glasses in her hands, drinking left and right as she walked and she came to where I was standing and as everybody was listening to music, or talking or making conversation, and Rine was standing on the balcony getting miserable, playing those games of love that are called *el mate* in Havana, she sat down on the floor and leaned against the sofa and as she drank she rolled about on the floor and then she stretched herself out flat with the empty glass in her hand and lay down along one side of the couch which wasn't a modern one but one of those antique Cuban sofas, made of wicker and wood and woven straw or *pajilla* and she got right under it and stayed there sleeping and I could hear her snoring underneath me sounding like the sighs of a sperm whale and Bustrófedon who couldn't or didn't see La Estrella said to me, Nadar, *mon vieux,* are you blowing up one of your balloons? meaning (I knew him too well) that I was farting and I remembered Dali said once that farts are the body's way of sighing and I almost started laughing because it occurred to me that sighing is the soul's way of farting and snoring is the sighs and farts of dreaming. But La Estrella went on snoring without anything like this to bother her at all. Suddenly I realized that tonight's fiasco was mine and only mine, so I got up and went to the kitchen to pour a drink which I tossed down silently and I went silently to the door and left.

Third session

Doctor, do you think I should go back to the theater? My husband says the only thing that's wrong with me now is that I have a surplus of nervous energy which I never use up. At least, before, when I was in the theater, I could imagine that I was someone else.

I HEARD HER SING

I don't remember how long I spent walking the streets nor where I was because I was everywhere at once and as I was returning home at two o'clock and was passing in front of the Fox and the Crow I saw a man and two girls come out and one of the girls was freckled and had big tits and the other was Magalena, and she greeted me and introduced me to her girl friend and boyfriend, a foreigner with dark glasses, who told me straight off that I looked like an interesting person and Magalena said, He's a photographer, and the fellow said with an exclamation that sounded like a belch, Agh, so you're a photographer, come along with us, and I wondered what he would have said if Magalena had told him I worked in a market: Agh, so you're a porter, a proletarian, how interesting, come with us and have a drink, and the fellow asked me what my name was and I said Moholy-Nagy and he said, Agh, Hungarian? And I said, Agh no, Vulgarian, and Magalena was dying of laughter, but I went along all the same and she walked in front with the woman, the wife she was of the man who was walking beside me, a Cuban Jew she was and he was Greek, a Greek Jew, who spoke with an accent which I didn't know where the fuck it came from, and I think he was explaining to me the metaphysics of photography, saying it was all a game of light and shadow, that it was so moving to see how the salts of silver (My God, the salts of silver: the man was a contemporary of Emile Zola!), that is to say the essence of money, could make men immortal, that it was one of the paltry (why not saltry) weapons that being had in its wars against nothingness, and I was thinking that I had the luck of the iris to be always meeting these well-stuffed metaphysicians, who ate the shit of transcendence as though it were manna from heaven, but we've just arrived at Pigal and are about to go in when Raquelita, sorry, Manolito el Toro runs into us and goes and kisses Magalena on the cheek and says, How're you, pal, and Magalena greets her like an old friend and this philosopher who's standing beside me says, She's very interesting, your lady friend, seeing her clasping my hand and saying, And how're you, you old Russian mulatto, and I tell the Greek by way of introduction and correction at the same time, My friend Señor el Toro, Manolito, a friend of mine, and the Greek says, That's even more interesting, meaning he had begun to know what I already knew, and as Manolito's leaving, I say, And how about you, Plato, so you like *efebos*? and he says, What's that you said? and I say, So you like young boys like Manolito, and he says, Young boys like her? I sure do! and we sit down to listen to Rolando Aguiló and his combo and soon the Greek is saying to me, Why don't you ask my wife for a dance? and I tell him I don't dance and he says, It's not possible, a Cuban who doesn't dance? and Magalena says, There's two of them because I can't dance either, and I tell her: A Cuban man and a Cuban woman, you mean, and Magalena starts humming "Fly Me to the Moon" which is what the band is playing but she stresses the word fly on every beat. Then she gets up, Excuse me, she says, emphasizing her *s*'s which is the attractive mannerism of some mulatto women of Havana, and the Greek Jew's wife, this Helen who launched a thousand ships in the Dead Sea, asks her, Where are you off to? and Maga answers, Just the Ladies', and the other woman said, I'm going too, and the Greek, who's a modern Menelaus who couldn't care less about being betrayed by an odd Paris or two, gets up and when they've left he sits down again and looks at me and smiles. Then I understand. Fuck me, I tell myself, this is the island of Lesbos! And when they return from the "Ladies'," this combination of two tones of the same color, these two women whom Antonioni would call Le Amiche and Romero de Torres would paint with his broadest brush and Hemingway would describe just a little bit more subtly, when they sit down I say, 'Xcuse me but I'm leaving, because I've got to get up early, and Magalena says, *Ay*, but you're going much too soon! and I follow the thread of her song and say, Part of you I take with me, and she laughs and the Greek gets up and shakes my hand and says It's been a pleasure meeting you, and I say the pleasure's all mine, then I take the hand of this biblical high priestess for whom I would never be a Solomon or even a David and I say, *Encantado* and I'm off. Magalena catches up with me at the door and says, Are you really going? and I say, Why do you ask? and she says, I don't know, but you're going so early and so suddenly, and makes a gesture which would have been charming if she hadn't made it so often and I say, Don't bother, I'm quite all right: sadder but wiser, and she smiles and makes the same gesture again, *Adiós amor*, I say, and she says, *Ciao*, and goes back to her table.

I think of going back home and wonder if there would be anyone still there and when I'm passing the Hotel Saint John I can't resist the temptation not of the *traganíqueles*, the coin-slot machines, the one-armed *bandidos* in the lobby which I would never put a dime in because I wouldn't ever get one out, but of the other Helen, of Elena Burke who sings in the bar, and I sit at the bar to hear her sing and stay on after she's finished because there's a jazz quintet from Miami, cool but good with a saxophonist who looks like the son of Van Heflin's father and Gerry Mulligan's mother and I settle down to listening to them play "Tonight at Noon" and to drinking and concentrating on nothing more than the sounds and I like sitting there at Elena's table and ordering her a drink and telling her how much I dislike unaccompanied singers and how much I like her, not just her voice but also her accompaniment, and when I think that it's Frank Domínguez who's at the piano I don't say a thing because this is an island of double and triple entendres told by a drunk idiot signifying everything, and I go on listening to

"Straight No Chaser" which could very well be the title of how one should take life if it wasn't so obvious that that's how it is, and at that moment the manager of the hotel is having an argument with someone who just a few moments ago was gambling and losing consistently and to top it off the guy is drunk and pulls out a gun pointing it at the head of the manager who doesn't even wince and before he could say bouncer two enormous fellows appear and tackle the drunk and grab his gun and give him two punches and flatten him against the wall and the manager takes the bullets out and slides back the bolt and returns the empty gun to the drunk who still doesn't know what's hit him and tells them to frisk him and they shove him to the door and shove him out and he must be some big shot as they haven't made mincemeat of him yet and Elena and the people from the bar turn up (the music has stopped) and she asks me what's happened and I'm just going to tell her I don't know when the manager waves them back saying *Aquí no ha pasado nada* and then with a flick of his hand orders the jazz-men back to their music, something the quintet more asleep than awake do like a five-man pianola.

I'm already on the point of leaving when there's another uproar in the entrance and it's Colonel Ventura arriving, as he does every night, to eat at the Sky Club and listen to poetess Minerva Eros, the alleged mistress of this assassin in uniform, she who bleats happily (for her and myself) in the roof garden, and after greeting the manager Ventura goes into the elevator followed by four gunmen, while another ten or twelve remain scattered around the lobby, and as I'm sure I'm not dreaming and add up all the disagreeable things that have happened to me tonight and see that they were three in a row, I decide it's just the right moment to try my luck at the crooked slot machines and I pull out of my pocket, which feels more like a maze, a coin that doesn't have a minotaur engraved on it because it's a genuine Cuban real not an American nickel and I put it in and pull the handle, the single arm of the Goddess of Fortune, and then put my other hand like an inverted horn of plenty in the chute to catch the silver rush to come. The wheels spin around and an orange comes up first, then a lemon and a little later some strawberries. The machine makes foreboding rumbling, stops finally and comes to rest in a silence that my presence renders eternal.

My door is locked. It must have been Rine who locked it, loyal as ever. I open the door and I don't see the friendly chaos that supplanted the alien order imposed by the cleaning woman just this morning, I don't see it because I don't want to, because there are more important things in life than disorder, because stretched out on the white covers of my sofa-bed, yes sir, no longer a sofa but entirely a bed, on those spotless Saturday sheets, I see the enormous, cetacean, chocolate-colored stain, stretched out like a hideous blot, and it is of course, you've guessed it: Estrella Rodríguez, this star of the first magnitude who dwarfs the white heaven of my bed with her expanding black sun's appearance: La Estrella is sleeping, snoring, slobbering, sweating and making weird noises on my bed. I accept it all with the humble philosophy of the defeated and take off my coat and tie and shirt. I go to the refrigerator and take out a pint of cold milk, and pour myself a glass and the glass smells of rum not milk, though its contents probably taste of milk. I drink another glass. I put the half bottle back in the refrigerator and throw the glass into the sink, where it sinks in a sea of glasses. For the first time that night I feel how suffocatingly hot it is: it must have been like this all day. I take off my undershirt and trousers and remain there in my underpants which are short, and I take off my shoes and socks and feel the floor which is almost hot, but cooler than the city and the night. I go to the bathroom and wash my face and mouth and see there's a great pool of water under the shower, a mere memory of the ice it had once been, and I dip my feet in it and it's only moderately cool. I go back to the only room in this idiot pad that Rine Loyal calls a studio apartment and look for somewhere to sleep: the sofa, the one of wicker and wood, is very hard and the floor is soaking, dirty and littered with cigarette butts and if this was a film and not real life, this film in which people really die, I would go to the bath and there wouldn't be an inch of water in the bathtub, it would be a clean well-whitened place where I could sleep comfortably, the greatest enemy of promiscuity, and I would wrap myself in the blankets I don't have and sleep the sleep of the just and chaste, like an underdeveloped Rock Hudson (surely underdeveloped for lack of exposure) and the following morning La Estrella would be Doris Day singing without a band but with music by Bakaleinikoff, which has the extraordinary ability to remain invisible while sonorous. (Fuck Natalie Kalmus: I'm beginning to talk like Silvestre!) But when I return to reality it is dawn and this monster is in my bed and I'm exhausted and I do just what you, Orval Faubus, and anybody else in the world would do. I get into *my* bed. Onto an edge.

Fourth session

It must have happened when I was a little girl. All I know is that I had a tin box, orange or red or golden, with chocolates or candies or cookies in it, which had a landscape on the lid, with a lake that was all painted amber and there were some boats on the lake, motorboats, or yachts that were traveling from one side to the other, and there were some opal-colored clouds and the waves looked gentle and easy to sail on they moved so slowly and everything was so peaceful that it would have been a pleasure to live there, not on the boats but on the shore, on the edge of the candy box, sitting there looking at the yellow boats and the peaceful yellow lake and the yellow clouds. They gave me the box one day when I was sick and I must have taken it to bed with me, because I dreamed that I was in that landscape and I still have that dream quite often. There was a song my mother used to sing that went: *"Rest your oars, mister boatman, because I like your way of rowing"* (then there was an unpleasant discussion between the beautiful woman enraptured by the rowing and this boatman who didn't want to rest his oars for fear of being shipwrecked, but I was no longer listening to this part, because I had gone to sleep, or whatever it was, I didn't listen) and I listened and listened to the song and I thought I was there on the edge of the lake watching the boats come and go without making a sound in that eternal calm.

MIRRORMAZE

I

Silvestre and I were driving my car down O Street coming from the Hotel Nacional and right now crossing 23rd to zoom out like a fart past the Cafetería Maraka when Silvestre said *Lights!* and I asked him *What?* and then he said *The headlights, Arsen, you'll get yourself a ticket* because it was already after seven and in the time it took to slide down the soft shoulder of O and into the bosom of 23rd it had already gotten dark and my car lights are not yet on because it's not easy to tell if it's day or night when you're in a convertible (*I* know somebody up there is going to ask me *if* I know what I'm talking about, don't I know that a convertible is an open car and you can see everything better from it including weather, climate and time? I *know* what I'm talking about and whoever the unknown person or persons are who are saying this let me tell them once and for all that all I said was, please see above, that "in a convertible it's not always easy to tell if it's day or night," that's all I said: I didn't go into any superfluous details: we are not Proustians, my friend and I, I mean *we'd* rather be Proustites: Silver and Arsenic soulfides: as a matter of fact I haven't even said whether the top was up or down: it is down but what I wanted to say and didn't is that anyone who is fortunate enough to own a convertible will know these infinite enumerations without me having to tell them, so I'm only saying this for the benefit of those who have never traveled in a convertible along the Malecón, between five and seven in the afternoon or rather evening on August 11, 1958, at sixty or eighty miles an hour: such privilege, such exaltation, such euphoria of the finest hour of the day with that summer evening sun going down red into a west indigo sea, between clouds which almost succeed at times in perfecting it to a flop, turning the sunset into a major production: the schmaltzy finale of a religious picture filmed in Glorious Technicolor, something which luckily didn't happen that day, though the city is now rosy at times, then amber, then salmon-colored above while below the blue of the sea becomes deeper, almost mauve, even purple, and it's beginning to cover the waterfront and penetrate the streets and the houses till all that remains afloat is the concrete skyscrapers all pink and cream like delicately spun frothy-beaten sugar-topped meringues for chrissake!—and all this is what I'm gazing at as I feel the evening air like a halo around my head and the speed between chest and shoulders like a second heartbeat when this fellow Silvestre had to come up with his thing about *The headlights*) and I turned the car lights on off course. But I switched the high beam on instead, who knows why, and the beam spurted straight ahead: a horizontal stream of flour, of smoke, of cotton candy whipping out of the wheel right to the end of the st. Silvestre said *Stop her on sight!* But I thought he was asking about the headlights again and I said *Can't you see them, you cunt!* and he said *Of corset I can see them cunts!* and he made his eyes round like two plates with an egg (his eyes are yellow yellow) on each of them and that no-neck of his was popping out of his shirt and he flattened his head against the windshield so much that I thought we had hit some invisible truck head-on and that I hadn't yet felt either the bang or the pull of the crash, because I was watching him all the time, seeing his bespectacled face flattened against the windshield: glass grinding glass. Meanwhile, back on the street, the car was hurtling down O on her own and when I looked (I knew that the street *was* empty: I hadn't been driving these past five years just for fun) I saw *Them!* I put my foot all the way down on the pedal and the car braked hard with a corresponding scream which the echo formed on the north face of the windowless buildings on Humboldt Street transformed into the Lorcan lament of a pedestrian (tube of Soulgate truthpaste) who has had his anima pressed out of his mouth on the spot. Consequently the street filled with people and I was obliged to stand up in my car like a politico at a whistle-stop (I even had it on the tip of my tongue to say "Romans, countrymen, lend me your lire") to shout with all my lungs *All right, folks, break it up! Everything's all right!* But the mob wasn't standing around because of us.

They were all watching the two blondes or the repeated blonde walk down the street and they used our noisy stopover as a pretext (though there was little need of one: the blondes were a real pretext in themselves, besides there is always this enclave of hipsters, hustlers, hombres, hotheads and homos saps at the encampment between the Maraka and the Kimbo *cafeterías* if you go south by southwest along the sidewalk from the Saint John to the Pigal, all of them congregating under the lamp or near the oyster stall, inside the den of coffee stand or in the yellow newspaper booth and around the other smaller coffee stand across the street or even crowding the doors of the twin eateries by just standing there hands akimbo: dugouts ready for trench whorefare) and they began wolf-whistling and bitch-calling and howling and shouting "Don't push, *cabrones!*" "Let me through pleassse!" *"Introito ad altarem Deae"* "Leave some of her for us assholes!" "Down with women!" and there was even someone hollering "The witches of Swatzerland." But the best catcall was shouted from the guts as someone made a bullhorn with his hands (it must have been Bustrófedon, who is always hanging out around here, because his voice was cold and hoarse very much like Bustrófedon's, but I couldn't tell), then this odd fellow, this spirit compass, yelled at the top of his mouthpiece *The blonde leading the blonde!* and every but every playboy in the western world roared with laughter, including Silvestre whose face was by now glued forever to the windshield (the blondes were not walking in our direction anymore: they were rather on top of the car because they came marching down the street and I realized then that they weren't tourists or American chorus girls but real Cubans—although it was not only because they were walking in the middle of the street that I knew it naturally: I knew it for the same reason as *el maestro* Innasio knew it thirty years back in New York, a city then as foreign as Havana now, when he taught us a new tune: "Those who do not walk with an easy pace, with an unequaled grace, those are not she-Cubans") because I'd braked so sharply and he was complaining of the blow on his head, so I told him *What about the state of grease you've left my windshield in.* I was joking of courses but he wasn't listening either to the beginning or to my final words *you graceball!* Neither would I have been listening if it hadn't been a voice from one of those women who make me another Ulysses lashed to the mizzen topmast stay so as to listen without falling into shark-infested waters or into lava or into a swamp with a brand-new white *dril-cien* suit on—or simply, falling in disgrace: which voice or siren song was calling *Arsen!* and I look up and see the double blonde who has stopped next to us and naturally what I see are two gowns of tulle or organdy (organza, one of the blondes corrects me later on, when her gown is all creased up, but it sounded more like orgazm then) or some very delicate durable-crispy material, that becomes four bundles beyond the blue horizon of my car, which is what I have right in front of my eyes, and where the two bloodless necklines come to a violet end (they are both dressed in purple) I see the beginning of two white bosoms, milky white, almost blue (like my car which is also white) in the tungsten lights of the street lamp and two long necks not swanlike but like two fine white and exactingly trained fillies, Lippizaner mares as it were, and then two super (haughty superb) chins, because they know that under them their necks are fine and long and pearly (white) and their busts so milky (white) or rather violet-colored that everybody stops to look at them (so do we: I for one can hardly take my eyes off them) before looking at the other certain wonders which this dumb car of mine now keeps hidden, and then (I *must* go *upward* on my journey) two broad red fleshy mouths (broad because the broads are smiling a smile which doesn't display their teeth as they know Mona Lisa is back in town) and the fine (I'm sorry, fellers: I have no other adjective—not at this moment) nostrils and, oh mah Gog, those *four* eyes! One pair of eyes is blue and laughing azuredly and has thick eyelashes that look like eye wigs (as the mouths look crimson and are really rosy) but in a few seconds I'll know, and so will you, that they aren't false, and then a high smooth forehead from which a true mane of blond hair begins, with one of those bouffant hairdos which are in fashion (which have only just begun to be in fashion and it had to be a woman who was pretty sure of her beauty and very much given to displaying it and very proud of being a modern belle to venture out in the streets of Havana with those puffed-outs, although up to now the skirtmishing terrain has been limited to the streets of El Vedado and La Rampa only, Havana proper immediately declared off limits) but right after the coiffure takes off puffing it is stopped short by a pale lavender bandeau, fencing her natural beauty in history: features framed by fashion. Oh what a perfect freak when a woman is a man-made monster!

Now, as for the other blonde, I don't think I need describe either her mouth nor her Joyconda smile nor her bouffant—nor even the lavender headband. The only way she's different (if you want to differentiate them) is that her eyes are green, her eyelashes not very long and her forehead not so high. *You shouldn't drive so fast, dear* the blonde on the right, who's the one I know, is saying: now that she moves back a little to let the purple para lights make her smooth gleaming cheeks turn phosphorescent (as sole makeup she's wearing an oily cream to show off her poreless Japanese-like complexion) I recognize her. *Livia* I'm saying *What a pity I didn't know it was you before! Otherwise I'd have run you over and the trip to the hospital would have been a pleasure cruise.* She laughs her guttural spurting laugh, her head shaking and thrown back as though she's gargling my joke on doctor's orders and says in a voice as phony as her laugh *Ah, Arsen, you're always the same: you never change!* Because Livia is one of those women who always expect a man to change his ways in the same way as she changes her hairdo or her hair dye. *It suits you very well, being blonde* I say. *That's a thing you should never say to a woman* (who to, then—Liberace?) *dahling* she says with a delivery as phony as her laugh: lips pouting and wet and at the same time she moves a hand deftly in my direction as though she were ready to strike my head with an imaginary fan: *That's naughty* she says. (If this scene, because it *was* a scene, had happened in Old Havana, circa 1858, the novelist Cirilo Villaverde would actually have seen a fan, guards made of carved mother-of-pearl, *brisé* sticks, leaf of black lace.) *Ay sí, you're naughty* says the other blonde, who has an echo of a voice. *Very naughty! Who are they?* Silvestre asks me *Anna and Livia Pluralbelles?* Livia turns her shortsighted look on him first and then her arrogant look and then her look of a femme fatale and then her look of acknowledgment and then her enchanting look and then her charmed look: Livia, as you can see, has quite an arsenal of looks, which, if they could be traded for hand grenades, would turn her eyes into the magazine of one of Batista's barracks. *You* she said, removing the pin of the look she keeps for the assault on well-known strangers and at the count of seven throwing it at Silvestre. The fused stare blows right in his face: *You must be one of Arsen's intellectual friends, aren't you? Yeh* I say *he's Silvestre Isla, the famous author of For Whom the Balls Tell.* Livia's lackey enters the war to tip the outcome of the battle in our favor: *Isn't it For Who the Bell Tolls?* she says. *Yep* I say *he wrote that one too: this is just a sequel. That tru?* Livia's altar ego asks, talking more to Silvestre than me. *Too true* Silvestre says poker-faced. She has just lost the war, poor thing. *It's also a fag, I mean fact* I say *that he wrote them both under a fruity pseudonym, though some historians insist that it was under a budding chestnut tree. Ay sí?* Livia thinks the moment has come for her to intervene as a great power and she hurls a fragmentation glance into the allied trenches which she follows up with an eye grenade at my public parts. *My dear* she explodes *can't you see that this couple is pulling your leg? I'm not pulling her leg at all* I say *rather I'm holding her hand though I'd like to seize her capital, violently if possible and end the war not with a whimper but with a bang. What's the name of the country in Spanish?* I'm not being facetious: Livia's altered ego has had her hand on the door of my car for some time now and for some time now my hand has been on her hand: for some time now our two hands have been on the door of my car one on top of the other: a fact that Livia's alter idem doesn't seem to register. Now, while I'm speaking, I'm looking at my hand as though I was looking at hers and device versa. She smiles. *Ay sí, its tru!* she says. She takes her hand from under mine and positions it a couple of inches nearer Livia as she says *Ay, you're being fresh, ain't you?* not looking at me, not looking at Livia either but at some vanishing point between us both and Limbo. *My name is*

Mircea Éliade. WHAT? Silvestre and I both start up in disbelief at the same time. *Mirtha Aleada* she repeats: we hadn't heard her the first time: that's what it was of coarse. *But my professional name is Mirtila. I chose it for her* Livia says. *It's a good name, isn't it, Arsen? Beautiful* I say in my best actor's voice: till a short time ago that's exactly what I was. *You've always been good at choosing names for people* I say. *Except my own* she says *which is my real name. O.K.* I say *all that's left is for me to introduce myself. No need to* says Mirtha Aleada or Mirtila. *You are Arsenio Cué. And how did you know it, Mirthful Mirtila?* says Silvestre. *Ay, because* vague gesture showing a total apprehension of culture *I watch television. Ay, she watches television* Silvestre says to me and Livia and to her he says *Do you go to the movies too?*

Ay sí Mirtila says *when I don't have to work evenings.*

Do you go alone, Mirtila? says Silvestre.

When I don't go in company, sí Mirtila answers with a smile that almost lets itself be a giggle and Livia almost laughs in solidarity: Livia Solidaria, that's her full name.

Ingenious ingenue I say. *But I don't know why, she reminds me of Maelzel's automaton chess-player* but Silvestre isn't interested any longer in my wit which becomes as intimate as masturbation: playing a private part.

Will you come with me, Mirtila? Silvestre begs.

Ay no Mirtila says.

(I thought of ye goode olde Doctor Johnson who always began his allocutions with the word Sir.)

Why not? Silvestre insists. *Would you be so kind as to inform me.*

(Overcultivated manner of speech, I explained. To no effect, because I was talking to myself.)

I hate men with glasses Mirtila says. *So there!*

Underneath I wear yellow eyes Silvestre says and I look at him. *Besides I look better in the movies.*

In what film? says Livia Innuenda.

I doubt it Mirtila says more stupid than cruel.

She doesn't believe in miracles, sonny boy says Livia Perfidia.

Silvestre was on the brink of taking off his glasses but this had already gone too far (and too long for Livia, who can't bear to go more than ten seconds without being the center of world-wide attention) and suddenly I hear a hideous din behind us which I can't imagine why it didn't make itself heard earlier: from the line of cars behind us waiting for me to move on or get out of the middle of the road. In the midst of this flashing of lights (making Livia look for a moment as if she is in the world premiere of the film she never made, waving her arms asking for recognition as she drowns in the luminous waves made by the headlights of celebrities) and blowing of horns I hear voices, particularly a recognizable one shouting quite distinctly *Early to bed and easy to arouse, makes a man out of a mouse!* Livia puts on an expression as though she senses something rotten in the Denmark of her illusions of grandeur and says, reverting to the language of the gutter like a nun returning to the world from the retreat of a dialogue among well-shod Carmelites *What a fucking nerve!* and Mirtila who hasn't heard or understood a thing (or both) feels obliged to say *Ay sí, darling, they've got a fucking nerve!* once more sliding her hand away from under mine. Livia says *Arsen, we have a dear loft* (I think she was talking of the rent but then I see she means dear in the sense of tender and isn't talking about money but about love, just as she always says loft and never apartment or pad like everybody else) *next door* and she just has time to lift and point a perfect livid arm *It's that magenta building on the corner.* I start off more propelled than compelled by the noise of our homemade jam. *Come up and see us sometime* and already I'm moving off rapidly carried on the noise of engines, exhaust fumes and tires turning the white waves of speed into gray blurs on the black asphalt of the evening. *It's on* and I hear Livia forgetting her famous tropical contralto and yelling in shrieking soprano *fifth floor next to the* a last cry which turns into a single word ascending on her voice

r
o
t
a
v
ele

a scream we can still hear as I make a turn to go up 25th Street. *What do you think of* Silvestre says. *Who*? I say pretending not to be on his wavelength. *Mirtila, who else* says Silvestre and lets his question which is not a question keep hanging above us like the real roof of the car or like the pale crown of the night, and under its weight or inside its dome we cross that somber area between 25th and N Street and L and 25th, which I've never particularly cared for, and now, safely in the hustling and bustle of the corner of the Havana Hilton and all those ancillary or ancient pensions and *cafeterías* or cafés around it, with people moving from neighborly modest street corner to mammoth hotel for tourists, and students coming with the alibi of drinking coffee to better sit the night out studying but actually to watch the parade going by with all these girls fluttering toward Radiocentro and La Rampa, I say *Mirtila, as a woman*? *Not bad. She's tall, elegant, cute without being coy* and because the lights turn green (traffic chameleon, mercy is your color not hope) I don't have time to finish what I'm trying not to say but when I see I'm still going up 25th I cry shit on my existence at the top of my inner voice because through saying little and thinking much while I'm talking I've continued down this street which goes past the School of Medicine and at the thought of so many naked dead given lodgings behind those useless iron railings, mortal men preserved in the hideous posterity of formol, I simply step on it. *But what do you think of her* Silvestre insists asking as we are heading toward the Avenida de los Presidentes *really*? feeling better here myself not because of the question but because we are riding now past the gardens which divide embellishing one of my favorite avenues. I must answer him right away or he'll go on asking me the whole fucking night: while we're having dinner in El Jardín, at the movies and after, having a refreshing pause or a coffee on 12 & 23, my favorite street corner, sipping black coffee or brown Cokes our favorite drinks while we're watching the last of the chickadees going home each one to her own bed and not, *ay!* to either of ours, until I drop him off at his house and I go home to try to sleep or to read all night till it be morrow or failing that to phone whatever easy say is in and ready to discuss my chosen subject for the wee hours of tonight, namely Quentian Theory—in other words, I would have to sit between the two prongs of his question the rest of the night. So it's better if I answer him now and then let Elia Kazan in *East of Eden,* with its sociometaphysical preoccupations in Cinemascope cum DeLuxe Color, entertain and move him and keep him happy in that never-world which is more real for him than this dark passage we have just negotiated without/apparently/as much as a scratch, leaving intact also my reputation as the sort of Cuban explorer who's a man to go in the jungle with. *You're naïve, believe you me* I say *you are fucking naïve!*

II

As the elevator wasn't working, I half turned around to go out again but finally I decided what the hell and go up by the stairs anyway. Now, this very moment, I hesitated for a moment being faced with the street glowing like the rays of a torch from these lower depths, and I mean horizontal depths because looking at the long corridor which was more like a tunnel I knew I was in one of the deepest darkest damnedest sulphur mines in the world, with three or rather two seams to exploit: one of them already exhausted (the elevator) and two that were still intact (the alley at the back where I could shout up at her window and the fucking staircase) and the possibility of vacations al fresco, in the free air of the evening, that transom/ransom of life now a parole of free will, alien and distant because I had myself chosen to come here—a nonparolee. There was also the occupational hazard of an aleatory escape of laughing gas. Why had I come here? From somewhere or other, from below maybe (though down below there could be no other living quarters than what Jules A. Vernus called the Hall of Winds Phenomenal, vulgo the airshaft), I heard sounds which couldn't be taken for an answer because very plainly they were hammer strokes plus the corresponding echo. They were mending the elevator evidently. I began to climb the stairs and felt an inverse vertigo/does such a sensation exist?/coming: if there's anything I hate more than going down a dark flight of stairs it's going up one.

Why have I come to see you, Livia Roz? (Is that your real name or are you perhaps called Lilia Rodríguez?) Did you really invite me to your house? If you prefer, if you are able, please answer the two frank questions and forget the pernicious parenthesis, would you? I could never have explained to Silvestre why I was counting these steps on a metaphysical flight with the tip of my shoe, while one of my hands/sweating/gripped the railings of the polished marble banister and the other/soft/was futilely trying to hold onto the sweaty wall of granite. I think I must have arrived because my invisible knuckles were knocking on a nonexistent door and a distant, piercing and recognizable voice was saying or shouting or whispering *Coming!* I remembered a dream of another door/other doors/and another answer to my knocking.

I could have told Silvestre many things. One of them was I used to know Livia Roz when she had black hair, which must have been some time ago. Her transparently white skin, so alive, had startled me, her dark blue eyes had delighted me and I wondered at her hair which I had imagined was naturally black. She remained standing holding my hand—or at least she held it in her own so long I forgot about her (her hand, I mean). I was introduced to her by Tito Lívido, who wasn't yet a film director but a cameraman for television. When she finished smiling and combing her hair with her hand and moving her neck rhythmically and pulling on my hand as though she wanted to play a game of tug-of-war, when she had spoken, perhaps a little before, or when she opened her mouth to say something, I knew that I had in my hand the foot of a peacock, the voice of a cockatoo, the waddling walk of a swan. *So* she said *you are* pause for breath of deep emotion *the famous* grimace of recognition *Arsenio Cué*? How could I possibly answer such a question? *No, I'm his brother of the same name*. The laughter was general (and C in C as well). Explanation of Tito *Arsen, a consummate joker* livid. *A joke of a consumer* I said. More laughter. I can't imagine why. *You* Livia said, lifting her ontological fan for the first time and employing it to strike me on my hard head *are naughty* putting on a tone of voice that was intended to be maternal *very naughty*. I really had no idea what to do, because she still hadn't let go of my hand. Then in one of the phases of the game/tug or war/she pulled me down toward her and while she was bending me over forward to look at my other hand, the left one, she said whispering in my ears and at the same time letting the whole world hear she was interested in culture: *Ay* exactly the same tone of voice Rodrigo de Triana had employed when he discovered America *you have a book in your hand!* (I know I'm making it sound complicated but you would have had to have seen it, seen and heard: I say and heard, because if you had only seen it, through a glass lightly for example, you might have got the idea that something obscene was going on.) *What is it?* I showed her the book. She read it like someone who has just learned how to read. Across-the-river-and-into-the-trees. Here she made a grimace almost of disgust. *Eminguey? You read Eminguey? Yes, sometimes* I think that was what I said. *Isn't he a little bit out of fashion?* I think I smiled: *The thing is I was sick when I was little.* Tito said, lividly, something in her ear and just as she was opening her mouth so it looked like an exclamation mark without a dot, I said *and now I'm catching up with my reading.* She was smiling now with her broad rosy lips (she wasn't wearing any makeup that day, I remember), and the smile spelled *I am so ignorant* but actually meant *Poor darling, you definitely are behind the times* and what she actually said was *Forgive me* delicate pause *may I call you tú?* a new and deeply intimate beginning.

Certainly I said *of curtsy you may* and as I said it she squeezed my hand as a token of gratitude. *Thank you:* she was also a friend of emphasis. She reached out for the book with her other hand. *Please lend it to me for a second* she said *I must go now* and she slipped her hand inside my jacket (it was then I realized she had let go of my hand, which remained hovering in the air, reminding me of that game children play of muscular reflexes and the arm against the wall: incipient dynamic tension) to fish out my pen *I'll give you my number* she said as she wrote *and you must give me a call.* She gave the pen and the book back (I looked at the phone number without seeing it) and smiled her smile marked Good-bye But Maybe See You Soon. *Ciao* was what she said, naturally.

I called her up one day just as I was finishing this moving novel for the third time, this canonic text which is both sad and happy at once, one of the few books genuinely about love that have been written this century, when I saw her name written above the phrase The End in a large hand, copybook but attractive: a yes she is no she isn't false/carefully written/male-looking. She wasn't there but I spoke to Her for the first time, She. I mean *Laura her friend* as a little too sugary voice told me *Livia isn't in. Can I take a message?* No, thank you, I'll call back another time. I hang up: strange, that, we hang up. We both hang up. We cut short our conversation like this, with a gesture, when we were just beginning to communicate. We hang up. I believe that never after (and there were plenty of occasions when we might have been) have we been so close to each other. She told me later that she had remained glued to the phone (which was on the main floor, near the dining room full of guests) that evening at a quarter past seven, waiting for me to call her back. This was what she told me one day when Livia introduced us opposite the TV station. She left the group of people she was with to greet me, because she knew I don't like groups. *Arsen* Livia said *there is a* pause *friend of mine who is longing to meet you.* I hadn't the slightest idea who she was and I was even going to say excuse me and get back into the car when I saw a tall girl, poorly dressed in black, very slender, with pale-chestnut-almost-sandy hair, standing by the staircase and smiling: I had glanced at her as I was passing, happy to see that lithe young perfect body, and I think that I'd have noticed her eyes which were gray or hazel or maybe green (no, I can't have even looked at them because I'd have remembered: it is her eyes, mauve, dark, a quality purple, that I'm unable to forget) and I was walking on by when Livia's possessive hand brought me back to the present, to present me: *Laura* she called her, and she came giving the first proof of that docility in front of Livia I was so often to reproach her with, so stupidly. *Listen, I want to introduce you to Arsen. Arsenio Cué/Laura Díaz.* I confess I was surprised by that simple Díaz among all the sonorous exotic and memorable names that pollute the show biz world, but I liked it as I like the fact that she still uses it today when she is famous. There was nothing special about the way she shook my hand: perhaps only good enough for shaking hands in the town square on Independence Day. I looked at her:

I looked at her face and I smile when I remember it, because where there is so much sophistication today, so many lips that pout like Brigitte Bardot, so much black eye shadow, so much morning/evening/and/or dramatic makeup, here instead was a simple, down-to-earth and open beauty, which was also serene, sad and trusting, because twenty-year-old beauties and total hunger are too much in competition with each other for the prize of Havana. Besides, she was a widow—a thing I didn't notice, of corpus, as there were plenty of other things I didn't notice and I think maybe I would have known more about her by phone than I do now that I have her here fixed in my memory: talking and laughing with the sun falling behind her flying hair and the sea, five hours later when I took her from Mariel from a late lunch by the bay and later on driving along the Malecón to her home.

Between this opening word (Between) and that final period there is another story, of which I only want to tell the ending. Livia gets crazes to use an ordinary word instead of tendencies, which is a medical term. One of them is to have roommates, another is always to get herself invitations (when someone passes by in a car, to anonymous dinners, to live in *any* friend's house), another craze she has is to "steal boyfriends from her girl friends," as Laura explained one day. Livia and Laura were more than just roommates, they were close friends now and went everywhere together and they worked twogether (Livia, with rare ability, turned Laura from an ugly small-town duckling—too tall, too skinny, too pale for Santiago—into a swan of Avon Inc.: now she was a model for ads and commercials and a mannequin for fashions and clothes in newspapers and magazines: she taught her how to walk, how to dress and how to talk, and not to be ashamed of her long white neck, but to hold it up "as though the Hope pearl were hanging from it, dear" and finally she got her to dye her hair Apache black—"raven's wing, darling" Livia would say if she was standing behind me and reading this page I'm writing) and they ended up by being like twin sisters: Laura and Livia/Livia and Laura/Lauralivia: one and the same thing. Livia also had another craze: she was an exhibitionist (Laura was one too, which makes me think that all the women I've known were exhibitionists one way or another:

inside or outwardly: shy or brazen—but then aren't I one myself too with my car and its lowered hood, this exhibition case on wheels, aren't we all, isn't man a creature who exhibits himself to the cosmos in this enormous convertible we call the world? But I'm getting metaphysical and I don't want to go beyond the physical: it's about the flesh of Livia and the flesh of Laura and my own flesh that I want to talk now) and she lived in a display window. One day, when I first knew them and I went up to their room in the boardinghouse for the first time, she insisted that Laura should try on a new model of bathing suit they were going to advertise next morning and she also tried on her bikini. Livia suggested *Let's make Arsen suffer* and smiled and Laura excited by the game asked *To see if he's a gentleman?* and Livia answered *To see if he's a man or only a gentleman* but Laura intervened *Please* she said, and after an embarrassed pause, *Livia* and she said to me *Arsen, s'il vous plait, go out to the balcony and don't look or come back in till we don't call you.*

I have seen too many MGM films not to have made the mistake of not wanting to be a typical Cuban in a moment like that, but rather to be like Andy Hardy meeting Esther Williams, so I turned around and went out onto the balcony smiling like a man who knows he is a gentleman or vice versatile. I remember I overlooked it all: Livia's insinuation which was so vulgar as almost to be an insult, the Melvillian sun outside, Laura's innocent double negative: with the elegance and almost the same walk as a David Niven of the tropics. I remember seeing some children playing in the park in the double sun of sky and cement while three Negro girls—their sitters presumably—were talking sitting in the shade of the young ficus in flower. I remember that I was trying to sit on an ideal bench in the shade of the trees of my dream when I actually heard them call me and I got the reality of the sun full in my eyes when I came back from my instant trip and turned around: it was Livia. When I went in Laura was wearing a white bathing suit, not a bikini or a two-piece but a "radiant white swimsuit," to use Livia's technical language: with a long white decolletage at the back plus the plunging neckline which joined between the breasts and was fastened at the neck: I have never seen her more beautiful than she was that evening—except naked except naked except naked. I said mistake (please see above) because from that day on, from that very moment, Livia in one section of her willful dream machine was manufacturing the desire, the anxiety, the necessity for me to see her naked: *I* know: since she called me and said *Arsen, could you fasten me here, please, it's slipping* pointing with her shoulder blades to the strap of her bikini which was hanging loose, her hands groping for it with a lack of cunning that had to be a put-on. I *knew:* since I could see in the mirror that Laura didn't like the way I lingered for a minute longer than a minute on that glamorous knot, that perfumed nudity, that ultimate in flesh fashion.

No, there was no love lost between Laura and me that evening, not as yet. There was love, there is, there will be as long as I live, now. Livia knew it, my friends knew it, the whole of Havana/ that is to say the whole world/ knew it. But *I* didn't know it. I don't know if Laura ever knew it. Livia, sure, *she* knew it: I knew she knew it because she insisted that I come in when I went to look for Laura on June 19, 1957. *Come on in* she said. *Don't be afraid, I'm not going to eat you.* I answered in a way that Livia thought was one more display of wit, you will take it as proof of sentimental shyness and all it is is a quote from Shakespeare: *Give me thy hand, Messala* I said. *This is my birthday* (*Julius Caesar*, Act V, Scene 1). Livia thought I was giving her a nickname and she laughed: *Ay, the things you say, Arsen darling. Me Messalina? The only Messalina in this house is Hope* Livialaura's cook-maid-washerwoman from Jamaica *who has a new boyfriend* (*loverboyfriend, you understand*) *every day*. I went in. *I'm alone* she said. *And the big black hope?* I asked as she sat on the sofa, settled a couple of cushions between her shoulders and put her feet up: she was wearing pants (slacks in Capri blue lastex for Livia) and a blouse of a masculine cut and she took off her shoes before answering *She's out, my love* combing her hair with her hand. *She has the day off*. She buttoned her blouse up to the neck and then she unbuttoned it again so I could end up seeing, to my surprise, that she wore a bra.

We talk: about my birthday which wasn't today but in three months' time, about the anniversary two weeks back of the day when Bloom's moll sitting on the bog had let flow a long stream of unconsciousness which would become a milestone, a millstone in the shape of a solid shit turd in literary history, of the photos that Códac had made of Livia and which were coming out in *Bohemia:* about everything—or almost everything, because a moment before I had made up my mind not to wait for Laura longer and to return home, when there emerged what Silvestre calls my Sub Topic. *Códac suspects* Livia said raising her collar with both hands *that some of the pics (the best ones off curves) won't get published. Really?* I said with about as much interest as Bertrand Russell, say, would have shown in the matter. *Why not?* She smiled, then she laughed and went through the motions of moistening and pouting her lips, and finally she said *Because I'm au naturel* of course that's not what she said—au naturel—but it's what the exotic noise she made resembled most. *They don't have the guts, the noel cowards:* my VOICE was roused in emphasis: *The bastards! They know not what they do.* I looked at her blue eyes, her hair beginning to turn platinum blond by the times and the black mole on her chin which she wore like a watermark to show, by transparency, the quality of her skin *Forgive them, Levia: alleviate their sins* her torso which was more bust than torso: fit for a pedestal or a museum or a bookshelf *make their hell cool and levitate their skins* her shapely legs, more insinuating than ever under those tightly stretched pants and finally her feet being intimately caressed by her finely formed long hand, an action a fashionable cold cream had turned into an erotic advance in every drugstore *EVERYWHERE she wears OILSKIN!* myself speaking with the voice of the announcer who spoke unctuously while her suggestive hands were vanishingcreaming her foot in the commercial on television and in films.

When she had left off projecting round belly laughs toward the ceiling like smoke rings of laughter, she said *Ay, Arsen, it's impossible to be serious with you* and she got up saying *Do you want to see them?* I didn't understand what she meant and she could see it written all over my face. *The photos, sweetie* she said, opening her arms in a parody of extreme exasperation. *What did you think I meant?* I looked straight at her. *The originals* I said *not the copies.* She laughed. *You're always the same* she said. *Do you or don't you want to see them?* I told her I did au naturally and she went into the next room telling me to *Wait.* I looked at my watch but I can't remember what time it was. But I do remember it was at just that moment that Livia called me from the bedroom. *Come on in Arsen* and in I went. The door was open and she was on the bed arranging the photos in which her breasts were displayed naked. They were large. I mean the photos: two or three of them almost covered the bed. She appeared in them:

naked from the waist up, arms crossed/ or
with shirt half-open to midriff/ or
wide open but not showing the nipples/ or
naked, from the back/ or
naked and hidden in pimpy shadows

but never could you see her compleat bosom. I told her so. She laughed and pulled one photo out from under another and said *What about this one then* as though she was asking a question and answering it yes at the same time. I tried to take a look but she hid it behind her body. *I didn't see it* I said. *You're not going to see it* she said. *The lady's not for seeing* and she laughed showing off her naked throat: she was a cockteaser or as the Spanish say *una calientapijas:* in Cuba we don't have a word for that: perhaps because we have so many of those—I mean women for that. I decided to leave. She knew. *Baby's getting ever so cross* she said aping a sob-sob. *If Baby stays just a leetle longer Baby get such a big present.* I stared at her and she stared back. *There!* she said and threw the photos on the floor: she was sitting naked, but now you could see her tits turned into udders by a wideangle lens that made them almost threedimensional: they were white and perfect and beautiful, so Livia was right to be proud of them, to be vain about the photos, to be angry at the negative for putting on print that wonder in which mere flesh is at the same time an aesthetic object and subject of passion. *I don't believe it* I told her all the same. *They're 3-D tits good only for Arch Oboler.* She froze in her tracks though she wasn't moving. *Who that?* she asked and seemed almost furious. *He directed Bwana Devil.* In a single movement she bent down, picked the pic off the floor, all the rest off the bed, put them back into the closet and went straight into the bathroom. *Don't go!* she said before closing the door. She came back again. Three minutes must have elapsed between her going in and coming out but it's all simultaneous in my memory. She was coming out naked. I mean, she had on only some black, brief panties and nothing else. *How about now?* she said and came to me tiptoeing, her breasts swelling and arms and shoulders thrown back, a trick she must have learned from Jayne Mansfield, but I didn't laugh it off because in front of me (and I mean in *front* of me) I had a beauty you can sense with all the senses, see/touch/smell/hear/taste: see with your hands, listen with your mouth, taste with your eyes, smell with every pore. *True or falsie?* she said. It was another voice, full of emotion, not mine, that answered: *Just a farce.* I looked, she looked, we looked: and there in the doorway was Laura with a round box in one hand and in the other the little hand of a small blond and ugly girl. It was her daughter.

I remember now (when the door of Livia's new house opens) another door that closed and the handy, hardy words Laura said and which her suddenly icy tone rendered truly dramatic: *Next time see that you close the door* and she left. I remember her ever-present indifference whenever I called her, called on her, whenever I went to see her at the TV station and the affectionate coolness in which our relationship ended: phrases like *How're you* and *See you soon* and *So long for now* taking the place of all our previous expressions of warmth, of affection—of love? *Sonnyboy, you're a sight for sore eyes!* Livia said. *Mirtila, look who's here* talking to the rooms/to the room she was entering leaving both doors open: walking in nothing but her panties as she sat down at the dressing table and said *Come on in, Arsen, make yourself comfortable* looking at me in the mirror *I won't be a minute* touching up her lips again with the same care and precision and mastery of the brush with which the books of reproductions say that Vermeer painted the mouths of Dutch women, though maybe more scantily dressed—she, Livia, not Vermeer or his miniature women. The voice from the bathroom said *Here I come* and it sounded like a voice shouting shoot! because the shower curtain opened right after her voice and there she came: Mircea Éliade, Mirtha Aleada—or just plain

Myrtle for you and for the press and for her friends, naked, yes, her as well: in her birthday suit and she said *Ay, Arsen* when she saw me *excuse me I didn't know it was you* and went back to the bathroom without closing the door, put on a bathrobe (transparent) and came out again (naked) and began slipping her arms that were steaming from the heat and the shower into the white blue-flowered sleeves. But she didn't fasten the bathrobe and she began rummaging for things in the closet/dressing table/medicine chest/suitcases on the living room floor/in the kitchen/refrigerator and every second moment she came back to the sofa-bed I was sitting on, to look out of the window and see if it was going to rain *I aint gonna wear my new raincoat today either fuck it* she said *Ay perdona Arsen but it's a REEL drag. There aint no seazns here nomore.* Livia got up and went to the bathroom and while she was carefully dampening her made-up face she said *She comes from the north, honey, from Canada (Dry, of corks).* Mirtila emerged from among the suitcases with the skimpiest sky-blue panties in one hand and a pair of low-heeled white sandals in the other. *No, I come from El Cotorro, but it's still true there aint any seazns here nomore* putting her panties on *and Livia, you know quite well that if a woman's gonna be reel elegant* taking off her pale-blue bathshoes and slipping her feet into her sandals as she talked *theres gotta be at least two seazns.* Livia burst out laughing. *Do you hear the way she talks, Arsen, and then she wants to be a speakerine* she said coming in and fastening her shoulder strap. *Have to, child, HAVE to* Mirtila sat herself at the dressing table *O.K. have to or gotta to its still tru an elegant woman has to show off her vestry* medieval vestiary I thought *and in this shit of a country* turning to me (in this cunt of a shitry) *if you don't mind me saying so, Arsen* turning to Livia *you can't even do that* getting up and yelling out of the window *YOU CAN'T EVEN DO THAT* louder *you can't do a goddamn fucking thing* and she went back and sat at the dressing table again and looked at me *Ay perdona tú but that's how it is: Im up to here in it* and she lifted her long skinny hand and pulled out a tuft of straw-colored hair dyed a hundred, a thousand times and quite dead now, embalmed in white dye, metallic, mineral, solid platinum: *la chevelure de Falmer* none other.

Can I describe her breasts? I saw them outlined in the mirror. One night they were large on the point of breaking the chastity brassiere and youthful, now they were flaccid, long and ending in broad dark purple tips: I didn't go for them. Livia's breasts, when I saw them, had changed too and not for the better and I didn't want to look at them again so I could keep the good/bad memory I'll always have of them: it's better to lose paradise for a deceiving red apple than for the dry, certain fruit of knowledge. At night, the other night, Mirtila looked like she was fifteen, sixteen, seventeen at most and now I couldn't say how old she was, all I knew was that some time, in her childhood, she'd had rickets, because her chest bulged sickeningly and she was not so much slender as suffering from malnutrition. Even without any makeup her lips were violet, like her nipples, only paler and though her nose was incredibly well-formed and her eyes were big and clear with long lashes, you could see she had a Negro granny left behind, behind the chemistry of her makeup and physics of incandescent light: like Livia she didn't go out anymore except at night, and with too much paint at that. I could see too that her eyebrows were shaven off altogether and this made her forehead much too wide. I didn't go for her: this wasn't the woman I'd volunteered to come for to this infernal heat on an August afternoon, to this twilight darkness, to this spiral of questions without answers that Mirtila as she was deciding how to paint her face throws at Livia who is just finishing making up hers and not paying any attention to:

Livia luv can you turn on the light? Livia do you think I should clean my face with this Elisabetarden stringinrefreshin creem or with Ponze vanishin creem/ Livia's not listening because she's in the hall, near the window, putting mascara on her lashes/ *Livia honey should I put on a base of Lildefrance or should I try the AmoretaCreem. D'you think the Velada Radiante's the best, don' forget I'm gonna use Ardeena on top/* Livia's sitting in the hall with a little lacquered box on her knees and is rummaging in it/ *D'you think Arden Pink or Golden Poppy's the best lipstick, I can't decide, I don' dig the taste. I don' know if the Revlon Louie Exvee is right for me. What kind of a nites it gonna be sweetie/* Livia is pulling out a baroque ring from the black box/ *The Rosyhorrora's reel fine but I don' know if it agrees with the rest of the stuff/* Livia's pulling out a pair of earrings to go with the fingerring and puts them on/ *I think after all I'll put on the Revlon choral Vynilla and forget it: I'm tired of choosing/* Livia's pulling from the lacquered box a long necklace of cultured pearls: everything Livia's wearing has a certain quality, but a fake/mediocre quality: once Jesse Fernández the photographer/who was taking a series of shots of her/told me: "Baby, O.K., so here in Havana she's a model, but in New York or L.A. she'd be nothing but a hundred-buck call girl"/ *Livia d'you think the Lena Rubysteen Caraseeds's better than the Mascaramatic or should I use the I shado or the Arden Cosmosticks/* Livia's going into the kitchen to pour herself a glass of milk, a minidinner for her pet ulcer/ *Now here's a problem. Lissen, sweetie, I topped off my bath with a bucketful of Morny salts, June Roses they were, and now I can't think what perfume to put on. D'you think I should use the Misdiorr or the Diorama. I think the Diorisimo is better/* Livia's sitting again on the same seat in the hall slowly sipping her glass of milk/ *But lissen, pet, Maggy de Lancon or the Lanvin Arpeege's reel nice too, but just fine. Right, I think I'll put on the Jivency Interday, cos it always brings me luck/*

I look at Livia and for the first time she looks back/ her mouth makes a four-letter word/ and she waves her hand in boredom. Mirtila gets up and puts on a black bra and a matching black pantie girdle, and begins rolling on her stockings (dark mauve) sitting on the edge of the stool at the dresser: I look at her closely and she looks like a praying mantis/a samurai warlord/an ice hockey goalie. *Let's go out this evening* I say, I can't think why. *We gotta parade some gowns* she says without stopping a moment the delicate work of sliding her long shapely legs back into their dark silky elastic cocoons. *How about later on?* I ask. *I'm comin right back here to sleep. Last night I didn' sleep no wink, not a wink, but not a one.* Now she gets up and looks at me. *How do I look?* I look at her and say *Great* and it's true she does, she looks real good: she is another woman. *And I still gotta put my dress on: its brand new.* I'm just going to ask her for the third time/ Everything happens in threes/ but I think what the hell. Luckily Livia calls me so I get up and go over. *Come back some other time, Arsen* Mirtila says. I don't know what I said back.

This peasant, she just comes from the sticks Livia whispers to me *and I get more and more sick of her. Every day she gets more and more cocky and she tries to give me lessons and all* and the whisper gets louder *ME who invented her!* Then right out loud *How do I look, loverboy?* she asks me. *Who's the fairest of us all?* I laugh. *Thou art, Your Majesty, but under Hollywood Snowwhite is alive and well and balling with the magnificent 7 dwarves.* She slapped me/deliciously/in the face with her invisible fan. *You're always the same* she says jokingly aping Mirtila. *No, I'm being serious, you're very beautiful. You're both beautiful. I don't know who to choose.* I open the door. *But I* Livia says *'ve always been your real lov*e and I go out. *Yes* I say from the corridor. *My one and only.* I bump against the railings and begin to go down the stairs cursing them: one foot in the void/ another foot into the abyss/ another one into nowhere. When'll they turn on the lights in this fucking house?

Fifth session

I remember when I was my husband's fiancée. No, I'm lying, I wasn't engaged yet, but he used to come and invite me out to the movies or take a walk and the day came when he invited me home to meet his family. It was Christmas Eve and it was already late, about eight o'clock, when he came to pick me up, and I was already beginning to think he wouldn't come and everybody in the building rushed to their balconies to see us and my mother didn't go to the balcony, because she knew they were all looking and she was very proud of me because my fiancé was rich and because he'd come to pick me up in a convertible to take me to dinner in his home and she told me, "Everybody in the neighborhood has seen him, child. He'll have to marry you now. See that you don't disappoint us" and I remember how disgusted I felt with my mother. It was Christmas Eve but it was very hot and I felt very distracted because I had put on the only presentable dress I had, a very summery one, and to show I had put it on for a purpose I said to my fiancé as soon as I got to the car, "It's really hot, Ricardo," and he said, "Yes, extremely. Would you like the top down?" He was very considerate and courteous and so kind.

When we got to his house I felt very good, because everyone was dressed informally, although the house was a very snazzy one in the Country Club and his father was delighted to have me and wanted to teach me to play golf the next day and we decided to eat in the garden though we drank our cocktails indoors. I felt very good with Arturo too, that's Ricardo's brother who was studying medicine, and with their mother who was very young and beautiful, a bit like a Cuban Myrna Loy, very distinguished-looking, and with Ricardo's father who was tall and handsome and never stopped looking at me the whole evening. I had had a little to drink and we were sitting in the living room, talking and waiting for the turkey to be golden roasted, and Ricardo's father invited me to go on a tour of the kitchen. I remember I didn't feel well and that Ricardo's father gripped me tightly by the arm as we went to the kitchen and as the house was half in darkness because of the Christmas tree the brilliant, almost white, light of the kitchen bothered me. I went and looked at the turkey and then I saw the girl who had brought us our drinks and who helped the chef (they were very rich and had a chef instead of a woman to cook for them) and then I saw she wasn't old and I remembered that Ricardo's mother had said something about her not being very experienced and I saw her in the light of the kitchen, as she was moving between the table and the sink and the refrigerator with the salads and she never once looked at us and I thought that her face was familiar and I saw that she was quite young and it was then that I realized she was a girl who had been at school with me in my pueblo before I came with my family to Havana and whom I hadn't seen for ten years. She was so old, doctor, so worn out and she was the same age as me, exactly the same age and we had played together when we were girls and we were very good friends and both of us had a crush on Jorge Negrete and Gregory Peck and we used to sit out at night on the steps of my house and make plans for when we were grown up and I felt so uncomfortable that I couldn't say hello to her, because it would make her feel so bad, and I had to leave the kitchen. Then, when I was in the living room again, I just about went back to the kitchen to say hello, because I thought I hadn't said hello to her because I was afraid Ricardo's family would see that I was from the country and had been very poor. But I didn't go.

The meal took a very long time coming, I don't know how long: something had happened to the turkey and we went on drinking and then Ricardo's brother wanted to show me all around the house and first of all I went to see Ricardo's room and then his brother's room and I don't know why but I went into the bathroom and the curtain of the shower was drawn and Ricardo's brother said, "Don't look," and I was so curious I opened the curtain and looked and there in the shower, drenched in dirty water, was a skeleton that still had bits of flesh on it, a human skeleton, and Ricardo's brother said, "I'm cleaning it!" I don't know how I managed to get out of the bathroom nor how I went down the stairs nor how I managed to sit at the table in the patio to eat. All I remember is that Ricardo's brother took me by the hand and kissed me and I kissed him and then he helped me across the dark room.

In the patio everything was very pretty, very green because of the lawn and beautifully lit up and the table was very well arranged with a very expensive tablecloth and they served me first because Ricardo's mother insisted on it. And what I did was to look at the meat, the pieces of turkey, very well cooked, almost burnt-looking in the brown gravy, and put my knife and fork across my plate, lower my hands and start crying. I spoiled their Christmas for them, these people who were so kind and friendly, and I returned home worn out and so sad and quiet that not even my mother heard me come in.

I HEARD HER SING

I dreamed I was an old man who'd gone out on a skiff into the Gulf Stream of the night and had gone 68 days now without catching any fish, not even a damselfish or a sardine. Silvestre had been with me for the first 66 days. After 67 days without a single fish Bustrófedon and Eribó and Arsenio Cué had told Silvestre that I was now definitely and finally *salao,* which is the worst form of salty. But on day number 69 (which is a lucky number in Havana-by-night: Bustrófedon says that it's because it's a *capicúa,* that's Cuban for a palindrome number, Arsenio Cué for a thing or two he knows about it and Rine for other reasons: it's the number of his house) on day or rather on night number 69 I was really at sea and all alone, when through the deep blue, violet, ultraviolet waters a phosphorescent fish came swimming. It was very large and bosomy and it looked like Cuba and then it became small and toothy and it was Irenita and then it got dark, blackish, pitch black and lissome and it was Magalena and when it bit my line and I caught it, it began to grow and grow and grow and it fought the line as it grew and it was as big as the boat now and it stayed there floating with strange sounds coming from its liver-lipped mouth, purring, groaning beside the boat, gaping, palpitating, making funny noises, noises more weird than funny like somebody choking as he swallows, and then the big fish was quite still, and then predatory fish began to arrive, sharks and barracudas and piranhas, all of them with faces I could recognize, in fact one of them looked very much like Gianni Boutade and another like the Emcee and it had a star on its mouth and yet another fish was Vítor Perla and I knew it was him because it had a throat like a tie made of blood and a pearl pinned on it, and I pulled the line quickly and fastened it to the side and, funny thing, I started talking to it, to the fish, Big fish, I said, fish that you are, fish, Nobel fish, I have lampooned you, harpooned I mean, it's true I caught you but I'm not going to let them eat you, and I began to haul it into the boat in a slow frenzy and I managed to get its tail into the boat and it was a radiant white now, the fish tail only, the rest of it being jet black, and suddenly I began to struggle with its soft, sticky, gelatin-flanks, gelatin because that side of it wasn't a fish but a jellyfish, an *aguamala,* but all the same I kept on pulling and suddenly I lost my balance and fell back into the boat, still pulling at its jelly side and the whole whale of a fish fell on top of me and the boat was too small for both of us and it, the fish not the boat, gave me no room to breathe and I was suffocating because its gills had landed on my face and over my mouth and nostrils and as this fish was all blubber it was spreading over me, smothering me as it sucked in my air, all the air, not only the air for breathing, the air outside but the already breathed air, the air *inside* as well, the air from my nostrils and from my mouth and from my lungs, and it left me with no air to breathe and I was suffocating badly, choking, asphyxiated. I was about to drown or choke when I woke up.

I stopped fighting the noble fish that was in my dream to begin another struggle, kicking and wrestling with a villainous sperm whale in real life which was lying on top of me and *kissing* me with its immense lunglike lips, kissing me all over my face, kissing my eyes and nose and mouth and who was now chewing my ear and biting my neck and sucking my breast and La Estrella kept sliding off my body and climbing back onto it again making unbelievably weird noises, as if she were singing and snoring at the same time and in between her groans she was speaking to me, whispering, gasping in her rasping baritone *mi amor* please kiss me *mi negro* please kill me *mi chino* come come come, things which would have made me die laughing if

I'd been able to breathe and I pushed her with what strength I had left, using a half-crushed leg as a fulcrum and making a springboard not of the bed but of the wall (because I'd been driven back against the wall by that expansion wave of fat, flattened, almost obliterated by that black universe that was expanding in my direction at the speed of love), I managed to give her a final big push and succeeded in putting her off balance and out of bed, *my* bed. She fell on the floor and there she stayed puffing and panting and sobbing but I leaped out of bed and switched on the light and then I *saw* her. She was stark naked and her breasts were as fat as her arms and twice as large as my head, and one of them fell over on one side and touched the floor and the other jutted out over the central breaker of the three great rollers that separated her legs from what would have been her neck if she had had one and the first roller above her thighs was a sort of canopied extension of her mons veneris and I could see how right Alex Bayer was when he said that "she depilated herself completely" because there wasn't a single trace of hair, pubic or otherwise, on her whole body and that couldn't have been natural, but then nothing was natural about La Estrella. It was then that I began to wonder whether she came from outer space.

If the dreams of reason beget monsters, what do the dreams of unreason beget? I dreamed (because I had fallen asleep again: sleep can be as stubborn as insomnia) that UFOs were invading the earth, not as Oscar Hurtado threatened in ships that touched down noiselessly on the rooftops or like Arsenio Cué's creatures quote hurld headlong flaming from th'Ethereal Skie/ with hideous ruin and combustion down unquote or as Silvestre feared infiltrating our lives in the form of microbes reproducing silently, but with definitely Martian shapes, creatures with suckers that could create total suction, as Rine would say, and adhere to walls made of air and then descend or ascend invisible steps and with majestic footfall could spread terror like an overflow of their black, brilliant, silent presences. In another dream or perhaps another form of the same dream these alien beings were sound waves which mingled with us and haunted us and enchanted us, like unseen sirens: from every corner a music gushed out that made men stupid, a paralysing song ray which nobody could resist and nobody could in fact do anything to fight this invasion from outer space because nobody knew that music could be the secret and final weapon, so nobody was going to stop his ears with wax or even with his fingers and at the end of that dream I was the only man on earth who could realize what was actually happening and I tried to lift my hands to my ears and I couldn't because my hands were tied and even my neck and shoulders were tied to the ground by some invisible menders and it happened that I must have fallen off the bed because I woke in a pool of sweat on the floor. I remembered then that I'd dragged myself right across the floor to the opposite end of the room and had gone to sleep right there near the door. Did I wake up with a motorman's glove in my mouth? I can't tell but I can tell that I had a taste of bile on my lips, and was terribly thirsty, and I didn't even drink so much as a cup of coffee because I felt like vomiting, but I thought twice before getting up. I wasn't at all keen to see La Estrella whether she was freak or foe, sleeping in my bed, snoring with her mouth open and half-closed eyes, rolling from side to side: nobody ever wants to meet the nightmare of the night before when he wakes up. So I began to work out how I could get to the bathroom to wash and return to look for my clothes and put them on and go out into the street without disturbing her. When I'd done all this in my mind I began to write a mental note to La Estrella to ask her more or less when she got up to do me the favor of leaving without letting anyone see her, no that was no good: of leaving everything as she'd found it, no that was no good either: of closing the door behind her: shit, all this was childish and besides it was quite useless because La Estrella might not know how to read, O.K. I'd write it in big bold caps with my grease pencil but who told me she couldn't read? Racial segregation, that's who, I said to myself as I was making up my mind to get up and wake her up and talk to her openly. Of course I had to get dressed first. I staggered to my feet and looked at the Castro convertible and she wasn't there and I didn't have to look for her very far because I could see the empty kitchen right in front of me and the bathroom door was open so I could see the bath was empty as well: she wasn't here, she'd gone. I looked at my watch which I had forgotten to take off last night and it was two o'clock (in the afternoon?) and I thought she must have gotten up early and left without making any noise. Very considerate of her. I went to the bathroom and as I was sitting on the can, reading those instructions that come with every roll of Kodak film which had been left on the floor I don't know by whom, reading this conveniently simple division of life into Sunny, Cloudy, Shade, Beach or Snow (snow in Cuba, they must be joking!) and finally Clear Well-lighted Indoors, reading these instructions without understanding them, I heard the doorbell ringing and if I'd been able to jump up without foul consequences, I'd have done so because I was sure it was La Estrella's triumphal comeback, so I let the bell ring and ring and ring and I managed to silence my gut and my lungs and the rest of my body so I became the Silent Don. But a Cuban friend is more adhesive than a Scotch tape and someone shouted my name through the airshaft between the kitchen and bathroom, not a difficult operation for someone who knows the building, has the physique of a trapeze artiste, the chest of an opera singer, the persistence of memory and a stunt man's daring to risk his neck by sticking his head through the corridor window. It wasn't the voice of a Martian. I opened the door after performing some hygienic rituals and Silvestre burst through the doorway like a white tornado, livid, shouting excitedly that Bustro was sick, seriously ill. Who? I said, picking up the debris of my hair after the wind of his entry had scattered it over a radius of my face, and he said, Bustrófedon, I left him in his house early this morning because he was feeling sick, throwing up and all that and I laughed at him because I thought he was able to take his drink better than that but he told me to leave him alone and take him to his place and not disturb him but this morning when I went to look for him to go to the beach the maid told me there was nobody at home neither the señor nor the señora nor Bustrófedon because they'd taken him to the hospital so Silvestre told me all in one breath without a comma. And the maid called him Bustrófedon, just like that? A question that was my token gift of shit to this morning already brimming with drowsiness, hangover and diarrhea. No, you cunt, she didn't say Bustrófedon but of course it was Bustrófedon, who else. Did they tell you what was wrong with him? I said on my way to the kitchen to drink a glass of milk, that oasis well in the morning-after desert of us nomad drinkers. I didn't know, Silvestre said, I don't believe it's serious but I don't think he's at all well either. I don't like the sound of his symptoms, it could very well be aneurysm. A new *rhythm*? I asked in mock-disbelief. No, hell no! Cerebral *aneurysm*, an embolism of the brain arteries, I don't know, and I laughed at his words just before he said I don't know. What the fuck are you laughing at now? Silvestre said. You're on your way to becoming a famous diagnostician, *viejito*, I said. Why, he shouted and I could see he was getting angry, why did you say that? Forget it, I said. So you think I'm a hypochondriac too? he said and I said I didn't, I was merely laughing at his vocabulary but admiringly, dazzled by his instant diagnosis and stunned by his scientific knowledge. He smiled but didn't say anything and I narrowly missed hearing yet again his story of how he'd already started or was about to start studying medicine when he'd gone with a classmate of his to the faculty and straight into the dissection room and had seen the corpses and smelled the smell of formaldehyde and dead flesh and heard the ghastly sound of bones creaking when a professor cut them up with a saw, a *common* saw for chrissake! And so on and so forth. I offered him a grateful glass of milk and he said, No thank you I've already had breakfast and from the word breakfast he went on to what comes before breakfast—which is not the morning after but the night before.

What happened to you last night? he asked and I've never known anyone to ask more questions than Silvestre: Why should be his middle name. I went out, I said. For a walk. Where? Nowhere special I said. Are you sure? What do you mean, am I sure? Of cures I'm sure! At least nobody else was in my shoes, or were they? Ah! he said, making a guttural noise to show he understood what I meant, how interesting! I didn't want to ask him any questions and he took advantage of my disadvantage to ask me some more. So you don't know what happened last night? Here, I said, trying not to make it sound like a question. No, not here, he said, in the street. We were the last to leave, I believe. Yes, the last because Sebastián Morán left before you returned with La Estrella as he still had to do his show (I thought I heard a musical note of sarcasm in his voice) and then Gianni and Franemilio left and we stayed and by we I mean Eribó and Cué and Bustrófedon and me, talking, shouting rather above La Estrella's snores and Eribó and Cué and Piloto & Vera left together and Rine had gone earlier with Jesse and Juan Blanco, I think, I'm not sure, so Bustrófedon and I took Ingrid and Edith with us. I mean, what happened was that after closing up shop in your place Bustro and I picked up Ingrid and Edith as we planned to go to the Chori and on our way to La Playa Bustrófedon was in true form, you should have heard him, but we were already on the heavy side of the river when he began to feel ill and we had to go back and Edith finally told the driver to stop on the corner and she went to bed all by herself, Silvestre said.

In the room I come and go talking to my guardian angelo as I look for my socks which only last night came in pairs and have now all managed to become single specimens. When I got tired of searching for them through the universe of my studio I returned to my own private galaxy and went to the closet and pulled out a new pair and put them on while Silvestre went on talking, telling me his story, and I was working out what do with the rest of that Sunday. The thing is, he said, that I was making out with Ingrid (and now I should explain that Ingrid is Ingrid Bergamo but that's not her name, that's her nickname, we gave it to her because that's how she pronounces the name Ingrid Bergman: she's a *mulata adelantada*, as she herself puts it when she's in a good mood, meaning she can easily pass for white, and she dyes her hair ash blond and puts on lots of makeup and wears the tightest skirts of anyone in this island where the women don't wear dresses in any case but body gloves, and she's a very easy lay, which didn't do anything to diminish Silvestre's pleasure because no woman is easy on the eve of her bedding), so I picked her up and took her to the *posada* on 84th Street, he said, and after we were already inside the patio she started saying no, no and no, and I had to tell the driver to please drive on. But, he said, when we were back in El Vedado and the taxi had gone through the tunnel for the fourth or fifth time, we started kissing and all that and she let me take her to the *posada* on 11th and 24th Street and the same thing happened there except that the driver said he was a cab driver not a pimp and that I should pay him there and then so he could go away and then Ingrid started arguing with him for not taking her home and the guy was so cut up that I paid him quickly and he shot off. Of kosher, he said, Silvestre said, I took Ingrid with me and there in the intimate darkness she staged a big row and we went out onto the street again arguing with each other or rather she was doing all the arguing as I was trying to calm her down, as reasonable and cool as George Sanders in *All About Eve* (Silvestre always talks like that, in filmese: once he made a frame with his hands playing the photographer, and he said to me, Whoa! Budge an inch and you go out of frame! and another time I arrived at his house, which was dark, with the doors of the balcony closed because the evening sun hit them hard and I inadvertently opened the balcony and he said, You've just exploded twenty thousand full candles in my face! and the time he and Cué and I were talking about jazz and then Cué said something pedantic about its origins in New Orleans and Silvestre told him, Don't cut in with that flashback now, *viejito!* and other things I forget or can't remember now), and there we were walking and quarreling and crossing El Vedado from north to south, you know where we finally ended up? he asked but didn't wait for my answer. We arrived at the *posada* on 31st Street and went in as though there was nothing to it. I believe, he told me, I won the game by default but this was only the first round and inside, once we were in the room there was a wrestling match between a heroine from Griffith and a Von Stroheim villain to get her to sit down, are you listening? just to get her to sit down and not even on the bed but in a chair! After she'd sat down she didn't want to let go of her handbag. Finally, he said, I got her to calm down and sit quietly, almost relaxed and I go and take off my jacket and she's up like a shot and runs to open the door to leave the room and I zoom in on the door and see her hand in big close-up on the bolt and I put my jacket back on and calm her down once more but in calming her down she gets so nervous she makes a mistake and sits on the bed and no sooner is she sitting than she leaps up as though it was a fakir's bed of nails and I, playing the part of a man of the world, very much a la Cary Grant, I manage to persuade her not to be frightened, there's nothing to be afraid of, sitting on the bed is only sitting, and the bed is just like any other bit of furniture, namely a chair, and like a chair the bed could just as well be a seat and she's much quieter now, so she gets up and leaves her handbag on the table and sits back on the bed again. I don't know why, Silvestre told me, but I guessed I could now take my jacket off, so I took it off and sat beside her and began to caress and kiss her and having got this far I pushed her back, so she would lie down, and she lies down only a second because up she pops like on a spring again and I go on pushing her down and she goes on sitting up and I insist she lie down until something's got to give and this time she lies down and stays down for good, very quiet and very much the ingenue in a romantic-but-risqué scene, so I decide to take a chance and begin telling her how hot it is and that it's a pity she's going to fuck—pardon—to wreck her dress and how it's getting all rumpled and how elegant it indeed is and she says, It's cute, isn't it? And with no heralding effect whatsoever she tells me she's going to take it off so as not to crease it, but that she won't take off anything more, that she will definitely keep her slip on, and then she takes her dress off. She gets back on the bed again and I've already taken my shoes off and I forget the Hays code, I start working on her body in medium shot, and I plead with her, I beg her, and I almost go down on my knees on the bed, asking her to take off her slip and I tell her I want to see her beautiful starlet's body, that she needn't wear more than just panties and bra, that it's only the same as a swimsuit except she's in bed not on the beach and I succeed in convincing her with this argument, *viejito,* and she takes her slip off though first she tells me that's all, she's not taking off anything more. But nothing. So then we start kissing and caressing and I tell her I'm going to get my pants rumpled unless I take them off so I take them off and I take my shirt off too and now I've got nothing on but my shorts and when I scramble back on the bed again she starts getting angry or pretends she's angry already and she won't let me caress her like before. But a minute later I'm touching her hand with a finger and then the finger climbs on top of her hand and then climbs up her arm not only one finger but two and then my hand climbs up the south face of her tit because it's there, and then I caress her body and we start feeling and fondling each other again and then I ask her, beginning in a whisper, almost in voice off, telling her, pleading with her to take off the rest of her clothes, or just her bra so I can see her marvelous breasts but she won't let me convince her and then just when I'm on the point of losing my cool, she says, O.K. and suddenly she's taken her bra off and what do you guess I'm seeing in the dim red light in the bedroom? That was the subject of another public debate: switching off the overhead light and switching on the bedside lamp. What I'm seeing is the eighth wonder of the world, the eighth and the ninth because there are *two* of them! And I start going crazy over them, and she starts going crazy and the whole atmosphere switches from suspense to euphoria like in a Hitchcock movie. The end of the sequence was, so as not to bore you with any more detail shots, that with the same or similar arguments that had become standard treatment by now I succeeded in persuading her to take off her pants, *but*, BUT, where old Hitch would have cut to insert and intercut of fireworks, I'll give it to you straight—I didn't get any further than that. Not even the Great Cary would have been able to persuade this poor man's Ingrid to do a love scene, torrid or horrid, and I came to the conclusion that rape is one of the labors of Hercules and that really there's no such thing as rape, because it can't be called a crime if the victim is conscious and only one person commits the act. No, that's quite impossible, dear De Sad.

I begin to laugh seismically but Silvestre interrupts me. Wait a moment, hang on a sec, as Ingrid says, that's not the end of the film. We spent the night, Silvestre tells me, or the bit of the night that was left on the best of terms and succored by her expert hands, satisfied more or less and in *Ecstasy,* a state of, I fell asleep and when I wake up it's already light and I look for my loved one and I see my costar has changed with the night, that sleep has transformed her and like poor Franz Kafka I call it a metamorphosis and even though it's not Gregor Samsa whom I find beside me it sure is another woman: night and kisses and sleep have removed not only her lipstick but the whole of her makeup, the lot: the once perfect eyebrows, the large thick lovely black lashes, the phosphorescent and pale complexion that was so kissable the night before are no more, and, wait a moment, don't laugh please: you ain't heard nothing yet, so hold on, I'll be rocking the boat: there, by my side, between her and me like an abyss of falsyhood, there's a yellowish object, round more or less and silky in appearance but not in texture, and as I touch it I almost leap out of bed: it's hairy! I pick it up, he says, in my hands, very cautiously, and hold it up to the morning light to see it better and it is, a last tremolo of strings attached plus a clash of cymbals, yes, a wig: my leading lady becomes the American eagle because she is hairless or, he said, bald, bald, bald, bald! Well, not *completely* bald, which is even worse because she has a few bits of colorless fuzz here and there, quite disgusting I must say. So there I was, Ionesco Malgré Louis, Silvestre said, in bed with the bald soprano. I must have been thinking this so hard I said it out loud, because she began to stir and then woke up. In the immediately preceding shot I'd left the wig where it was, had lain down again and feigned sleep, and as she wakes up now the first thing she does is to put a hand to her head and in a frenzy she frisks around, she *leaps* around, looking for her hairpiece everywhere and she finds it and puts it on—but *upside down, chico,* upside down! Then she gets up, goes to the bathroom, closes the door and turns on the light and when she opens it again everything's in its place. She looks at me and then she does a double take because she was so worried about losing her hair she forgot I existed and it's only now she remembers she's in a *posada* and with me. She looks at me twice, Silvestre said, to make sure I'm sleeping, but she looks at me from a distance and there I am fast asleep with my eyes half opened, seeing everything: I'm a film camera. She picks up her handbag and her clothes and goes into the bathroom again. When she comes out she's another woman. Or rather she's the same woman you and I and everybody else know and who gave me such a hard time last night before she consented to let me be present at her unveiling, at her total striptease, *au dépouillement à la Allais*.

All this time I couldn't contain my laughter and Silvestre had to narrate his Odyssey above my guffaws and now the two of us laughed together. But then he signaled me to stop and said, But don't you laugh at Barnum, old Bailey, because we're both partners of Browning in *Freaks*. What do you mean, I say. Yes siree, you've been making love with the Negro nation's answer to Oliver Hardy. What do you mean, I repeat. Yes, yes. Listen, after I'd left the lie-detector chamber I took that delectable little blonde back to where she once belonged in an early taxi and after I'd seen her safely home I went off toward the sunrise and beyond, where my house is, and as I was passing here, it must have been about 5 o'clock A.M., there was La Estrella walking along the sidewalk up 23rd Street, looking real cross, and I don't mean her hair but her looks. So I called her and picked her up and took her home but along the way, my friend and lighting cameraman, she told me that a horrible thing happened to her on her way to stardom and she proceeded to tell me that she'd fallen asleep in your camera obscura and that you came back drunk and had tried to sodomize her, and she ended by swearing to me that she'd never never never put a foot inside your house again, and I'm telling you, she was really mad at you. So you see one freak equals another and a farce mirrors a fiasco or *fracaso,* failure's saddest form. Did she actually say that? I asked. No, not her but probably Carlos or Ernesto. Come on! Is that what she told you, is that what she said? Well, said Silvestre, she said you tried to bugger her, that's what she told me but I'm not keeping to the text. I'm giving you a fair film copy instead.

As I had no more laughter left in my body, I left Silvestre sitting on the bed or the sofa and went to brush my teeth. From the bathroom I asked him which hospital Bustrófedon was in and he told me he was in Antomarchi. I asked him if he was going to see him in the evening and he shook his head and said that at four o'clock he had a date with Ingrid the woman from Bergamo and he thought that today he shouldn't put off till tomorrow what he should have done yesterday. I smiled but without conviction now and Silvestre told me I shouldn't smile like that because it wasn't her body he was after but only that naked soul of hers and that I should also bear in mind her antecedents in film myth: Jean Harlow also wore a wig. Made by Max Factor of Hollywood.

Sixth session

Doctor, how do you spell psychiatrist? With or without a *p*?

VAE VISITORS

THE STORY OF A STICK
(*With Some Additional Comments by Mrs. Campbell*)

The Story

We arrived in Havana one Friday around three in the afternoon. The heat was oppressive. There was a low ceiling of dense gray, or blackish, clouds. As the boat entered the harbor the breeze that had cooled us off during the crossing suddenly died down. My leg was bothering me again and it was very painful going down the gangplank. Mrs. Campbell followed behind me talking the whole damned time and she found everything, *but* everything, enchanting: the enchanting little city, the enchanting bay, the enchanting avenue facing the enchanting dock. All I knew was that there was a humidity of 90 or 95 percent and that I was sure my leg was going to bother me the whole weekend. It was, of course, Mrs. Campbell's brilliant idea to come to such a hot and humid island. I told her so as soon as I was on deck and saw the ceiling of rain clouds over the city. She protested, saying they had sworn to her in the travel agency that it was always, but always, spring in Cuba. Spring my aching foot! We were in the Torrid Zone. That's what I told her and she answered, "Honey, this is *the* tropics!"

On the edge of the dock there was this group of enchanting natives playing a guitar and rattling some gourds and shouting infernal noises, the sort of thing that passes for music here. In the background, behind this aboriginal orchestra, there was an open-air tent where they sold the many fruits of the tropical tree of tourism: castanets, brightly painted fans, wooden rattlers, musical sticks, shell necklaces, earthenware pots, hats made of a brittle yellow straw and stuff like that. Mrs. Campbell bought one or two articles of every kind. She was simply enchanted. I told her she should wait till the day we left before making purchases. "Honey," she said, "they are souvenirs." She didn't understand that souvenirs are what you buy when you leave a country. Nor was there any point in explaining. Luckily they were very quick in Customs, which was surprising. They were also very friendly, although they did lay it on a bit thick, if you know what I mean.

I regretted not bringing the car. What's the point of going by ferry if you don't take a car? But Mrs. Campbell thought we would waste too much time learning foreign traffic regulations. Actually she was afraid we would have another accident. Now there was one more argument she could throw in for good measure. "Honey, with your leg in this state you simply cannot drive," she said. "Let's get a cab."

We waved down a taxi and a group of natives—more than we needed—helped us with our suitcases. Mrs. Campbell was enchanted by the proverbial Latin courtesy. It was useless to tell her that it was a courtesy you also pay for through your proverbial nose. She would always find them wonderful, even before we landed she knew everything would be just wonderful. When all our baggage and the thousand and one other things Mrs. Campbell had just bought were in the taxi, I helped her in, closed the door in keen competition with the driver and went around to the other door because I could get in there more easily. As a rule I get in first and then Mrs. Campbell gets in, because it's easier for her that way, but this impractical gesture of courtesy which delighted Mrs. Campbell and which she found "very Latin" gave me the chance to make a mistake I will never forget. It was then that I saw the walking stick.

It wasn't an ordinary walking stick and this alone should have convinced me not to buy it. It was flashy, meticulously carved and expensive. It's true that it was made of a rare wood that looked like ebony or something of that sort and that it had been worked with lavish care—exquisite, Mrs. Campbell called it—and translated into dollars it wasn't really that expensive. All around it there were grotesque carvings of nothing in particular. The stick had a handle shaped like the head of a Negro, male or female—you can never tell with artists—with very ugly features. The whole effect was repulsive. However, I was tempted by it even though I have no taste for knickknacks and I think I would have bought it even if my leg hadn't been hurting. (Perhaps Mrs. Campbell, when she noticed my curiosity, would have pushed me into buying it.) Needless to say Mrs. Campbell found it beautiful and original and—I have to take a deep breath before I say it—*exciting*. Women, good God!

We got to the hotel and checked in, congratulating ourselves that our reservations were in order, and went up to our room and took a shower. Ordered a snack from room service and lay down to take a siesta—when in Rome, etc. . . . No, it's just that it was too hot and there was too much sun and noise outside, and our room was very clean and comfortable and cool, almost cold, with the air-conditioning. It was a good hotel. It's true it was expensive, but it was worth it. If the Cubans have learned something from us it's a feeling for comfort and the Nacional is a very comfortable hotel, and what's even better, it's efficient. When we woke up it was already dark and we went out to tour the neighborhood.

Outside the hotel we found a cab driver who offered to be our guide. He said his name was Raymond something and showed us a faded and dirty ID card to prove it. Then he took us around that stretch of street Cubans call La Rampa, with its shops and neon signs and people walking every which way. It wasn't too bad. We wanted to see the Tropicana, which is advertised everywhere as "the most fabulous cabaret in the world," and Mrs. Campbell had made the journey almost especially to go there. To kill time we went to see a movie we wanted to see in Miami and missed. The theater was near the hotel and it was new and air-conditioned.

We went back to the hotel and changed. Mrs. Campbell insisted I wear my tuxedo. She was going to put on an evening gown. As we were leaving, my leg started hurting again—probably because of the cold air in the theater and the hotel—and I took my walking stick. Mrs. Campbell made no objection. On the contrary, she seemed to find it funny.

The Tropicana is in a place on the outskirts of town. It is a cabaret almost in the jungle. It has gardens full of trees and climbing plants and fountains and colored lights along all the road leading to it. The cabaret has every right to advertise itself as fabulous physically, but the show consists—like all Latin cabarets, I guess—of half-naked women dancing rumbas and singers shouting their stupid songs and crooners in the style of Bing Crosby, but in Spanish. The national drink of Cuba is the daiquiri, a sort of cocktail with ice and rum, which is very good because it is so hot in Cuba—in the street I mean, because the cabaret had the "typical Cuban air-conditioning" as they call it, which means the North Pole encapsuled in a tropical saloon. There's a twin cabaret in the open air but it wasn't functioning that night because they were expecting rain. The Cubans proved good meteorologists. We'd only just begun to eat one of those meals they call international cuisine in Cuba, which consist of things that are too salty or full of fat or fried in oil which they follow with a dessert that is much too sweet, when a shower started pouring down with a greater noise than one of those typical bands at full blast. I say this to give some idea of the violence of the rainfall as there are very few things that make more noise than a Cuban band. For Mrs. Campbell this was the high point of sophisticated savagery: the rain, the music, the food, and she was simply enchanted. Everything would have been fine—or at any rate passable; when we switched to drinking whiskey and soda I began to feel almost at home—but for the fact that this stupid *maricón* of an emcee of the cabaret, not content with introducing the show to the public, started introducing the public to the show, and it even occurred to this fellow to ask our names—I mean *all* the Americans who were there—and he started introducing us in some godawful travesty of the English language. Not only did he mix me up with the soup people, which is a common enough mistake and one that doesn't bother me anymore, but he also introduced me as an international playboy. Mrs. Campbell, of course, was on the verge of ecstasy!

When we finally left the cabaret, after midnight, it had

stopped raining and wasn't as hot and sticky outside. We were both pretty loaded, but I didn't forget the stick. So I gripped it with one hand and grabbed Mrs. Campbell with the other. And the cab driver took it upon himself to take us to another kind of show which I wouldn't be talking about if I didn't have the excuse that both Mrs. Campbell and I were dead drunk. Mrs. Campbell found it very exciting—as she did almost everything in Cuba—but I have to admit it was pretty boring and I think I even slept through half of it. One of the by-products of the Cuban tourist industry is that the cab drivers double as salesmen. They carry you off somewhere without asking you and before you realize it you're inside. This was a house like any other, but once you're inside they take you through to a hall with seats on all sides, like one of those theaters that were fashionable in the early fifties, a theater in the round, except that there's no stage in the center, only a bed, a circular bed—or rather, in the round. They serve drinks—which are more expensive than in the most expensive cabarets—and then when everyone has found their seats, they turn off the lights and switch on a red light, and also a blue one above the bed, but you can see everything perfectly, and then two women come in, stark naked. They lie down on the bed and start caressing each other, making love and other things which are disgusting and unhygienic. Then a man comes in—a Negro, of course, but looking blacker than usual in this lighting—with an excessively long member and all three of them seem to get a big kick out of all sorts of variations on the theme. Some naval officers were also watching, which I thought was very unpatriotic, but they seemed to be having a good time and it's none of my business if they get their kicks in or out of uniform. When the performance was over someone turned on the lights and—what a nerve!—the two women and the Negro greeted the audience. This fellow and the women made some jokes at the expense of my tuxedo, about the fact that I was wearing black and that the walking stick was black too. They were standing right in front of us stark naked and the naval officers laughed a lot and naturally Mrs. Campbell seemed to think it was funny. Finally the Negro went up to one of the officers and told him in a very Cuban English that he simply hated women, and then made some obscene suggestions, but the sailors roared with laughter and Mrs. Campbell laughed too. A round of applause.

We slept until ten o'clock Saturday morning and at eleven we went off to this resort called Varydero, which is about fifty miles from Havana, and spent the whole day sprawled on the beach. The sun was scorching, but the sea with its changing colors and the white sand and the old wooden bathing huts seemed ideal for color film. I took a lot of pictures and Mrs. Campbell and I had a very pleasant day. But in the evening my whole back was covered with blisters and I was suffering from indigestion because of all that Cuban cooking crammed with shellfish. We returned to Havana with Raymond at the wheel, and he left us in our hotel after midnight. I was happy to find my walking stick waiting for me in the room, though I hadn't needed it all day because the sun and the sea and the fact that the heat was less humid had made my leg much better. Mrs. Campbell and I sat drinking in the hotel bar till very late, listening to more of that absurd music Mrs. Campbell finds so enchanting, and I felt very good because I'd come downstairs walking stick in hand.

The next day, Sunday morning, we sent Raymond off until it was time to return to the hotel and collect our things. The ferry left at two o'clock. So we decided to take a walk through the old part of town and have a look around to buy some more souvenirs, for the benefit of Mrs. Campbell. We bought some things in a store for tourists opposite the ruins of a Spanish fort which is open every day. Then, since we were loaded down with packages, we decided to stop at an old café and have a drink. Everything was peaceful and I liked the old-fashioned, civilized atmosphere of Sunday in the old part of town. We sat there drinking for an hour or so and then we paid and left. After a couple of blocks suddenly I remembered I'd left my walking stick in the café so I went back to pick it up. Nobody had seen it, which didn't surprise me: this sort of thing happens. I returned to the street, too upset for words and much more than so insignificant a loss could justify. But then I was equally surprised and overjoyed when as I turned the corner of a narrow street and walked toward a taxi stand, I saw an old man with my stick. When I caught up with him I saw that he wasn't old but of indefinable age, and definitely mongoloid. There was no possible way of communicating with him in English or even in Mrs. Campbell's precarious Spanish. The fellow didn't understand a thing and stuck to the stick.

I was afraid a slapstick situation would develop if I did as Mrs. Campbell suggested as a last resort and grabbed hold of the stick, because I could see that the beggar—he was one of the many professional beggars that infest countries like this—was no weakling. I tried to make him understand by signs that the stick was mine, to no avail—all I got for an answer was some strange noises from his throat. For a moment it reminded me of those native musicians and their guttural songs. Mrs. Campbell suggested that I buy the stick from him, but "It's a matter of principle, dear," I told her, trying to block the beggar's retreat with my body at the same time. "That stick belongs to me." I wasn't going to let him keep it just because he was a congenital idiot and still less was I going to buy it from him, because that would have been submitting to blackmail. "I'm not the kind of guy who gives in to *chantage*," I told Mrs. Campbell, as I stepped off the sidewalk into the street, because the beggar looked like he was trying to cross over to the other side. "Of course you're not, honey," she said.

Soon we had a small crowd of local residents around us and I was getting nervous because I didn't want to be the victim of a lynching mob, especially since I must have looked like a foreigner who was abusing a defenseless native. The people, however, were well-behaved, considering. Mrs. Campbell explained the situation as well as she could and one of them, who spoke very little and very primitive English, offered to act as mediator. He tried, without success, to communicate with the idiot. The latter made no response except to grip the stick tighter and make signs and noises to indicate that it was his. Like all crowds, the people were sometimes on my side and sometimes on the beggar's. My wife, however, still tried to explain the situation. "It is a matter of principle," she said, more or less in Spanish. "Mr. Campbell is the rightful owner of the stick. He bought it yesterday, he left it in a café this morning, this gentleman," she said, pointing to the cretin, "took it, and it doesn't belong to him, no, *amigos*." The crowd was now on our side.

Soon we became a public nuisance and a policeman arrived. Fortunately it was a policeman who spoke English. I told him what had happened. He tried to disperse the crowd, but the people were as interested as we were in the solution of the problem. He spoke to the idiot, but as I've already explained there was no possible way of communicating with this character. Of course the policeman lost his patience and pulled out his gun to threaten the beggar. There was a sudden hush and I feared the worst. But the idiot seemed to understand and he handed the stick back to me, with a gesture I didn't like. The policeman put his gun back and suggested I give the moron some money, not as compensation but as a gift "to the poor man," so he said. I refused point-blank: this would be agreeing to a social blackmail since the stick belonged to me. I explained this to the policeman. Mrs. Campbell tried to intervene, but I saw no reason for giving in: the stick was mine and the beggar had no right to take it, to give him money was like paying someone for not stealing. I refused to budge. Someone in the crowd, Mrs. Campbell explained, had suggested a collection all around. Mrs. Campbell out of pure simpleminded generosity wanted to contribute from her own pocket. It was time to put an end to this ridiculous situation so I gave in, although I shouldn't have. I offered the idiot some small change—I don't know how much exactly but it was almost as much as the stick had cost—and I was ready to give it to him without showing any hard feelings, but the beggar wouldn't take it. Now it was his turn to act as the offended party. Mrs. Campbell tried to mediate. The man seemed on the point of accepting the money, but then he thrust it back, making his usual guttural sounds. Not until the policeman took the money and offered it to him did he accept. I didn't like his face at all, because he stood there staring at the stick when I took it with me, like a dog watching a bone. The disagreeable incident was finally brought to a close and we took a taxi on the spot—which the policeman hailed for us with dutiful courtesy—and someone cheered as we drove off and a few even waved us a friendly good-bye. I was glad I couldn't see the expression on the cretin's face. Mrs. Campbell didn't say a word the whole journey and she seemed to be counting her purchases mentally. I felt great now that I had my walking stick back, since it had risen to the category of souvenir-cum-anecdote, much more valuable than the mountain of presents Mrs. Campbell had indiscriminately collected.

We got back to the hotel and I told them in the lobby that we were checking out in the afternoon but we would have lunch in the hotel. I asked them to make out the bill for us and we went upstairs.

As always, I opened the door and let Mrs. Campbell in first, and she turned on the light because the curtains were still drawn. She went through our sitting room and into the bedroom. When she turned on the light in there, she gave a sharp cry. I thought she might have had an electric shock, knowing how dangerous high voltages can be in foreign countries. I also thought she might have been bitten by poisonous vermin or discovered a thief. I rushed into the bedroom. Mrs. Campbell was rigid, unable to speak, she was on the verge of hysteria. At first, seeing her there in the middle of the room in a catatonic state, I couldn't understand what had happened. But she made some noises with her mouth and pointed to the bed with her hand. There, on the glass top of the night table, black against the pale-green painted wood, was *another* walking stick.

Mrs. Campbell's Comments

Mr Campbell, who is a professional writer, got the story wrong, as usual, of course.

Seen from the boat Havana was dazzlingly beautiful. The sea was calm, a pale blue, almost the color of the sky at times, with a broad purple belt across it which someone explained was the Gulf Stream. There were a few little waves with crests of foam, looking like sea gulls in an inverted sky. The city came up suddenly, breathtakingly white. There were a few ominous clouds in the sky, but the sun was shining and Havana wasn't a city but a mirage, or the ghost of a city. Then it opened at both sides and a rapid catalog of colors appeared which merged in the general sun-drenched whiteness. It was a panorama, a CinemaScope of reality, a real-life Cinerama: I say this to please Mr Campbell, who is a movie-lover. We sailed between buildings that were more mirrors than buildings, reflections that could swallow the eyes of those who gazed at them, past parks where the grass was either burnt or intensely green, on toward another city, older, darker and still more beautiful. Slowly, inevitably, a pier moved toward us.

It is of course true that Cuban music is primitive, but it is nonetheless lively and enchanting, flavored with so many delights and then always, up pops a violent surprise. It is an indefinable poetic quality which goes up and up, propelled by the rattlers and the guitar, while the drums beat it down to the ground and the *claves*—two sticks which make music—are like a stable horizon linking them.

Why all this fuss about his bad leg? Maybe he wants to sound like a war veteran. What Mr Campbell suffers from is rheumatism.

The walking stick was a perfectly ordinary walking stick. It was made of a dark-colored wood and it may or may not have been beautiful, but it certainly didn't have any grotesque carvings on it or an androgynous head for a handle. It was a walking stick of the kind you can find anywhere in the world, of unpolished wood, with a certain picturesque charm: that's all, nothing special. I imagine many Cubans carry a similar stick. I never said the stick was exciting: this is a blatant Freudian insinuation. Besides, I wouldn't commit the obscenity of buying a walking stick.

The stick cost very little. The Cuban peso is worth the same as the American dollar. The beach near Havana is called Varadero not Varydero—which he pronounced predictably Verydeer-o.

There were plenty of things I found enchanting in the city but I've never been ashamed of my feelings and I can say exactly what they were. I liked the old part of the city. I liked the nature of the people. I liked Cuban music very much, of course. I liked the Tropicana—despite the fact that it is a tourist attraction and knows it: beautiful and exuberant and evergreen, a perfect image of the island. The food was passable and the drinks the same as anywhere else but the music and the beauty of the women and the unbridled imagination of the choreographer were unforgettable.

Mr Campbell attempts, in his narrative, to make me the prototype of the average woman: in other words, a spiritual cripple, with the IQ of a moron and the importunity of a pawnbroker at a wake. I have never said things like Honey, this is the tropics or They are souvenirs! He's been reading too many "Blondie" comic strips—or else he's had an overdose of "I Love Lucy."

The word "native" appears many times in the course of the narrative but Mr Campbell shouldn't be blamed for this. I suppose it is inevitable. When Mr (it must bother him that I omit the period after his title since he is absolutely obsessed with punctuation) Campbell heard that the management of the hotel was "ours" as he called it he smiled a connoisseur's smile, because in his eyes people who live in the tropics are perpetually lazy. Also, they're difficult to tell apart. For example: the cab driver said quite clearly that his name was Ramón García.

I never thought it funny that he took this stick every time he went out into the city. When he left the Tropicana, he was completely drunk and in the short time it took to cross the entrance hall he dropped the stick three times. It was embarrassing. He was enchanted, as he always is, that they mixed him up with the Campbells who are multimillionaires and he still insists that they are relatives of his. It wasn't the bit about the international playboy that made me laugh but his phony disgust when they called him "the millionaire of the soup industry."

It's true that Raymond (I gave up in the end and called him that) suggested the excursion to see the *tableaux vivants,* but only after Mr Campbell's insinuations. He forgot to mention that he had bought a dozen pornographic books in a French bookstore, among them a complete edition of a novel of the last century published in English in Paris. I wasn't the only one who enjoyed the show.

He didn't "find" the stick in the street, walking by the side of a man like one of Gogol's thing-people: it was in the café itself. We were sharing a table (the café was full) and upon getting up Mr Campbell grabbed a walking stick that was leaning against the table next to ours. It was dark and knotty: similar to his own. As we were leaving we heard someone running after us making noises: it was the rightful owner of the stick, only we didn't know it then. Mr Campbell wanted to give it back and it was *I* who opposed the idea. I told him he'd bought the walking stick with good money and that even if the beggar was an idiot, he wasn't going to take advantage of us, using his mental condition as a pretext. It is true that a small crowd gathered round us (mostly regulars of the café) and that an argument followed, but they were on our side the whole time: the beggar could not talk. The policeman (he was a tourist policeman) was passing by chance, I think. Naturally, he also took our side, so much so that he arrested the beggar. Nobody proposed a collection and Mr Campbell didn't pay any recompense: I wouldn't have allowed it in any case. The way he tells the story it sounds as if the walking stick was a magic wand which suddenly turned me into a fairy godmother. None of this is true: in actual fact it was I who insisted that he shouldn't give up the stick. It should be obvious by now that I never suggested he grab hold of the stick. (The whole "sequence," as Mr Campbell describes it, sounds like something out of an early Vittorio de Sica film.)

My Spanish is not perfect, but I can make myself understood.

There was never any melodrama. Nor lynching mobs nor cheers, and if the beggar did make an ugly face, we didn't see it. Nor did I scream when I saw the other stick (I find these dramatic italics of Mr Campbell in very poor taste: "*other* stick." Why not simply "other stick"?). I merely pointed at it without any hysteria or catatonia. I thought it was terrible, obviously, but then I also thought that error and injustice were easy to correct. We went out again and found the café and learned from the clientele where the precinct was, since they'd arrested the beggar for theft: it was Mr Campbell's ruined fortress. He wasn't there. The police officer had released him at the gate, to the accompaniment of the laughter of the other policemen and the tears of the thief, who was himself the only one who had been robbed. Nobody, of course, knew where we could find him.

We missed the boat and had to return by plane, together with the two walking sticks.

THE TALE OF A WALKING STICK WHEN FOLLOWED BY MADAME CAMPBELL'S CORRECTIONS IN THE COMIC STYLE

The Tale

We arrived in Havana on a Friday afternoon and a very hot afternoon it was, with a low ceiling of dense heavy dark clouds. As soon as the boat entered La Bahía[1] the pilot very simply switched off the breeze that had refreshed the crossing. It had been cool and now suddenly it wasn't. Just like that. Ernest Hemingway, I presume, would call it, a marine ventilator. Now my leg was bothering me like the devil and it was with a great deal of pain that I walked down the gangplank, but I disguised it well for the benefit of our hosts and guests. (Should I say natives and discoverers?) Mrs. Campbell came behind me talking and gesticulating and amazing herself over everything the whole saintly time and she found every little thing enchanting: the enchanting blue bay, the enchanting old city, the enchanting and picturesque little calle[2] near the enchanting dock. Who, me? I, what I was thinking was that the humidity must have been 90 or 95, and I was more than sure that my saintly leg was going to give me terrible trouble the whole condemned weekend. It must have been the devil's own idea that brought us for a

1 Spanish. The bay.
2 Spanish. Street. Road in a city.

restful vacation to this ardent,[3] moist island that was bleached white by the sun wherever it wasn't entirely scorched. Dante's *Invierno,* no less. Of course it had been Mrs. Campbell's project in the first place. (A design by Mrs. Campbell, with a HERS embroidered behind, I am tempted to add.) I warned her as soon as I was on the upper deck and saw the dome of black clouds hung up over the city like a sword of Damoclean rain over my leg. She protested indignantly and said that the travel agent had sworn on his postered heart that it was *always* Spring in Cuba. Spring, my poor bloody big toe! The travel agents! They must all have been in *Trader's Horn* with Carey and Renaldo and picked up Booth's disease. (Edwina Booth, I mean. She is a woman's disease.) We were well planted in the Torrid Zone, infested with mosquitoes, endemic malarially and populated by forests of rain. I said so to Mrs. Campbell and she had to have the last word: "Little dear, this is *the* Tropic!"

Upon the dock, like an essential part of the machinery of disembarkation, there was a trio of those enchanting natives scraping at a guitar and shaking two castanets shaped like calabashes and banging bits of wood one against the other and uttering certain savage cries such as pass for music here. As décor[4] for this orchestra of aborigines someone had erected an open air stall where they sold all the fruits of the tree of knowledge of tourism: castanets, colored *habanicos,* the instruments that looked like gourds, little musical sticks, necklaces made of shells and bits of wood and seeds, a mediocre menagerie scraped from the bottom of the barrel, and hats made of hard, brittle yellow straw: Tutti frutti.[5] *Madame* Campbell bought one or two examples of every item. She was radiating with pleasure. De-lighted. Static. I advised her better to leave all these purchases for the last day on land. "Little dear," she said, "they are *souvenirs*."[6] She couldn't grasp the point that the *souvenirs* are supposed to be bought only when you leave the country. Thank to God, we managed to get through the custom very quickly, a fact which, I have to admit, surprised me much. They were also

3 An instance of hyperbole, presumably. White hot, originally.
4 French. In the context the word means background or context.
5 Italian. All the fruits.
6 French. Memories.

very amicable, even if they did lay it on a bit too thick, if you know what I mean.

I regretted that I hadn't brought my Buick. What good is it going on a ferry if you don't take your car with you? But Mrs. Campbell decided at the last moment, that we would have wasted a lot of time learning the traffic regulations. If the truth is to be known, she was really afraid we would have another accident. Now she had one more argument to add: "Little dear," she said, "with your leg in *that* [pointing to it] condition, you couldn't possibly have driven a car. We'll take a cab."

We hailed a cab and some natives (more of those than were strictly necessary) helped us with the baggage. Mrs. Campbell was very full of this so-called Latin courtesy. Proverbial, she called it. Putting tips in extra hands, I considered how pointless it would be to tell her that it was a courtesy that was proverbially well paid for. She will continue to find them just wonderful, no matter what they do and/or prove on the contrary. Even before arriving I knew that everything was going to turn out wonderfully well. When our cases and the thousand and one things Sra. Campbell had bought for her were in the cab, I closed the door (in fierce competition with the driver, who was obviously a cousin of Jesse Owens) and went around to the other side to get in. Ordinarily, I get in first and Mrs. Campbell follows me, to make the things easier for me. But this gesture of obsolete good manners which Mrs. Campbell was enraptured by, and said was *mucho latino*,[7] induced me to a mistake I will never forget. It was then (on the other side) that I saw the walking stick.

It was not a common walking stick and I shouldn't have bought it if only for that reason. Quite aside from the fact that it was a thing ostentatious and twisted, it was also expensive. It is true that it was made of some precious hard wood, ebony or something similar and it was carved with tedious care. (An exquisite hand, Mrs. Campbell said.) In terms of dollars, of course, it wasn't expensive. Under a nearer inspection, the carving was nothing more than grotesque designs with no particular significance. The stick ended with a head that was

7 *Sic.*

cut into the shape of a *Negro* or a *Negress* (you can never tell with these artists), whose features were strikingly ugly. In toto,[8] it was a little on the repellent side. Like a fool, it immediately attracted me, although I can't exactly say why. I am not a frivolous man, but I think I would have bought it even if my leg had been hurting or not. Who knows, maybe Mrs. Campbell would have finally pushed me into buying it, seeing my interest. Like all women, she is in love with buying things. She said that it was beautiful and (hold your breathing) *exciting*. My God! *Los mujeres*.[9]

In the hotel, our luck she was still running good and our reservations were found valid. We went up and took a shower and ordered a speedy lunch from room service. The service was rapid like the lunch was good and then we took a satisfactory short nap, the Cuban *siesta*—when in Havana . . . No, it was very hot and sunny and noisy outside and inside it was a clean, cool lighted place. A good hotel, quiet, with excellent air-conditioning. True it was expensive, but it was worth it. If there is anything the Cubans have learnt from us Americans, it is a feeling for comfort and El Nacional is a comfortable hotel and, even better, it's efficient. We got up late, at the fall of night and took a turn around the vicinity.

In the perfumed gardens of the hotel we made the acquaintance of a sort of the driver of a taxi who offered to be our guide. He said he was called Ramón something or other and he produced a very filthy wrinkled identity card to prove this. He then proceeded to drive us through a labyrinth of palms and parked cars in the direction of that broad avenue which the *haveneros*[10] call La Rampa, with her stores and clubs and restaurants on both sides and her neon signs and heavy traffic and people going up and down the ramp which gives the avenue her name. It isn't at all bad, a bit like Frisco. We wanted to see the *Tropicana*, the Night-club which bills itself as "the most fabulous cabaret in the world." Mrs. Campbell had almost made the journey specially to visit it. We, or rather she, decided we would have dinner in there. Meanwhile, we went to see a movie

8 Latin. Altogether.
9 *Sic*.
10 *Sic*.

which we had wanted to see in Miami and had lost. The movie house was near the hotel and it was new and modern and was air-conditioned.

We returned to the hotel to change ourselves for the occasion. Mrs. Campbell insisted I should wear an evening dress. She would put on her finest evening gown. As we were leaving my leg started to hurt again, probably because of the cold air in the movie house and the hotel, and I took the stick with me. Mrs. Campbell raised no objection. On the contrary, she found it peculiar.

Tropicana is localized outside the town. It is a sylvan cabaret. The gardens grow right up to the roads leading to it and every square yard is overgrown with trees and bushes and lianas and *epiphytes* which Mrs. Campbell insisted were orchids, and classical statues and fountains with running water, everywhere, and spotlights with occult colors. The nightclub can be described as physically fabulous: that is its highpoint, but the spectacle for the most part never gets airborne and is simply dull, like in every Latin cabaret, I suppose, with naked half women dancing the rumba and mulattoes shouting their stupid songs and pretentiously dressed singers struggling with the style of old Bing,[11] in Spanish, of course. The national drink of Cuba it is called a *Daiquiri*, a mishmash which can best be described as a rum ice-cream-soda-cum-cocktail-on-the-rocks, good for the general Cuban climate which is not far from a hot oven. In the streets outside, I mean, because this cabaret had inside the "typical Cuban air-conditioned," so they told us, which is the same as saying that they take the temperature of the North Pole and box it up in a room. There is a twin cabaret without a roof beside in the *aire libre* which one wasn't using this particular night because they were waiting for rain at about 11 o'clock. These Cubans are good meteorologists. We had just begun eating one of those meals that Cubans call international, catholically greasy and full of things cooked in deep fry and the meat is too salty and the desserts are too sweet, when the rain started falling down so strongly we could hear it above the sound of the music. I say this to suggest how violent a Cuban storm can be

11 Bing Crosby.

because there are few things on this earth that make more noise than a typical Cuban band. For Mrs. Campbell this was the climax, the high pinnacle, the acmé of the evening, what with the sophisticated savagery of the environments, the jungle, the rain, the music, the food and the sylvan pandemonium she was quite simply enchanted. We might have been visiting Las Encantadas. Everything would have come out passable or even pleasant upon switching to bourbon and soda[12] when it almost began to feel like home, if only then this emcee[13] who was a real maricón[14] had not started introducing the artistes to the public and the public to the artistes and everyone to everyone else and finally, to round it off, this hick or idiot of an emcee sent someone off to ask us our names proper and introduced us in that incredible English of his. Not only did he take me for one of the soup people, which is a frequent and supportable mistake, but he also said (over the loudspeaker, what's more!) that I was an international playboy. What barbarity! Maybe he meant the *Playboy of the Western World.*[15] But it didn't look at me that way. And what do you imagine Mrs. Campbell had been doing all this time? She was laughing, in stitches, laughing till the tears rolled down her face. Having a delirium!

It was well after midnight when we left the cabaret, and it had stopped raining and the air was cool and fresh, a new day scrubbed clean. We were both intoxicated, but I didn't forget my stick. I grasped it in one hand while with the other I did the same for Mrs. Campbell. Our chauffeur-guide-physical counselor, this Virgil of the Inferno of the night, insisted on taking us to see another class of show. Mr. and Mrs. Campbells were *bien borrachos*. D,r,u,n,k. Mrs. Campbell found it very exciting, which didn't surprise me. I have to admit that for my part it was a disagreeable and boring function, and I believe I slept over a piece of it. The *function*, as they call it, is a local by-product of the tourist industry by which the cab drivers double up as men or salesmen at the same time. They take you there without asking you and before you really realize what's happening, there

12 Cocktail. *Bourbon* is a rye whiskey made in Kentucky.
13 Phonetic abbreviation for M.C., master of ceremonies.
14 Spanish. Homosexual, fairy.
15 Reference to a play by the Irish dramatist, J. M. Synge.

you are *inside!* By *inside* I mean that you are in a house that looks like any other on this street, but when the door closes behind us visitors they take you through a corridoors[16] to an inner sanctum or penetralia, like a living room but with seats all around the circumference like one of those off-Broadway theaters that were so after a fashion in the mid-fifties, a cross between an arena and a theater, only this time the arena isn't a stage but an enormous round centrally-placed bed. A Ganymede[17] offers you some beverages (which you pay for, of course) and they are much more expensive than the drinks at the Tropicana) up to the high balls ~~(?)~~ and later but not much later when all the guests have arrived and every body is accommodated, they put out the light[18] and then put on the lights (one red and the other blue) above the bed, so you can see the scene with discretion and at the same time forget the presence of your neighbor which you might find somehow embarrassing. Then the two women come in, severely naked. They go to bed together and compromise themselves in some really unhealthy gymnastics, which are indecent and completely unhygienic. At the climax, the lights flash on and off and the couple becomes a single woman, screaming, because such cries are the most common form of expression in Cuba. Then a third actor is brought in, a ~~Negro~~ Black, naked, pitch-black now because of the lights an Othello in search of profit, a professional Lothario, Supermán they called him, with an exaggeratedly large penis which he wields shamefully to add to that terribly intimate love play that the double (or quadruple because there is a broad focal mirror on the platform) Desdemona is playing, and they seem to get a great deal of pleasure out of the final act. There were a number of ~~Officers of the marines~~ naval officers in the public and it all seemed very anti-American, but they were also enjoying the show and it's not part of my business whether the Armada go there in or out of uniform. After the show they turned up all the lights and there goes a nerve! the two little

16 Joycean portmanteau word composed of corridors and doors.

17 Ganymede, acc. the Concise Oxford dictionary, cupbearer, youth.

18 Shakespearean wordplay. See *Othello,* Act IV, Scene 2. There are other references throughout the text to Hemingway, William Blake, Melville, John Millington Synge, *et al.*

girls (that is because they were very young) and the ~~negro~~ black bowed to the audience. This Samson Sex and his young associates made some jokes at the expense of my dinner jacket and black tie and the walking stick, in Spanish of course, and with appropriate gestures, standing right in front of us completely in the skin, and the Marines were dying of laughter while Mrs. Campbell tried hard, but without success, not to laugh. Finally the ~~Negro~~ Black went up to one of the officers and said to him in a very effete and fractured English that he hated women most and this time the marines cracked up and Mrs. Campbell did the same. Everyone applauded a round of applause including me.

We slept late on Saturday morning and went out nigh on eleven o'clock to go to Varadero, a beach exactly at a hundred and forty-one kilometres to the East of Havana and we stayed there the rest of the day. The sun was as relentless as usual, but the sight of the calm, open multicolored ocean and the dazzlingly white dunes and the pseudo-pine trees and the sunshades made of palm fronds and the wooden villas along the shore with their late Victorian mannerisms were something that Natalie Kalmus could have imitated. I took out many photos in color of course, but also some in B & W,[19] and I was very glad I had gone there. There were no people or music or porters, or cab drivers or emcees or ~~who~~ prostitutes to make me look ridiculous or despicable and/or just plain silly. Paradise Gained? Not quite. At the end of the day I had blisters all over my shoulders and arms and a terrible heartburn to match, the product of eating an excessive amount of shellfishes at lunch. I tried vainly to prevent them with Bromo-S[20] and cold cream—tossing the stomach powder down with water and rubbing the ointment all over me, not vice versa. To no avail. Dusk also brought with it a horde of Transylvanic[21] mosquitoes. We beat up a hasty retreat to Havana.

I was delighted to find my walking stick waiting for me in my room, neglected and almost forgotten because the sun and the

19 Black and white.

20 Bromo Seltzer. A digestive powder.

21 Transylvanic, from Transylvania, the avowed home of Count Dracula. Metonymy for vampires.

sand and the redoubled heat had alleviated the pain in my leg. All our sunburn, and other discomforts were forgotten and Mrs. Campbell and I went downstairs and stayed in the bar until very late, listening to more of this extremist music which gives her so much pleasure and which was a little softer now, muffled by the night and the curtains of the room, and I felt very good with my walking stick by my side.

The following morning and a beautiful sunday morning it was too we sent Ramón away until it was lunch, when he would return to the hotel to pick us up and take us away for ever. The ferry was programmed for navegating at three in the afternoon. Then we decided to visit *Havana Vieja*[22] and grab a last look at the neighborhood and buy some more *souvenirs*. You will see that once more hers it was rather than our decision. We bought them ("Now there", said Sra. Campbell, "that's just the place for you") in a tourist shop opposite an old Spanish fort which had fallen into disrepair. *Abierto Cada Día* it said, *Including Sundays. English spoken.* Laden with cadeaus[23] we decided to sit down impromptu and have agreeably cool drinks in an old *café*, which Sra. Campbell had spotted on the other side of the *plaza*, two blocks distant. *El Viejo* Café it was called redundantly, but it fitted in perfectly with the calm, picturesque, suffocating atmosphere of a civilized sunday down there in the old part of the Spanish city.

We sat there for about an hour or so drinking, and then we asked for the check and paid and left. We had gone about three blocks when I remembered that I had left my stick in the café and I went back. Nobody seemed to have seen or noticed it and nobody seemed particularly surprised. ~~So strange an occurrence hardly raises an eyebrow in these countries.~~ I went out again feeling mortified and far more depressed than I should have been by such trivial a loss.

"The world is full of walking sticks, darling", Mrs. Campbell said and I remember seeing myself looking at her fixedly, not coldly or out of the corner of my anger but in a state of trance,

22 *Sic.* ch. *Sic.*
23 French. *Sic.*

incapable of turning away from the glorious splendor of this Doctor Pangloss of an emancipated woman.

I went off at a quick walk looking for a taxi stop and rounded the corner again and stopped and looked in front of me and behind and then I saw a look of astonishment on Mrs. Campbell's face, an astonishment which was a mirror of my own. There, in a narrow alley was an old colored man walking with my walking stick. On closer inspection I saw that he was not so much old as ageless, obviously a mongoloid moron. There was no question of reaching an understatement with him either in English or in Mrs. Campbell's precarious Spanish. The man couldn't comprehend any idiom and this, dear reader, is Nemesis for the foreign traveler. Now he was shipwreckedly gripping onto the stick with both hands.

I feared that a *slapstick*[24] situation would develop if I resolved myself finally to grab hold of the stick, as Mrs. Campbell advised me to do, as I was afraid of the beggar (he was one of those professional beggars whom you can find anywhere abroad, even in Paris) who was a very strong man. I tried to make him comprehend by using signs that the stick was mine, but I failed miserably and he answered me with some strange growling sounds which were as foreign to me as human speech was to him. I was reminded of those native singers and their lyrical throats. He also disproved the current scientific notion that claims that every mongol is cheerful, affectionate and a lover of music. Somewhere or other a radio was playing at full blast some even fuller Cuban songs. Above all the (noise), Mrs. Campbell, now completely Cubanized, was shouting the suggestion that I should buy the stick from him, which of course I refused to do. "Darling", I howled in exasperation, holding up ground as I tried to block the dark passage of the beggar with my enormous skeleton, "it is a matter of principle, that stick he belongs to me", and I didn't feel how quietly I was conveying my meaning since a shouted principle immediately ceases to be one. In any case, I wasn't going to let it go with him just because he

24 Situation of silent comedy. Blow and Knock. Literally, slap and stick.

was a moron and I was not going to surely buy it, thus robbing myself. "I'm not a man for blackmailing", I told Mrs. Campbell now in a lower tone, stepping below the sidewalk as the beggar was threatening to cross the street. "I know, little dear", she said.

~~But the nightmares of Savannah are the exact facts in Havana~~. As it is a custom, we soon had a small crowd of local inhabitants surrounding us and I got very nervous as I didn't want to be the victim of any outbreak of lynching. To all appearances I was a foreign tourist grabbing advantage of a defenseless native and I saw more than one face of dark skin in the circle of Cubans. In the center this Lutheran[25] stood firm, a solitary Maximalist combating the irrational with alien reasons.

The people however behaved very well considering (the circumstances). Mrs. Campbell explained the situation in her best possible manner and there was even one of the spectators who spoke a fractioned English and who offered in his primitive manner to act as mediator. This self-made Hammarskjold tried without any evident success to communicate with the mongol, moron or Martian. All he did was to retreat a couple of steps, grasping, holding onto, embracing the walking stick and muttering some story in an unknown idiom full of sounds and fury—signifying, of course, nothing. Or rather meaning, always inferring that the walking stick was his private property. The crowd, like all mobs, was on our side some of the time, and other times on the side of the beggar. My wife was still insisting on my rights. "It is a material of principle", she said, in her broken Spanish. "señor Campbell here is the legitimate owner of the stick of walking. He bought it yesterday and abandoned it this morning in an old café. This gentleman", she was referring to the moron, pointing at him with her left index, "took it from where my husband", pointing at me with her right index, "left it in spite of not belonging to him", shaking her currently blonde head to and fro, "no, no, amigos". A dubious suggestion of theft, by means of amphibology, the equivocal suggestion, the ambiguous phrase (who did what to who?), but the oratory of this

25 Reference to the well-known Protestant theologian of the 16th century.

female Portia won the support of the sidewalk court and the jury was now decidedly on our side.

Soon we were a public nuisance and a policeman arrived. We were doubly fortunate in that he was a policeman who spoke English. I explained everything to him. He tried in vain to disperse the rabble but the people were as interested as we were interested in finding a solution to the problem. He spoke to the mongol, but there was no way of communicating with this Mr. Nobody, as I've already said. Of course the policeman lost his temper and took out his gun to compel the beggar. The multitude grew, suddenly silent and I feared the worst. But the moron seemed, finally, to comprehend and gave me the walking stick back with a gesture that I didn't like one bit. The policeman put his gun back in its holster and made the suggestion of me giving the beggar some money. "Not as a recompense but ~~in~~ as a gift to the poor man", to quote his own words. I opposed. This would be truly accepting a social blackmail, because the stick was certainly mine. I said as much to the officer. Mrs. Campbell tried to intercede, but I saw no reason to give in. The stick was mine and the beggar took it without it belonging to him. To give him money for its return was to lend my endorsement to a robbery. I refused, absolutely to placate him.

Someone in the crowd, so Mrs. Campbell explained, had suggested a voluntary contribution all around. Mrs. Campbell, who is so foolworthy and gold-hearted, wanted to help him out of her pocket. However it was, I had to put an end to a situation so ridiculous and I relented, which I shouldn't have done. I offered the moron a few pieces of change (I can't remember exactly how much, but I'm sure it was more than I had originally paid for the stick) and I wanted to give it him, without any hard, feelings, but the beggar didn't want even to touch it. Now it was his moment to play the character of Human Being Offended. Mrs. Campbell interceded once again. The man appeared to accept it but then he had second . . . thoughts and rejected the money making more of his ancient guttural noises. It was only when the policeman put it in his hand that he clenched it with a rapid gesture. I didn't like the look on his face one bit, because he stood there looking (fixedly) at the stick when I took it away with me like a dog abandoning a bone he has buried/unburied. The disagreeable incident was now over and we took a cab on the spot, product of the policeman, courteous as it was his duty to be. One of the crowd cheered when we went off and someone waved goodbye, benevolently. Mrs. Campbell (for the first and only time in the whole trip) didn't say a word and she seemed to be busying herself making a mental reckoning of her many gifts—those man-made ones, not the one Nature had given her. I felt well about the company of my recovered walking stick for it was now a souvenir with a tale interesting to tell, much more valuable than all the things that Mrs. Campbell had bought by the dozen.

We returned to the hotel. I told the clerk in the lobby that we were leaving early in the afternoon, and asked him to have the check ready for us when we came down, I told him also that we were going to have lunch in the hotel and that we would pay for it at the cash-desk in the restaurant. Then we went upstairs.

As always, I opened the door to let Mrs. Campbell go in first and she switched on the lights, since the blinds were down. She went into the sitting room and proceeded through to the bedroom and I went to raise the blinds, praising the peace and quiet of the Tropical sunday as I went. When she switched on the bedroom light, she let out a high penetrating scream. I thought she might have received an electric shock, knowing how dangerous the currents are abroad. I was also afraid there might be a poisonous snake. Or perhaps another robber caught in fragranti.[26] I ran into the bedroom. Sra. Campbell seemed stiff, rigid, unable to speak, almost on the point of hysteria. I couldn't understand what could have happened seeing her standing there in the middle of the room in a state of catalepsy. She pulled herself together and with some strange guttural sounds, pointed with her little finger to the bed. The bed was empty. There was no *mapanare*, or robber, or facsimile of Superman on it. Then I looked at the night-table. There, resting upon the glass top, black on the surface painted green, conspicuous, relevant, incriminating, ultimately disgusting, was the other *walking* stick.

26 *Sic.*

Señor[1] Campbell, a professional writer told the story wrong, "as always."

Havana looked dazzlingly beautiful from the boat. The sea was calmed, and its surface was a clear blue, almost cobalt at times and criss-crossed with a broad deep blue belt which someone explained was the Golf Stream. There were a few diminutive waves, like seagulls made of foam skimming peacefully across an inverted sky. The city appeared suddenly, completely white and vertiginous. I saw a few dirty clouds above it but the sun was shining outside of them and Havana wasn't a city but the mirage of a city, a specter. Then it opened up on both sides and began to define itself in fixed colors that dissolved instantaneously in the whiteness of the sun. It was a panorama, a real Cinemascope, the Cinerama of life! I say this to please Mr. Campbell who is excessively fond of the movies. We continued to navegate between buildings of mirrors, like flashes of light, like gaseliers,[2] scintillating inside the eye, past a park where the grass was either burned or a brilliant green, towards another town—old, dark, and even more beautiful. Irrevocably a dock came up to us.

It is perfectly true that Cuban music is primitive but it has an enchanting gaiety, an unexpected violence which is always kept in reserve and something poetic about it which is not possible to define and which soars high on the *maracas* and the guitar and the falsetto[3] voices of the males or—from time to time—and with a harsh oscillation, similar to the *blue*[4] singers, a repetition of the harmony as valid for Cuba and Brazil as it is in the South because it is a tradition that comes from Africa, while the *bongó* and *conga* drums tether it to the ground and the *claves*—the mysterious "banging bits of wood together" of Mr. Campbell's

1 In spanish in the original.

2 Gaselier, lamp suspended from the ceiling with many points of light. From *gas* and *chandelier*.

3 Italian. Small falsy, speaking of the human voice.

4 Song of the Southern States in the U.S.A. (Dixie).

narrative, is neither a superstitious liturgy nor a secret code but two little batons not to conduct but for to make music, delicate percussion instruments beaten one against the other *col legno*[5] —c.f. the notes on the sleeve of John Caged's LP[6] Percutante percusión AG0690—these "musical sticks" are always stable, like the horizon.

Why all this dramatization of his leg which was in a bad state but hardly at all useless? Perhaps he wants to sound like a disabled veteran of war. In actual fact, Sr. Campbell is a victim of rheumatism.

Strictly speaking the walking stick was just a stick for walking ordinary. It was made of a dark and probably hard wood but not unless I'm much mistaken of ebony. There was no rich carving on it nor an androgynous head on the hilt. It was a walking stick like thousands of others you find sticking[7] around the earth, a little crude, but with a certain picturesque appeal: nothing out of the ordinary. I imagine that many Cubans have had an identical walking stick. I never said that the walking stick was exciting: this is a vulgar Freudian innuendo. Moreover I wouldn't buy obscenity from a walking stick, never.

The stick costs a few centavos. The Cuban peso is equivalent to the American dollar. I should mention in passing that *abanico* is the Spanish word for a fan, not *habanico*. Probably a confusion because of his sympathy for the word *La Habana*. You never say *haveneros* for the same reason as you don't write Havena. The adjective *mucho* is always shortened to *muy* when it is used as an adverb. And he should have said *las mujeres*, not *los*, *las* being the feminine form of the definitive article. But you wouldn't expect finesse[8] from Mr. Campbell when it is a question of *mujeres*. Women, that is.[9] By the way of the beach you say Varadero not Varydero and much less to pronounce it, as he did, Verydearo—in the sense of expensive. There were many things in the city I thought were enchanting but I have

5 Italian. Lit. with wood.

6 Long-play, gramophone record of extended duration.

7 Pun intended in the original.

8 French. Untranslatable. The nearest English equivalent is good manners.

9 Idiomatic joke based on the similarity in pronunciation between *women* and its Spanish equivalent, *mujeres*.

never been embarrassed by sentiment and I can say exactly what they were. I liked—no, I *loved* the character, or rather the temperament of the people of Havana and of everywhere else. I was very much in love with Cuban Music, spelt like this, with capitals. It was love at first sight between the Tropicana and myself. In spite of the fact that it is a tourist attraction which everyone has heard of, it is genuinely beautiful and exuberant and vegetal, a perfect image of the island. The food is edible which is the only quality that food needs and the drinks are the same as drinks everywhere. But the music and the beauty of the chorus girls and the sylvan unbridled imagination of the choreographer I think of these things as unforgettables.

The master of ceremonies was a typical Latin very elegant tall and dark with green eyes and a black moustache and a dazzling white smile. A true professional, with a deep baritone voice and an attractive American accent—there was nothing of a *maricón* about him, contrary to what Mr. Campbell wrote, running the risk of libel suits as the word means queer or queen in English.

With the best will in the world Mr. Campbell entangles himself in his own verbal gymnastics—the only kind he is capable of—in trying to make me into a prototype: the only kind: the common female of the species. In other words a mental invalid with the IQ[10] of a simpleton, a cretinous Girl Friday,[11] a moronic Straight-Woman,[12] a female Doctor not Pangloss but Wattson, with the extra quality of being like a merciless loanshark at the deathbed of a client. I'm more Shylock than Portia. He might just as well have called me Mrs. Camp *toute courte*.[13] I never said things like Little dear this is the Tropic or They are *souvenirs* darling or any other petty snaps. He has been reading too many "Blondie" comic books or he has seen all the Lucille Ball shows on television. I wouldn't mind in the least being Lucille if only he had the glances of Desy Arnass[14]—and the same age as well.

10 Intelligence quotient.

11 Literary ref. Mrs. Campbell is addicted to them. See Daniel Defoe's novel *Robinson Crusoe* where there is a character named Friday.

12 Feminization of Straight-man.

13 French. In short.

14 *Sic*.

In the (under) development of the narrative you can read on many occasions the word "native" used in a derrogatory sense. Please don't blame *El Viejo* Mr. Campbell and his tautologies. It is inevitable, I suppose. When Mr.—he, that is, this Mister Comma Mister Period Mister Hyphen who is so enamored of punctuation marks that he gets really distressed every deliberate time I leave out the period after his title, Mr "there *you* are"—Mr. Rudyard Kipling Campbell heard that the management of the hotel was "ours" as he called it meaning they were Americans, he smiled the broad smile of a conoisseur[15] in a museum. For him the hoi polloi[16] of the Tropics are always a crowd of loafers, inescapably so, people who take siestas all the time. Also they are arduous to tell apart. The cab-driver said perfectly clearly that his name was Ramon Garsia.[17]

I didn't find funny his goings and comings all over the place walking stick in hand all the time. In the Tropicana, when we were leaving the dining room not i,n,t,o,x,i,c,a,t,e,d but helpless drunks yes, with his walking stick falling to the ground one and another time in the course of crossing the short well-lit crowded space of the entrance-hall and his precarious balance when he picked it up it was he who was—really and truly this time—a "public nuisance."

He simple adores being mistaken for one of the Campbell millionaires. He always does. He even insists that they are narrow relations of his. I didn't laugh the title of Playboy International, but I had nothing but contempt for his phony disgust when he heard them calling him the millionaire in soups. He's such a lousy actor.

His exaggerated and sometimes completely fictional custom of drinking which he makes such a fanfare of and many other literary characteristics, these are all copied from Hemingway, Fitzgerald *et al.*[18]

There was no sexual abduction. What is true is that Ramón—I had to give up in the end and call him that—offered to take us to see the live demonstrations, but only after Mister Campbell's

15 French. One who knows.
16 Greek (classical). Lit., the people.
17 *Sic.*
18 Latin. Lit., and the others.

multiple doubles entendres.[19] He has never mentioned the fact that he bought books of the Obelisk and Olympia Presses,[20] by ~~a cor~~ the dozen in a bookstore in calle Belga,[21] and that he showed me the notes which said that they were not for sale in the UK[22] or in the USA, and he even insisted on buying a costous and voluminous French novel, *Prelude Charnel,*[23] illustrated throughout in color and which I would be able to translate for him at some future date in the bedroom. He didn't mention the title of the film we saw, *Baby Doll.*[24] He didn't propose the *tableaux vivants*[25] and the exhibitions of sexual prowess, but he certainly did make one or two dubious remarks about the Marines and the red light district around Barrio de Colón. No comment on his version of Lust's Labors Lost or on the tropical *Sexe, Son et Lumieres.*[26] I will say that it weren't this poor little depraved one of me who enjoyed alone the show of Lothario/Othello/Superman to borrow Mr. Campbell's use of names and punctuation. And I will add, to finalize, that he is the one man on this earth since the days of No Eyelids Sing[27] who is capable of sleeping with both his eyes wide open.

He didn't "find" the stick on the street, wandering along with a stranger like Gogol's nose,[28] a literary Person-Thing, a genuine walking walking-stick.[29] The walking stick never left the cafe, which was without any doubt at all called Lucero Bar. We had both been sitting in a crowded room. When Mr. Campbell got up to leave quite simply and naturally he took a stick from the next table: a dark stick knotted exactly like his own. We were standing in the door when we heard someone running

19 French. Double meaning.
20 English publishers of pornographic books in France in English.
21 She must be referring to the Casa Belga, a bookstore in old Havana.
22 United Kingdom.
23 French. Untranslatable, but fleshy prelude gives a rough idea.
24 Film by Elia Kazan. It was called "Muñeca de Carne" (fleshy doll) in Cuba.
25 *Sic*. French. Living pictures.
26 French. Sex, Sound and Lights. Ref. to the technique of using lights and stereophonic sound to exploit points of interest for tourists.
27 Famous pirate of the China Seas?
28 Ref. to Nicolai Gogol's famous short story, "The Nose".
29 *Sic*.

after us and uttering the strange then and familiar now noises. We looked behind and saw the real owner of the stick only of course we didn't know that at that time. Mr. Campbell made a gesture as though he was going to return it, but it was I who opposed. I told him that he bought the stick with his own good money and just because the beggar was an idiot we weren't going to let him go outside with it, as though his mental malformation was an excuse for the robbery. It is quite true that we soon had a mob around us, for the most part customers of the "café", and that a number of debates broke out. But there were always arguments on our side: the beggar, if you remember, was unable to speak. The policeman—who came from the tourist division—turned up and intervened through pure chance. Inevitably he was always for us, decidedly thus, and he took the beggar toward jail without ulterior discussion. Nobody suggested a collection and Mr. Campbell didn't pay any compensation because there wasn't any. However if it had been, I wouldn't have let him. The way he tells the story he makes it sound as though the walking stick was a magic wand which suddenly converting me from witch to saint.[30] Nothing like this happened. In actual fact it was I who was the most insistent that he shouldn't let the walking stick go away just like that. I detest idiots, Mr. Campbell is the only one for whom I have the slightest patience, which wears itself out as he wanes crasser through the years. I never suggested he take the stick as an end and the whole scene is told as though Sr. Campbell was a script writer for the Italian screen of the late forties.

My Spanish is not, I swear to God, a perfectly spoken idiom but I can easily make myself being easily understood. I was in Paradise High under Professor Rigol and Mr. Campbell is only being jealous.[31] I also gave it a good scrubbing before coming to Cuba. I will never exhibit outside a language I do not well know. Incidentally, *on dit* sword of Damocles, *pas* Damoclian sword.

30 Word play or pun, apparently.
31 Salacious pun.

There wasn't any melodrama. Mr. Campbell's story, as told, is not only incompetent but also infested with halfs of the truth and lies. There never was any General Campbell's Last stance nor any lynching-mobs nor applause nor any final face of the pitiful beggar. We couldn't have seen him anyway from the taxi. I never screamed when I saw the other—I find these italics disgusting, nothing but drama and sugar-bathing, like a metaphor for the whole story: "*other* walking stick": why not just "other walking stick"?—the other walking stick, nor did I have an attack of catatonia. There were no hysterics; I simply limited myself to showing him the walking stick that was presently ours. I thought that a terrible mistake had been made of course, but then I thought that the mistake and the injustice were reparable still. We went straight again to the café and by questioning the people in there we found out where the police station was: it was Mr. Campbell's Spanish fort that had fallen into disrepair. The beggar was not longer there. The policeman had released him at the gates while his colleagues laughed and the robber who was himself the only one who had been robbed wept inexhaustible tears. Nobody, "of course", knew where to find him.

We missed the boat and had to return by plane—with our luggage and books and souvenirs plus two walking sticks.

Seventh session

I told you a lie on Friday, doctor. A really big lie. That boy I was telling you about, we never got married. I married another boy who I didn't even know and he never married anyone, because he was a homosexual and I knew it from the day I met him because he told me. What happened was that he invited me to go out with him because his parents suspected that his best friend was something more than just his best friend and they had threatened that they would send him to a military academy if he didn't offer to marry me. But I was never his fiancée. And they didn't have to send him to an academy after all.

BRAINTEASER

Who was Bustrófedon? Who was/is/will be Bustrófedon? Boustrophedon? Thinking about him is like thinking of the goose that laid golden eggs, of a riddle with no answer, a spiral without end. *He was Bustrófedon for all and all for Bustrófedon was he.*

I don't know where the fuck he got that 7-plus-4-letter name from. All I know is that he often called me Bustrofoton or Bustrophotomaton or Busneforoniepce, depending deepening my current hangup, but I always answered his mastery voice, and Silvestre was Bustrophoenix or Bustrophoelix or Bustrofitz-herald, and Florentino Cazalis was Bustrofloren long before he changed his name and began writing in the papers bustroper-ously as Floren Cassalis, and his girl was always called Bustro-fedora and his mother was Bustrofelisa and his father Bustro-father, and I just don't know if his girl friend's real name was Fedora or if his mother was really called Felisa or whatever. But I guess he must have picked that word, *the* word at random (house) out of a dictionary like the way he took the name of a medicine (with Silvestre's help?) to bustroform the continent of Mutaflora with its metafauna of bustroffaloes composed of hunting bustrophies sent back alive.

I remember one day we'd gone out to eat together, he and Bustrofedonte (which was Rine's name that week, because his name wasn't just Man's Best Friend but also: Rinecerous, Rinaidecamp, Rinaissance, leading to general Rinformation and Rineffulgence followed by a Rinegation and back to Rinessentials and Rinephemera, Rinetcetera, Rineffervescent, Bonofarniente, Bonosirviente, Busnofedante, Bustopedant: rineing ringing the changes on his name to show the ring & range and changes in their friendship: casting words in a spellometer) and me, and when the two of them came to find me in the newspaper office he said, Let's go eat in a Bustrofeteria, because he loathed expensive restaurants and chandeliers and paper flowers, and when we found a B-eanery and before we'd sat down he'd called the waiter. Bustroboy, he said. You know what they're like, the waiters in Havana early in the evening or late at night: all bums, so they don't like to be called by their name: neither waiter nor boy or Charlie or even come here you flunky, that kind of thing, and so this fellow came up with a face as long as a boa's tail and almost as cold and scaly and he clearly wasn't a boy any longer if he ever had been. C-come on, old b-boy, w-we w-want s-some b-bustrofood, said putting on a sturm und s-stammer this Bustrofunfare, and the waiter (if that's the right word) looked daggers at him, more cobra than boaish or boyish or boorish, and I shoved a paper napkin (it was a modernstyleatery) in my mouth to drown my laughter, but my laughs could crawl and do breast and back and breathstroke so the paper towels were beginning to taste like papertigertale, and as fuck or late would have it, B., whose name was Bustrophate that moment, said to me, We should of off invited Bustróphoelix, and my laughter was Bustrofoaming around the floodgates of the next of napkin and then he asked me, What you think, Bustrophotoflood? and I answer Fure fof fourse and my napkin flies off fike a pfeiffer fjet followed by a superzanic bang composed of a chain eruction of vocal or oral or auroral farts and in the trajectory it follows the servjette sets itself on a collision main course with the waiter's face, taking the whole length of his long lonely face like a landing strip, finally striking his jaundiced eyeball like a yellow bullseye and the fellouch refuses to serve us and gets off our cloud to plunge icariously into the horizontal chasm of thiseatery and starts bellyaching in the backroom to the Poseidowner and we're still there in the hearafter drowning of laughter on the shores of the tablecloth, almost nausicated, with this unbelievable public proclaimer Bustrophone herald tribunely crying out, You were a Bustro-phenoNemo, a Bustrofonbraum, crying out loud, Bustyphoon, Bustornado, Bustrombone, outcrying himself, Bustrombam-arina, crying to left and right, sydneyster-and-dexterly, ambi-dexterritorially. Of curse the wan and ownly oner had to turn up right then & there: a fat bald little fellow even shorter than the waiter, so short that be hecame shorter as he approached us and when he finally arrived at the table he seemed to be walking on his hands not his feet. A moveable feat. A bust. Or was it a buster?

—WASSA MATTA?

—We wonly want to weat, Bustro said, turning a doldrum profile toward him.

—You won't get anything to eat if you fool around like that.

—Like what? Bustrofastidious asked and as he was a tall skinny fellow with a real ugly mug and thismugly of his was cratered with an acme of an acne or

huge pox Americana or
by time and tide and its ruins or
meteorites or
vultures or

by all these things together:

MACNEPOXVLTURETEORUINITES

he stood, got to his feet, doubled tripled, B' telescoped himself for-ward looking more like an unjolly green giant every miniminute till he almust touched the ceiling, roof or rafters, so big was he.

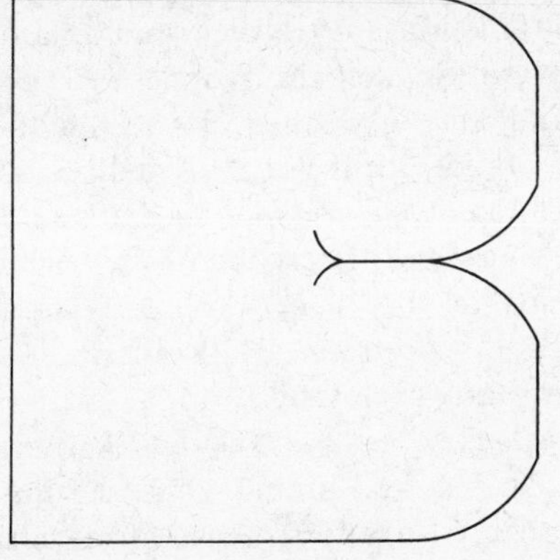

AND THE OWNER GOT SMALLER AND SMALLER AND
SMALLER AND YET SMALLER IF IT WAS STILL POSSIBLE AND MAN
was but so incredibly shrunk he was only the size of my
thumb or my little finger which is a very little finger:
he's in fact a genie of the bottle in reverse and now he
went on getting littler and littler, as tiny as anyone
can be, even tinier and tinier: the tiniest tim on
earth, and tinier even: tm: till amazing us with
his shrinking bouts & feats: and he was no
longer visible, not quite yet invisible: so
final-ly he stood up to vanish down a hole
by the door: a mouse-whole by-by by
the way by the door: a house of a
doormouse so very Butso housey
this mousey-hall did not begin right
& there it began somewhere
els somewhere elsie: it
began with—oh no! oh
yes!—but no! but yes,
sire, it began it
yessiree! but hole it,
mate! hold it a
moment for this
hole begins
here but
and / or,
ah so
an
o

and it reminded me of Alice in Wonderland and I said just that to Bustroformidable crytone and he began to entertain certain sentences and us and he delit and regaled us: the brief and regal night of Frank Masonry: Alice in Funland, Alice in Thy-land, Alice in Mytime, Alice in Wonder, Alice in Wanderlush, Alice the one and last, My Alice, Malice, Malice Forathought, Alice and Eve, Malice and Varix, Evealice, Avarice, Avaricia and Malicia and Malaysia and Melanesia and Macromicia and Micronisia and Microlicia, Microalice in the hole, in the whole, in the hold, Alace in the hole, Alichole, Alls-hole, Alasthouse, Alasose, Alicetose, Alicetosis, Halicetosis, Helixhose, Helax-hoses, Elaxtosis and shrinking and growing up again and shriveling back to seize he—B—B1—B1? Why not B2? B or not 2B—him began sitting and singing and seizing and sizing me up and down with my Fure fof fourse, furoff coarse, my Four de

Force and with his Alliteration his Alcemptation his Alicevocation, merrily marrying, Marryling my self and Cuba and Martí and the Wanton nightmare I Want-a-name-'ere La Guantanamera, that Martían song with its tropsical rhythm that goes wroughly like thus, dedicated to the one I hate:

(*instant pretension or interpoleation or inpernetration by M.S.*)

Yo soy un hombre sincero
I'm a man without a zero
De donde crece la palma
From the land of the pawn-trees
Y antes de morirme quiero
And 'fore lay-dying I xerox
Hechar mil voces del alma.
One thousand copies of me.

Con los sobres de la piedra
With the sour sickle of this hearse
Quiero yo mi muerte hinchar
I want to share man Mao
El apoyo de la Sierra
The reivers of the Sierra
Más compras hace que el mal
I like butter, then some tea.

Mi anverso es un verde claro
My grin is a dear sun-tan
En un jardín encendido
Gotten in a flaming garden
Mi reverso un muerto herido
My torso is a wounded fountain
Que luce en el norte un faro.
That looks for shells in a maiden.

BUT NO, it's no good: you'd have to hear it, you'd have to hear him in Bustroperson as you'd also have to hear his *Poe(t)'s Ravings:*

Twice beneath a mudtime weirdly ponderous I spoke in faerie
Over (and o'er) a voluminium of unwritten law (oh lore!)—

While I nodled, noodled, nundled, trundlingly I come
unsundered,
As if someone howsomever, rapping, crapping at my do'er.
" 'Tis a widershins," I mongreled, "crapping at my own
undo'er—
Who unstuck my nether moor?"

Undustunctly I rumumbled it were dìssembling Decembled;
And each humbled, blundering embryo fell upon its dying floor.
Ungrately I wished tomorrow; or tomorrow and to borrow
In mine bones was Caesar's horror—horror for a long lost
bore—
For the bare and fair and barren former maiden whom I bore—
Quoth the waiter, "Medium raw."

And the silken, sullen slinking of each skulking purple passage
Thrilled and spilled and filled and chilled me with a drafty
corridor;
So that howsoever bleating my heart stopped but natheless
cheating
Went on beating, eating sleeting (a self-wind heart it was I
swore)
The whore it was I mildly swore.

Incessantly my soul glue longer; so I longered more languorous,
"So said I," I said, "you Modman, come inside me and explore;
But in sooth, in truth, 'tis proof, you spied me at my knightly
crapping,
I'm a ghostwriter, thou knowst well, inscribbling on inphantile
floor
Whatsomever rhymes Unreason hath in his untimely maw—
Bottomless, I ask for more.

And so on incessanter till breath do us phart. And it was in that same Bloke Decembryo that Rogelito Castresino took the opportunity to go down the street and we started singing all the variations on all the names of the people we know. A secret game—until the chambermate or whatever his name is came and interrupted the ceremony and Bustrofacetious hailed him like a long lost bugger, doing what he called, poor Bfellow, his namaste, but he did it not with the palms of his hands, but with the back, like this:

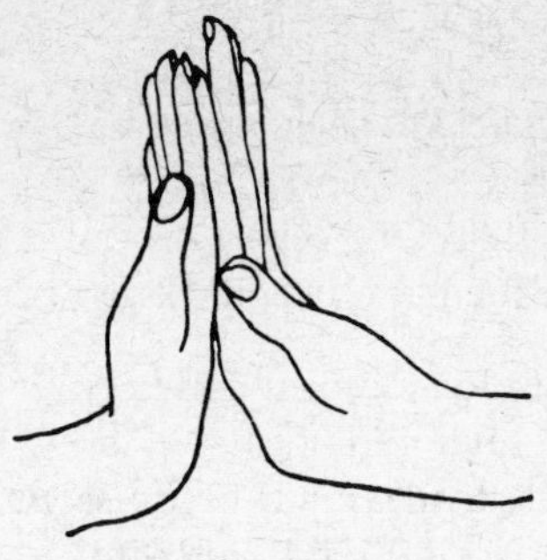

and we ordered dinner. He did.

Bustrobeans said Bustrofacile said he With white rice I tried to say but he said a T T T-bone or Bustrofilet and a cup of BustrofedonT said Bustrofidelis said Bustrofricassee said Bustrofartingissuchsweetsighing and Bustrordered them all at once because it was always he who was talking and he said it all looking at the waiter in the eye (or eyeball to youball), face to farce, looking him in the I's, condescending the stares because though he was still seated he was taller than the other even though he had generously shrunk himself a little, and when we'd finished he ordered dessert for us all too. Tootsyfruitsy. Bustroflan, he said and then he said, Bustrofocee (you focoffee yourselfish, said I) and then trying to serve as gobetween (they also serve who only stand as waiters) said quickly, Three coffees, but when I tried to say, pleasantly, If you please, I said Piss you eve and something Elsie, I'm not sure and I'm not sure either how we managed to make a getaway without someone accusing us of being terrorists what with all the implosion and explosion of laughter, like slaughters off the avenue and when they brought us the coffee, we drank it in pieces and paid and left the restoroom all systems à gogo singing the Quistrisini Variations (copyright Boustrophedon Inc.) on that jittery Festineburg that Bustroffenbach had composed. Here's to Frenchsip!

Last aald acqaaantanca ba fargat
And navar saan agaan
Wa'll drank a cap af kandnass yat
Far tha sanka afaald Lang Sana.

Lest eeld acqeeentence be ferget
End never seem egeen
We'll drenk e cep ef kendness yet
Fer the neskefe eeld Leng Sene.

List iild icqiiintinci bi firgit
Ind nivir siin igiin
Wi'll drink i cip if kindniss yit
Fir thi sikihi iild Ling Sini.

Lost oold ocqooontonco bo forgot
Ond novor soon ogoon
Wo'll dronk o cop of kondnoss yot
For tho so kopho oold Long Sono.

Lust uuld unquuuuntuncu bu furgut
Und nuvur suun uguun
Wu'll drunk u cup uf kundnuss yut
Fur thu sucus uf uuld Lung Sunu.

with me prohividing the reuthmic accompanist, misstaking probing that mon is evolting into mankey by drinking the mild of humonkeydniss: lone leave monkind!, phlaying my chimpanum to Eribó's baboongo, mandrilling a little cynosure of old eyes, making negular roises (at least I think so: I was zoo drunk I insisted I got rhythm) with my fingerprints and a glassdarkly and spooneristmus in my handshake and later outlawside with my handsoff and fingertrips and the mouthfool and for feetall coming in from thime to tyme crying !$£!!!¿¿% +=&&&! Ah ah ah! AH! What a wallz we had that night, that Knight of the Balls, we really did have a goot dime and Bustroform in grate shape invented the most twattwisting and frensyfree and sample tongtwisters like that one this one it *Was he Houdini who wrote whodunits for women humorously wondering under humble exhumed human uteruses and humeruses*? hand hall those Madam I'm Adam's, like that so hold hand beewtifutile hand clocksickall hand heternal *No evil live on,* and these three he cuntcockeded, on the stop, spot. after laying a bed for a chit with Ryne: *Now a gas saga won* number one *Wonder Eve's amoral aroma severed now* number two *Emit a tit a time* number three whitch are sample and seasy and are half-Cubist and half-Quexotic or completely a toxic for an ekuedistant third partying is sock sweet surrey, and they sourprised me because Rhine's reinforced feet (two, said Bustrofaraway, the left and the wrigth, degauche et malraudroit) were three, ad pedem litter: Havana, the name of a city which is just a beautyfoul corruption of Savanna/ Sabannah/ Sabana/ Abanna/ Havannah/ Havana/ Habana/ La Habana/ *Avana* in Italics Cyrillically Gabana, and the Sbanish panner (why? because we were crossing Central Park between the three centers, the Galician center and the Asturian center plus the off center) and mulatto she-woman walked on by and there was another horny foot (B. said that that made a quadruped, a Nu or Gnude or New) which was our eternal theme then, La Estrella of cursed, and Bustrofactored it into more anagrams (a word he broke up into: A ram sang) with the phrase *Dádiva ávida: vida* which when written in a ringaroundarosy, in an *encierro:* is the serpent that eats itself: is the ring that is an ankh: is a magic circle, cyclic shift which continually makes a cipher of the zephyr of life and deciphers its ways anyway and which you can begin reading with any one of the words and it is a wheel of fartune: *David, ávida, vida, avi, vid, ida, dádiva, dad, ad, di, va:* beginning again, turning and turning and turning the till undtil you come to the wheel of aloneliness with its still center out of which it can tale us its tell, and which can also and as well and so well be used with La Estrella because the wordwheel, the life sentence, the three-times-four-letter anagram which also makes twelve words a twelf-word:

was a star and

He recited gray darkened passages from what he called his Dicktionary of Contaguous Words end Andless Idees, which of source I cannot remember in their entitirety, but I can give you many of his past words and the explanations, not definitions which their author indented: Aha, Anna, deed, Eve, gig, Hannah, noon, poop, radar, wow, which upsidedome explains why I'm sodown, and finally regretting in passing away the fact that Adam wasn't called Adá in Spanish (would he be called like that in Catalá? He wondered) because then not only would he be the first man but he'd also be perfect and the only man right enough to name things, and declaring that noon was logically the zenith of the day just as deed when it is written done has a completeness which says what it means and the number 101 should be praised one hundred times because it was like 88 (glory be) a total number, round, identical to itself eternity cannot change it nor space wither nor time stale and however you look at it it is always the same, another one, even though the plus perfect of perfect numbers was, *is*, the 69 (to Rine's great Joy) which is the absolute number always differing and never the shame, not only Pythagorically (which, but exactly, bugged Cué) Platonically as well and (which tickled Silvestre: a mystic bond of broaderhood made them both one, Don One) Alcmeonic, because it closed in on itself and the sum of its farts plus the sum of the sound was equal (Cué walked out at this point) to the last figure and I don't know how many other pseudo numberical complications which always drove C. crazy and when he was leaving B. called at him in the doorway with Cuban Malice, And what does that innuend, gentlemen!

Bustrofrankbuck spent all his time hunting wild words in the dictionaries (his semantic safaris) when he went out of sight, and out of mind (his not ours) and shut himself up with a dictionary to bring 'em words back alive, and any dictionary, it didn't matter which, in his room, driving into the rough sketches of letters, became his dictumnary, eating out of it at oddmeals, taking a bath with/in it sleeping with/on it with words as a pillow waiting for sunup/or/down: It by His side sliding in and out of It, not a book- but a dictionary-worm, because dictionaries were all he read and he said, he said to Silvestre that they were better than dreams, better than masturboratory fansies, better than glu movies. Better than Hitchcock o belie me! Because the dictionary created its suspense with one word lost in a wood of words (not like needles in a haystack which are easy to find, but one particular pin in a pincushion) and there was the wrong word and the word innocent and the word guilty and the word-assassin and the word-police and the word-chase and the word-rescue-patrol in the last word-reel and lastly the word end, and because the suspense of the dictionary lay in seeing oneself looking desperately for a word up and down the columns until one found it and when it turned up seeing that it meant something different, this was better than one's surprise at the last real, and the one thing he truly and reely regretted was that the dictionary the dictionaries have hardly any obscenities in them as this Bustrofunkandwagnalls knew them all by heart as he also knew by heart and played by ear the definition of the word dog in the Diccionario Manual Ilustrado de la Real Academia Española (2a.ed., Madrid, 1958, p.1173/a): *M., domestic mammal of the family of canidae, of varying size, shape and color according to the breed, but which always has its tail shorter than its hind legs* (and he paused at this pointer) *one of which the male of the species lifts in order to urinate,* and he went on with his happy trip around the words:

Tit
eye
nun
kayak
level
sexes (everything starts with them three)
radar
civic
sos (the most helpful)
gag (the funniest)
boob

and for years he missed Miss Gardner lovesickly because he said, Ava was the ideal woman, and he went crazy over the simihilarity between allegory and allergy and causality and casualty and chance and change, and how easily farce becomes force, and he also made a list of words that read differently in the mirror:

Live/evil
part/trap
flow/wolf
diaper/repaid
reward/drawer
drab/bard
Dog/God!

and from this *blast*phemy he used to jump into concussions, what he called his anagogic anagrams:

cats scat
risk irks
wells swell
Spain pains
cars scar

to end his high IQ in hai-kus:

I saw, I was
Psychic, chic spy.

Eve, Adam's rib:
A maid, a bride:
Eve!

BUT

Eve's mad:
A river's dam
Is bad:
I've made *bras!*

and he showed the changes in muted and/or mutant syllables like anon and onan and navel and venal and late and tale in endless alchemies, and he explained and expounded and explosed as he played with words till three in the morning (we knew what time it was because they were playing the waltz Three O'clock in the Morning Waltz) when he hit the jackity-jackpot of the spot that tops the post with a stop of pots and puns. That was the night that was exactly the same as another night when he wore Cué out with his new system of discontinuous numeration based on a proverb he'd read (probably B. would prefer to say heard) I don't know where about (we ignore his presidents whoreabouts, Ho Ho Ho!) a figure being equal to a million and in which the numbers have no value fixed or determined by their position or order but they have an arbitrary and fluctuating or totally fixed value, and you could count, for example, from 1 to 3 and after the 3 or course the 4 didn't come but 77 or 9 or 1563 and he said that some day they would discover that the whole system of postal addresses was in Error, that the logical thing would be to give numbers to the street and a name to every house and he declared that the idea paralleled his new system for baptizing brothers in which they'd all have different last names but the same first name, and aside from Cué being completely pisstaken (I'm sorry, there's no other word for it, a pissword) it was the short and happy night of frank comradery until the we ours, and wee were all amused (said B.: I'm not amused, am used) when in the Dewville Silvestre picked up a card that a croupier had discarded, the two of diamonds, and he said he could say what was the up or the down of the card, not the obverse or reverse, but that he knew how to set it right, put it on its feet, fix it, by pure intuition, so he said, meaning that the two of diamonds, it's well known, always falls on its two feet and Bustro was delighted to find a graphic palindrome and defied Silvestre to destroy it once he knew its true position and Cué said Silvestre was cheating and Silvestre got bugged and Bustrófedon took his side saying it was impossible to cheat with a single card and he persuaded Silvestre to show us the game of polygamy (that was what he called it) and Silvestre asked us all, aside from B., if we knew exactly what was a hexagon and Rine said it was a six-sided polygon and Cué said it was a solid object with six surfaces and Silvestre said it was a hexahedron and then I began drawing one (Eribó wasn't there, of courset: otherwise he'd have done it) on a piece of paper

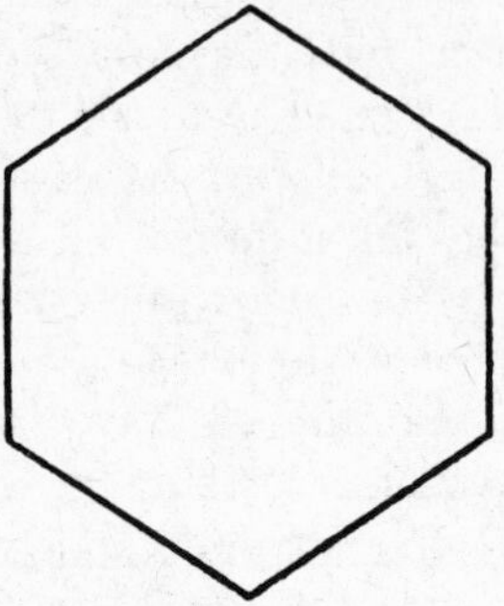

And then Silvestre said that really it was a cube that had lost its third dimension and he completed it like this

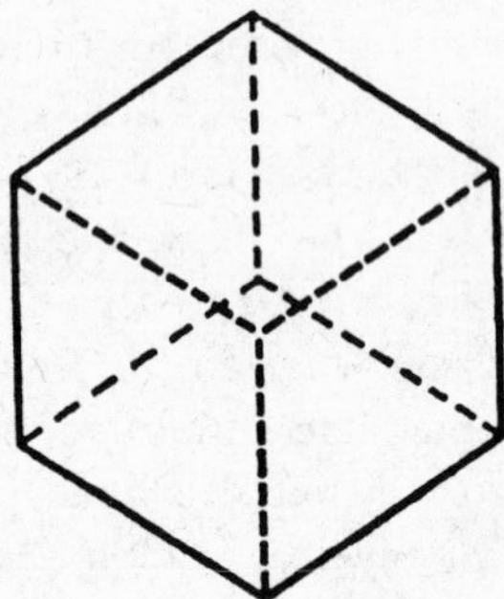

and he said that when the hexagon found its lost dimension again and we knew how it did it, we'd be able ourselves to find the fourth and fifth and other dimensions and travel freely between them (along the diMason Avenue, B. said, pointing to Eribó's former pukebiscity aliency) and enter a picture, across the frame and into the motion picture, then to move frame by frame at twenty-four paces a second, and one more step and stop on a point as on a full-stop, then travel from present to future or to past or to that side of paradise just by opening a door, and Rine took the chance to talk about his inventions, like the machine that would turn us into a light ray (into a shadow ray too, I said) and it would send us to Mars or Venus (that's where I'd like to go, said Vustrofedon) and far away and long will be another machine would turn us re, would make the light beam into lights and solid shadows and so we'd become tourists of time-space, and Cué said it was the same technique as the stage coaches and B. said they weren't the stage but the space coaches man-aged by H. G. Wells Far-go & Co., and Cué made the error (which B. spelt misstake) of telling how he'd once thought of a love tale in which a man on earth knew there was a woman on a planet in another galaxy (Bustrófedon was already saying she'd gone the way of all milk, translating from cow Latin) whom he was in love with and he went crazy with love for her and they both knew that it was the genuine love because they would never-never meet and they'd have to love each other in the silence of infinite space and of corpse Bustrófedon brought the skeletal evening to a closet bugging Cué by saying they were Tristar and Isolstice, and so we all blundered and stumbled off each to his humble home, homble for short (by way of the desert, for short-cut) when, by a strange chance (change-stance), we met up in Las Vegas with Arsenio Cué, who'd been evading our invasion (or invading our evasion) all evening because he was with a woman vulgo tore or wart (and if I talk like Bustrófedon from now on till the end of mine I'm not sorry except that I do it consciously & conscientiously and the only thing I regret is that I can't talk normally and naturally and all the time (by all the time I mean time past as well as time future) like this and forget about the light and the shadows and the chiaroscuro (about photos for shot, because one word from him is worth a thousand images), a blond, tall, white, white-white, real, pretty, photogenic, a, model, who was a silk-screen repro of herself and Cué put on his leaden face and his radiant voice and B. told him the club was full of simple elements and that we'd probably turned his saturnalia into a saturnine joint, and it was then that Bustrope invented that criminal slogan of Arsenic and old lays, which we turned into a hymn to the night until the night ended and when I wanted to go on hymning and make it into a humn to the dawn of the Magi, Rine said you're an haurora bore all is, so I'd shot my bolt and I shut my mouth and shat my ass silently but on kulchur which always comes and balls things up (if you're having a ball) with its sadometaphysicks.

That was the last time (if I forget what I want to forget, which is why I put in this apparent thesis, to put a period to my memory: Saturday night and Sunday mourning) that I saw Bustropharaoh (as Silvestre sometimes said) and if you don't see him alive you don't see him, and it was really Silvestre who saw him last. Alive. The very evening before this Bustrofilmfan as he was called that week by us, not by everybody or for all time, just by us, had turned up and told me that B.'d been taken to the hospital and I thought they were going to operate on his eye because he had a bad but not evil eye that squinted, squandered and wandered in the jungle of the night: one of his eyes aimed, as Silvestre always said, at lettre and the other at le neon or at the nothing in being, at nothingnest, and this chameleon seeing was terrible, he said but not complained, a puzzle for his brain so he always had headaches, great sustained, stable and migratory migraines which the poor fellow B. called his paracerebellum or the Brutalcephalalgias or the Bustorrential Brainstorms, and I thought of going to the clinic on Monday at midday when I finished my nightshift, which B., more economically or with less ceremony, called my shight sometimes and other times my nift. But yesterday on Tuesday morning Silvestre calls me and tells me straight out that Bustrófedon had just died and I felt that the phone was telling something that meant the same whichever way round you put it, like one of those games he invented, and I saw that death was a far-out joke: an unknown combination: a palindrome that spilled out of the viscious holes of the eternally in mourning phone stopbathing my soul with a shower of muriatic acid: the ultimate spoilsport.

And it was at the phone, by a casual or causal chance of life, that Bustrophoneme, Bustromorphosis, Bustromorphema began really to change the names of things, really and truly, for he was already sick, not like in the beginning when he mixed everything up and we couldn't tell when it was a joke and when it was a yoke. But now though we didn't know if it was meant to be funny or phony we suspected it was serious, grave, gravely ill. Because it wasn't only the *feca con chele* for *café con leche* he'd taken from the Argentinian lunfard-language in New York (where he'd met Arsenio Cué off course: he was the first to see, the first to hear him, his disc-overer), as from gotan, which isn't Gotham but the reverse of tango, he derived the barum which is the opposite of the rumba to be danced in reversed gear, with the head on the floor and moving the knees instead of the hips. Or his recitation of his Numbers (more, later) which are: Amerigoes Prepucci and Hareun al-Hashish and Nevertitty, and Antigreppine the mother of Nehro and Dungs Scrotum and el con de Orgasm and Sheets and Kelly and Fuckner and Scotch Fizzgerald and Somersault Mom and Julius Seizure and Bertolt Bitch and Alexander the Hungrate and Charles le Magnate and Depussy and Mayor Wagner who wrote the Lord of the Rings and that cockieyed musical compositor Igor Strabismus and Prickasso and the philosopher avec le savoir-faire De Sartre (also called Le Divan Maquis) and Georges BricaBraque and Elder de Broiler and Gerónimo Ambusch and Versneer and Vincent Bongoh (to bug Silvio Sergio Ribot, better known as Eribó, thanks to B period) and wanting to write a roman a Klee, about a painter that lost its tale, and things-stings like forming an airway company to rivald Aer Lingus and with cunning call it Cunny Lingus, and likenesses like calling Atanasia by the name of Euthanasia (she was the cook at the Cassalis', so she only cooked Cassalores) or his cuntpetitions with Rine Leal, whom he once beat by a short head (Rine was lowering his I-brows at the time) saying that the Ukrainians had U-shaped heads and that their real name was Ucraniums, or just Craniums, if they happened to be non-U) or his put-ons like turning up saying he'd come implacably dressed when he meant dressed to kill or cuempeting with Silvestre to hear who could make the greatest number of variations on the name of Cué, on cue, or for X sample pseudonaming me Códac (it was a second baptism for me, a baptism of fireworks because the first initialtory write had washed off after the immersion, so the logo of Kodak, once revealed, blew up and superimposed on my prosaic habanero name the uninversal and graphic mark of my trade) saying, Come forth, Lazarus Ludwig the Second, knowing, as he knew, everything there is to be known about Ido and Volapuk and Dr.

Esperanto and the Neo and Novial and after Idiom Neutral the beautiful front of Novesperanto with its Saussuges plus playing his Peano's and using & abusing the Basest English (for Forforeigners) and easing out the easiest and most perfect language, Malayalam, and expounding his theory that contrary to what happened in the Muddle Edges, when seven (7) languages all different came out of a single language like Latin or German or even Slav, in the tense future these twenty-one (he stared at Cué as he said it) languages would turn into one single long language based on or sticking to or on a guided turn with English, and man (and/or woman) would speak at least in this partition of the world and till eternity do us part an enormous lingua frangla, a sensible, possible, stable Babel. But at the same time and in the same breath this man B. was a termite attacking the scaffolding of the tower before they'd even thought of building it because every day he laid the Spanish language waste saying in imitation of Vitor Perla (whom he called Von Zeppelin because of the shape of his helium-filled head), saying sotisphicated and etoxic and decilious or boasting he had asex to the innard depths of a subject or complaining that they didn't understand his mal-or-odous humor in Cuba but taking a comforter in the thought that he'd be praised overseas or in that abroad of time which is the future. Because, he Mused, no man is a mofette in his own country.

When I'd finished listening to Silvestre, without saying anything, before hanging up, hanging up the suddenly black terrorphone, in morning that mourning, I said to myself, Fuck and shit, the whole world dies! Meaning the happy and the sad, geniuses and morons, the open and the inhibited and the cheerful and the gloomy and the ugly and the beautiful and damned and the bearded and the shaven and those with five-o'clock shadows and the tall and the short and the vicious and the innocent and the strong and the weak and the meek inheritors and the immortal and all the bald people too: everybody and even people like Bustrófedon who could make out of a couple of words and four letters a hymn and a joke and a song, these people, they also die and their memory dies too and even their songs die too, a little bit later perhaps but they die and ideas also die, so I said, Fuck! And nothing more—and right after that I said shit.

It was later, today, right now that I learned that in the autopsy before the funeral, which I refused to go to because Bustrófedon stuffed away in there, in that coffin, wasn't Bustrófedon but something else, just a thing, a useless bit of trash preserved down there in a strong box out of custom, when they'd finished trepanning Bustrófedon's skull in the form of a question mark for science and they pulled his brains out of their natural resting place and the psychopathologist had taken it in his hands and played with it and scratched its surface and patted its top as much as he felt like and had discovered finally that he had a lesion (he, poor guy, would have called it a lesson) since he was a kid, or earlier, from birth, or before he was even formed and that a bone (what do you think, Silvestre and Cué: an aneurysm, an embolism or a bubble in the humorous vein?), a knot in the spinal column, something like that, which pressed on his brain and made him say all those marvelous things and play with words so he ended his life as a new Adam, giving everything a name as though he really was inventing language (him talking to Dragon Lady, to Death: Madam I'm Adam) and Death proved him right, not *him* but that doctor who killed him, who didn't murder him, no, please don't get me wrong, he didn't even want to kill him, he wanted to *save* him, in his fashion, a scientific fashion, a medical fashion, because he was a philanthropist, a humanitarian, a Doctor Sch (you know who) whose Lambsarena was the orthopedic hospital where there were so many deformed children and paralytic women and invalids in his care, who opened the skull shaped like B. to get rid of once and for always (terrifying word, that: *always*, eternity, the fucker) the repetitions and changes and alliteration or alterations in spoken reality, what the doctor called, to please Silvestre where it pleasured him most, bang in the middle of his hypocondria, tickling his scientific ribs, almost imitating Bustrófedon himself, but of courses with his medical qualifications, his diploma for genescide, the Dr and period among all the ornamental lettering and little drawings and signatures guaranteeing the impossible, using longer technical and medical words which all went to prove that all experts are liars but as people always believe in them they are always the greatest liars, saying Aesculapius' jargon, with Galen's stone (a philosopher's stone, or a touchstone or, more simply, a gallstone or a Keystone, or a tombstone, Arizona?), saying "aphasia," "disphasia," "ecolalia," things like that, explaining, very pretendentiously. So Silvestre said, that it was *Strictly speaking, a loss of the power of speech: of oral discrimination or if you prefer me to be more specific, a defect not of phonation, but derived from a dysfunction, possibly a decomposition, an anomaly produced by a specific pathology, which in its last stages dissociated the cerebral function from the symbolism of thinking by means of speech, or*—no no no for chrissakes! it's perfectly clear just as it is and you should leave him in peaces, can't you see doctors are the last elephantine pedants left, the only mammoths of palaeolitery pedantry still alive now that the megaesoteric J'aime Joys and Earza Pounk and Teas Eliot are gone—with the possumble exception of the foulaired George Ludwig Borgid? These are the hypocritical pretexts, the diagnosis to camouflage the perfect murder, the Hyppocratic alibi, the medical excuses, but what he actually wanted was to see in what corner of Bustrófedon's skull (his Bucranium as Silvestre the disciple called it zoo aptly), to find the particular habitation and place where ordinary clumsy language and commonplace logic and everyday words (our daily breath) were so marvelously changed into Bustro's magic nightwords, which you couldn't even preserve in that formol of memory called nostolgia because I, who am, was, the one who saw most of him, wasam very bad at keeping words when they don't have anything to do with the photo (above right) and even then it's a wreckedched caption I write with caution and I always have to have it corrected by somebody—like this one. But if the games, the dursty yokes as Cassalis' mother used to say, are all lost and so I can't repeat them, I don't want to forget (so far as I preserve them: not in the memoria memoranda of Silvestre—his formol logic—nor in Arsenio Cué's feedback in anger nor in Rine's criptical mass, nor in the exact photocopy I've never been able to make, but in my tallboy drawer, alone among the negatives of a memorable half-Indian half-Negro woman, mon violon d'Indegro, the picture, the naked affiche-davit of her white flesh against black light, her Rubensian flash as Juan Blanco would say and one or two letters that have and have not any importance other than what they had when written and the telegram from Poppy Fields, my god, what kind of a pseudo-pseudonym's that, the telegram that was once blue and is now yellow and which still says in a Spanish learnt on the radio: TIME AND DISTANCE MAKE ME UNDERSTAND I LOST YOU STOP: write this, gentlemen of the jury, and give it to the telegraph officer at Santiago—doesn't this show that women are either right out of their heads or that they have more *cojones* than Maceo e-ponymust and his heroic horse's balls as well?) his parodies, those we taped at Cué's place, which Arsenio taped rather and which I then copied and which I never wanted to return to Bustrófedon, still less after his discussion with Arsenio Cué and the radical decision they both made to wipe the tapes clean—each with a different and opposite motive. That's why I kept this thing that Silvestre wanted to call memorabilia, and which I now return to its rightful owner, folklore. (A nice sentence, ain't it? Too bad it's not mine.)

THE DEATH OF TROTSKY AS DESCRIBED BY VARIOUS CUBAN WRITERS, SEVERAL YEARS AFTER THE EVENT—OR BEFORE

José Martí
(1853–1895)

THE HATCHET JOB

Legend has it that the stranger didn't ask where he might eat or drink, but only where he could find the house with the *adobe* wall around it; and that, without so much as shaking the dust of his journey off both his feet, he made for his destination, which was the last retreat of Leon Son-of-David Bronstein: the prophet of that new-time religion who was to become the eponymous founder of its first heresy: messiah, apostle and heretic in one. The traveler, one Jacob Mornard, warped and twisted, and accompanied only by his seafaring hatred, had finally arrived in the notorious sanctuary of the Exile whose family name means stone of bronze and whose frank, fiery features were those of a rebellious rabbi. Furthermore, the old man was distinguished by his haughty and farsighted gaze underneath his horn-rimmed glasses; his oratorical gestures—like those of the men of the Greek *ágora* not of the Hebrew *agora*; his woolly and knitted brows; and his sonorous voice, which usually reveals to ordinary mortals those whom the Fates have destined, from the cradle, to profound eloquences: all this and his goatee gave the New Wandering Jew a biblical countenance.

As for the future magnicide: his troubled appearance and the awkward gait of the born dissident were sketches of a murderous character which would never, in the dialectic mind of the assassinated Sadducee, find completion to cast, in the historical mold of a Cassius or even a Brutus, the low relief of an infamous persona.

Soon they were master and disciple; and while the noble and hospitable expatriate forgot his worries and afflictions, and allowed affection to blaze a trail of warmth in a heart that had anciently been frozen with reserve, his felonious follower seemed to carry in the stead of a heart something empty and nocturnal, a black void in which the slow, sinister and tenacious fetus of the most ignoble treachery was able to take roots and strike. Or perhaps, perchance it was a mean cunning that looked for revenge; because they say that at the back of his eyes he always carried a secret resentment against that man whom, with faultless subterfuge, he was in the habit of calling Master, using the capital letter that is reserved only for total obedience.

On occasions they could be seen together and although the good Lev Davidovich—we can call him that now, I suspect, even if in his lifetime he concealed with an initial this middle name that spelled yarmulke, and carried false credentials—took extreme precautions—because there were not lacking, as in the previous Roman tragedy, evil omens, the revelatory imagery of premonitions, or the ever-present habit of foreboding—he always granted audience in solitude to the taciturnal visitor, who was at times, as on the day of misfortune, both adviser and supplicant. This crimson Judas carried in his pale hands the manuscript in which his treachery was patently written with invisible ink; and over his thin blueish and trembling body he wore a *Macfarlane,* which would, to any eye more given to conjecture and suspicion, have given him away on that suffocatingly hot Mexican evening: distrust was not the strong point of the Russian rebel: nor systematic doubt: nor ill will a force of habit: underneath the coat the crafty assailant carried a treacherous hoof-parer: the magnicidal adze: an ice pick: and under the ax was his soul of guided emissary of the new Czar of Russia.

The trusting heresiarch was glancing attentively over the pretended scriptures, when the hatchet man of the Party delivered his treacherous blow and the steely shaft bit deep into that most noble head.

A cry resounded through the cloistered precincts and the *sbirri* (Haití had refused to send her eloquent Negroes) ran there in great haste and eager to convert the assassin into a prisoner. The magnanimous Marxian still had time to advise: "Thou shalt not kill," and his inflamed followers did not hesitate to respect his instructions to the hilt.

Forty-eight hours of hopes, tears and vigil the formidable agony of that luminous leader lasted, dying as he had lived: in struggle. Life and a political career were no longer his: in their stead glory and historical eternity belonged to him.

José Lezama Lima
(1912–1965)

THE NUNCUPATIVE WILL OF A CRUSADER

+++MOST-TRANSPARENT-REGION-OF-THE-AIR, July 16 (NP)—Lev Davidowitch Bronstein, the onomastic vicar forane of the Bolsheviki, presently ambulating under the pseudonym of Troztky [*sic*], died today in this megapolis in Wagnerian angst, amidst the profoundest sympathies of sycophants and seneschals alike, exhaling rounds and catches like ecumenical melismata after his *protégé,* an uncertain Jacopus Mornardus or Merceder [*sic*], pulled out with scholastic secrecy from a vesture feignedly discipular but in actuality deceitful and traitorous, a deicidal weapon conveniently hidden under that tautological cloak to end abruptly the ne'er-yarmulked diaspora which has had its inception, by just analogy, on the island of Prinkipo. The assassin did not employ, as reported, a bare bodkin. There were faint murmurs that the pseudo apostate drew out on that crepuscular Valpurgis nach [*sic*] a killer pick or puncheon or perhaps a malevolent-cum-endwishing alpenstock, and nailed it with murderous intent to that *tête* so heavily laden with thesis and antithesis and para-diaboloid synthesis. The sharp-edged tool dived deep into the stubborn, dialectical tufty mane of the *Steppenlowe,* or feline of the steppes, whose roaring was as philosophically shallow as ideologically *naïve:* obliterated this image, formerly so aurorean and now vespertine, which validates the symbol of the orthodox and later heretical father, terminating with extreme political prejudice such singular opposition. Of course, Mollnard [*sic*] himself ended up by solely imposing his *favori* to his companions, just one more incipient inmate in the mysterious and innumerable corridors of Lecumberri, locked minotaurically in his duplex labyrinth of silence and allegiance: a shrewd sicarius or an autistic automaton? Lew Davidovicht [*sic sic*] before exhaling his final, so revelatory and apocalyptic last gasp, it is known here to have said, in a sort of spoken twilight of the gods in exile, in a Marx-Engelian Strugund-Drame [*sic sic sic*], in a materialist version of the Last Supper, or rather like another John of Pannonia taking exception to the violent intrusion of the arguments of a new Aurelian in his ideological privacy, these infamous last words quote I feel like one possessed who has just been penetrated bodily . . . by a soft assegai unquote+++

Virgilio Piñera
(1914–1966)

AFTERNOON OF THE KILLERS

I believe with my heart crossed that nobody ever knows whom he is working for. This handsome young man, Mornard (here and *entre nous*, I can say that his real name is Santiago Mercader and that he is Cuban; I mention it because I know that all this is food for the gossipmongers), went to Mexico to kill on purpose Leon D. Trotsky, this lion of Russian letters, while he was showing the master some of his writings for him to read and criticize. Trotsky never knew that Mornard was working as a ghost writer for Stalin. Mornard never knew that Trotsky was working like a dog for literature. Stalin never knew that Trotsky and Mornard were working like slaves (excuse the simile) for history.

When Mornard arrived in the lands of the Aztecs the night was as dark as an inkpot and his intentions were black as ink or as the night, good only for moonshining. The assassin was not, as is usually the case with epigones, an original mind. He has of course his historical antecedents, as the history of this vale of tears is full of violence. This is why I have so great a hatred for historians, because I detest violence with all the strength of my soul. But violence seems to be the motivating force of this *piccolo mondo* that we live in. Although there is violence and violence. And then some.

For example, there is no doubt that the French aristocracy was in a state of decadence when the Revolution and Danton, Marat and company decimated it. But only a little before it had what is called its golden age, *son age d'or*. This is an epoch which I know inside out, because I haven't neglected to read a single one of the memoirs that were written during that epoch or before or after and . . . but not to weary you with an erudition that I detest as I detest all specialists, scholars, etcetera, I must say I am thoroughly acquainted with all the tittle-tattle of the *Aristocratie*. An aristocracy which, let it be said in passing, was rotten through and through, like the Palais de Versailles, which had to be abandoned every six months while everyone went to the Louvre, because the staircases and corridors and salons had been converted into a pigsty with all the feces and stools of nobles and aristocrats. The same thing happened six months later with the Louvre. Did you know that the royal dentist of that time instead of pulling out a back tooth of Louis XIV extracted a piece of bone the same size from the soft palate and the poor man contracted so great an infection that he had such a case of halitosis that nobody was able to go near the Sun King for fear of getting nasal sunstroke? Just like that. But this could never have been sufficient justification for a *quid pro quo* like the guillotine, because cutting off your ruler's head is not the best way of curing him of bad breath.

But *revenons a nos moutons* . . . and to those who make mutton of them. This young fellow, Mornard, came to kill Mr. Trotsky, who was writing his memoirs—in a style which, to be strictly truthful, was much better than that of Stalin, Zhdanov, and the other Cossacks. It wouldn't surprise me if they had ordered him to be killed out of envy, a sin that grows like poisonous ivy in literary circles, otherwise why would Antón Arrufa say that a book should be a pistol? Obviously to aim the book at me and shoot, literarily speaking, point-blank. But Piñera lives!

This is the problem that all the masters have to face with their disciples, epigones, followers, etc., and L. D. Trotsky should never have tried to teach these people how to write. Teaching (above all in literature) doesn't pay. And here we come to the "kernel" of the problem. I presume that when Trotsky decided to write his drama—because to say it once and for all and unreservedly, the memoirs of the men who make or have made or will make history are nothing other than historical dramas—a drama, I repeat to say it again, which treats of the antagonism between master and disciples, and in which he was forced to choose between a realistic, a social realist, an epic or a symbolic treatment, he chose the last. And why did he choose the symbolic? those who are inclined to ask questions will ask.

He chose it then because he preferred the symbolic and he chose it so to speak like an animal, instinctively, for the same unreason as we choose stewed meat instead of baked fish when confronted with the menu containing both items—simply because we prefer our meat stewed. So it was that, to put it as crudely as possible, Trotsky ordered stewed meat. Now, does the choice of stewed meat or of the symbolic presuppose the existence of a master-disciple antagonism or a literary mayhem—or mythifying and mystifying and mystimythifying and mythimystifying of the occasioners of this antagonism or combat between baked fish and stewed meat? Or, to say it with as little pedantry as possible, the ichthyosarcomachy. Made mincemeat, as it were. Only this. In a setting (and it was nothing else—let it be said once and for all, this *château* or fortress in which the criminal assassinated his victim *was* a stage) that was realistic or socialist realist or social realist they appeared demystified and demythified and demystified or demythimystified; in an epic they would divide the roles, technically speaking, of heroes and villains. In Trotsky's tragedy he was a sort of Russian Agamemnon while the Soviet Union was Clytemnestra—Russia—they are mythifiers and mythimystifiers or mystimythifiers of their own political persona. But the antagonism would be the same, to be perfectly precise about it, in the two or three or four possible conceptions.

It raises, as if with a hand, the following, and very hard, penetrating question: that of the good or bad conscience of the writer. Did Trotsky gamble away his "bad conscience" by choosing the symbolic conception of his assassination? Should he, instead, have had recourse to his "good conscience" by choosing the realistic or social realist or socialist realist or epic conception of the above-mentioned act, so terribly personal?

These two questions prompt us to make the following reflection: would the conscience of the assassin have a seamy side, a loose seam where to hem and haw on both sides? Would the good conscience of the assassin, on choosing these two sides of every question, not at the same time be turning itself into a bad conscience because of the exclusion it made of the third or divine conception—that is to say the ideal conscience of the master—the way you turn a glove inside out? Would the man who was being assassinated not impose his own limits, in this case the toughness of his skull resisting the assassin and his piercing instrument, which amounts to the same thing: that is to say this insistent pick? There are here, as a good housekeeper at the marketplace would put it, fruits to be had.

And by reason of what symbolic conception would he have to obey the bad conscience on the part of the assassin? Or of the assassinee, which amounts to the same thing? In that death in the afternoon of the killers (they won, the killers, the matadors, the assassins, I have to say, because they completed their *faena* and in this moment of truth or *minute de la verité*—in the manner of a toreador the disciple delivered the death blow with a *puntilla* to his bull or father-master-leader) the master-disciple antagonism was brought suddenly to a conclusion. At no point did the conflict or agon (with a child-author this tantrum would have been solved by a good caning from the teacher-father) suffer any diminution, nor, to use the language of the professional parlor magician, was there any sleight of hand; at no point did the expiation of the masters and the *hubris* (or "cockiness") of the disciples seem less honest than it would have been in the realist or socialist realist or social realist or epic conscience; at no point did the feigned or pretended bad conscience of Trotsky develop, as with his disciples, into the mystimythifying or mythimystifying and mythifying and mystifying of an antagonism proper. Which amounts to saying, anything alien to the *genre*. Artistic form, ideological content and motivation are fused in one and the same thing: the aired conflict. Or as a gossip columnist would put it: the private feud. Or literary mayhem, as it were.

Finally, and it seems to me that it is of the utmost interest: it is very possible that the parents of Mornard (and with them many other parents, including Stalin's parents, which is the same as saying his own parents, because Jacques Mornard *is* Stalin, as is well enough known) will say: What a naughty boy! Lookee here, to do something so very naughty, like for instance murdering this good old man! . . . This is to define bad conscience in common language. It happens because of an illusion or *mirage* frequent enough in human beings, that the assassin is mistaken for the persona of the assassin and they pass judgment on both of them with all the mythifyings and mystifyings and mythimystifyings or . . . (oh, botheration, I'm getting fagged, or *fatigué!*) as if imposing simple meanings on a double murder or vice versa. Such a *mirage* or illusion alters the terms of the equation and the "good consciences" automatically pass over into being bad. By automatically I mean through inertia, or mechanically, or maybe that such a "bad" conscience has no existence without the subjectifying of the conscience of the assassin. That is to say, gossip is the old wives' gospel.

Speaking of stevedores, I almost forgot to tell you that during the fifteen years I lived in Santiago de Cuba, near the port (I enjoyed it all enormously), I was acquainted with Caridad Mercader, or Cachita, as her neighbors insisted on calling her, the mother of the assassin or disciple *par excellence*. In her youth, a pretty, young unmarried mother, Cachita, when she gave birth to little Santiago (or Santiaguito), who was then what midwives at that time called a bastard, that is a son without a father, hence the name Mercader, which is clearly much more Cuban than Jugazhvili. Caridad Mercader, cradling this future Saint Iago (Santiago, *Iago,* Saint—get it?) in his cradle, said or repeated (when she said it more than once) a sentence which I heard and which perhaps I should have taken for a premonition, an act of prescience or prophecy or, who knows, even a gossip of time future. She said (as my sister Luisa would say), this exemplary mother:

—When my son grows up, he will be a big man.

But if Trotsky né (or better, *ci-devant*) Bronstein is dead (which seems, after all, possible) and there is nothing to be done about it because what we call the hereafter doesn't exist or at least it doesn't exist for those of us who are, as Borges' cook calls it, in the here-before. As the here-before doesn't exist for those in the other-world or, to coin a phrase, in the icebox. Mornard, it seems, is still alive or at least so they keep him in the Lecumberri prison, and that is sufficient. What Santiaguito Mercader should do is to ask for paper and ink and start writing his memoirs, because literature is the best sedative that I know. I remember that when I was in Buenos Aires, where I spent sixteen bitter summers, writing was my sweetest consolation. And by writing I mean making literature or, at least in my case, great literature. —V.P.

Lydia Cabrera
(1900–)

THE INITIATE TAKES THE CUP THAT WILL MAKE HIM A CUPBEARER

He had already forgotten the rounded negative of Baró, the *babalósha* (chief) of old Cacha (*Caridad*), his mother from Santiago, when she asked him if she could borrow his *nganga* to carry out a "work" on the "guampara," on the day that the powerful chief or *orisha* arrived bringing with him none other than the terrible and powerfully magical caldron which he kept hidden in a black sack—*blako-sako*. The spirit (*ghoulo*) that dwelt in this man had shown that he was good (*groovu*) because the "moana mundele" (white woman, Cachita Mercarder, in this case) had asked him to do her a favor by protecting her son and the mission (*noissima*) that he had before him. The old man made haste to carry out that petition (*f'avoru*) because his *nganga* also gave its approval (*iesseri*). The witch doctor calmly authorized him to accomplish the sanctification—"with permission of the pledge"—if such was his desire. *Burufutu nmobututu!*

It was a *nganga* in its own right and as the white man was a keen photographer (*fotu-fotu fan*), he wanted to make a likeness of the noble old man Baró (he remembered that in Santiago he had had a Negro "tata" or Negress) but not before this man had asked permission of *Olofin* intoning a liturgical song or *litu-kanto.*

Olofin!
Olofin!
Tendundu kipungulé!
Námí masongo sílanbása!
Silanbáka!
Bika Dioko Bica Ñdiámbe!
Olofin!
O!
LO!
Fi!

—What do the shells (*cauris*) say, old and noble Baró, asked the white man, troubled. —Is it possible?

The noble and old Baró smiled his African and naturally enigmatic smile.

—Yes (or *no*)? the troubled white man asked again.

—The *cauris* (shells) speak well of it, said the old and noble Baró. —*Olofi* is pleased.

—May I take the photo now? asked the troubled white man.

—NO! the old and noble (or noble and old) Baró answered sharply.

—Why not? asked the troubled white man, looking troubled.

He had refused him this favor not because he mistrusted his good intentions nor because he was afraid that his image would fall into the hands of another witch doctor, who as owner of his portrait could cast a spell on him (*Ungawa!*) or easily put an end to him by sticking pins (*it hurts*) into it nor because the *nganga,* quite apart from the profanation, would have been bound and weakened by it. Nor because he was afraid of the troubling witch eye of a camera. Nor because he mistrusted the white man. Nor . . .

—Why not then? asked the white man.

Noble and old and black Baró looked at him with his African eyes and then (also with his African eyes) looked at the camera and at last he spoke:

—This magical machine to make many little Barós in B & W by means of light reflected on sensitized paper, it's an Asahi Pentax Spotmatic, of course, with a CdS photometric lens, and a 2.8 aperture. Old and noble Baró never look good in photo made with it.

What a difficult situation! There remained (*Ol-lef*) no other (*nozinguelsu*) solution (*Ungawa!*) than to go away (*fokkoffo*)!

The white man left for Mexico to fulfill his pledge. He was dressed in a white suit, a white shirt with white buttons, a white tie with a white tie pin, a white belt with a white buckle, white socks, white underclothes and white hat and shoes. The clothes of those who "incarnate" "a" "saint"—and have the money to buy themselves a trousseau. He also wore a red handkerchief in his top pocket. Part of the liturgy? No, perhaps it was for adornment or a note of political color to break the monotony of the white. But there is another theory. The man who was dressed entirely in white was called Santiago Mercader and he was preparing himself to kill Bwana Trotsky, a powerful chief with great powers. Perhaps the handkerchief was a sign for some color-blind accomplice (*ínfomma*).

The white man (*Molná mundele*) arrived, saw Leon (*Simba*) Trotsky and killed him. He nailed him on his "coco" (head) with the "guampara" and dispatched him to his "In-Kamba finda ntoto" (icebox). To ensure the accuracy of the final blow, the *orishas* were always consulted first.

GLOSSARY

Asahi Pentax Spotmatic: commercial term in Latin, English and Japanese. Photographic camera.

Babalao: babalósha in Lucumi.

Babalósha: babalao, also in Lucumi.

Baró: a man's given name. Also a surname.

Bwana: father or father figure. Equivalent to the Russian word for "little father."

Guampara: wampara, Swahili. From the Arab word *wamp'r.* Approx. *assegai.*

Mensu: opposite of *nganga.* Roughly, *Juju.*

Moana mundele: white woman. Acc. Pierre Berger, "tongue which walks pale."

Nganga: from the dialect of Dahomey, *oroko.* Amulet.

Olofi: Beloved God. Sometimes. At other times, devil. He is represented normally in his normal position. But occasionally he appears face-downward.

Orisha: from the Bakongo word *orisha. Babalao* or *babalósha.*

Tata: nurse, wet nurse. Sometimes, mother.

Lino Novás Calvo
(1905–19??)

HOLD THAT TYRANT!

Hold that man for me! Fasten him well. Don't let him go. Hold him right there! So he doesn't get away. Look what he's done. This thing (because it's nailed there, a thing, yes, that one there—*not* that one! *that* one!—made of iron, not wood or stone or pumice-stone or plastic but iron, cast-steel some would call it, rooted, riveted, right through the bone between frontal and parietal lobes, close to the occipital bone, not calculated coldly and precisely but skillfully wielded and flailed and nailed to the head of this man—that is to say, of myself—who will soon be done for, soundly and with fury, with a cold rage spurred on by hatred and envy and political enmity, making two men into one single thing by that connective iron which is an extension of his hand, like an inimical gesture or rather the caricature of a gesture or if you insist the gesture itself of stretching out a hand in friendship it seems but in fact made into a homicidal weapon and now both men are one single man, or rather two: executioner and victim, because of that caricatural gesture) which I have on my head is no *mantilla* high comb. No siree. Lay hold of him. There! So he doesn't get away. That's no ornament. What I have on top of my head. Nor is it a ceremonial skullcap. Hold him tight! That's right. Nor is it some rebellious tuft of hair. It is an ax. Nailed right here. To the skull. As simple as that. Hold that man, for my sake. That's it!

(Because he remembers, because he's not able to forget, because he still remembers, because he still hasn't forgotten, because the past appears to him as a stream of photo images, discontinuous, fragmented but in movement, truth moving at sixteen frames a second, like the track of an old movie shown in a movie house in Luyanó or Lawton-Batista, on the outskirts, or even farther out, where the roof gardens are called rooftops and gardens become tiled roofs and the telephone numbers are no longer an initial letter and then the numbers, where there are not even numbers on the phones because they are not needed, neither initials and then the numbers nor the numbers themselves. Because there are no phones. There is no need of one. All you need is to shout. Instant connection.

In those outskirts where we played soldiers, Allies and Germans, and like Allies and Germans behaved in fact the cab drivers and the drivers of what when time passed were to be called buses but which now are not yet called buses but something else, omnibuses or whatever they are called, and I had to play the baddie when one day the chick appeared at the stand, popping up between two jalopies and saying, between two jalopies, that she was pregnant, and I had to ask her, "So you're definitely and finally knocked up?" and she answered me, still between two jalopies, that she was, nodding like this. Her head moving in a vertically repeated and disgusting movement, up and down. Like this. Nodding. So, after all, she was. Pregnant. So I know what memory is as I know that the man, that one over there, that man, remembers. But what he remembers is of no importance. To me. Because they are his, this man's.

Memories. And nothing else. But it's criminal, nevertheless. This I, Claudius, doing such a thing! Sending this man where he sent him to dispatch him where he dispatched him, sent, dispatch him over there and then like Rosencrantz and Guildenstern rolled in one person leave him alone. Because there was no ransom. For him. Not even a faint hint of a remote intention to ransom him and his cell was a fortress within the fortress that is the Lecumberri prison, so nobody is ever going to come to his rescue. A King Claudius! That's what he is. This other fellow, this bestial tyrant, this executioner of peoples, this man, Stalin, that's who. None other. He was. The man who sent him. *I* know it well. How couldn't I? It was me who took him in my jalopy and drove him to the Machina docks to catch the last ferry one night when the *nona* moon was shining. Yessir, that's the man. Him.

Nonesuch. The killer. The man, because he is a man not a woman nor a child nor a queen in drag but a man, because he goes around dressed as a man even though he has committed the act of a woman, a treachery, and has put certain imaginary projections of the brow on the other man's head, doing that to an old man and when he was reading his manuscripts to boot. And to have done it behind his back.)

From behind the chair, suddenly, with a movement that was the slow-motion version of a movement, a frozen action, a delayed advance which was the denial of a movement, but a movement after all. The killer, Jacob. Santiago, Iago, Diego. Whatever his name is. This man, that man, the one who stands here. *There*. Mornard, Mercader or whatever the hell his last name is. That one, James Mollnard. It was he who was my killer. How do I know? *Hombre!* because we were, the two of us, here in this room, alone, and I was sitting here, in this armchair or rocking chair or whatever chair I am now in slowly drifting into death, in an agony neither sweet nor bitter nor painful nor sad nor happy nor serious but perhaps grave, slowly drifting off slowly toward that place with no name and no number and no phone where they are calling me from, passing away without even having a blind vision like Tamaría did or the motorized death rattles of Ramón Yendia or even the obscene relationship which old Angusola had with his daughter the sweet mulatress Sofonsiba (pretty names, aren't they? I took them from Faulkner who in turn took them from any encyclopedia or whatever, and we both took it misspellingly from Sophonisba Angusciola, that Italian woman painter in the Renaissance) or anything. Nothing. Just like that. So he was standing there behind me and I was sitting here in front of him and the one (him) stood behind the other (me) and so it was one behind and the other in front, with me doing all the sitting and he doing all the standing, and the reading, the examination or whatever it was would have proceeded perfectly pleasantly if only it hadn't occurred to this man to jump me, his eyes bulging, and strike me, with whatever he's done it, on the head, on top of the head, back on top or top of the back, and I here with my eyes (and perhaps also my gray matter underneath my gray hair) bulging as I lay dying while you stand there asking questions or you are standing there asking questions and questions as I die laying asking questions and questions and questions and questions and questions (you) and all the questions being asked of me and none to this man because all you are capable of is stretching out your fists (clenched) to his face, to his eyes (still bulging), beating, browbeating and blackjacking him, without even asking (us) if what is hurting me is also hurting him. Or whatever.

That's right. Hold him! Don't let him escape! Don't let him get away. Lay hold of him and tie and fasten him (which is more or less the same). Do it. Well. Hold. Him! So. He doesn't get. Away. That's right! Hold that man, for Marx's sake! Hold him! Hold or hem him in! Hem him in! Hem! Hem hem!

Alejo Carpentier
(1904–1882)

LOT'S STEPS[1]

To be read in the time it takes to play the *Pavane pour une infante defunte,* at 33 rpm

I

L'importanza de mio compito no me impede de fare molti sbagli. . . . The old man paused perusingly over that sentence infinitively split by an aftertaste of shame, while he thought: "I hate dialogues" and translated it mentally into French to see how it sounded, and sketched on his venerable, venerated, venerating features a smile like a sniff of licorice, perhaps because through the open window, with its shutters recently painted white and now folded back in their frame, across the drawn venetian blinds, the upper part of which could be seen through the flimsy curtains of muslin imported from Antwerp, beside the golden hinges, the curtain cords also of the same yellow-bronze color, their metallic glare contrasting with the

1 *Avis au traducteur: Monsieur, Vous pouvez traduire le titre—"Explosion ex cathedra."* S.V.P. —L'Auteur

dazzling whiteness of the wooden paneling, of shutters and shutterbolts, all made of Canadian walnut wood whitened with cadmium powder dissolved in linseed oil, and over the spacious window seat, adorned with flowerpots which they had sown with Cuban lilies and sunflowers, though he did not see the flowers either in front or behind the snow-white glare and it was because they were not planted in the embrasure of the window but outside in a plot of red tiles that caught the implacable sun, extending beyond the sheltering line of the penthouse roof, in the heat of the day, as Atanasia, the chambermaid, would have said in her Avernal vernacular: through the luminous cavity there entered unexpected and extravagantly sweet melodies. The music came from beyond the gramophone which regurgitated the tunes of his native land with their melismatic savor, neither fifes nor lutes nor dulcimers, citterns, sistrums, virginals, rebecks, flageolets, zithers or psalteries, but a balalaika, plucked so as to draw from it the sonorities of a Theremin, in the manner of Kiev, "Kievskii Theremina," which brought with it the memory of the campaigns in the Ukraine. "*Je déteste les dialogues,*" he said, in French, wondering how it would sound in English. The man, the younger of the two, because one of the men was young and the other old and by the law of comparatives one of them *had* to be younger than the other who was older and it was this one, the younger one, who was looking at him and laughing now with forced explosions of pleasure, the sentence meant to be a quotation someday. The old man, because there was an old man and if there were two men in that bedroom, carpeted with shaggy weaves from Irkutsk, one of them had to be the older, by weight of years and remembrances, and it was this one who was looking back and then upward, seeing the other foreshortened with the enormous open mouth of his discipular factotum in the visual *auris sectio,* noted mentally while he was taking notes, lips (two), palate, back teeth, uvula, pharynx, tonsils (or a gap where there were tonsils, because they had been taken out in early tonsillectomy), a politically red tongue and teeth (nearly thirty-two), teeth properly so called in the lower and upper maxillary, incisors, canines, premolars, molars and wisdom teeth and as he was still laughing, with no other motive now than the natural sycophancy of a follower, he saw wrapped in the surrounding humidity the soft palate, raphe, uvula (again), larynx, anterior supports for the soft palate, the tongue again (or was it another tongue?), the tonsular gaps and posterior supports for the palate, and odontologically exhausted he returned to his book. The young man, because it was the younger of the two men who was looking at the opus magnum which the hateful and hated master held in his hands, registered the following things on his watchful, resentful retinas: box, book covers, tile, corner plating, back, backing, ribbing, rosette, letter heading, headband cord, cloth binding, paper binding, stitching of quinternions and sheets of paper, trimming at top, at bottom, trimming at side, illustration, head margin, outside margin, mouth, second cover, cover, and glided a swift glance over the text. Now he passed from the art of bookbinding, the bibliographical references, the nomenclature of books to feel under his waterproof trenchcoat, which he wore conveniently buttoned up despite the winds of a tropical heat wave which were blowing over the *altiplano,* and over his well-cut jacket he was able to examine with elbow and forearm the sharp, well-honed edge of the ax at the end of its short shaft of polished white teak. He looked away from the book and at that noble white head and thought that he would have to perforate the hair-covered skin, the occipital bone and cut through the meningeal membranes (*a.* dura mater; *b.* aracnoid; *c.* pia mater) to cleave through the cerebrum to pass through the cerebellum and perhaps arrive at the oblong medulla, so that everything depended on the initial force of the blow, on a momentum capable of transforming his homicidal inertia into action. *"Tengo un santo horror a los diálogos,"* the old man said again, this time in Russian but thinking how it would sound in German. It was this leitmotif sentence, this refrain, this ritornello that moved the young man to strike.

II

He hurled away his cigarette, rolled in corn paper, because somehow it smelled of the custard porridge, made with American maizena, eaten for breakfast in his infancy, of pounded cornmeal served up for desserts, of the preprandial polentas called *tayuyos* in his native Santiago of yesteryear, and the yellowish maize-made missile hit against the fence formed by lined iron bars hammered into spears with artistic intent no doubt, for, toward the top, they resolved themselves in symmetrical deles, calligraphic signs, borders exquisitely filleted and painted gold, and other ornamental ironwork here and there, not thrown in haphazardly but for good measure. The gate was a grooved portcullis set in motion by pulleys, cables, springs, bolts, turnstiles, block pulleys, racks, axle shafts, bolt holes, toothed wheels, ratchets, mortises and, finally, handles plus the occasional hand of whatever Cerberus was on duty, to whom the simple and memorable password, which he recited in his brazen baritone, should suffice:

Queste parole di colore oscuro
vid'io scritte al sommo d'una porta;
per ch'io: "Maestro il senso lor m'e duro"

congratulating himself warmly on the splendid Italianate pronunciation that slipped from his lips like a swift Gregorian train. But the smile into which his Dantesque terza rima flowed died the very moment he half heard the gatekeeper, who, for a reply, nonchalantly chanted Avernal words in his perfectly archaized Tuscan dialect:

Qui si convien lasciare ogni sospetto;
ogni viltá convien che qui sia morta
Noi siam venutti al loco oy'io t'ho detto
che tu vedrai le genti dolorose,
c'hanno perdutto il ben de lo'nteletto.

Now there was nothing left he could want except that occult and primitive lifting mechanisms would start raising the ferrous door with its bristling iron spikes locked in their base of premonitorially reinforced concrete. He walked down steeply sloping bifid paths bordered by volcanic rubble and gazed at the imposing *château-fort* which already towered above him. He saw facades that mingled a delirium of styles, where Bramante and Vitruvius disputed the primacy with Herrera and Churriguera and where traces of early Plateresque were fused with a bold display of late Baroque, and if the pediment appeared to be in the classical Greek sharp-edged triangular style it was only an idle guessing game, because you saw immediately that the edge of the portico was in no wise triangulated, and in parts of the entablature, between the screens and the architraves, he noticed some friezes and on the left and right wings there were side arches which supported Catalan vaults that looked like empty crypts, although some of the fascia revealed a certain usefulness or at least a pretension toward being aesthetic, but it disturbed him greatly that the intrados made the voussoir provocative of unforeseeable meditations. It was the upper bracket, with its projecting buttresses which suffered an excess of molding, the element which brought him back to the sumptuous bracket carved with all the delicacy of the Rococo. But what was the reason for the three ogives that were so conspicuously asymmetrical: one of them equilateral, another flamboyant and the third Moorish? Did it mean that the convex moldings with their quarter-circle profile were oval? Would they not be the pivots for still more digressions? Eccentric and possibly paradoxical methods of constructing a facade, because the quarter-round molding instead of being concave molding that we can all recognize at first glance, and which seemed clearly from its profile to be a quarter of a circle, faded away at the edges and on joining the capital adopted circular eccentricities but on descending the column was replaced by a certain formal nonsense, while the facade was at once infested with columns of every order: Ionic, Corinthian, Doric, Doric-Ionic, Solomonian, Theban and between capitals and plinth there extended curiously flutings and grooves, and our visitor was astonished to see the plinths between the base and lower cornice, around the pedestal and not between the frieze and the architrave as other previous visitors who had praised the architects and masterbuilders of these exotic lands had told him. The keystone of this construction system was provided, a rare thing, by the keystone of the building carved in *capellanía* stone and it was then that he realized that he had been on the right track from the start, and that he made no mistake, because here were the purplish rounded moldings he had expected, the architraves of porphyry he was told to expect and the apophyges with their striations so unexpectedly executed in chartreuse and magenta. This *had* to be the place of his appointment with historical destiny, and he felt that instead of blood and plasma there was quicksilver flowing mercurially in his peripheral and minor arteries. He arrived at the entrance with its overlapping and superfluous denticles overhanging festoons of cretonne and little cords which imitated an awning so well, and he decided to call out. But first he gazed at the memorable door which did not need the inscription "*Per me se va ne la cittá dolente* . . . *lasciate*, etc."

III

A curious door, he said to himself half aloud, while he gazed at the transom, whose frame was classical, though made of quartz, feldspar and mica, elements which, he knew that when combined formed granite, and the door leaves, covered with a coating of metal of a consistency which if it hadn't been made of steel would have made him think it was iron, with a protective plaque in the place that the keyhole should have occupied, although the door knocker—made of bronze—was exactly where it should have been: above the sash, dividing the lower from the upper panels and indicating one of the three hinges, which were also gilded. He didn't knock. Why? To have done so he would have to have been wearing an iron gauntlet.

They opened up, surely by putting an eye beam or photoelectric cells into action, and he went in, passing over the threshold and under the lintel without either difficulty or surprise. But no sooner had the heavy doors closed behind his shoulders than he began to feel afraid and he tried to find some support between the door jambs and on feeling his shoulder striking against paneling of steel from Akron, Ohio, he fell back instead against the bevels. The sight before his eyes was indescribable. From the street the whole mansion had the appearance of a castle, fortress or casemate visible because of the absence of triglyphs and metopes over the convexities of the echinus with its apparently Doric frieze, because the soffit did not ascend in the ruled inverted steps, because some parts of the openwork were ramparts, because there were corbels that were reinforced at the angles, and which were not only through their irregularity capable of destroying any order, but also because he noticed watchtowers, loopholes, projections, posterns that had the appearance of sally ports, portholes that gave little or no ventilation, merlons that seemed like parapets over the facing, fortifying the roof tiles and flat roofs above the fluted molding, and inside the patio very strong buttresses and counterforts protected the solid thickness of the wall not far from the innocence of latticework suggesting the mysteries and jealousies of an arbored bower and surrounding it, trellises of flowering judases! Higher, higher up, on the roof, the guttering was disguised with burlap and barbicans for the *trompe-l'oeil* of the termination of the impluvium, while turrets in an Assyrian-Romanic style were made to look like Gothic flying buttresses and between double windows and lanterns and embrasures that were evidently excessive, rusty catapults and stone cannons, anachronistic gun carriages and short carbines had appeared at some epoch, and between the acroteria, gargoyles and hippogryphs there could well emerge the fearful asymmetry of an opportune *franc-tireur*. All this made him think that he was among comrades: armed men. But now, once he was inside, all was a *cauchemar* of inebriated interior decorations. True, the nightmare had already begun in the left wing of the patio where, in order to make a pendant to the austerely priveted gazebo, there was a crumbling monopteric shrine and through the intercolumniation, across the delicately stylish portico, between silent pilasters, a stone block could be seen that was evidently dedicated to funerary rites. But *this, this!* Would it be better to beat the air or rather a hasty retreat? Impossible, since the door had closed hermetically, and it was protected by bolts, spring latches, iron levers, crossbars, linchpins, padlocks and square bolts that would provide obvious resistance to any sudden assault, however Herculean, and besides all he would achieve by it would be to stain the sleeves and shoulders of his *impermeable*, bought in Paris, which protected the steel-headed pickax that was to deal justice—or murder most foul, if we are to believe the opinion either of exegetes or of detractors.

The memory came to his mind now that he had forgotten in his closely detailed observation certain florid architraves, and foundations of granite supported on socles of broken cockles and the eye measurements of the divisions of the foundations (wretched rhyme) of the facade. He returned to the present reality and gazed at the floor with its green glazed tiles, a Grecian fret on a white mosaic, and confronted his doubts with determination by walking toward some archivolts where helicoidal figures reclined on fascias of fluted stone. This was a mere peccadillo compared with what would happen afterward, when his eyes were to fall on the salon which was vestibule, lobby and labyrinth at the same time, on the profusion of half arches, or horseshoe arches, trilapses, ogee arches, lanceolates, mitrals, quarter arches and curves of arches, in silent promiscuity with neoclassical pilasters, *art nouveau* paneling, internal spandrels, side arches that supported imitation vaults and intrados that had been painted every color of the spectrum and some more besides, a hallucinatory fuchsia opposing itself to the complementary and equally dazzling colors of the denticular ornamentation, shaped like pearls, garlanded, fretted, ring-shaped, of grooving entredos, of meshwork and network, and below festoons and dosserets made of *acajú* that separated the interior friezes or socles which the natives had endeavored to pass off as valances, these last hung with tassels of mauve silk. At the end of the room near the monumental staircase and as though presiding over this formal chaos, erect, with his arm as pale as his pointed little beard, with mongoloid features, dressed in a greatcoat, wearing shoes or a wide cravat, still eloquent or at least gesticulating, standing on a pedestal, was Vladimir Ulitch Ulianov or his marmoreal likeness whom an inscription, also in marble, under the eponymous effigy identified in Cyrillic characters as Lenin. Gazing at candelabra, counting steps of variegated marble, lowering his observant eyes to banisters of calcareous stone, lost among volutes, spirals, curves, foliated ornamentation and the vertical joists of the ironwork of the handrails and balconies, he was dozing off, but not before he had first approached in perpetual astonishment a glaringly obvious Marcel Breuer sofa, in which he buried himself comfortably.

IV

The noise of footsteps on the tiled floor awoke him and he glimpsed through the nets of his dream or of his eyelashes what he thought were buskin boots, then he went on to wonder whether they were sandals or perhaps *huaraches* and finally he saw that they were ordinary shoes composed of sole, together with lining, first sole, welt, inner sole—*cambrera,* as the country people here call it—heel, heel piece, upper and tongue, also known as "ear" in these remote byways of South America. In them a man was walking wrapped in clothes that had the color of old engravings. By his side was another man and he saw that one of them had a thick neck consisting, he suspected, of: hyoid bone, thyrohyoid membrane, thyroid cartilage (concise pronunciation key:), cricoid and thyroid membrane, cricoid and tracheal cartilage, and as he gazed at him with his single eye (he wore an eyeshade over the other in the style of the Princess of Eboli or of, in the future, Moshe Dayan) and knew that it was only one eye that was looking but that this eye was also a functional collection of: cornea, iris, choroid, crystalline lens, sclerotic, superior nasal artery, inferior nasal artery, papilla of the optic nerve, interior temporal artery and macula lutea, and from the yellow stain of this last he knew that the other, at least, saw him in two dimensions but in color.

Of his companion he saw appear no more than an ear and although the unexpected rhyme troubled him not a little he enumerated to dismiss any unpleasant sensation the parts of it that were visible which were the helix, antehelix, cochlea, lobule, tragus and antitragus, a pinna that certainly covered a duct smeared with cerumen, vestibule, tympanum like anvil and hammer, external and medial ear and labyrinth. One of them stretched out his hand to him and he didn't know which (man or hand) it was, but he did know that it was not only hand or man that was greeting him, but: wrist, hypotenary eminence, palm, little, ring, middle and index fingers, thumb and ternary eminence, not to mention tarsus and metatarsus, fingers and any dead ringers (*merde!*), tendons, muscles and protective skin. He raised his hand to return the greeting and when he had finished this gesture he turned it over palm up and saw the lines and zones of logic, instinct, will, intelligence, mysticism, of Jupiter, Saturn, Apollo, Mercury, of Fortune, of heart, of health, of Mars, the lines of the head, the Moon, the life line and the line of Venus, and wondered whether he would have good fortune or not and at the same time whether the red stains localized near his Mount of Venus were warts or tetters.

He could hear that the thugs were talking on the square tiled floor of various warlike subjects and that they were making verbal comments thereon, and he couldn't avoid his old analytic habit of making a synoptic chart for everything that is in this world. So when he heard the word *rifle* he thought of cannon, gunsight, breach, ammunition box, ramrod, bolt, trigger, trigger guard and butt; *bullet*, he knew that it could be made of lead or steel, that it could be incendiary or a tracer, perforated, 4. *Print.* a heavy explosive or for hunting and that they always had a casing of brass, and a nucleus of lead, niter and the fuse; *grenade*, he remembered the firing pin, the safety catch, the washer on the safety catch, the stopper made of an alloy of lead, the detonator and firing mechanism—and not once did the idea come to his mind of what their target was or whether they might be aiming at him. They went on their way and he was left alone again, but not for long because he was soon kept company by the buzzing of an intrusive and aboriginal insect, of which he could discern the following parts: head, faceted eyes, feet (first pair), prothorax, feet (second pair), sting, abdomen, metathorax, notum (noted?), the lower wings, the upper wings and feet (third pair). Could it be a wasp? He felt he suddenly had a transparency of spirit, that his fear was seen as metaphorical and his intentions were thus revealed by his own concealing. From this point to inferring that an intrusive hymenopterum would produce so great an upset and even greater revelations, was no more than one step and that not a wasted or lost step, not a one and a two-step lost but Lot's a trouble because at once they will be brought to associate his phobia with perverse intentions, and they will see that he was a sort of ichneumon, this wasp which in the jungles of the Orinoco hunts tirelessly for its spider, so as to jab its mortal sting into its nucha. Or could it be a bee, queen or worker or drone? To distract himself from the terrors and anxiety of these last considerations, he looked away to the other end of the room, where he observed some banners, but well before he could discern whether they were the initial and orthodox banners of the Party he saw that they were divided, like all banners, into splice, sheath, cloth, stitching, selvedge, pendant tassels, selvedge (the other one), seam and tip, and as it was not a triangular pennant nor a galliard or heraldic colors but a square flag, he knew that it was *the* one, the Venerated, although he couldn't pick out any sickle and crossed hammers on the background which he now saw was blue and not red. Could he have been suffering from Dalton's disease? To test whether this assertion was certain or uncertain (more of these anacoluthic alliterations!) he looked at the four escutcheons dexter and sinister that seemed to guard the flags and before he came to the conclusion that one of them was Spanish, another French, another Polish and the fourth the Swiss Guard, he observed the different quarterings: canton dexter of chief, chief, canton sinister of chief, flank dexter, heart (or abyss), flank sinister, canton dexter of point, point, siege of honor, and he began looking at the navel (of the escutcheon, of the four, four different navels and only one true navel) and went on to note gold or or (fuck!), argent, gules, azure, vert, m., purple, sable, stones which served as base or distinction to: oaks, chains, lashed trees, enguiched cornets, enguled bands, crowns enfiladed, enclaved escutcheons, dentate, quartered, capes, burels, bordured, quartered coats, vairies, chequereds, lozenges, rustres, potences, parties, orles, borders and pumas and eagles rampant and meandering snake.

He was going closer to make out the differences when an usher, aide-de-camp, seneschal, secretary or amanuensis came in and told him that he could go up, that the Master (those were his very words) would receive him, that he was already waiting for him—and he might well have added that patience is a preamble to impatience, or in the proverb of this man's own people: he who hopes loses hope, because he saw (and observed) his pertinent or impertinent grimace. He made a quarter turn exactly over one of the fleurs-de-lis inscribed on the circumference of the central mosaic and went off with the feigned walk of a disciple toward the quarters of the *hereticus maximus*. He went up the flight of steps step by step, stopping a moment to observe that above the balustrade, as an extremity to it, was the handrail and that the veins mixed with slate in the ambered marble coincided with the tiles which veined with slate the marble, also amber, of the staircase, although he had under his feet the red felt carpeting and not the marble steps, on which cord straps and bronze hinges contrasted brilliantly. Opposite him on the first landing he found a suit of armor from the *quattrocento*, complete with visored casque, gorget, pauldron, rerebrace, couter, vambrace, tasse, demi-tasse, poleyn, fauld, greave, cuisse, cuirass, shield (or eschutcheon), and hauberk with a Toledo steel on a shaft of oak wood. But though he paid little attention to the cuirass with its bas-relief moldings or to the ribbed vambrace, he wanted to know whether the casque was an entire helmet or only a morion with a gorget that extended upward, and he went closer to the suit of armor, almost (he was prevented by the wall) went right around it, and saw on drawing closer that the above-mentioned gorget was rather a broad beaver or perforated bassinet with a sort of felt in the visor and he concluded that it was a headpiece rather than a helmet—and as his raincoat got caught on the hauberk, halbert or halbard as it is sometimes called, he remembered that he had to go up sooner or later and challenge his opponent—it was in the midst of making this decision that he was struck by the rose window on the landing. But he summoned his strength to resist this foliated attraction and began climbing the stairs again. Up above he arrived at the entrance, which consisted of a portiere of carefully worked colonial carving, and he saw that the door and with it the frames (or posts), the panels, the framework, moldings and lintel were of Spanish oak and although there was no protective plaque there was in compensation a lock and a door knocker, both in thick bronze with gudgeons of the same alloy, and he ran his historical hand over the protecting moldings before closing a Marxist fist on them and knocking with vigorous nervous knuckles.

V–LV

(SUMMARY OF THE PLOT OR RATHER, BRIEFING

After having reviewed and subsequently made an inventory of the room and all its furnishings and other fixtures, Jacques Mornard shows Lev Davidovitch Trotsky his "discipular stanzas," as Alejo Carpentier calls them, and while the said Master is absorbed in reading them, he succeeds in pulling out his murderous adze—not forgetting to enumerate every one of the anatomical, sartorial, idiosyncratic, personal and political peculiarities of the great dead, because the magnicide—or author—is suffering from an acute case of what is known in French literary circles as Le Syndrome d'Honoré.)

Nicolás Guillén

ELEGIA POR JACQUES MORNARD (EN EL CIELO DE LECUMBERRI)

Era duro y severo
grave la voz tenía
y era de acero
su apostasía.
(Era, no, es,
que todavía que todavía
está el hombre entero.)
Es.
De acero.
De acero es.
¡ Acero!
¡ Eso es!

TROTSKY: ¡Iba yo por un camino cuando con la muerte di!
(Leía la frase "un camino" cuando me dieron a mí.)
MORNARD: No sé por que piensas tú
León Trotsky que te di yo.
Al hacha que tenía yo
diste con tu nuca tú.

Nicholas Guillén

ELEGY FOR JACQUES MORNARD (UNDER THE SKIES OF LECUMBERRI)

He was hard and severe
grave was his voice
and his apostasy
was forged of steel.
(He was, no, he is,
for to this day for to this
day that man still lives.)
He is still
forged of steel.
He's forged of steel.
Of steel!
That's how he is!

TROTSKY: I was goin' 'long a road when I saw Death come up suddenly!
(I was readin' the words "a road" when someone struck me certainly.)

MORNARD: I don't know why you think that I
did strike you, Leon Trotsky, dead.
The hatchet I was holding you
seized and planted in your head.

CORO (Zhdanov, Blas Roca y Duclos):
Stalin gran capitán
que te proteja Changó
y te cuide Yemayá!

TROTSKY: Isla de Prinkipo mía yo quiero tenerte entera
y quiero (cuando me muera)
tener en mi tumba un ramo de hoces y una bandera!

MORNARD: Ve cogiendo ahora tu ramo
de hoces y tus banderas
y no esperes a que mueras:
ya te maté con mi mano.

TROTSKY: Si muero en la carretera
no me pongan flores!
Si pido bortsch con lentejas
no me le echen coles!

MORNARD: No pidas bortsch con lentejas
y olvídate de las flores,
de las hoces y las coles:
no estás en la carretera,
sino en casa de Tenorio
donde hay ya su buen jolgorio
celebrando tu velorio
con un juego de abalorios.

TROTSKY: ¿Muerto yo?

MORNARD: Sí, pues mi hacha te mató
y al que doy por muerto yo
¡no lo salva ni Paré (Ambrosio)!

TROTSKY: ¡Ay, qué imbroglio!
¿Y no hay vida en la otra vida?
Mira que no he completado
de Stalin la biografida.

MORNARD: Lo siento viejo León
Lion, Lowe, Leone, Lev
Davidovich Trotsky né
Bronstein. Estás como Napoleón,
Lenín, Enjels, Carlomar.
Estás más muerto que el Zar:

CHORUS (Zhdanov, Blas Roca and Duclos):
Stalin, great captain,
may Changó protect you
and Yemayá watch over you!

TROTSKY: Island of Prinkipo, I want to possess you entire
and I want (when I expire)
a branch made of sickles and a flag to fly over my grave!

MORNARD: Branch of sickles and flags to wave,
you're going to find them right now
so please don't wait till you've expired:
by my hand you're dead and tired.

TROTSKY: If I should die upon the road
on my grave I want no flowers!
If I ask for borsch and lentils
please don't give me cauliflower!

MORNARD: Do not ask for borsch and sickles,
and forget 'bout caulis and flowers,
you are not dead upon the road
but down in Blue Beria
's office with its cork-lined walls
and skeleton-closeted halls
where everyone will have a ball
drinking toasts to your downfall
and dance mazurkas at a call
—before they're sent to Siberia.

TROTSKY: Me dead?

MORNARD: Yes, since my hatchet's done you in,
and when I kill a man not even
Paré (Ambrosius) can reprieve 'im!

TROTSKY: Ah! It's too damn bad you intruded.
Is there no life the other side?
Listen, I've not yet concluded
Jo Stalin's biographicide.

MORNARD: I sure am sorry, old boy, Leon,
Lion, Lowe, Leone, Lev
Davidovitch Trotsky né
Bronstein. You've hit the dirt
like Lenin, Engels or Bonapart.
You're as dead as the long gone Czar:

Kaputt tot, dead difunto
mandado pal otro mundo,
ñampiado, mort, morto profundo.
Diste la patada al cubo.

TROTSKY: ¿Y quien habla, macanudo?
MORNARD: Tú. Es decir, tu in-cubo.
TROTSKY: ¿Y esa luz?
MORNARD: Es un sirio funerario.
TROTSKY: ¿Y esta voz?
MORNARD: Es un turco literario.
TROTSKY: ¿Sirio? ¿Turco?
¿De qué hablas, insensato?
MORNARD: Bueno, *cirio, truco.*
(¡Este viejo literato!)
VOZ: Haciendo tu biografía
teniendo tan pocos datos
no esperes ortografía.
TROTSKY: ¿Y este otro interlocutor?
MORNARD: Isaac Deustcher, el doctor.
TROTSKY: Por favor,
que no entre, que me muero.
Me muero, sí. Es mejor
morirse de cuerpo entero
que quedar para profeta
sin greyes ni escopeta
y en la testa un agujero.
¡Muero!
(*Muere al darle una zapateta.*)
CORO (Deustcher, Julian Gorkin y Gambetta,
que ha venido por la rima y el entierro):
A llorar a Papá Montero!
Zumba, canalla rumbero!
Ese Trotsky fue un socialero.
Zumba, canalla rumbero!
A Pepe le dio con el cuero.
Zumba, canalla rumbero!
Y Yugaz vil le hizo un agujero.
¡Zumba, canalla, rumbero!
(*Exeunt all except Hamlet.*)

kaputt, muerto, bumped off, defunct,
you're making tracks for another world,
worms are crawling thru your head.
Moreover you've kicked the bucket,
so you're tot, mort, morto, dead.

TROTSKY: What the fuck was that you said?

MORNARD: You, not me. Your alter ego said it.

TROTSKY: And what's this light you've just lit?

MORNARD: It's a funeral caper.

TROTSKY: And that voice?

MORNARD: It's a literary vice.

TROTSKY: Vice? And before, caper?

MORNARD: O.K., *taper*, then, *device*, not vice.
(These old literary guys!)

VOICE: Writing your damned biography
with little known or no data
don't expect orthography:
you just put up with errata.

TROTSKY: And who's this interlopercutor?

MORNARD: Isaac Deustcher, a so-called doctor.

TROTSKY: Please make sure he doesn't fetter
me, who is almost dead.
No, I'm dead already. It's better
to die completely than become
a prophet without flock or gun
and a big hole in my head.
I'm dying, CCCP, dying!
(*As he dies his limbs start dancing a corrido.*)

CHORUS (Deustcher, Julian Gorkin and Gambetta,
who came along to rhyme with better):
Let's cry for Papa Troki the brave
and dance until dawn on his grave!
He was a socialist hero and brave.
(We'll dance until dawn on his grave!)
Only himself he's unable to save.
(But we'll dance until dawn on his grave!)
His head was bashed in by Yugaz, that slave.
(And we'll dance until dawn on his grave!)
(*Exeunt all except Hamlet.*)

HAMLET (En realidad es Stalin con peluca rubia, calzas, jubón y en sus manos un bogey bear u oso ruso):

Ah, si este sólido Trotsky
pudiera derretirse, fundirse
y luego convertirse en Rocío . . .
Perdón, en rocío.
(*Entonando de nuevo*)
Cuan vanas, vacías, ostentosas e inútiles
se muestran a mi vista las prácticas todas de Malthus . . .
(*Con hastío*)

¿No habrá otra manera de librarse de ese canalla, traidor, infame, etc., sin disfrazarse ni tener que recitar tales sandeces?

HAMLET (*In actual fact it is Stalin wearing a blond wig, trunk hose, a doublet and holding a Russian or bogey bear in his hands*):
Oh, that this too too solid Trotsky
would melt, thaw and resolve himself
into a Jew . . .
Pardon, a dew.
(*Continues*)
How weary, stale, flat and unprofitable
seem to me all the practices of Malthus . . .
(*With disgust*)
Is there no other manner of ridding myself of this villain, traitor, slave, etc., without disguising myself or reciting such stupid lines?

Translated by Earl Russell Browder

At this moment, as though it were a play by Shawkspear and not by V. I. Vishinsky, the voice of Molotov is heard first far off and then close at hand, or vice versus:

Extra! EXTRA! MORNARD KILLS TROTSKY! Read all about it! Pics and details inside! Extra! Extra! Read all about it!

The voice is hoarse and sounds African but Stalin recognizes it as the voice of Molotov and not of Bebo the news vendor on 23rd and 12th. He removes his disguise (Stalin, not Bebo or Molotov and certainly not Trotsky) and runs off, happy and naked, down the corridors of the Kremlin. In the distance he starts jumping up and down: someone has left some thumbtacks on the floor. Cries are heard of:

Kamenev! Zinoviev! Rykov!

(They are the dirtiest words in the Russian language aside from Trotsky.)

Then:

Parallel Center United by Nails!

A purge! A purge! A purge!

Lady Macbeth (the one from the district of Msknz) enters rubbing her hands (it is cold) and sleepwalking. Her hair is tied up in a Slavic topknot and she is carrying a bottle of castor oil on her head. Taking advantage of a momentary thaw, she stops rubbing her hands and draws from her breast the complete works of Marx, Engels and Lenin, a magnifying glass and a teaspoon. She puts the books on the floor, succeeds in making a fire of them with the aid of the magnifying glass and the Russian midnight sun and warms the castor oil over it. Then she tries, without success, to give a spoonful of the purgative to Stalin, who wrestles with her, stamps his foot, frees himself and runs off through the Kremlin, shouting still more obscenities which a secretary by his side jots down in a treatise on linguistics. In the tumult which follows, the ghost of Lunacharsky appears from doors, corridors, walls and cupboards with the ghost of Radek by his side calling him "Lupanarsky, Lupanarsky," while he is telling a counterrevolutionary joke to the ghosts of Arnold and Piatakov (on his other or right side):

"Socialism in one country! It won't be long before we have Socialism in one *street!*"

Piatakov and Arnold laugh, but the ghost of Bukharin, who has crept up behind them, warns him:

"Watch out, Radek, that little joke has cost you your life once already!"

Arnold, Piatakov and other lesser ghosts disappear discreetly and leave Radek, who continues imperturbably to tell his infra-Red jokes to himself, at the same time turning his head every now and then to shout "Lupanarsky" over his shoulder to no effect (on the shoulder, not Lupanarsky, who trots off with his tail between his legs).

In less time than it takes to say Obedinennoe Gosudarstvennoe Policheskoe Uprardenie, the corridors of the Kremlin are filled with tens, with thousands, with millions (a hundred or so) of political phantoms. Above the whispering of the ghosts Stalin's obscenities can be heard (in Georgian now) accompanied by the complaints of Yugazbilly the Kid in Interprole, the idiom of the international proletariat:

"Would that Trotskyism had only one head!"

"My premiership for a pale horse!"

"Liberty, how many statutes have been erected in thy name!"

"Etcetera!"

CHORUS (Aragon, Éluard, Siquieros, Sholokhov and Brecht accompany Guillén):

Stalin!
Great Captain!
May Shango protect you
and Jemaja watch over you.
Of course they will!
Just like I'm telling you!

The voice of Arsenio Cué on the reality of the tape recorder or of parody shouts, in a loud voice, What the fuck are you saying, that's not Guillén and Silvestre's voice can be heard, and Rine Leal's, phantasmal, in the background, and my own voice, superimposed on each other, but the voice of Bustrófedon is heard no more and this was all that Bustrófedon wrote if this could be called writing although if Origen (Silvestre's suggestion) and Early Stanley Gardner (my own modest contribution) had done the same twenty centuries late, then why not him? But I don't believe that he had the intention of *writing* (Arsenio Cué's italics) at all but rather to teach Cué himself a lesson by absolutely refusing to write a single line however much Silvestre insisted and at the same time to point out to S. that C. was wrong—even if he was wrong also—and that literature is no more important than conversation and that neither of them are more important than the other and that being a wrighter is the same as being a reeder as B. called them and that both was nothing to write home (or anywhere else) about, after all or before nothing. Although Bustrófedon had said very plainly on this and on other occasions that the only possible literature was written on walls (increment out of excrement), when Silvestre said that he had already said just that thing and that he had written an essay with that title (B. excreted on him ferociously when he said it and explained him exactly what the similarities and differences could and should be between essay and assail and hustle and asshole) Bustrófedon said that he was talking about the walls of public conveniences, men's or gents', bogs, W.C.s, johns, cans, loos, escusados, shit or pisshouses and he gave a recitation of his analectasy or selected pieces of Faecetiae (recited, of course, by Arsenio Cué) such as In these old and 'allowed 'alls/ Use the paper not the walls or My mother made me a homosexual—if I buy her some wool will she make me one too? Or Here's no place to snore or slumber/ Piss and shit and fart like thunder/ Or Lawrence was a dune bugger/ Or I am 7 inches long and 2 round—that's O.K. but what size is your cock? Or those little ads with their microscopic print which promise to Cure gonorrhea, soft sores and syphilis EVEN *OVER* 20 YEARS. We assure you Complete Pripacy and also an *Instant Curé* (de campagne?) or the posters against Testicular Debility or Lack of Virility? Impotence? Monosexuality? Visit *Dr. Arce's Institute of Sexology*—Modern Scientific Methods—CULS GUARANTEED and after all this the colophon written by hand: a hand job: If you can't get an erection/ Try our friendly persuation. The other, B. was saying now, the other literature should be written on the air, in other words you make it simply by talking, if you want my advoice, or if you are concerned with your posteriorty, he was saying, you should record it on tape, so, and then rub it out, so (doing the two things that very day, with the exception of the specimens above) and so everyone remains happy. Everyone? I'm not so sure. The rest of the tape is taken up with the noises which is what we all have been of Bustrófedon: Cué, at least, says with some authority that these garblings, rumblings, scratches, gratings and scrapings are what is generally known as parasite noises.

Bustrófedon really didn't write anything more, if we discount the memoirs he left under the bed with a chamberpot as paperweight. Silvestre made me a present of them and here they are without so much as a comma or colon missing. I believe that to a certain extent (as S. would say) they are important.

SOME REVELATIONS

A joke? And what else was the life of Bustrófedon if not that? A joke? A joke within a joke? In that case, gentlemen, it's a grave matter. And the problems he set Silvestre, driving him to the point of despair (Silvestre S. De Spair, who told him You are the Capablanca of invisible writing. How come? asked Bustrófedon. Did he play on an all-white board with chessmen made of ivory towers? No, said Rine laughing, instead of square 64 he preferred 69! Not at all, serious Silvestre answered seriously because he couldn't allow a joke when he was talking gravely or vied versa. He wanted to make the so-called game-science more difficult because it seemed to him too much a game and too little a science or vice versatz, and Bustro, who said, It's just that I'm a Capablanca who watches the chessmen playing by themselves: I write with sympathetic ink), and the subsequent delight of Bust, who seemed like a jockey in a steeplechase race (words which bugged this Eddie Arcaro of the dictionary, as did phrases like the desert of the Sahara and Fujiyama mountain or the city of Leningrad, which always bugged him like crazy whenever somone said them, except when he said them himself which seemed to relieve him), or rather: he himself was the master/designer of literary obstacles and he proposed then a literature in which the words would mean exactly what the whim of the author decided, so that all he needed to do was to state in a prologue at the beginning that whenever he wrote night one should read day or when he said black one should assume he meant red or blue or colorless or white and if he stated that a certain character was a woman the reader should understand man by it and after the book had been written he would suppress the prologue (at this point Silvestre always did a running jump: salto alto, Sp.) before publishing it or he would stick other letters on the typewriter at random (this phrase typewriter at random would delight B. if he read it, I'm quite certain) and then type out these words: skw flowjns woda. ¿2/ ;qwertyuiop?%==+Ñ−***"1££&$) ("' !!!!!¿¿¿¿Z or long for a book written entirely back to front, so that the last word became the first and vice verses, and now that I know that Bus has taken a trip to the other world, to his opposite, to his negative, to his anti-self, to the other side of the mirror, I think that he will read this page as he'd always have wanted to: thus:

A joke? And what else was the life of Bustrófedon if not that? A joke? A joke within a joke? In that case, gentlemen, it's a grave matter. And the problems he set Silvestre, driving him to the point of despair (Silvestre S. De Spair, who told him You are the Capablanca of invisible writing. How come? asked Bustrófedon. Did he play on an all-white board with chessmen made of ivory towers? No, said Rine laughing, instead of square 64 he preferred 69! Not at all, serious Silvestre answered seriously because he couldn't allow a joke when he was talking gravely or vied versa. He wanted to make the so-called game-science more difficult because it seemed to him too much a game and too little a science or vice versatz, and Bustro, who said, It's just that I'm a Capablanca who watches the chessmen playing by themselves: I write with sympathetic ink), and the subsequent delight of Bust, who seemed like a jockey in a steeplechase race (words which bugged this Eddie Arcaro of the dictionary, as did phrases like the desert of the Sahara and Fujiyama mountain or the city of Leningrad, which always bugged him like crazy whenever somone said them, except when he said them himself which seemed to relieve him), or rather: he himself was the master\designer of literary obstacles and he proposed then a literature in which the words would mean exactly what the whim of the author decided, so that all he needed to do was to state in a prologue at the beginning that whenever he wrote night one should read day or when he said black one should assume he meant red or blue or colorless or white and if he stated that a certain character was a woman the reader should understand man by it and after the book had been written he would suppress the prologue (at this point Silvestre always did a running jump: salto alto, Sp.) before publishing it or he would stick other letters on the typewriter at random (this phrase typewriter at random would delight B. if he read it, I'm quite certain) and then type out these words: skw flowjns woda. ¿2/ ;qwertyuiop?%==+Ñ−***"12£&$) ("" !!!!!¿¿¿¿Z or long for a book written entirely back to front, so that the last word became the first and vice verses, and now that I know that Bus has taken a trip to the other world, to his opposite, to his negative, to his anti-self, to the other side of the mirror, I think that he will read this page as he'd always have wanted to: thus:

And his Geometrics of the Spirit in which a spiral terminating in an arrow is the sign for a geometric nightmare, in many arrows in vectors which always bring one back to the center (risotorna vincitore, B would sing), compulsively-convulsively, like a lifer, while the line of the spiral retreats continually under one's feet, like a helix? And his sign for geometric happiness: a circle, a glossy sphere, or better still: a crystal ball, and his sign for serene stupidity: a square, and for primitive and mobile solidity (a geometrical rhinoceros, he called it): a trapezium, and for obsession: a simple spiral, and for neurosis: a double spiral, and for

brevity: a period
continuity: a line
origins: an ovoid
fidelity: an ellipse
psychosis: excentric circles?

And his proposal that first thing in the morning Unesco should be renamed Ionesco? President: Marx, Groucho. Secretary General: Raymond Queneau. Members: Harpo Marx (or his statue), W. C. Fields, Dick Tracy and the vis-president of Viscose, Mr. L. Aztec. And the tragicomedy of AA, as he called it, when Antonin Artaud met his apotheosis in Mexico, which was at Tenhampa or at Guadalajara-de-Noche and the band of mock-mariachis greeted every customer in turn and were really living it up, and one of the group, Fernandel Toro, said to the guitarist, The gentleman here's the great French poet Antonin Artaud, and when the mariachero went back to his group, Fernandel shouted out: Hermano, let's give him one from Jalisco! and the Mexican, pulling down the brim of his sombrero and smoothing his enormous Zapata mustaches, screamed at the top of his voice over the uproar and downroar, and all the drunk tequila, Damas y caballeros, we have the pleasure of dedicating our next number to the great French poet who is here among us tonite, honoring us with his presence: EL GRAN TOTONÁN TOTÓ!, and he Bustrofinished by saying that Groucho Marx and Quevedo and Perelman were so much alike they had to be different people! Ampersend?

Bally Dancers

Alicia Marxova
Alice Wonderlova
Marx Platonoff
Vaslav Vijinsky
Nishinski
Jules Supermansky
Isadore Drunkasse
Adella Mort
Margo Fountainpen
Pat Dedeux
Ruth de Loukin-Glass
Sue-Anne Lake
La Passionaria
Jack d'Angoisse
Hilda Capo
Joe Lemon
Shirt Villeya
Ussrlanova
La Boyassianna
Rudolf Vagentina

Authors of Poperas

Strauss & Strauss & Strauss
Rodgers & Hart
Rodgers & Hammerstein
Rodgers & Rodgers
Rodgers & Trigger
Leopold & Loeb
Rosencrantz & Guildenstern
Boyassian & Mammassian
France Les Halles
Vincent Yahooman
David Ricardo Strauss
George Gehrswing
Call Porter!
Oftenback
Jerome Kern Jerome
RCA Victor Herbert
Offend Bach
Irving West-Berlin
Silver & Gullivant
Tinkers & Evers (& Chance)

Copywrighters

True Person
Water Lilliput
James Reston Peace
Theo Ligarchy
Nails Hardener
Herbal Mathé
Daily Carnage
Urban Clearway
Bruce Lipps
Barry Kaids
Art Buchenwald
Joseph Awfulsop
Jack MacRaker
Shirley Boyassian
Anna Coluthon
A. Pancho Lyse
Dick Takenaback
Hellin Laurelsong
Waltered Winches
Cliff Anger

Famous In Books (or In Famous Books)

Crime and Puns, by Bustrofedor Dostowhiskey
Under the Lorry, by Malcolm Volcano
Comfort of the Season, by Gore Vidal Sassoon
In Caldo Brodo, by Truman Capone
Against Impenetration, by Su Sanstag
The Company She Peeps, by Merrimac Arty
Mutter Carajo!, by Bert Oldbitch
By Left Possessed, by Lord Brussell
Ruined Vision, by Stephen Spent
Troubles with My Cant, by Green Grams

Philosuffers

Aristocrates
Empiricles
Antipaster
Presocrates
Ludwig Offerbach
Luftwaffe Feuer-Bang
Marxcuse
Ortega and Gasset
Julius Marx
Giordano Brulé
Des Carter
S. Boyassian-Mamassian
Lysergicus
Sophocrates
Duns Scotlandiard
Lao Tse-tung
Phlato
Abelard & Helloise
Platinus
Unomono

Musickians

Sans-Sense
Wanter Pistol
Artur Blitz
Ephrem Timbalist
Igor Stavisky
Handels Messiaens
Rhythmic Kossackov
Demeter Pumpkin
Aaron Copuland
Cecilia Chorus van Antwerp
Laurence de Rabbia
Yehudi Minuet
Ladonna Oldsmobile
Doremy Fazoll
Siberius
Morris Rebel
Wonderland Dowski
S. B. Mamasian
Hector Bidet
Proto Iliac Chachaicovski

Arstits

Whistler
Singer
Remembrandt
Le Murillo
El Grotto
Picabbio
Lenin Riefenstahlin
Vincent Bang Ugh
Bob Motheriswell
Anti Warhole
Silver Dalli
Edgas
Mizarro
Purillo
Uccillo
Sophonisba Angusciola
Gioya
Uffizi
Sargent
& Constable

Immentionables

Menasha Troy (in Canada)
Shiram Boyasian Mamasian (in Cuba)
Cuca Valiente (in Venezuela)
Concha Espina (in Uruguay)
Chao Ping-ah (in Cuba)
Nora Condom (in Cuba, Spain and the USSR)
Walter Piston (in the USSR)
W. C. Fields (in the USA)
Lev Davidovitch Bronstein (in the USSR)
Ervana Cacanova (in Ancient Rome)
Sean Connery (in France)
Shiram Boyasian Mamasian (in Cuba)
Lucille Ball (in Harvard)
Ernest K. Gann (in Spain, Cuba, Mexico and Argentina)
Dmitri Tiomkin (in Tanglewood)
Felo Bergaza (in Mexico)
Giovanni Verga (in Mexico)
and Shiram Boyasian Mamasian (in Cuba)

And what he and Silvestre called The Blaster Cast, with a thousand irrepeatable & unrecallable names? Ah: BUT NO: stop: basta: whoa: it's tooo much. And, my God, to think that all this, all this (and seven too) has died up there in the opera, operating theater, where he deceased to exist (and to be or not to be and to think, and to cast a shadow?), the Great Totonán Totó, Dalai, the Mostest, and that the doctor, that vampire, would never have the satisfaction of knowing what would happen when he gave back what was left of B. to the others, to the vultures or next of kind, to the century, like a Doctor Frankenstein in reverse. But (but: this word, *but,* always ends by coming in between) later during the autopsy or butchery (because they even laid him out on a marble slab), in the camera obscura of revelations, the doctor knew there that he had his practical reasons, that his pedantic prognosis (or proboscis) was certain and that was the only thing Oldfucker was sure of. As for me, an anonymous scribe of latterday hieroglyphs, I could tell you something else, I could tell you this one last thing : he opened Him up (I no longer have even the and Up Him Closed and Him at looked and)name His say to right he didn't see Him: he saw *nothing*—because he never knew, but a just was table dissecting the on was there all that, never sewing machine and an umbrella *full stop*

Eighth session

I dreamed that I was an earthworm, pink all over, and that I was going to visit my mother in her house on Calle Empedrado and I was going up the stairs, but I was walking upright, on my feet like I always walk, and nobody seemed surprised. I went up the stairs and although it was daytime it was very dark and on one of the landings there was a black worm who raped me. Afterward I was on a stone in the middle of a river with my little worms and they were all pink like me, except for one little worm who had black spots and who was also the one most attached to me. I gave him a shove with my tail but he came back and I kept on shoving him. I wanted to keep him away from the other worms and he looked at me with such a sad little face, but the more unhappy he looked the more angry I became. Suddenly I gave him a big shove and I pushed him into the water.

I HEARD HER SING

Bustrófedon died yesterday, or is it today?

Is life a concentric chaos? I don't know, all I know is my life was a nocturnal chaos with a single center that was Las Vegas and in the center of the center there was a glass of rum and water or rum and ice or rum and soda and that's where I was from twelve o'clock on, and I turned up just as the first show was finishing and the emcee was thanking his charming and wonderful audience for coming and inviting them to stay for the third and last show of the night and the band was striking up its theme song with a lot of noise and nostalgia, like a circus brass band but changing from the umpa-pa to the two-four or six-eight beat of a *charanga* trying out a melody: the noise of a ragtime band coming on like a Kostelanetz string orchestra, something which depresses me even more than knowing I'm already talking like Cué and Eribó and all the other six million soloists of this island called Tuba and while I'm rubbing the glass in my hands and digressing that sober little man who sits inside me and speaks so low nobody but me can hear him tells me I'm losing my footing and as that genie of the bottle I am has just said very softly now *Cuba,* and Hey presto! there she was greeting me, popping out of nowhere to say, Hi there honey and at the same time giving me a kiss just there where the cheek meets the neck and I looked in the mirror, mirror on the wall (of bottles) and I saw Cuba, every inch of her, bigger and more beautiful and sexier than ever and she was smiling at me so I turned around and put my arm around her waist, And how're you Cuba baby, I said and I kissed her and she kissed me back and said, Be-au-ti-ful, and I didn't know if she was okaying the kisses she was testing with that sex sense she carries on the tip of her tongue or if she was extolling her soul, as Alex Bayer would say, because her body sure didn't need any padding. Or maybe she was simply glowing over the evening and our chance meeting.

I left the bar and we went over to a table but first she borrowed some change from me for the jukebox which was already playing none other than her "Sad Encounter" which is her theme song just as this music-killing band's is "The Music Goes Round 'n' Round," and we sat down. What are you doing here so early, I asked and she said, Didn't you know dear I'm singing now in the Mil Novecientos and I'm their star dear and I don't care what you say what matters is what they pay me and I'm sick and tired of the Sierra, and here I'm at the center of everything and I can get away to the San Yon or the Gruta or where I feel like between shows and that's what I'm doing now, capeesh? Sure I understand, you are the center of my chaos now Cuba I was thinking but I didn't say it though she knew what I meant because I was fondling her tits right there in the ultraviolet darkness where shirts and blouses turn into the shrouds of a pale ghost and faces turn a deep purple or can't be seen at all or else they look like wax it depends on their complexion or race or what drinks and where people slip away from one table to another and you see them crossing the dance floor deserted now and being first in one place and then another and doing the same thing in both, in other words making love, or *matarse* which means making death, a much better word because they were lethally exciting themselves to death and these gauche movements from one table to another changing company but not jobs made me think we were in a fish bowl, all of us, including me, though I thought, believed, allowed myself the luxury of thinking it was the others who were the fish in the bowl and suddenly we were all fish so I decided to drown myself, plunging into Cuba's cleavage, her melons coming out on their own from her blouse to surface to the open market, diving under her armpits left unshaved a la Silvana Mangano I think or a la Sofia Loren or some other star of the Italian screen, swimming, ducking under, totally immersed in her and suddenly I thought I was the Captain Cousteau of night waters.

And then I raised my face and saw an enormous fish, a galleon navigating underwater, a submarine of flesh that stopped short of colliding with my table and sending it sinking to the surface. Hey there baby said a voice deep and bass and shipwrecked as my own. It was La Estrella and I remembered when Vítor Perla, may he rest in peace, no, no, he's not dead but the doctor ordered him to go to bed early or he'd never get up again, I remembered that he knew what he was saying when he said that La Estrella was the Black Whale and I thought that one night she must have appeared to him just as she did to me now, and I said, High Estrella, and I don't know if it slipped out or if I just said it, the fact was she began lurching and swaying and she placed one of her hands like a black tablecloth on my table and recovered her balance again and said to me, as she always does, La, La La and for a moment I thought she was just warming up the tuba of her throat but she was correcting me so I said always willing to oblige, Yes *La* Estrella and she let out such a bellow of laughter it stopped the people in mid-table and I think it even froze the jukebox in mid-turntable and when she got tired of laughing she went off and I have to say that neither she nor Cuba had exchanged so much as a word because they weren't on speaking terms, I suppose because a singer who sings without music never speaks to someone whose singing is all music or more music backing that is than singing and with apologies to her friends who are also my friends Cuba reminds me of Olga Guillotine, who is the favorite singer of all those people who like artificial flowers and satin dresses and nylon-covered furniture: the fact is I like Cuba for other reasons than her voice anything but her voice definitely not her voice but for visual reasons, for the eye has reasons that the ear never knows, for reasons that not only can be seen but can be touched and smelled and tested, something that can't be done with a voice or perhaps only with one voice, with the voice of La Estrella, which is the voice that nature jokingly preserves in the excrescence of its pupa of flesh and fat and water. Am I still being unfair, Alex Bayer, alias Alexis Smith?

It was dancing time and I was falling all over the floor in rhythm and the voice I was holding in my arms was saying between giggling fits, You're pretty far gone, you know and I looked hard at her and saw it was Irmita and I wondered where Cuba had gone to but I didn't wonder how I came to be dancing with Irenita, I-re-ni-ta, Irenita that's her name, Irena if it really is her name and not an alias because I'm like Switzerland surrounded by allies and it was Irenita who said, You're going to fall over and it was the truth, I noticed it the moment I was telling myself, She must have come out from under the table, yes, that's where she comes from because she was always under the table where she fits very neatly but does she fit? She isn't as tiny as all that and I don't know why I had thought she was so tiny because she comes up to my shoulders and has a perfect body, perhaps her thighs or what you can see of her thighs are not so perfect as her teeth or what you, me I mean, can see of her teeth and I hope she's not going to invite us both to laugh together because I've no wish to see her thighs as far back as I've seen her teeth when she laughed and showed me her missing molar, but she had the cutest and best figure I've seen and the face of a swinger and her face was the mirror of her body missing molar excepted and I forgot about Cuba completely, totally, absolutely. But I couldn't forget La Estrella because she didn't let me. A great uproar exploded in the submerged cathedral, that is to say in the back room, and everybody was running toward it and we ran too. On the sofa near the entrance, next to the door, in the darkest corner of the room was an enormous black shadow shaking and roaring and falling on the floor and heaving it back onto the sofa and It was La Estrella, helplessly drunk and throwing a fit of crying and shouting and raving and as I went to see what was the matter with her I stumbled over one of her shoes lying on the floor and I fell on top of her and when she saw it was me she folded her Doric columns around me and held me tight and then she was giving me a missing molar with her crying, hugging me and saying, Ah *negro* it's hurting me, it's really hurting and I thought there was something in her body hurting and I asked her and she repeated it's hurting me, it really hurts and I asked her what it was that was hurting and she said, Ah *mulato* he's dead he's dead and she was crying and not saying who or what was dead and I managed to free myself and then she cried out, My little son and finally she said, He's died! Ay how I miss him! and she fell to the floor and stayed here and looked as though she had died herself, or passed out but she was only asleep because she began snoring as loud as she'd been shouting and I slipped away from the group, come on all together now, which was still trying to lift her back onto the sofa and I groped my way toward the door and went out. I missed La Estrella as much as you miss a missing molar when it's still there and it hurts.

I walked the whole length of Infanta and when I got to 23rd I met up with this moveable coffee vendor who's always around and he offered me a cup and I said, No thanks I have to drive and it really was because I didn't want any coffee because I wanted to stay drunk and go around drunk and live drunk all my life which is the same as saying I wanted to drink myself to life. And as I didn't want just one coffee I took three and I got talking with the portable vendor and he told me that he worked nights from eleven to seven up and down La Rampa and I thought that's why we never run into each other because it's the same time I do my Rampa beat and I asked him how much he made and he told me 75 pesos a month no matter what he sold and that every day or rather night he sold between 100 and 150 cups of coffee and he told me, This, tapping his Goliath of a thermos with his David of a hand, makes about 300 pesos a month and I'm not the only vendor and it all goes to the boss. I don't know what I said to him about his missing molar of a boss because now I was drinking not coffee but a rum on the rocks not the beach rocks as you might imagine but bar rocks and I thought I would phone Magalena and when I got into the phone booth I remembered I didn't have her number but then I saw a whole telephone directory written over the walls and I selected a number because in any case I had already inserted a coin and I dialed it and waited while the phone rang and rang and rang and finally I heard a man's voice very weak and tired say Hello? and I said, Is that you, Hellen? and the man replied in his voice that wasn't a voice, No, señor and I asked him Who then, her sister? and he said, Hello hello and I said Ah so you're a double Hellen, and he said, almost screaming, What's the idea, waking people up at this time of the night! and I told him to go fuck his missing molar and hung up and picked up my fork and began cutting up my steak very carefully and I heard music behind me and there was a girl singing and lingering over the words and showing off her missing molar and it was this queen of musical suspense Natalia Gut (iérrez was her real name) singing a version of "Perfidia" that sounded like "Porphyria," and I realized I was in Club 21 eating a T-bone steak and when I eat I sometimes have this habit of suddenly lifting my right hand so the sleeve of my shirt can disentangle itself from the sleeve and from the food and fall backward and when I lifted my arm a searchlight blinded me and I heard them saying a name which turned out to be my professional name and I stood up and people were applauding me, many people, an audience, but the light on my face went out and it hit a table several tables away and then someone said another name and I was eating the same steak but in a different place because I was in the Tropicana but not only do I not know how I got there whether on foot or in my car or whether they took me there and not only that but I no longer know if all this happened the same night and the emcee is continuing to present the guests as though the place was full of celebrities and fuck it! somewhere or other in the world there must be an original for this shitty parody, in Hollywood I bet, a word that gives me a missing molar, not only to pronounce but even to think of and I get up to go out and fall into the missing table between two tables and with the help of the captain of waiters I reach the patio and give him a military salute and say permission to go overboard sir, before going off, permission granted.

I return to the city and the cool night breeze makes me see the streets again and I reach La Rampa and continue along it and turn the corner into Infanta and park near Las Vegas, which is closed and there are two cops at the door and I ask them what's up and they tell me there's been trouble and ask me to keep moving pronto and I say I'm a reporter and they come on friendly and tell me they've arrested Lalo Vegas, the owner, because they've just discovered he's been pushing drugs, *Just?* C'mon, show me your missing molar I ask one of the cops and he laughs and tells me, Please *periodista* don't give us a hard time and I tell him there aren't any hard times telling him *No hay problema* just that and I go on my way past Infanta and Humboldt, on foot, and I come to a dark passage where there are some garbage cans and I can hear a song rising from the garbage cans and I walk around and around them to see which garbage can is singing so I can introduce her to her wonderful one-man audience and I go from one garbage can to another and then I realize that the honey-toned or honky-tonked words are rising from the ground, from among the scraps of food and filthy bits of paper and old papers which make a missing molar out of the words Sanit. Dept. written on these cans and I see that underneath the papers there's an iron grille on the sidewalk which must be the air vent of some joint down there under the street or in a basement or maybe it's the musical circle of hell, and I hear piano music and cymbals playing and a slow moist clinging bolero and then some applause and more music and another song and I stay there listening and feeling the music and the rhythm and the words climbing the legs of my pants and flowing into my body and when it stopped I realized that what was coming through this grille was the warm air pushed up by the air-conditioning of the Mil Novecientos and I turn the corner and go down the red staircase: the walls are painted red, the steps covered with red carpeting and the handrail striped red velvet and I shift toward the red to plunge down into the music and the noise of glasses and the smell of alcohol and the smoke and sweat and rainbow lights flooding the place and the people and I hear the famous finale of that bolero that goes "*Lights and liquor and lips/ Our night of love has ended/ Adiós adiós adiós*" which is one of Cuba Venegas' songs and I see her bowing all elegant and beautiful and dressed in sky blue from tits to toes and bowing again and displaying those great rounded half-uncovered breasts of hers that are like the lids of two marvelous stewing pots under which is bubbling the only food that makes men into gods, femmebrosia, and I'm happy to see her bowing and smiling and that her incredible body is swaying and that she's throwing back her breastaking head and above all that she's not singing anymore tonight because it's better, much much better to see Cuba than to hear her and it's better because anyone who sees Cuba falls in love with her but anyone who hears and listens to her can never love her again because her voice is her missing molar.

Ninth session

Didn't I tell you I'm a widow? I married Raúl, the boy who invited me to the party. His whole family was at the wedding, which we had in Jesús de Miramar, and the church was full of society people and I went dressed in white and as it was a *misa de velaciones* ceremony my fiancé remained under my veil while they were saying Mass and he kept on looking and looking at me, he was so nervous. He got married to me when he found out that I was—how shall I put it, doctor?—that I was . . . You remember the story I told you about his brother, the one who kept a skeleton in his bathtub? Well, after that night he came to look for me one day at drama school and we went out together several times and we became pretty intimate and in the end I got, I was pregnant. His name was, and still is, Arturo and he refused to have anything to do with me after that so I went to see his brother Raúl and told him everything and there and then he decided to marry me and that's how we got married. But on the wedding night, we went off to spend our honeymoon in Varadero, in his parents' house which they had left us to be alone in, and his father had given him a new car as a wedding present. On the wedding night he stayed up talking to me very late and when I went up to bed he stayed downstairs alone, saying he'd come up later. I was waked up three hours later by the phone ringing, someone from the police who told me that he had had a car accident. He hovered between life and death for three days and then he died. The first thing he did when he recovered consciousness in the hospital, after the accident, was to say my name, but he didn't say anything else though during his delirium he said a number of things and words that nobody could understand. I told his family that he had gone out to find me something to eat and that that was why he was out on the road so late. There were two things I couldn't explain very well though: that he had gone out to the street when the house was full of food and what he was doing on the main highway to Havana two hours later. His family always treated me very coldly afterward, but they were very kind when my daughter was born and even more kind when two years later they succeeded in taking her away from me to New York by telling the judge I was leading the immoral life of an actress. The child had the same face as Raúl but this time in the right body.

I HEARD HER SING

Now that it's raining, now that I have to look at the city lost in the smoke of the pouring rain, this city somewhere behind the vertical mist on the other side of my office window, yes, now that it's raining I remember La Estrella. Because the rain erases the city but it cannot erase memory and I remember La Estrella's hour of glory as I also remember when she fell from glory and where and how. I don't go to the nitecaves, as La Estrella called the nightclubs, any longer because the censorship has been lifted and they have moved me from the entertainment supplement to the front page and I spend my time taking pictures of political prisoners and bombs and Molotov cocktails and dead bodies the police leave lying where they fell to serve as an example, as though the dead were able to stop any other time than their own, and I'm again on night beat but it's downbeat.

I stopped seeing La Estrella I don't know for how long and I hadn't heard anything about her until the day I saw the copy about her opening at the Capri and I don't know to this day how her quantity of humanity had managed to make this great leap forward in quality. Someone told me an American impresario had heard her in Las Vegas or the Bar Celeste or at the corner of 0 and 23rd and had made a contract with her, I don't know, all I did know was her name was in the paper, my *own* newspaper, and I read it twice because I didn't believe it and when I was convinced it was true I felt really happy for her: so La Estrella has finally made it I said to myself and I was frightened like hell to see that her unshakable self-assurance had proved more prophetic than pathetic because I'm always alarmed by people who make a one-man crusade out of their destiny and who while denying luck and chance and even destiny have a feeling of certainty, a belief in themselves that's so deep it can't be anything but fate and now I saw her not only as a physical phenomenon but as a metaphysical monster: La Estrella played the Luther of Cuban music and she had always been dead right, as if she who couldn't read or write had in music her sacred scores.

I sneaked out of the city office that evening to go to the opening. Somebody told me she had been nervous during the rehearsals and although she was always on time at the beginning she missed out on one or two important rehearsals and they penalized her and almost took her off the program and if they didn't do it it was because of all the money they'd spent on her. This guy also told me she had refused to sing with a band, but what happened was that she'd paid no attention when they read her the contract which made it perfectly clear that she had to accept all the clauses of the company and there was a special clause in which they mentioned the use of transcriptions and arrangements, but she didn't know what the first word meant and it was quite clear she hadn't any notice of the second because underneath, next to the signatures of the managers of the hotel and the company, there was a gigantic X which was her signature in her own hand, and so she had to sing with a band. This is what Eribó told me. He's the bongo player at the Capri and he was going to play with her and he told me all this because he knew I was curious about La Estrella and he came to the office to explain things and patch up a fight we had because of something he did which almost killed this story and me with it. I was on my way from the Hilton to the Pigal and was just crossing N Street when I saw Eribó. He was standing under the pines near the car park facing the Retiro Médico skyscraper and talking to one of the Americans playing at the Saint John and I went up to them. He was the piano player and they weren't just chatting but arguing about something and when I greeted them

I saw the American had a strange look on his face and Eribó took me aside and asked me if I spoke English, and I told him, Yes, a leetle, and he said, Listen, my friend here is in a tight spot, and he took me over to the American and in this weird state he formally introduced me and told the piano player in English that I would look after him and then he turned to me and said, You've got a car, haven't you? and I said sure and he said, Could you do me a favor and find a doctor, and I asked what for, and he said, This fellow needs a shot badly because he's in terrible pain and he can't sit down at the piano in the state he's in and he's on in half an hour, and I looked at the American and I could see from his face he really was in pain and I asked Eribó, What's the matter with him? and Eribó said, Nothing, he's just in pain, do me the favor will ya, look after him because he's a nice guy, and I got to go play because the first show is just about over, and then he turned to the American and explained what he'd said and turned to me and said, See you soon, and he left.

We went off in the car, me looking for a doctor not in the streets but in my mind, because to find a doctor during the day who's willing to give a junkie a shot of heroin is hard enough, let alone during the night, and every time we ran over a hole in the road or crossed a street the American gave a groan and once he screamed. I tried to get him to tell me what was wrong and he finally managed to get through, over, across to me that it was his anus. Your what? My asshole, man! and at first I thought he was just another pervert and then he told me it was only hemorrhoids and I told him I would take him to an outpatients' clinic, to an emergency clinic nearby, but he insisted all he needed was a shot to kill the pain and he'd be O.K. again and he was writhing on the seat and sobbing and as I'd seen *The Man with the Golden Arm* I hadn't the slightest doubt where it was hurting. Then I remembered that there was a doctor who lived in the Paseo building who was a friend of mine and I went and woke him up. He was scared because he thought it was someone wounded in a gunfight, a terrorist who'd been busted by his own petardo or drunk a Molotov cocktail or whatever or maybe someone who'd been hunted down by the S.I.M., but I told him I didn't get mixed up in things like that, I wasn't interested in politics and that the closest I'd been to a revolutionary was at a focal lens distance of 2.5 and he said all right, all right he'd have to go to his office and he gave me the address and said he'd follow us. I got to the office with the man fainting all over the place and as luck would have it a cop turned up just as I was trying to wake him so I could get him into the house and sit him down in the *portal* to wait for the doctor. The cop came up and asked me what was wrong and I told him he was a pianist and a friend of mine and that he was in pain. He asked me what was wrong and I said he had hemorrhoids and the cop repeated the word, Hemorrhoids? and I told him, Yes, piles, but he thought it was even weirder than I did and said, Are you sure he's not one of those guys, meaning was he dangerous, like a terrorist or something, and I said, Oh come on, he's a musician, and then this guy came round and I told the cop I was taking him inside and whispered to him he should try and make it by himself because this cop here was suspicious and the cop must have heard what I was saying, because he insisted on coming with us and I can still remember the iron gate creaking behind us as we entered the silent patio and the moon shining on the dwarf palm tree in the garden and the cold-looking iron garden chairs painted white and the strange group we made, the three of us, the American, the cop and myself sitting on the terrace in Vedado as the dawn was about to come up. Then the doctor arrived and when he turned on the light in the *portal* and saw the cop and us sitting there, the piano player in a half-swoon and me thoroughly frightened by now, he made the face Christ must have made when he felt Judas' lips on his own and saw the Roman sbirri over the apos(tate)tle's shoulder. We went in and the cop with us and the doctor got the piano player to lie down on a table and made me wait outside, but the cop insisted on staying and he must have inspected the anus with a vigilante's eye because he came out perfectly satisfied when the doctor called me and said, This fellow is very sick, and I saw that he was asleep and he said, I gave him an injection now, but he has a strangulating hemorrhoid and he'll have to be operated on at once and of course I was astonished then because I was lucky after all: I played the wrong number and it came up. I told the doctor who the piano player was and how I met him and he told me to go away, that he would take him to his clinic which wasn't far and he'd take care of everything and he walked me out and I thanked him and also the cop, who returned to his beat smiling.

At the Capri there were the same people as always, maybe a little more crowded than usual because it was Friday and an opening night, but I managed to find a good table. I was with Irenita who always likes to pay visits to fame even if she has to go by the way of hate to get there and we sat down and waited for the stellar moment when La Estrella would ascend to her musical heaven which was the stage and I kept myself busy looking around at the women in their satin dresses and the men who looked from their faces like they wore long underpants and the old women who would go crazy over a bunch of plastic flowers. There was a rolling of drums and then the emcee had the pleasure to introduce to the charming audience the discovery of the century, the greatest Cuban singer since Rita Montaner, the only singer in the world who could be compared with the greatest of the great in the world of international song like Ella Fitzgerald and Katyna Ranieri and Libertad Lamarque, which was like a salad for all seasons to be had with a soupçon of seltzer. Lights out and a searchlight tore a white hole in the purple backdrop and between the folds salami fingers were groping their way in and behind them there appeared a thigh in the shape of an arm and at the end of the arm La Estrella arrived with the black hand mike lost in her hand like a metal finger between those five nipples full of fat that are her actual fingers. Finally every inch of her sprawled on stage singing "Noche de Ronda" as she expanded forward in the general direction of a little round black table with a tiny black chair beside it, both shaking with more than stage fright as they waited for her freight to crash-land on them, and La Estrella spread out toward this suggestion of café chantant precariously balancing on her head a coiffure that Madame de Pompadour would have judged too much. She sat down and chair and table and La Estrella were within a thin inch of falling together to the ground and offstage, but she went on singing as though nothing had happened, steadying the tumbling table, silencing the creaking chair and drowning the loudsy band, all done with her voice, recovering from time to time her sound of yesteryear and filling the whole of that great hall with her incredible *voce e mezza* and for a minute I forgot her strange makeup, her face which was no longer ugly but simply grotesque up there, a purple mask with great scarlet-painted lips and the same defoliated eyebrows as before painted across in straight thin lines over the slitty eyes: all the ugliness the darkness of Las Vegas had always concealed. But a minute can only last a minute. If I stayed on until she had finished it was only out of solidarity and pity but all through the show I couldn't help thinking Alex Bayer would be doubly happy at this star-struck moment later known as the apotheosis of La Estrella.

When the show was over we went backstage to congratulate her and of course she didn't allow Irenita into her dressing room with its great silver star pasted on the door, the edges still sticky. I remember it well because I had time to study it in detail while I was waiting for La Estrella: I was the last person she deigned to receive. I went in and the dressing room was full of flowers and fairies and two little mulatto acolytes who were combing her pompous pompadour and arranging her clothes. I greeted her and told her how much I had enjoyed her singing and how good she looked on stage and what a great singer she was, and then she offered me her hand, the left one, as though it was the Pope's hand, and I shook it limply and she answered with a sidewinding smile and didn't say a thing, but nothing, nothing, nothing, not a word: all she did was to smile her frozen lopsided smile and preen herself in the mirror on the wall and demand constant attention from her sycophants with a megalomania which like her voice, like her hands, like herself, was simply monstrous. I left the dressing room as best I could telling her I would come and see her again some other time when she wasn't so tired or nervous or busy, I can't remember which, and she smiled her lopsidewinding smile at me like a period or like a full stop.

Later I knew her Capri show had folded and that she moved to the Saint John, with only a guitar for backing, but the guitarist was not Niño Nené but somebody else. She had a genuine success there and she even cut a record (*I* know: I bought it and *listened* to it), and after that she went to San Juan, P.R., and to Caracas and to Mexico City and everywhere she went people were talking about her voice more than listening to it. She went to Mexico against the advice of her private doctor (no, *not* Alex Bayer's private doctor) who told her the altitude would kill her and she went in spite of his advice and in spite of everything she overstayed herself until one evening she ate a huge dinner and the next morning she had acute indigestion and called a doctor and the indigestion became a heart attack and she spent three days in an oversize oxygen tent and on the fourth day she got worse and on the fifth day she died. There ensued a legal battle between the Mexican impresarios and their Cuban colleagues about the cost of transport to take her back to Cuba for burial and they wanted to ship her as general freight and the air company said that a coffin wasn't general freight but came under special transport and then they wanted to put her in a frozen-goods container and have her sent the same way they fly lobsters to Miami and her faithful acolytes protested, outraged by this ultimate insult, but finally they had no other alternative than to leave her in Mexico to be buried there.

I don't know if all this is true or false but what is true is that she's dead and that soon nobody will remember her and that she was very much alive when I knew her and that now nothing remains of that fabulous freak, that enormous vitality, that unique human being but a skeleton like the hundreds, thousands, millions of true and false skeletons there are in Mexico, a country peopled by skeletons, once the worms have gorged themselves on the three hundred and fifty pounds of living flesh she bequeathed them. It is God's truth that she is gone with the wind which is the same as saying she's fucked and farted and that nothing remains of her but a lousy record with a shitty sleeve in obscenely bad taste on which the ugliest woman in the world appears in full sepia color: eyes slitting and mouth wide open between liver-colored lips and cradling a microphone in her hand very close to an avid muzzle, and although we who knew her know damn well this is not her, this is definitely not La Estrella, and the dead voice of that godawful record has nothing to do with her own live voice, this is all that remains of her and within six months or a year when all the dirty jokes about her photo finish and the micockphone she is about to blow in it are past and gone and forgotten, within two years at the most she will be completely forgotten herself—and this is the most terrible thing of all because the one thing I feel a mortal hatred for is oblivion.

But not even I can do anything, because you can't give a stop bath to life, so life must go on. Not so long ago, just before they transferred me to the front page, I went to Las Vegas on leave (yes, the nightclub has reopened and is continuing with its grand show of the evening and its *chowcito* and the same people go there every night and every dawn and on into the morning as before *familia*) and there were two girls singing there, new ones, two pretty little Negro girls singing and swinging without any backing. I instantly thought of La Estrella and her voice revolution in Cuban music and of her style which is a thing that lasts longer than a person and a voice and a revolution. La Estrella lives in these girls who call themselves Las Capellas in a homage that doesn't dare disclose its name, and they sing very well and in pluperfect pitch and what is more, they have a lot of success. I took them out, along with this critic friend of mine I don't know if you remember him, Rine Leal, to drive them home that same evening. On the way, right at the corner of Agua-dulce, when I stopped at the red lights, we saw a boy playing the guitar and anybody who had eyes for music could see he was a kid from the sticks, a poor lonely kid who liked music and wanted to make it himself instead of having it canned or slaughtered on the premises. Rine made me park the car then and there and compelled us to go down under the May drizzle and into the *bodegabar* where the boy was, and I introduced him to Las Capellas though I didn't know him from anywhere and then told him the girls were crazy about music and that they sang but only in the shower because they hadn't yet dared to sing with accompaniment, and the kid with the guitar from the sticks was very humble and naïve and goodhearted and he said, Come on, let's try and don't be shy because I'll follow you and if you make a mistake I'll cover up for you and if you stray I'll go after you and bring you back to the bar, and he repeated, Come on, why don't you try for once, come on. So Las Capellas sang with him and he followed them as best he could and I think the two beautiful Negro singers had never sung better than at

Aguadulce which once meant fresh water but not anymore, and Rineleal and I applauded and the owner of the place and the other people who were there applauded too, and then we went off running under the drizzle which had suddenly become a shower and the kid with the guitar followed us with his voice, shouting at Las Capellas, Don't be shy because you're very good and you'll go a long way if you want to, and we left Aguadulce running and got into my car and drove up to their house because Las Capellas are *decentes* but we stayed in the car waiting for the rain to stop or merely as a pretext for staying because after it had stopped raining we went on talking and laughing and so on and so forth until there was an inti*mate* silence in the car and it was then we heard outside, quite distinctly, someone knocking on a door. Las Capellas thought it was their mother trying to attract their attention to order but they were surprised beyond belief because, as one of them said, their mother was very sensible and we heard the knocking again and we stood still and we heard it again and we got out of the car and the girls went into the house to find their mother sound asleep and nobody else lived with them and we could see the neighborhood was very quiet and orderly at that early or late hour. It was real spooky. Las Capellas began talking about dead people and the living dead and ghosts and Rine played some verbal games with the Bustrophantoms so I said I must split because I had to get to bed early, which was true, and we returned, Rine and I, to Havana and on my way back I thought of La Estrella but I didn't say anything not because it was uncanny but because it was unnecessary. Anyhow, when we got to the center of town which is La Rampa of course and we got out to have a coffee and so to bed, we met Irenita plus some nameless friend of hers who were just leaving Fernando's Hideaway and straight to bed so we invited them to go to Las Vegas where there wasn't a show or a *chowcito* or anything by now, only the jukebox and some very distant relatives so we only stayed there for about a half hour drinking and talking and laughing and listening to some unknown records till it was almost dawn, when we took them both to a hotel on the beach.

Tenth session

Doctor, I can't eat meat again. It's not like the last time, when I saw in every steak a cow I once saw in my village that didn't want to go into the slaughterhouse and dug its hoofs into the ground and got its horns stuck in the door of the slaughterhouse, and struggled so hard that in the end the man came out and gave it a blow with his knife right there in the street and the blood flowed in the gutter like water when it's raining only soiled with a different hue of red. No, and the cook has orders to fry my meat until it's charred black. But do you know what happens: I chew and chew and chew but I can't swallow it. I simply can't. It won't go down. Did you know, doctor, that when I was a girl and went out on dates I had to go on an empty stomach, otherwise I would vomit?

"I make this explanation for the reason
that without it many readers would suppose
that all these characters were trying to
talk alike and not succeeding."

MARK TWAIN

BACHATA

I

It will be a pity Bustrófedon didn't come with us because we were going along El Malecón at forty, fifty, eighty miles an hour coming from the Almendares, that Ganges of the West Indian, as Cué called the river, and on the left was a double horizon: the jetty and the piece of invisible stitching that must be the scar left by the division of the waters, that illusory blue line at exactly two point six miles offshore. It was a pity Bustrófedon won't come with us to see, when the twin horizons of cement and sunlight allow it, the motley ocean: the green blue indigo violet deep purple bands of the Stream, so well blended that not even Pym's knife could separate them. It is indeed a pity Bustrófedon isn't coming with us along the Malecón this evening with Arsenio Cué and me in his car which glides along like a travel shot from the fort of La Chorrera to the *frontis* of the Vedado Tennis Club, the continuous sea wall of the jetty now flanking us on the left but only until we turn around and go back (as we always do). On the right our boundary line is as of now the Hotel Riviera (a square soap dish with an oval bar of soap on one side: the veined egg of a roc: the gambling saloon's pleasure dome) and seconds later the service station opposite the often murderous roundabout, this bleached gas station which becomes an oasis of light in the black desert of the Malecón-by-night, and in the background the sea forever enacting a fallen backdrop. Over it all there is another dome: the never-ending vault, an infinite bar of blue soap, the egg of a cosmic roc. The shimmering sky.

To travel with Cué means to talk, think, free-associate like Cué, but as he is silent I take advantage of this fleeting moment to be myself for just a second and look around: I watch the ferry from Miami head toward the channel of the bay evidently pilotless because it is cruising along the jetty: visibly mistaking the wall for the sea after emerging blind drunk from horizontal clouds that form a natural atomic growth, a drinkable mushroom the salty, thirsty Gulf Stream will gulp down, then seeing how that evening sun turns every single window on the thirty-story Focsa building into a nugget of gold, alchemically changing the obscene pile of masonry into an Eldorado by putting gold fillings in the cavities of that mammoth inhabited tooth: gazing at it all with that unique pleasure you get from approaching a given point at a uniform and constant speed: the secret of the movies since Griffith, a sensation heightened now by listening to a melody that could be our soundtrack, and Cué's voice, his actor's delivery completes the illusion, destroying it at the same time:

—What do you think of Bach at sixty? he says.

—*What*?

—Bach, Johann Sebastian, the baroque bang-up husband of the revealing Anna Magdalena B., the contrapuntal father of a harmonious son, the blind man of Bonn, the deaf man of Lepanto, the one-handed wonder, the author of that instruction emanuel for every spiritual prisoner, *The Art of the Fugue,* he says. —What would the old boy Bach say if he knew that his own music was speeding along the Malecón of Havana, in the heart of the tropics, at sixty miles an hour? What do you think would scare him more? What would he find most shocking? The time not the tempo over which his basso continuo has traveled? Or space, the far places his organized sound waves have reached?

—I don't know. I hadn't thought about it—and it was true I never thought about it, then or now.

—I do, he says. —It has occurred to me that this music, this elegantly gross concerto (and he leaves an empty space between his pedantically dramatic phrases for the music to fill) was created to be listened to in Weimar, in the eighteenth century, in a German palace, in the baroque music room, by candelabra, in a silence that was not physical but historical: a music for eternity, in other words, for the ducal court.

The Malecón slid away under the car and became an asphalt plain bordered by houses pitted with brine and the interminable sea wall, and the overcast or partly overcast sky above and the domed doomed sun itself sinking irresistibly but unnoticed, just like Icarus, toward the sea. (Why this mimesis? I always end up by being like the others: tell me how I speak and I'll tell you who I am, which is like saying whom I've been seeing.) I was listening to Bach now in the intervals of Cué's notes to the program but in fact thinking about the verbal games Bustrófedon would have made if he'd been alive, that is with us now: Bach, Bachata, Bachanal, Bachelor, Bachillus (which are found in the air interrupting the spatial continuum of a Bacuum), Bachalaureat, Bacharat, Bacations—and I was actually hearing him make a dictionary out of a single word.

—Bach, says Cué, —who smoked tobacco and drank coffee and fornicated like any *habanero* is traveling beside us now. Did you know that he wrote a cantata to coffee (was he asking me?) and another to tobacco, and that he dedicated a poem to it which I know by heart: "Every time I light my pipe/ To pass the time by smoking it/ And sit down and take a drag, my thoughts return/ To a sad and gray and tenuous vision/ Which proves how well I get lost/ In smoke like any other ghost"—he left off citing and reciting. —What do you think of the Old Man? I'll be doggone if that isn't a Montuno melody he's playing. He fell silent to listen or make me listen. —Listen to this sudden *ripieno,* Silvestre *viejo,* doesn't it become Cuban when you hear it on the Malecón and it's still Bach but not exactly Bach? How do you think the physicists would explain it? Maybe speed is a musical continuum? What would Albert Schweitzer say about it?

In Schwahili? I was thinking. Cué was driving and at the same time humming to the music, his hands pushing forte with closed fists or following a pianissimo with butterfingers, then descending an invisible musical scale. But what he really looked like was an expert in deaf-and-dumb language translating a speech. I remembered *Johnny Belinda* and he almost reminded me of Lew Ayres, the most honest of dramatic cl i chés written on his face, carrying on a silent conversation with Jane Wyman accompanied by the ignorance or admiration, in any case silent, of Charles Bickford and Agnes Moorehead.

—Can't you hear how old Bach plays on the tonality in D, how he builds up his imitations, how he makes his variations always unpredictable but only when the theme allows and suggests it and never before, never after, and how despite that he always manages to take you by surprise? Doesn't he seem like a slave with all the freedom in the world? Ah, *amigo,* he's better than Offenbach, because he's *ici, aquí, hier,* here in this *tristeza habanera* and not in any *Gaieté Parisienne!*

Cué had this obsession with time. What I mean is that he would search for time in space, and they were nothing but a search, our continual, interminable journeys along the Malecón, a single infinite journey like this one, but at any time of the day or night, traveling over this decaying landscape of old houses between Maceo Park and La Punta, which will end up becoming what man took from the sea to build it: another barrier of reefs, bitten by the brine, salted by the spray whenever there is a wind and by the waves on those days when the sea breaks over the street and dashes against the houses seeking the coastline that has been stolen from it, creating it, making another shore for itself, and then the parks in which the tunnel begins now and where the coconut palms and the fake almond trees and catkins do not entirely blot out the appearance of a goat's pasture which the sun produces by burning and toasting the green grass till it's yellow like straw, and the excessive dust becoming another wall in the sunlight, and then the waterfront bars: New Pastores, Two Brothers, Don Quixote, the bar where the Greek sailors dance arm in arm while the whores look on and laugh and the church of San Francisco, the convent church, facing the Stock Exchange and Customs, pointing out the different times of history, the successive foreign occupations carved in this plaza which in the times and engravings of the Capture of Havana by the English looked like a parody of Canaletto, and the bars which mirror the entrance of the Alameda de Paula reminds you that in Havana the docks begin and end the promenade by the sea. Following the sweet curve of the bay we would go on every trip to Guanabacoa and Regla, to the bars, and look at the city from the other side of the port as if we were in another country, listening to and watching the *vaporetto* that makes the crossing every half hour. Later we would go back the whole length of the Malecón as far as 5th Avenue and the Playa de Marianao, unless we drove to Mariel or plunged down into the tunnel under the bay and reemerged in Matanzas for dinner and then on to Varadero to gamble and then return at midnight or dawn to Havana: talking all the time and telling jokes or gossiping all the time and always, and also philosophizing or aestheticizing or moralizing, but always: the thing was to make it look like we didn't have to work because in Havana, Cuba, this is the only way to be *gente bien* or high society, which is what Cué and I wanted, would have wanted, tried to be—and we always had time to talk about time. When Cué talked about time and space and when he went over all that space in all our time I thought that he did it to divert us, and now I know: it was: to do something different, to make one thing of another, and while we were going over space he succeeded in evading what he always avoided, I think, which was to go over another space outside of time. Or to be precise—remembering. The opposite of me, because I like remembering things better than living them or living things knowing they can never be lost because I can always evoke them again—*there must be time. This is the thing that is at present the most troubling and if there is the time that is at present the most troublesome the time-sense that is at present the most troubling is the thing that makes the present the most troubling. There is at present* . . . I can live them over again by remembering them and it would be good if we used our word *recordar,* which means to remember, in the way the English do—to record—instead of *grabar,* for cutting a record or making a tape, because that is what it is, which is the opposite of what Arsenio Cué does. Now he was talking about Bach, about Offenbach and Ludwig Feuerbach as well (of the baroque as the art of honest plagiarism, and of how he could reconcile himself to that Austrian and joyful Parisian because he said he knew that in the forest of music he would never be a nightingale, and praising the latter-day Hegelian who had applied the concept of alienation to the creation of the gods), though this had nothing to do with remembering, but with its opposite. That is to say with memorizing.

—*Te das cuenta, viejo*? This man was a sum total and he looks like a multiplication. Bach squared.

At that moment (yes, exactly that moment) universal silence fell: upon the car, the radio and Cué, all because the music had stopped. The announcer was speaking—he was a lot like Cué, at least voicewise.

"Ladies and gentlemen, you have just been listening to the Concerto Grosso in D Major, opus 2 number 3, by Antonio Vivaldi. (Pause) Violin: Isaac Stern; viola . . ."

I bellowed with laughter and I think Arsenio did too. The speaker just transformed his contrapuntal rumination into musica falsa.

—Culture in the tropics, *chico!* I said. —How about that? *Te das cuenta, viejo*? I said, imitating his voice, but making it sound more pedantic than friendly. He didn't look at me but said:

—Fundamentally I'm right. Bach spent the whole of his life plundering things from Vivaldi, and not only from Vivaldi (he wanted to save himself from perdition through erudition: I could see it coming) but also from Marcello, he said in his clipped voice, Marchel-lo, —and Manfredini and Veracini and even from Evaristo Felice Dall-Abaco. That was why I was talking about a sum total, or summa.

—You'd have done better by saying remainder or subtraction, wouldn't you?

He laughed. What's good about Cué is that he has a more developed sense of humor than he has of ridicule. "This program in our series Great Composers of the World was dedicated to the work of—" Off he switched the radio.

—But you're right, I said, temporizing or contemporizing. I'm the Contemporizing Cid. —Bach is the father of them all and Music is his lawful wedded wife, but Vivaldi winks at Anna Magdalena from time to time.

—Viva Vivaldi! Cué said, laughing.

—If Bustrófedon were with us in this time machine he would already have said Vibachvaldi or Vivach Vivaldi or Bivaldi and he would have gone on like that all through the night.

—Then, what do you think of Vivaldi at sixty?

—That you've slowed down.

—Albinoni at eighty, Frescobaldi at a hundred, Cimarosa at fifty, Monteverdi at a hundred and twenty, Gesualdo flooring the accelerator . . . A pause followed, more exalted than refreshing, and he went on: —It makes no difference; what I said is still true and I'd like to know what Palestrina would be like in a 707 jet.

—A miracle of acoustics, I said.

II

The convertible rode on, as though on rails, along the expanding curve of the Malecón and I saw Cué concentrating once more on driving, another appendage of the engine, like the steering wheel. He was talking to me then of a unique sensation, in other words one I couldn't share (like dying or defecating), not only because it was a religious experience but because I didn't know how to drive. He said that there were times when the car and the road and he himself disappeared and the three became one and the same thing, the ride, space and the destination of the journey, and that he, Cué, felt as though the road was as much his as the clothes he wore and that it gave him the same pleasure as wearing a fresh clean and newly ironed shirt on his body, and that it was a physical pleasure as deep as fucking and that at the same time he, Cué, felt detached, as though he was in the air, flying, but without a machine to mediate between himself and the elements, because his body had disappeared and he, Cué, *was* the speed at which he was traveling. I spoke to him about the bow and the arrow and the archer and his target, and I lent him the little book and all, but he told me that Zen talked about eternity and he was talking about the moment, so discussion was useless and mark my words never the twain would meet. At the red light at La Punta he finally came out of his trance.

I looked at the park, at what remained of the Martyr's Park (also known as the Lovers' Plaza) since the tunnel had been opened up under the bay. Now the whole park had become just one more ruin, like the remains of that prison and the fragment of that wall where they used to hold executions in the nineteenth century, and the park, like the museums, had become a relic. Suddenly, in the reflection of the evening light, sitting under an almond tree, but, as always, in the sun, I saw her under. The Summering sky. I told Cué.

—What of it? he said. —She's just a nut.

—I know that. But it's incredible that she's there, that she's always been there for the past ten years.

—She'll still be there for a good while longer.

—You know, I told him, —that it's about ten years. No, not ten: seven or eight . . .

—Or five or maybe yesterday, Cué interrupted, because he thought I was joking.

—No, no, I really meant it. I saw her for the first time some years ago and she was talking and talking and talking. I sat down close to her and she went on talking, because she didn't see me, she didn't see anything at all and I thought it was so special, symbolic, what she was saying that I went to a friend's house, one of my classmates, Matías Monte-Huidobro, who lived nearby and I asked him for a pencil and paper, without saying a word about it because he was also writing or wanted to write at the time, I returned and picked up a fragment of the speech, which was exactly what I heard before, because when she got to a certain point, like the roll on a pianola, she repeated the whole thing over again. The third time around, I had copied down what she said, convincing myself nothing was missing except the punctuation, and then I got up and left. She was still carrying on with her speech.

—And where did you put it?

—I don't know. It must be around somewhere.

—No, I mean I would have thought you'd make a story out of it.

—Oh no. First of all I lost it, and then I found it again and it no longer seemed so fascinating, and the only thing that surprised me about it was that the writing had gotten fatter.

—*What*?

—Yes, it was the ballpoint I'd used, one of the old ones, and the paper was very porous so the writing had become swollen, and I could no longer read what I'd written.

—Poetic justice, Cué said and he started up and as we drove slowly past watching the mad woman sitting on her bench I took a good look at her.

—It's not her, I said.

—What d'you mean?

—That it is not her. It's someone else.

He looked at me as if to say, Are *you* sure?

—Sure I'm sure. It's somebody else. It's another woman. She was a mulatto.

—This one's a mulatto too.

—Yes, but the other looked Chinese. It's not the same one.

—If you say so.

—If you like I'll get out and look.

—No. What for? You're the one who knows her, not me.

—It's definitely not her.

—Maybe she's not mad either.

—Maybe. Maybe she's just a poor woman who came to take in some fresh air.

—Or sun.

—Or to be near the sea.

—This is the sort of coincidence I like, Cué said.

We drove on and when we were going by the amphitheater he suggested we have a drink at the Lucero Bar.

—It's a long time since I've been there, he said.

—Me too. I already forgot what it's like.

We ordered a beer and *saladitos*.

—It's funny, Cué said, —how the world changes its axis.

—What d'you mean?

—There was a time when this was the center of Havana both day and night. The amphitheater, this part of the Malecón, the parks from La Fuerza to the Prado, Misiones Avenue.

—It's as if Havana was becoming once more what it was in the times of *Cecilia Valdés*.

—No, it's not that. This was the center then, and there was nothing more to be said. Then the center moved to Prado, as before it must have been the Cathedral Plaza or Plaza Vieja or City Hall. With the years it moved up to the corner of Galiano and San Rafael and Neptuno and now it's reached La Rampa. I wonder when it will stop, this walking center which moves, and strangely enough, like the city and the sun, from east to west.

—Batista's trying to move it across the bay.

—No future in that. You wait and see.

—What, Batista's regime?

He looked at me and smiled.

—What are you getting at?

—Me? Nothing.

—You know I never talk about politics. That's my policy.

—But I know how you think.

—Well, that makes two of us.

—That's what I think, I said. —Nobody can make this city cross the bay.

—Off Kursk not. Look how Casablanca and Regla are declining.

I looked at Casablanca and Regla declining. I looked at La Cabaña. I also looked at the Morro Castle. Finally I looked at Cué, who was drinking his beer as he did everything, like an actor posing in all positions and even sometimes in profile. Sons & lumière.

III

We spent a while talking about cities, one of Cué's favorite subjects. He has this idea that the city wasn't created by man, but quite the contrary, and communicating that sort of archaeological nostalgia with which he talks about buildings as though they were human beings, where houses are built with a great hope, in novelty, a Nativity, and then they grow with the people who live in them and decline and are finally forgotten or they are torn down or fall to pieces and in their place another building rises which begins the cycle all over again. It's pretty, isn't it, this architectonic saga? I reminded him that it sounded like the beginning of *The Magic Mountain.* Enter Hans Castorp in act one with what Cué calls "the arrogant carefree drive of life itself" and arrives at the sanatorium, petulantly sure of his own obvious good health, a cheerful tourist in white hell—to learn a few days later that he too is tubercular. "I like that," Arsenio Cué said, "I really like that analogy. That moment is like an allegory of life. You go—or come—in with all the self-confidence of the young immaculate conception of the pure life, whole and hearty, and in next to no time you discover that you too are just another sick man, that the same shit has fallen on you as well, that living means decaying: Dorian Gray and his portrait."

I used to come to this park when I was a child. This was where I would play and I would sit on the wall to watch the warships coming in and out just as I am now watching the pilot's launch making its way out to the open sea and here, there, near the Castillito, this little castle which is nothing more than the ruins of a water closet in the old wall, I was teaching my brother to ride a bike one day and I pushed him very hard and he went off at full speed and crashed into a bench and the handlebars hit him in the chest and he fainted and vomited blood, he was like dead for half an hour or maybe ten minutes, I don't know. But what I did know was that it was I who had done it and a year or two later when my brother got TB I continued to think that it was all my fault. I told Cué about it, then. I mean now.

—You aren't from around here, Silvestre, I mean from Havana?

—No, I'm from the country.

—Where?

—From Virana.

—How d'you like that. I'm from Samas.

—It's very close.

—Yes, it's right next door, as the crow flies, as they say in the country.

—Thirty-two kilometers and a hundred and six curves on a small highway, which should really be called a dirt road.

—I used to go to Virana quite a lot during vacations.

—Really?

—We could even have known each other there.

—When was that?

—During the war. Forty-four or forty-five, I think.

—Ah, no. I was already living in Havana. Although, I'll tell you, I often used to go there for vacations, when we had money. But we were really poor.

The waiter came and interrupted us by bringing some fried prawns. And I was grateful to him. Doubly grateful. We went on drinking. I noticed the black spots in front of my eyes which had begun to appear recently. Like mute flies buzzing about. Probably another side effect of nicotine, toxic spots. A drag. A dreg. A critical precipitate. That's where all the bad movies I've ever seen must be gathered, so it could be a meto-p8-ysical—that's how my typewriter spells metaphysical—sickness. Or cosmic burns on the retina. Or Martians whom only I can detect. They don't bother me too much, but there are times when I think it could be the beginning of a fadeout and that someday a black light will be projected on my screen. A thing that will happen sooner or later, but I'm talking about blindness not death. This total blackout will be the worst possible fate for my movie eyes—but not for the eyes of memory.

—Do you have a good memory?

I almost jumped out of my seat. Arsenio Cué sometimes displays the most unexpected inductive talents. Unexpected in an actor, I mean. Shylock Holmes is his name.

—Good enough, I said.

—How goodonov?

—A lot. More than enough, it's very good. I remember almost everything and what's more I often remember the times when I remembered something.

—You should be called Funes the Memorious.

I laughed. But I was gazing at the port and thinking that there must be some relation between memory and the sea. (It is called *el mar* in Spanish. Mar, mere, memory. The sea of Marmory.) Not only because the sea is vast and deep and everlasting but it also is always there and somehow manages to return every other second in successive, incessant waves identical in themselves changing it instantly and yet eternally. The castle of Everness submerged emerging as a cathedral of my mind. Neverness. Now I was sitting on this terrace firma drinking a beer and a breeze blew in, that warm wind from the sea that picks up in the late afternoonca, and my memories of this evening air came to me in repeated gusts, but it was a case of total recall because in a copula of seconds I had remembered all the afternoons of my life (don't bother, I'm not going to list them for you, dear reader) that I would be sitting in a park reading a book and would lift my head above the printed surface to feel the evening air blowing across the pages on my face or lean against a wooden balneal house listening to the wind in the palm trees or lying on the beach eating a mango that stained my sandy hands mellow yellow or sitting by a bay window during an English lesson about the present participle or visiting my uncle and sitting in a rocking chair made of beach wood with my feet reaching now not reaching the ground with my new shoes getting heavier and heavier and heavier by the second, and on each occasion this warm gentle briny breeze would be blowing all around me. It must be the Aeolus of memory blowing over my sea of troubles and by opposing it make Marcelled waves. I should be called Mister Memory the Funneous.

—Why did you ask?

—No particular reason. It's not important.

—No, tell me why. We were probably thinking the same thing.

My only weakness, trying to think the same thing everybody else is thinking. Arsenio stared at me. His eyes squinted sometimes when he stared. It wasn't a defect but an effect he achieved with his eyes. I thought of Códac who said that in every actor there is an actress struggling to get out. He spoke, some seconds after opening his mouth in the shape of a liquid consonant. The Marlon Brando school of thought.

—Listen, can you remember a woman well?

A well of a woman.

—Which woman?

I was taken aback. Was it another inspired guess that will never abolish the future?

—Any woman. Take your pick. But it must be someone you've been in love with. Have you ever been in love? I mean, really in love?

—Yes, off courts. Same as anybody.

More than anybody was what I should have said. I tried to remember various women and I couldn't think of any and when

I was on the point of admitting defeat, it wasn't a woman I thought of but a girl. I remembered her sandy hair, her high forehead and her clear, almost yellow eyes, and her wide fleshy mouth and her chin which had a dimple and her long legs and the sandals on her feet and the way she walked and I remembered waiting for her in a park and remembering as I was waiting how she laughed and how perfect her teeth were when she smiled. I described her to Cué. A wishing well of a woman.

—Were you in love with her?

—Yes. I think so. Yes.

I should have told him that I was hopelessly in love, lost and found in a love that I never had again, before or since. But I said nothing. A woman is a well of love, bottomless.

—You haven't been in love, old boy, he said. A well of loveness. Lovelessness.

—What did you say?

—That you've never, never been in love, that this woman doesn't exist, that you've just invented her.

I should have been furious, but I can't even get mildly irritated when the whole world is foaming at the poles with anger.

—Why do you say this?

—Because I know it.

—But I told you I was in love. Isn't that enough?

—No, no, you believed, you thought, you imagined you were. But you weren't.

—Really?

—Really.

He paused for a moment to take a drink and wipe the drops of sweat and beer off his lips with a handkerchief. It seemed like a studied gesture.

IV

Those shoulders (these shoulders because I can see them here or, as people say, I have them right in front of my eyes), those/these shoulders, these and those shoulders of the woman, of the young woman, of the girl who was, uselessly, my fugitive love—will they return? I don't think they will. There is no need for them. Others will return, but that moment (her shoulders bare under the black décolletage, the satin evening gown clinging to the body and with flares below like the skirt of a Spanish gypsy or a rumba dancer, the perfect legs with ankles that never came to an end, her dress cut low at the front and her long neck continuing down between her breasts, and her face and her blond/straight/unbound hair, and the timid malice of that smile on her fleshy lips that smoked slowly and talked and sometimes burst out laughing so they revealed in her large mouth teeth that were equally large and even and almost edible, and her eyes her eyes her eyes always so indescribable, impossible to describe but unforgettable that night and the/her glance that was like another outburst of laughter: the eternal glance) will not return and this is exactly what makes moment and memory precious. This image assails me violently now, almost without provocation, and I think the best way of recapturing time past is not one's involuntary memory but the violent irresistible memories, which don't need any madeleines dunked in tea or the nostalgic fragrance of the past or an identical faux pas, but which come up suddenly like a thief by night and smash the window of our present with a blunt memory. It is then not uncommon that this memory induces vertigo: that sensation of being on the edge of a precipice, that sudden, unpredictable journey, that bringing together of two planes by the possible violent drop (the planes of reality by a vertical physical drop and the plane of reality and memory by the imaginary horizontal drop) shows us that time, like space, also has its laws of gravity. I would like to marry Proust off to Isaac Newton.

V

that's right, man (Cué was still talking) because if you had, if you had been in love you wouldn't remember a thing, you wouldn't even remember if her lips were thin or fleshy or broad. Or you might remember the mouth but you wouldn't be able to remember her eyes and if you remembered their color you wouldn't remember their shape and what you would never,

never, but never be able to do would be to remember hair and forehead and eyes and lips and chin and legs and feet and sandals and a park. But never. Because it would either not be true or else it would be that you weren't in love. Take your pick.

I was getting tired of this croupier in memories. Why should I have to take my pick? I remembered the end of *The Treasure of the Sierra Madre:*

Gold Hat Bedoya: *Mi Subteniente ¿Me deja coger mi sombrero?*

Sublieutenant: *Recójalo.*

Offshot voices are heard saying Ready! Aim! Fire! in Spanish and then a volley of Mexican rifle fire. Listen! If you had really been in love you would be trying, you'd be killing yourself trying to remember something as little as Her voice—*the* voice, and you wouldn't be able to or you would see her eyes right in front of your eyes suspended in the ectoplasm of memory—"ectoplasm of memory": that's what Eribó says too. Who could have invented it? Cué? Sese Eribó? Edgar Allan Kardec?—and all you could see would be her pupils looking at you. The rest is literature. Or you would see the mouth coming closer and feel the kiss, but you wouldn't see the mouth or feel the kiss because her nose would be in the way or run across like a referee, but it wouldn't be the nose of that time, but another nose, the one of that time when you saw her in profile or the time you saw her for the first time (to be continued).

He went on talking and I had fallen back into my habit of looking first to one side and then to the other side of the face of the person talking to me and I looked over his head and saw behind the coconut palms and above La Cabaña a Mediterranean flock of pigeons which was really a mirage, an optical illusion, white flies in my eyes—and the sky is not a peaceful roof but a violent ceiling of clarity, a mirror turning the white light of the sun into a burning, blinding blue, a deadly glare streaming like quicksilver under the pure, innocent blue of a heaven by Bellini. If I had a feeling for prosopopeia (Bustrófedon would have called me Prosopopeye the Sailor) I would say that it is a cruel sky—and I would be like that pathetically falacious Gorky, who said that the sea laughed. No, the sea does not laugh. The sea surrounds us, the sea envelops us and finally the sea washes our shores and flattens us and wears us away like pebbles on the beach and it survives us, indifferent, like the rest of the cosmos, when we are sand, also called Quevedo's Dust. It is the only thing in the world that is eternal and in spite of its eternity we can measure it, like time. The sea is another time or it is visible time, another clock. The sea and the sky are glass bubbles of a water clock: that's what it is, an eternal metaphysical clepsydra. Now the ferry was steaming away from the sea, from the Malecón, and entering the narrow channel of the port, almost sailing against the traffic, along the drive, and I saw its name clearly, *Phaon*, and Cué's voice, which had been trained for the air, came to me out of the sea of time saying:

—And you don't see Her, what you see is pieces of Her.

And I thought of Celia Margarita Mena, of Landrú's women, of all those jigsaw-puzzled ladies famous only because they have been hacked to pieces. When he stopped to catch his breath, I said:

—You know, Códac, the Photographer of the Stars, was right. In every actor there's an actress struggling to get out.

He understood the allusion. He knew I wasn't accusing him of being effeminate or anything like that, but that I knew his secret in part or in toto and he shut his mouth. He put on so serious an expression that I felt sorry and cursed myself for my habit of telling people the best right thing at the wrong time or the wrong thing at the right time. Or how to have bad timing in twenty easy lessons. He returned to his drink and didn't even tell me to go fuck myself or that it was impossible to talk to me, but he remained silent looking at the yellow liquid that made the glass yellow and which going by its color and smell and flavor must have been beer, beer warmed by time and memory and the evening. He called the waiter.

—Two more and make them cold, maestro.

I looked at his face and still saw the fire which Kallikrates or Leo must have had when he met Ayesha and knew it was Her. She, I mean.

—I'm sorry, *chico,* I said and I meant it.

—It doesn't matter, he said. —I have committed fornication, but that was in another country and besides the chick is dead—

and he smiled, Marlowe (Christopher, not Philip) or culture had saved us. I remembered a time when a woman was lost for culture or the lack of. It was Shelley Winters who pantingly said to Ronald Colman in *A Double Life*, "Put out the light," as she was going to bed with him, and poor old Ronaldo, dead as he is now, in real life as in films, who had gone mad in this film from playing Othello on the Broadway of film and he could not distinguish between the theater and real life (or real film), this Ronaldello turned the light off and said, "Put out the light and then put out the electric light:/If I wench thee thou flaming mister &c. . . . but once put out the light/ Thou cunting'st pattern of excessive nature/ I know not where is that Promiscuous heat . . ." and thus (that in Alejo once) he threw himself on Shelley, the poor wench, and smote her by error & trial. (What the hell are you doing you a sex maniac or what ughh oughhhh!) Shelley who was more innocent than Desdemona because she hadn't even heard of Othello or Iago or Shakespeare, not to mention Cassio, being an ignorant waitress albeit a New Yorker. It was this—being totalliterate, the opposite of an elephantine pedant—that actually killed her. On Literature Considered as a Fine Murder.

VI

We went up Calle San Lázaro for a change. I don't like this street. It's phony. I mean that at first sight, at the beginning, it's like a street in a city like Paris or Madrid or Barcelona and then it becomes mediocre, profoundly provincial, and when it gets to Maceo Park it broadens out into one of the most desolate and ugly avenues in Havana. Under the sun it is pitiless and by night it is dark and hostile and the only places that relieve its hideousness are the Prado and the Beneficencia orphanage and the steps of the university. But there is one thing I like about San Lázaro and that's the unexpected view of the sea you get on the first few blocks. Crossing Havana in the direction of El Vedado and if you have the good luck to be a passenger, all you have to do is follow the cadence of the blocks, turn your head and catch a glimpse, on the right-hand side, of a side street, a piece of wall and beyond it the sea. The surprise is dialectic: there is a surprise, there shouldn't be a surprise and finally without surprising me the sea assails me. A bit like Bach-Vivaldi-Bach for Cué just a while back. Besides, there is always the fear or hope that the wall of the Malecón might rise, might somehow become higher (by the whim of several commissioners of public works) and you'd no longer be able to see the sea so you'd have to guess it was there by looking at the sky which is its mirror.

—What are you looking for? Cué asked.

—*La mer.*

—What?

—*La mer, mon vieux, toujours recommencée.*

—Excuse me, I thought it was L'amour. You know, as in Dorothy Lamour.

—I haven't seen a single woman lately who's worth looking at twice or fucking once. Only the sea is worth looking at now.

We laughed. It was clear that we had our own keys to dawn and sunset. Then Cué with his actor's memory would go through a rosary (mumbled like a rosary) of quotations which he would declaim for the rest of the journey.

—"But now as August like a languorous replete bird winged slowly toward the moon of decay and death . . ."

What did I tell you?

—". . . they were bigger, vicious."

It was Faulkner and he was making fun of my admiration. A righteous revenge.

—Man, what a way to talk about mosquitoes! A little more and he'd say they were vampires open day and night.

I laughed. No, I smiled.

—What do you want? I said. —That's his first novel.

—Really? You don't say! Suppose I quote you something more recent? *The Hamlet* for example? "This happened during the autumn that preceded the winter at the beginning of which people, when they grow old, start counting time and dating events."

—But that translation is horrible, you know that. Remember also . . .

—Listen, kid, you know better than I that . . .

—That he's talking about an event that is as tragic and didactic as . . .

—Faulkner translates like an angel and in English it must be a damn of a lot worse.

—Faulkner is a poet, like Shakespeare, it's another world and you can't read it looking for purple patches. Shakespeare also has his Phamous Lynes as they call them on Radio Reloj.

—You're telling me! Cué said. —I haven't yet forgotten the scene, which still seems incoherent no matter how much I see it, the scene in the grave of the unhappy Ofelia (played by Minín Buck-Jones) where the vehement Hamlex Bayer leaps into the grave, which becomes for a few moments a dried-up version of the Mindanao Trench, and berates the contrite Laertes because he doesn't know how to pray!—to which the grief-stricken most brotherly brother (yours truly on that occasion) obligingly replies by seizing the petulant prince by the neck and without a moment's hesitation Amletto comes out with (in Luis Ah! Baralt's translation) an "Os ruego que quitéis vuestros dedos de mi cuello." Just like that, cool, calm and collected.

—So what are you trying to prove?

—Nothing. I'm not trying to prove anything. We're just talking, right? Or do you think I'm some kind of Elizabethan word-finder general?

He lowered the shades and fished in his pocket for the wraparound sunglasses he wore day and night and night and day he used to put on and take off, alternately, to show off his expressive eyes and his photogenic gaze, and later to cover both gaze and eyes with a mantle of moody modesty. The sin of lumière.

—"And the blessed sun himself a fair hot wench in flame-colored taffeta . . ." It should've been you doing the quoting or should I say quothing?

—*Quo Modo*?

—Because they are the words of a prince like you to a buffoon like me, who is, what's more, a better counsellor than you and me put together.

—I don't follow you.

—Don't follow me, follow Shakespeare.

"Marry, then, sweet wag, when thou art king, let not us that are squires of the night's body be called thieves of the day's beauty . . ." That's Falstaff, and man, is he something. The fellow he's talking to is Prince Hal. *Henry the Fourth,* act 1 scene 2.

Cué has a stupendous (or stupid) memory for quotations, but his English only escapes from the Caribbean singsong by falling into a light Hindu intonation. I thought of Joseph Schildkraut, the gone guru in *The Rains Came*.

—Why don't you write? I asked him suddenly.

—Why don't you ask me rather why don't I translate?

—No. I think you would be able to write. If you wanted.

—I used to think so once too, he said and fell silent. Then he pointed to the street and said:

—Look.

—What is it?

—Over there. He pointed more precisely (with his finger) and slowed down.

It was a billboard belonging to the OP which said SITE FOR PUBLIC WORKS OF PRESIDENT BATISTA, 1957–1966. HE IS THE MAN! I read it out aloud.

—*Plan de Obras Públicas del Presidente Batista, mil novecientos cincuenta y siete–mil novecientos sesenta y seis. Ese es el hombre.* So what?

—The numbers, not the *hombre*.

—There are two dates. What about it?

—The two figures add up to twenty-two, which is the day I was born, and my name and my two family names together add up to twenty-two (he said veintidós and not ventidós like any other Cuban for twenty-two). The last number, the sixty-six, is also a perfect number. Like nine.

—Pass me the corollary, please.

—The more I know about letters the more I like numbers.

—You can stuff it, I said and I thought, Shit! Another tiger with infinite stripes. But what I said was, —You're a cabalist.

—Pythagoric elixir, anodyne used against literary spasms. Or cramps, as they say in our own eastern province.

—Do you really believe in numbers?

—It's almost the only thing I do believe in. Two and two will always be four and the day they make five, start running.

—But you haven't always had these problems with mathematics?

—The problem is not the numbers but the way the numbers are treated. It's a bit like the lottery, which is the exploitation of numbers. The Pythagorean theorem is less important than Pythagoras' advice on not eating beans or killing a white cockerel or wearing the image of God on a ring or putting out a fire with a sword. And there are three other things which are even more important: not to eat the heart of an animal, not to return to your country if you have left it and not to piss facing east.

I laughed and the street suddenly opened out onto Maceo Park and La Beneficencia. But not because I laughed. Cué let go of the wheel and shouted:

—Thalassa! Thalassa!

He made one more joke and humming the Mexican waltz "On the Waves" circled Maceo Park three times.

—Look at it, Xenophobon! he said.

—Don't you like the sea?

—Would you like to hear a dream I had?

He didn't wait for me to say yes.

VII

Arsenio Cué's dream:

I am sitting on the Malecón and looking at the sea. I am sitting on the wall facing the street, but I am looking at the sea even though my back is turned. I am sitting on the wall and I can see the sea. (That tautology is part of the dream.) There is no sun or very little sun. In any case the sun is pleasantly warm. I am feeling good. It is obvious that I am not alone. A woman is sitting beside me who would have a face of great beauty if only I could see it. She seems to be with me, to be my companion. At least I don't feel any sensation of tension or desire, only the contentment one gets from the company of a woman who was very beautiful or desirable and is so no longer. She must be wearing an evening dress but I am not at all surprised. Nor do I think that she might be eccentric. The Malecón is no longer close to the sea: a broad white beach separates us from it. There are some people sunbathing. Others are swimming or rowing in the sand. There is a group of children playing on a large flat dazzling white strip of concrete near the wall. Now the sun is strong, very strong, too strong and we all feel like we are being crushed, flattened, shriveled up by this unexpectedly strong sunlight. Something suggests that we are in danger or there is an uncertain suggestion which then becomes a reality: the beach—and not only the white sand but the sea as well which is no longer blue, but white, not only the land, the water as well, are rising—folds over and climbs on top of itself. The sun is so strong that the black dress my companion is wearing begins to burn and her invisible face is black and white and ashes all at once. I hurl myself off the wall toward the beach or toward what was the beach but is now a field of ashes and start running without so much as giving a thought to my companion, forgetting in my fear not only my affection for her, but also the pleasure of having her with me. We are all running except her, and she stays where she is, on top of the wall, burning quietly. We run run run run run run toward the beach which has now turned into an enormous umbrella. To save ourselves involves running under the shelter of the umbrella. We are still running (there is a child who falls over and another who sits down on the ground, worn out maybe, but it's of no importance even to his mother, who continues running, although she looks behind her for a moment as she runs) and we have almost reached the umbrella of white sand and white sea and white sky as well now. At the same moment as I see that the shade of the umbrella is being wiped out by a white light, I also realize that the pillar is not shaped like an umbrella but like a mushroom, and that not only is it no protection against the murderous light, but that the pillar itself is the light. In the dream, this moment seems to have come too late or is no longer important. I keep running.

VIII

—It's the myth of Lot in the light of present-day science. Or of its dangers, I tell him and at the same time I'm saying it I realize how pedantic I'm being.

—Possibly. In any case you can see now that neither myself nor my subconscious nor my atavistic fears have any liking for the sea. Neither the sea nor nature nor outer space. I believe, as Holmes says, that concentrated spaces are an aid to the concentration of thought.

—Boethius is the cell he lived in. The consolations of claustrosophy.

—Not quite, because you could talk about the groves of Academe and about Plato and fuck up my argument. But it's true I've never seen an open-air lab. I'm thinking of ending my days in a cubicle at the National Library, of course.

—Reading everything from Pythagoras to Madame Blavatsky.

—No. Interpreting dreams and decoding ciphers and playing the numbers.

—What would Eliphas Levy say?

We had finally left the Malecón and I saw how the clouds had drifted away from the city and formed a white and gray and occasionally pink wall between the sea and the horizon. Cué was doing a thousand.

—You know that Cuban literature has never concerned itself with the sea, even though we are condemned to what Sartre would call islienation?

—That doesn't surprise me. Haven't you seen the equestrian statue of Maceo and how it turns its hindquarters toward the Pontos? And people sitting on the wall do what I did in my dream and turn their backs on the seascape, completely absorbed in this landscape of asphalt and concrete and passing cars.

—But the strange thing is that even Martí said: "The stream of the mountains pleases us more than the sea."

—And you're going to rectify this rhetorical rebuff?

—Dunno. But someday I'm going to write on the sea.

—Shit. The joke is that you don't even know how to swim.

—So what? According to you the only poet who could do it would be Esther Williams.

—See? You're beginning to understand why some of my best friends are numbers.

I searched all along the far-off/black/breezy archaic arches around the Carreño building, beyond the Tower of San Lázaro, and in the very exclusive mock-castle where Mercedez Bens on street level had all you need for traveling (spare parts & accessories inc.), which would have excited Cué, and upstairs Mary Tornes had her famous brothel for rich people, where you had to ask for an appointment by phone and prove your identity as a client first and where you were offered all you need for loving (spare parts & accessories inc.), which excited me without tempting me overmuch and where one day I met a girl who was beautiful but had only one arm and was dumb because of her almost eternal profession and I went on scanning the length of the porticos now where the sun was casting a placable shadow and when we pulled up at the MiTío service station I had my revenge and Arsenio Cué his nemesis: a lottery vendor holding up a vertical multicolored display leaflet with the ticket numbers in one hand, while with the other he offered the tickets and proclaimed all you need for winning in a voice we couldn't hear. I pointed to him and told Cué:

—Sad end for a philosophy.

IX

Is space in space? Arsenio Cué seemed to want to prove it and the fact that he contradicted me quoting Holmes was proof just as now he was driving along the Malecón in the opposite direction or, like a pendulum, swinging back to the way we came. He was concentrating on the driving and now that the scenery wasn't broken by his histrionic profile, I gazed at the brilliant sky and the low-hanging, far-off and deceptively solid clouds that looked like unreal islands and the sea which lay spread out a little way beyond the window and the sea wall. La Chorrera slipped by again, like the signal to leave your seat in a continuous program at the movies. Cué didn't enter the tunnel but went around it and up to 23rd and he pulled up alongside the traffic signals there and pressed the button to lower the top, which slid back like a moveable sky. I remembered the Verdun movie house and its moveable roof. We started up again with the air enveloping and oppressing and holding us back: it was the only boundary in our new-found freedom. From the bridge over the Río Almendares, with the dense thickets of trees on its banks and its wooden piers and the sun's reflection on the muddy current, it all looked like a river out of Conrad. We went down Mendoza and after a while took a right and continued down the Avenida del Río. Once more we saw the handwritten sign saying *Think twise—would you thro bricks to woman with baby*? and Cué said, —Nobody but W.C.! Fields could have done it, like that other sign on the Via Blanca which read OPEN ONLY TO GANCEDO meaning you couldn't turn except into Gancedo Street, and Cué said that it was one more exclusive property of the industrialist of the same name, or in the Biltmore where another sign read SLOW DOWN—YOU ARE RISKING THE LIVES OF OUR SONS and one night he had wanted to substitute the letter *s* for a *c*, or when he passed the sign on the Cantarranas highway which said DELICIOUS BLACKS AND DELECTABLE MOORS. DRIVE IN, an ad for black beans and rice, called "Moors and Christians" in Havana, he said it was a standing invitation for André Gide—which he pronounced André Yi until I asked him who this distinguished Chinese pederast was. We talked about billboards and signs like that surrealist one on the beach, which said RIDERS ON THE SAND PROHIBITED. Synge at Guanabo perhaps? Or the unconscious humor of Alfredo T. Quílez when he ordered that on the walls of the house where they printed *Carteles* magazine the traditional notice NO CARTELES, which means no posters, should be replaced by one saying NO LAMPOONS. Or the enigmatic DON'T THROW IN YOUR DOGS on the gate of a villa on Línea Street, which was absurd but for the little-known fact that an heiress turned her manor into an asylum for dogs and anyone who wanted to get rid of an undesirable cur would throw it over the gate—a sudden and unexpected airy sanctuary. And what about the sign outside a glassware shop which would have made all the difference in the world, if not for P'ui at least for the Dowager Empress: WE SPECIALIZE IN THE RESTORATION OF

CHINA. Or when Cué wanted to write on the notice in the El Recodo bar which said HOT DOGS HERE! the words *Cave Canem!* Or to add to the numerous ads reading PROPOSALS WELCOME on sites that were up for sale the word DISHONEST for an opener. It was he who also found this last beautiful piece of Sign Buddhism in Mexico, which notified truck drivers carrying building materials: MATERIALISTS ARE FORBIDDEN TO STOP IN THE ABSOLUTE. Arsenio Cué always predictable and always surprising and renewing himself. Like the sea.

We came out on Seventh and crossed Fifth Avenue (Cué called it Filthy Ava Nude) and went along up First: he offered me another San Lázaro Street and I saw the sea again, this time cut into fragments between Californian villas and hanging balconies attached to châteaux and family villas and hotel de posh and the Blanquita Theater (the Very Illustrious Senator Viriato Solaún y Zulueta wanted to be the owner of the largest theater in the world and asked, Which is the greatest theater on earth? Radio City, they told him. It has six thousand seats: well, the Blanquita has twenty seats more) and private and public balneal beaches and a vacant lot (Proposals wel) where the grass grew up to the shoreline, and at the end of the street, as we turned back toward Fifth Avenue, going all the way down Third so as to join the avenue by the tunnel and flying up along this street with its trees and lawns, hurtling through these vertiginous gardens at 60 mph, I realized what made Arsenio run. Under the simmering sky.

He didn't want to eat up the miles as we say here (and it's curious how many things in Cuba go in through the mouth and not only do we eat up space, but to eat a woman means making love and balls-eater and shit-eater is a synonym for an idiot and to eat rope means to go hungry, to be down and out and a fire-eater is a goon and to eat out of someone's hand is to let oneself be tamed by an adversary and when someone does something well or extraordinary, we say he ate it up, *se la comió!*), it was more like he was going over the word mile and I thought his intention was the same as my pretension to remember everything or as Códac's temptation wanting all the women to have a single vagina (though vagina wasn't exactly the word he used) or like Eribó who got an erection whenever he heard distant drums or the late Bustrófedon who wanted to be a living language. We were totalitarians: immortals to be by uniting the end and the beginning. But Cué was wrong (we were all wrong, all of us except, perhaps, Bustrófedon, who could well be immortal by now), because if time is irreversible, space is irreducible and what's more infinite. This was why I could ask him:

—Where are we going?

—I don't know, he said. —You choose and I'll obey.

—I don't have the slightest.

—How about Marianao beach? Cué said.

I was delighted. For a moment I thought he was going to say Mariel. One of these days we are going to come to blows with the blue dragon or the white tiger or the black turtle. Cué will also find his Ultima Thule. What did I tell you? We braked violently on 12th Street because the lights had changed to red. I had to hold on tight.

—"The air invents the eagle": Goethe, said Cué. —"The traffic signals invent the brakes": I. Myself.

X

We continued under the shade of the trees (laurels or false laurels, jacarandas, flowering chestnuts and in the distance the enormous fig trees of the park—cut in two by the avenue whose name I can never remember and from which these holy green giants look like a single Bo tree repeated in a blasphemous set of mirrors) like a roof over our heads and when we got to the pine trees nearer the shore I scented the sea, briny and penetrating like a shell opening up, and I thought, like Códac, that the sea is a sexual organ, another vagina. We saw Las Playitas slip past, and the amusement park which is called, inevitably, Coney Island, and the Rumba Palace and the Panchín and the Taberna de Pedro (which by night is a musical oyster with Chori as its black pearl singing and playing and making fun of himself and of everybody else as well: he's one of the clowns most deserving of world fame and perhaps the most anonymous) and the little bars, cafés and fried-food stands that meant, as on Avenida del Puerto, that the street was coming to an end or a beginning, and on Biltmore Avenue the date palms of Fifth Avenue turned into royal palms and I knew now where we were going—along the Santa Fe trail. Soon (because Cué stepped on the accelerator) we had left Villanueva behind and the picken-chicken (picking chicking), which became memorable one night, and the golf courses so we could see the roadsteads and the yachts at anchor and behind them the gulf and beyond the horizon the barrier of heavy white and solid clouds that formed the wall of another Malecón.

—Do you know Barlovento?

—Yes, I think I've been there with you. It's that allotment . . .

—I mean the Bar Lovento, Cué said.

Jaimanitas is a popular beach, but from the Santa Fe highway it's no more than a few flat ugly concrete houses, a first-aid hospital and one or two run-down bars and a river surrounded by mangrove swamps with stagnant water neither blue nor brown nor green but a dirty gray that glitters in the sun because the sea although you can't see it is only half a block away and the breeze comes up the channel of the river as though up a chimney.

—I don't remember it, I remember I told him. —Is that its name?

—No. It's called La Odisea.

—And I suppose the owner's a guy called Homer. Why not Aeneid Bar?

—You'd be surprised, but the bar's called Laodicea and that's the name of the owner, Juan. Juan Laodicea.

—Surprise is the cradle of poetry.

—It's a great place. You'll see what I mean.

We took a right turn, down a new avenue where the asphalt was still black, with tall curved concrete street lamps that bent over the road like Scott Fitzgerald's flappers over love, like the necks of antediluvian beasts over their prey, like Martians spying on our peripatetic way of life. At the bottom there was a hotel or the unfinished structure of a hotel, a square edifice. We took a turn to the left, and rode parallel to the sea, like the canals of this rich man's Venice whose happy owners could keep their automobiles in the carport and their motor launches in the yacht port and feel hemmed in by all you need for flight. I knew this was the paradise of the Cués. The project (or its realization) was false, or fictitious, but like everything in this country nature lent it its true beauty. The Traveler was right. The place was incredible for more than one reason. We arrived at the bar, which was on a wooden bridge on one of the side canals, and had a view of a large lagoon, also artificial, where the sun was reflected and multiplied in nuggets, in threads, in veins that formed a gold coast. In front of the bar was a maze of little coves and marine pines. I saw five palm trees whose trunks were covered with gigantic growths of lianas and on the sixth palm the fronds had died so that it appeared naked among its neighbors.

—This is my amen, Cué said. I thought he meant to say his acme.

—Drive back, I asked him.

—What for?

—Drive back, please.

—You want to go back to Havana.

—No, I just want you to drive back, twenty or thirty yards. To drive backward, not to turn around.

—In reverse?

—Yes.

He did so. So fast we shot back something like fifty yards.

—Whoa! Now go forward. Slowly. Slow as you can.

He did so and I closed one eye. I saw the canals, the roadsteads and the sea filing slowly past and finally I saw that the bar and the swamp and the vegetation all merged in one dimension and although there was a variety of color and I remembered everything as I had seen it just before, in depth, the light vibrated over the landscape and I felt I was in a movie. Like Philip Marlowe in a Raymond Chandler novel. Or rather, Robert Montgomery-Marlowe-Chandler in the few unforgettable moments of *The Lady in the Lake*, which I saw in the Alkazar on September 7, 1946. I told Cué. I had to let him know.

—Jesus Christ, you are completely nuts! he said and got out. —Nuts nuts (he was walking away). You've got the movies, that's what! he said as a parting diagnosis. But I followed him closely. Lumière & Son. We walked under a trellis of honeysuckle and past a lawn not of grass but of sea moss. We went into the bar. It was a dark room and I saw a dark rectangular strip of rough water at the far end which I realized afterward was a fish tank. At the back there were some doors which opened onto the still blinding light from which we'd come. Someone behind us, a woman's voice, said, —He who has ears to hear let him hear, and an invisible crowd of men and women, voices with no flesh on them, laughed. Cué greeted the barman or owner, who returned his greeting as though he hadn't seen him for ages or as though he had just left him in his house, with affectionate astonishment. Cué explained to me who he was, but I wasn't listening, so fascinated was I by the fish tank where there was a horny ray swimming around in circles eternally. It was what we call an *obispo,* a bishop, and you—yes, *you!*—call a devilfish. Cué told me that they always had one and that it was always dying so they always changed it for another, but that he couldn't distinguish them, and that this one could be either the earlier model or a stand-in.

We were drinking. Cué ordered a daiquiri without sugar and lots of lemon. Actor's diet, I said. No, he said, just doing what you should be doing: following the Gran Maestro. I ordered a *mojito* and amused myself looking at it, jiggling it, holding in my hands this Cuban mint julep which is a metaphor of Cuba. Water, vegetation, sugar (brown), rum and artificial cold. Mix and strain, stir till glass frosts, spin rim in sugar (white). Serves seven (million) people. Should I tell Cué? It would unleash his wit. Hughes says that a bound man is much more frightening than a free man and maybe it's because he can free himself at any moment. I was equally afraid of Cué's wit. But my name is Fearless Fosdick: I told him. After calling the waiter or his friend and asking him to bring us another round (first warning him, as he always did, not to take away his glasses even if they were empty), Cué untied himself, no: he burst free to juggle with life and man and the eternal: Promis-Cuetheus Unbound. I'll spare the reader the explicit crap of Cué's dialogues and offer instead his complete works. Or rather, his pandects. I don't know if they are worth anything. In any case they will serve to kill what Cué hates most: time.

XI

CONFESSIONS OF A CUBAN OPINION EATER

On opium:[1]

Quotation from the Monk of the Six Fingers (Si-tse Fing-ah; Fu-kyu-tuh dynasty):

"Opium is the religion of the Chinese."

From Marx (he asked me if Marx had read Hegel? Groucho. Groucho Marx, not Groucho Hegel):

"Work is the opiate of the people."

From Berkeley (the non-U, Busby):

"Movies are the opiate of the audience."

From your servant Silvestre (Mu-vee dynasty):

"Opium is the cinema of the blind."

Four centuries before Sartre, Christopher Marlowe:

Faustrus (he pronounced it like that, then in earnest):

FAUSTUS: Where are you damned?

MEPHISTOPHELES: In hell.

FAUSTUS: How comes it then thou art out of hell?

MEPHISTOPHELES: Why, this is hell!

Dies Faustae:

There are many exegeses on The Strange Case of Doctor Jekyll and Mister Hyde: some of them intelligent (Borges), some popular (Victor Fleming), and still others disconcerting (Jean Renoir). Note that I am talking to you about fiction, film and television. In other words present-day culture. There must have been many other interpretations which have escaped my notice, but I don't believe any of them—either the magical or the psychoanalytical or the rationalist—succeeds in unveiling the original mystery. (Pause. Arsenius Wolfgang Guéthe was giving dramatic stress to his words, a second glass in his hand.) Stevenson's short novel, Silvestre, is, let it be carefully understood, another version of the myth of Faust.

1 Arsenio de Quéncy was reeking with opinium. It was coming out of his ears. (*Titles by commentator*)

Art and its disciples:

> Neither the lunar nor the solar spheres,
> Nor the dry land nor the waters over earth,
> Nor the air nor the moving winds in the limitless spaces
> Shall endure ever:
> *Thou alone art! Thou alone!*
>
> RAG MAJH KI VAR
> *The Sacred Writings of the Sighs*

Cuévafy:

"And now what shall become of us without any barbarians? Those people were a kind of solution."

Mansportret:

"The condom is a mechanical barrier used by the male."

> ELIZABETH PARKER, M.D.
> *The Seven Ages of Women*

What would the authoress of *Caoba, the Guerilla Chief* say?

A question I always hear ringing in my ears late at night, said in an Italianate voice: Wasa there ever sucha a person as Vittorio Campolo?

The English in their bath:

The Eureka bathtub (Shanks & Co., Ltd., Barnhead, Scotland: see the Siracusa Hotel on El Caney beach) would have considerably facilitated the creative labors of Archimedes. Or is this merely one more example of the unpluggable humor of English plumbers? (Videlicet: a toilet nicknamed Shark, a bowl labeled Niagara, a urinal called Adamant, et cacaetera, faecetera.)

Nothingness is the other name of Eternity:

There is more nothing than anything. Nothingness is always here, in latent nonform. Being has to manifest itself expressly. Something comes out of nothing, struggles to become manifest and then disappears again, into nothing.

We do not live in nothing, but nothing lives in us, in a sense.

Nothingness is not the opposite of being. Being is nothingness expressed in other terms.

Musa paradisiaca or what cut Cué's knotted knot:

The discoverers mistook our manatee (order *Sirenia,* genus

manatus: a siren with hands) for a mermaid: their breasts, their almost human face and their method of coitus (a two-backed beast), all contributed to the analogy. But other more Cuban symbols escaped attention because they were of a vegetal order.

The palm tree, with its feminine trunk and the green tresses of its leaves, is our Medusa.

The cigar (a Havana, also called panatela, breva, corona or cheroot) is an avatar of the phoenix: when it seems to be extinguished, dead, the fire of life rises from its ashes.

The banana tree (muse of paradise) is the tropical Hydra: if one cuts off its head of fruit another rises to replace it and the plant acquires a new life.

Cantata to tea, Coffee concerto, Maté motet:

Coffee is a sexual stimulant. Tea is intellectual. Maté is the bitter primitive residue of a hungover dawn in New York circa 1955. (I am speaking for myself and also for you, Silvestre. I don't care what the scientists say. For this reason my example should be seen as both personal and remote.)

A coffee sipped on the corner of 12th and 23rd, at dawn, or just before, the morning wind from the Malecón still on my face, stinging my senses and the speed (the thing about speed that is so intoxicating is that it turns a physical action into a metaphysical experience: speed turns time into space—I, Silvestre, told him that the movies turn space into time and Cué answered, That is another experience that physics cannot comprehend), the speed, I myself, buffeted head-on and in profile by this dawn wind, exhaustion and an empty stomach making you conscious of your body, with that beauteous lucidity of insomnia after a night session cutting endless bars of soap operas, cut in your mind, it is then that a coffee—a simple coffee costing three centavos—a strong black coffee drunk when El Flaco, that long thin shadow, leaves his night shift, after scandalizing the workers going early to their work, the nightwalkers, the exhausted night watchmen, the night whores standing drenched in dew and sperm, all these, all this fauna of the night zoo you find at the gates of the Colón cemetery, all these people hit by his Tchaikovsky his Prokoviev his Stravinsky (and let his megamelomania go as far as Webern and Schönberg and—but, my

God, they'd lynch him!—Edgar Varèse), names which El Flaco, flaccidly, would hardly be able to pronounce, playing them on 23rd and 12th (and note that 23 and 12 make 35 and 3 and 5 make 8 while the sums of 2 and 3 and 1 and 2 respectively make 5 and 3, which also make 8: this street corner is perpetually condemned to traffic with the dead: 8 means death in the *charada,* as you know: this explains why the cemetery being on 12th and Zapata, a very long block away from 12th and 23rd, 23rd and 12th is a common synonym in Havana for cemetery), playing them on that pitiful portable phonograph of his which scratches all his records—this half cup of water and aroma and blackness is transformed (in me) into an urgent need to go in search, Eribó of the actresses, of them, call them N or M or M or N, or whatever her name is, call on them, on her, and wake her from her dreams of scenic grandeur and what with her heavy somnolence and my keen-edged wakefulness and the tumescent heat of this eternal summer's morning, to make love to make love to make love to, her to make to.

Tea always makes me work, think, want to get things done—intellectually, that is.

There must be some scientific explanation, something connected with excitation of the lobes or the circulation of the blood or what the phrenologists would call a perfusion under the cranial cortex and also with the titillation, out of sympathy, of the solar plexus. But I don't want to admit it, I don't want to have anything to do with it, I don't want to know this hypothesis. Don't tell me, Silvestre. Please, no. *Ay! Que no quiero saberla!*

I commiserate with Macedonio Fernández, with Borges and maybe also with Bioy Casares, although I'm quite prepared to congratulate Queen Victoria Ocampo: you can't grow a culture on maté. It will still be a hybrid—Biorges, Borgasares, Defeata Ocampo. A Matedonio.

Godspeed:

The idea of listening to Palestrina in a jet made you laugh. Yes, Padre Vitoria is my copilot and all that mass. But have you thought what effect speed might have on literature? Just focus your two point eight attention on this phenomenon alone: a plane flying between London and Paris arrives five minutes before it left when the jet makes the return flight from London to Paris. What will happen when man can travel at five or six thousand kilometers an hour and finds that he thinks less quickly than he moves? Is such a man the same thinking reed that Pascal thought he was? (Man, that is, not Pascal.) And yet, it often seems to you that I drive fast.

Why I am not a writer:

You often ask me why I don't write. I could answer you by saying that I have no sense of history. It costs me an entire day's effort to think about the next day. I could never say, following Stendhal, People will be reading me in the year 2058. (Which adds up to 15 or 33, because they both add up to 6, an even number which has an odd number imaging it in the mirror: a 9.) *Domani è troppo tardi.*

Besides, I haven't the slightest reverence either for Marcel Proust (which he rhymed, distinctly, with pooh), or for James Joyce (Cué pronounced it Shame's Choice) or for Kafka (it sounded like caca in his otherwise well-behaved voice). This is the Holy Trinity, whom you must adore if you are to write in the twentieth century—and as I wouldn't be able to write in the twenty-first . . .

Is it my fault if Bay City moves me more than Combray? Yes, I suppose it is. How about you? You should call this Chandler's Syndrome.

Speaking of Laura Cton?

Flowers corrupt. But corruption deflowers.

Way of livink:

I live between the provisory and disorder, in a state of anarchy. This chaos must be come what may another metaphor for life.

Who could be my ventriloquist?

Somebody up there Cues me.

The Time Killer:

The Duchess of Malfi pardoned her executioners because they did no more than catarrh would have done. Why so much hatred for Hitler, then? The majority of the people whom he killed would be dead now anyway. A campaign should be launched in the UN, and everywhere else as well, to declare Time a genocide.

(EICHMANN, showing Hitler the gas ovens, etc.: Now, Meine Führer, vad do you zink of my final solution?

FÜHRER: It's a gas, Adolf!)
Example of metaphoric or vital chaos:

A tale of Helius and Caballus: I was engaged in dubious battle with Juan Blanco, alias Jan DeWitte, the composer of "Canción Triste," who writes music under the nom de flute of Giovanni Bianchi. We leave his house at eight in the evening and go to the corner of Paseo and Zapata. Juan orders a chocolate milk shake, I a tomato juice. He, a custard apple ice cream, Arsenio Cué: strawberries and cream. JB: a pineapple juice and then a V-8—me, a hamburger. Juan eats a steak sandwich: he knows that the Era of Solid Commodities is dawning. I order a rice pudding: there is a time to live and a time to die, a time for entrées and a time for dessert. Juan Blanco devours a bread pudding, I peck at a cheeseburger. Job orders a *masarreal,* moi a guava pie. (Shit, we've exhausted both list and lust!) Ivan a pinta milka, Siberianly chilled, sybaritically sipped. As I watch him I make signs of Gangway!, and go out at a run, pale and cerulean, to the white john. It's all too clear that I've lost the battle. My kingdom for a cow! When I return, Juan, Sean, Johannes, John, João and this buncha guys are taking the Alkaseltzer of Segovia. But the pint is empty, *hélas! et j'ai bu tous les litres!* They will preserve the bottle cast in platinum and iridium in the museum of moderate pinting. Ave Ioannis Vomituri Te Salutant. SPQIB.

We go back again to his apartment. This night is filled with pupils from the conservatory. They are coming to hear for the third time, my God, the Ninth Symphony of that "monster in chains," as a musical nymph said the other day in this very place, meaning Beethoven. Don't be upset, Silver Tray, because another she-pupil insisted on describing LVB as the Blind Man of Bonn. And as it is still very early for Bonn and too late for the goils, there was yet another (they function by a process of internal convulsion) musical gal who carried me off to the balcony—I rubbing my venereal hands. But all we did was to confirm, yet again, the theory of relativity. She pointed to a light. Venus, she told me, the Morning Star. What made me unhappy was not that it was night and not morning nor that I was engaged in an erotic fiasco, only that I looked and could see neither Venus nor Mars but a brilliant yellow ordinary light bulb lighting up somebody's terrace. My tower of lust came tumbling down but I didn't say a word, believing with Brecht that truth shouldn't be told to everybody.

That night of the navel battle we went out again at midnight, all of us, to eat something after the Muses were silent. The girls insisted, melomaniacally, that we shouldn't eat anything solid after the spiritual nourishment that the tortured soul of Ludwig van and the well-salaried technicians of RCA Victor had provided. We put on an appearance of being convinced and hummed to cover up our belches.

Ah Oscarwilderness:

"There is a land full of strange flowers and subtle perfumes . . . a land where all things are perfect and poisonous."

The charge of the night brigade:

He returned to his numbers which were his charge of the 666. Arsenio Cué was as much enamored of numbers as he was of himself. Or vice-roy.

The 3 was the Great Number, almost Number One, because it was the first of the prime numbers which can be divided only by themselves or by unity. (Cué said Unity.)

Doesn't it seem strange to you that 5 and 2 are numbers that are so different and yet so similar? (I didn't disagree with him and he didn't tell me why.)

The number 8 is another of the keys to the Mystery. It is made out of two zeros and is the first number to contain a cube. The Big Step, that is to say the 2, is its cube root and 8 is at the same time 2 times 4, which is the geometric or Pythagorean number par excellence. All this & more it is vertically and in the Cuban *charada* it spells death, and 64, in the Chinese *charada*, is the Great Dead, *Muerto Grande*. $8 \times 8 = 64$ as you *should* know. (I told him I did, nodding the head of my tail.) In antiquity it was the number dedicated to Poseidon, that god Neptune who has streets and statues and lighthouses named after him here in Cuba, and whom you love so much. *Calle* Neptuno, if you remember, begins in *Central* Park.

It is this number that when it gets tired and lies down, stretches itself, has no end, it is infinity. (Or its symbol, which is the only finite thing we know about infinity, I told him. He didn't hear me.) Space is a Procrustean bed.

The five (sorry, Cué, my boy, the 5) is a magic number in

Chinese numerical mythology: it was they who invented the five senses, the five organs of the body, etc.

The 9 is another number that behaves "strangely." It is, of course, the square of 3, which is the first true odd number, given that the 1 is unity, the base of all things, our mother. (And the zero? I asked him.) It is an Arabic convention, he said. It isn't a number. (But it is our infinite, I said. We begin from it and we end in it. He smiled. He also made a zero sign with his fingers, that popular *mudrá* which indicates besides that everything is going or has gone well—or that there isn't anything.) 9 added to itself makes 18 and multiplied by itself makes 81. Back to front and counting from the right, the same number in a mirror. As you can see, if you add each one of its digits you find a 9 again.

Do you know that the prime numbers are strange compared with the even and odd numbers? (No, I didn't.) Yes, their series is discontinuous and arbitrary and it is still not complete. It will never be completed. Only the great mathematicians and the great magicians discover prime numbers—or are able to discover them.

(Where, in this company, would Arsenio Cué stand?)

I will show you the one number which is truly perfect. (He paused and looked at me.) Doesn't it seem strange to you that on almost all typewriters, certainly on yours, the sign for numbers is above the 3, as if to say this is The Number? It is the great square.

(With great ostentation he picked up a paper napkin and pulled my pen out of my pocket. He started drawing numbers.)

4 9 2

(He paused. I thought he was going to add them up.)

4 9 2
3 5 7

(He stopped drawing numbers and looked at me. They are all prime numbers, he said.)

4 9 2
3 5 7
8

(Let's hope the last one isn't as drunk as you, I said. Or at the slightest provocation we will be in the clutches of infinity.)

4	9	2
3	5	7
8	1	

(Stability for you, he said, smiling, and for me too.)

4	9	2
3	5	7
8	1	6

(He looked at the piece of paper triumphantly, as though he had invented or was about to invent this numerical square.)

There you are. The magic square. It's worth as much as a circle. He looked at me as though waiting for me to ask him why. (Why?) Because however you add it up you will get the number 15. Vertically, diagonally and horizontally it makes 15. You can see also that the sum of these digits, 1 and 5, is 6, which is the last number in the series and if you subtract 1 from 5 you get 4, which is the first number of the square.

As you can see, the 0 is missing. Historically this proves that the square existed before the Arabs, because formerly it was made of letters which served as numbers. For me this is the square of life.

(I wanted to tell him that he was a latter-day Euclidean, but I saw an early Pythagorean in his answer.)

This is the denial of your nothingness. Of 0.

Aleatory literature:

(At this point I began criticizing him—a pluribus unum: I am always like that: I react against the thing I have in front of me, even if it's my own mirror image—reproaching him for allowing himself to be carried away by numbers, and he answered me with a quotation:)

I only trust in things uncertain
All things plain seem clouded over
I only doubt the truth that's certain
Only in chance do I feel sure
And when I win, then I'm the loser

FRANÇOIS VILLON
Ballade du Concours de Blois

(That's literature, I think I said.)

No, literature is this Possible Masterpiece; it would be necessary to rewrite *Le Rouge et le Noir,* page after page, line by line, sentence by sentence, word after word, letter by letter. It would even be necessary to put periods and commas on top of periods and commas, in the same place, avoiding the original periods and commas with the utmost care. One would have to place the dots on the *i*'s (and on the *j*'s, I said) over the *i*'s, without displacing the original dots. The man who did this and succeeded in writing a radically different book, the same but different, would have achieved The Masterpiece. The man who signed such a book (Pierre Menard, I interrupted—Arsenio didn't disagree with me but said: You too thought it was him!) with the name of (here a borgesian pause followed)—of Stendhal would have achieved the Absolute Masterpiece.

(It's a blueprint drafted with sympathetic ink.)

No. Nor is it a program. The only possible literature for me would be an aleatory literature. (Like random music? I asked.) No, it wouldn't have a score, just a dictionary. (I must have been thinking of Bustrófedon because he immediately corrected himself:) Or rather a list of words that wouldn't have any order at all, in which your friend Zeno wouldn't simply join hands with Avicenna, which is too easy because they are opposites, but both of them would find themselves in the company of cabbage soup or shotgun or moon. Along with the book the reader would be provided with an anagram to make a title out of and a couple of dice. With these three elements anyone would be able to make his own book. If he throws a 1 and a 3, then he can look for the first and third words or even for word number 4 or even the thirteenth word—or for all of them together, and these could be read in an arbitrary order so as to abolish or increase the element of chance. The arrangement of the list of words would also be arbitrary, and both this and the reader's rearrangement would be decided by the dice. Perhaps in this way we would get real poems and the poet would once more become a maker or a troubadour. The aleatory would then no longer be merely an approximation or a metaphor. *Alea jacta est* means the die is cast, as I hope you know.

(You know El B has an idea that's not so different from yours?)

Really? What is it? Do I know it?

(Was he worried by what I said or simply interested? That's what I thought but I said: He thinks or rather thought that it would be possible to make a book out of three or two or even *one* word! He told me once he had succeeded in writing a whole page consisting of precisely one single—and he stressed: *not* married—word.)

Chano Pozo got there before, circa 1946, in his *guaracha* "Blen blen blen." Remember? It didn't have any lyrics except:

Score

Blen blen blen blen blen blen blen blen blen blen
blen blen blen blen blen blen blen blen blen blen
blen blen blen blen blen blen blen blen blen blen
blen blen blen blen blen blen blen blen blen blen
blen blen blen blen blen blen blen blen blen blen
blen blen blen blen blen blen blen blen blen blen
blen blen blen blen blen blen blen blen blen blen
blen blen blen blen blen blen blen blen blen blen
blen blen blen blen blen blen blen blen blen blen
blen blen blen blen blen blen blen blen blen blen
blen blen blen blen blen blen blen blen blen blen
blen blen blen blen blen blen blen blen blen blen
blen blen blen blen blen blen blen blen blen blen
blen blen blen blen blen blen blen blen blen blen
blen blen blen blen blen blen blen blen blen blen
blen blen blen blen blen blen blen blen blen blen
blen blen blen blen blen blen blen blen blen blen
blen blen blen blen blen blen blen blen blen blen
blen blen blen blen blen blen blen blen blen blen
blen blen blen blen blen blen blen blen blen blen
blen blen blen blen blen blen blen blen blen blen
blen blen blen blen blen blen blen blen blen blen
blen blen blen blen blen blen blen blen blen blen
blen blen blen blen blen blen blen blen blen blen
blen blen blen blen blen blen blen blen blen blen
blen blen blen blen blen blen blen blen blen blen
blen blen blen blen blen blen blen blen blen blen
blen blen blen blen blen blen blen blen blen blen
blen blen blen blen blen blen blen blen blen blen
blen blen blen blen blen blen blen blen blen blen
blen blen blen blen blen blen blen blen blen blen
blen blen blen blen blen blen blen blen blen blen
blen blen blen blen blen blen blen blen blen blen
blen blen blen blen blen blen blen blen blen blen
blen blen blen blen blen blen blen blen blen blen
blen blen blen blen blen blen blen blen blen blen
blen blen blen blen blen blen blen blen blen blen

What would Mary MacArty say about this?

What would Susana Domingo have to say?

What about Virginia Beowulf, whom you could call Nirvana Cacanova?

"You and I together in earth, in smoke, in dust, in shadows, in nothing."

How to kill an elephant: aboriginal method:

In Africa there are few rivers so deep that an animal as enormous as the elephant is obliged to swim and it is common enough to see migratory herds wading across the current. Often the water doesn't rise above knee level (the knees of an elephant, that is), but sometimes it completely covers the animal. Then they walk along the bed of the river, with only their trunks appearing above the surface, like breathing periscopes.

The black hunters can then without any difficulty take advantage of the elephant when he is crossing a river. They tie a weight to a spear and hurl it at the snorkel of flesh from a canoe. The weight causes the trunk to sink and De Oliphant to drown.

Eight hours later (not by a watch: by African time) the gases inside the carcass of the elephant make him float to the surface. He remains there like a harpooned whale and the natives can then easily capture their prey.

(It was, obviously, a quotation. Where the hell did he get it from, this metaphysical Charlie McCarthy?)

Popuhilarity:

Someone once said that the popularity of the word metaphysics is due to the fact that it can mean whatever you like.

Pascalm:

& People mistake what are only the Virtues for their virtues. Ethical superstitions.

& When somebody says, I have no respect for those who are powerful, what he means is that *one shouldn't* have any respect for those who are powerful. All of us pay respect to the strong and accept it from those who are weak. This last, despite any false declaration to the contrary: I hate flattery. This was Hegel's one really remarkable discovery (an ad hoc grimace from me, Silvestre), this immemorial relationship between slave and master, a discovery so profound that it makes one forget that the same man once said: "What one knows is greater than what one doesn't know."

The French make a virtue out of lucidity which is really nothing more than a vice: an ideal vision of life, which is in reality confused. At least, my life (which is the only one I know more or less well) is confused.

There are people who see life as ordered and logical, the rest of us know that it is absurd and confused. Art (like religion or science or philosophy) is just one more attempt to focus the light of order on the gloom of chaos. Lucky you, Silvestre, who can (or think you can) get anywhere with words. Passwords.

& It is a pity that art endeavors to imitate life. Dopey & Happy the times when life copies art.

The only thing eternal is eternity:

& Death is a return to the point of departure, a completing of the circle, a way back to a total future. In other words, to the past, to the past as well. In other words, to eternity. If you like you can add something from T. S. Eliot (Or Tess Elihoo, as he pronounced it), like Time present and time past or that quotation from Gertrude Stein you are so fond of. (Did I tell you it sounded like Get tru Stem?)

& Life is the continuation of death by other means. (Or vie se reversa, I said.)

& A life is nothing more than one half of a parenthesis waiting anxiously for the other half. We can put off the Great Arrival (or the Second Coming, as you would call it, Silver B. Yeats) only by opening up other parentheses in the middle: by creative work, by sport or by study—or by that Great Parenthesis, sex. (That's where your Second Coming should really come, I said. He laughed.) This is the orthography of life: Silvestre Isla (1929–   ). The second act is first a cipher, a void, then nothingness.

& Death is the great leveler: the bulldozer of God. (Or the bullgoader of Oz, said I. What about the Goddozer of bull?)

& The invisible tiger, as the Burmese call it. For me it is an invisible vehicle not a tiger. My invisible convertible. Someday I'm going to crash into It or It is going to run me over or I will throw myself out of It down Eternal road, 100 mph.

Do you know the Tale of the Long-haired Boy and the Bald

Woman, La Pelona, which is Cuban for death? It is a Creole version of *Appointment in Samarra.* A long-haired Boy was walking along main street when he saw Death but She didn't see him. Then he heard her saying, Ise gonna get me a long-haired boy today. He rushed into the nearest barber's shop and said to the barber, Shave it all off! He went back to the street feeling very cool, what with his head shaved to the skin and the evening breeze. Death, who had been searching up and down for a boy with long hair all day long and was simply dead tired, said when she saw the boy who had had his head shaved, O.K., so Ise not goin' to find me a long-haired boy, I'll grab hole of this skinhead instade!

Moral: All men are mortal, but some men are more mortal than others.

& Freud forgot the wise remark of that other Jew, Solomon: sex is not the only engine that drives a man between life and death. There is another, vanity. Life (and that other life which is called history) has been driven further by the wheel of vanity than by the piston of sex.

& Ortega (José Ortega y Gasset, not Domingo Ortega) said, I am myself and also my circumstance. (A Jew would say, I said, I am myself and my circumcision.)

& Evil men always win: it was Abel who was the first loser.

& It is not necessarily true that God supports local evil when there are more bad guys than good guys. It is rather that one baddy is equal to a crowd of goodies.

& It is better to be the victim than the executioner.

& Rine says, putting everything on stage as usual, that evil doesn't know how to organize a plot, that evil people can always make a magnificent first act, a good second act, but that they always break down in the third act. It's like a version of boy meets girl/boy loses girl/boy finds girl of one's life. The baddies always come to dust in a play by Shakespeare—in the fourth or fifth acts. But what happens to one-act lives?

& Vices are more convincing than virtues: we find Ahab more credible than Billy Budd.

& Good is afraid of evil, but evil laughs at good.

& Hell may be paved with good intentions, but everything else in it (its topography, architecture and decoration) is made of bad intentions. And hell's not just a cold-water flat, you know. (Try reading Dante's *Inferno* as a textbook in town planning: S.)

& Evil is the last resort of Good. (And vicious versa, a very low, drunken voice made itself said.)

& Yes, evil is the continuation of good by other methods. (And vice hiccup!)

Aren't we back to where we started?

(I don't know nor will we ever know, because at this point I got tired of being a Plato for this Socrates.)

XII

I was looking at the fish tank. There were a number of anonymous little fish which I didn't see because the ray kept swimming around and around incessant, obsessive, ghostlike, its sick white face lighting up as it reached its hideout between the stones. Then it would disappear in the dark stagnant water and reappear once more, always moving, never stopping for a moment. I thought it was cruel treatment but it wasn't surprising since it was only a fish. It is a devilfish Captain Cuésteau had said. He also informed me that they never lived longer than a month in captivity, not even in big pools, like sharks, which refuse to swim and run aground, to die of suffocation. One of the absurdities of nature, a fish that drowns. Neither sharks nor rays are fish, lectured Cuélinnaeus. I thanked him for this information about the life cycle of the ray, and he said you're welcome. Was I? What about the cruel sojourn of the ray in its mortal pool, was it welcome? He didn't say because I had forgotten Kuérkegaard the next minute and was remembering Count Dracula instead, the unforgettable Bela Lugosi, whose image I saw superimposed on the devilfish flapping his great mantle, covering his weird ghostly features with a cloak, obsessively traveling to and fro between the shadows and the dazzling glare of the aquarium (*We will be leaving tomorrow evening*), and I also saw beautiful ill-fated Carol Borland in *The Mark of the Vampire,* costarring with old Bela (Bela and La Belle, as Bustrófedon would say), him going through a Romanesque cobweb (The spider is spinning its vebb for the unvary fly) descending the Baroque staircase and stopping for a century at a peaceful Gothick window to watch over the victim who was sleeping promiscuously between Romantic curtains on an Art Nouveau sofa, and without giving a moment's reflection to this mad mixture of styles (Dracula, despite appearances to the contrary, is not an interior decorator) throwing himself on that deliciously tempting neck: that promised land of white flesh, that walking blood bank, that object of grief and love that would have given such pleasure to our Divine Markiss sitting on his nail-studded seat in the Charenton theater, enormous, bloated and greedy, drinking *sangría* (I never drink . . . wine) and eating gobbets of raw liver as though they were pink popcorn, and then as the devilfish flashes back again through his submarine cathedral I see the doubly immortal Lugosi terrified for all his infinite wickedness by a little crucifix and in the same memoryshot I see my young uncle who had once in a sudden fit of blasphemous rage broken his rosary and stamped on it and hurled it into the patio during a family quarrel one evening and later, at midnight, when he returned from the movies, where he had seen *The Vampire*, he was wandering around the patio like the Mad Doctor with a lamp in his hand, like a hunchbacked Christian Diogenes who only comes out at night, looking for the crucifix all over the orb of the orchard and he didn't go to sleep until he had found it and that dark night nothing happened in the patio, upon which I kept a close vigil with my eyes wide open peering over the blankets, watching for any ghostly sheets, but even if some evil creature had gone past I wouldn't have seen it since it was as dark as any night in the country when there is no moon, but when the moon is full and the *Marifasa Lupina Lumina* in flower, the werewolf comes to sow terror in London and steals along a gallery, a long corridor illuminated by the moon, and every time the shadow of a column falls on his face he grows more like a wolf and less like a man (an ingenious idea they used in movies before they perfected the fadeout-cum-reversed-makeup, the trick they used to transform Creighton Chaney into Lone Chaney, Jr., a lupine actor) and then he runs off ferociously through the garden speeding across it like an erratic arrow, leaping over hedges and running across fields and through some ghost-pale trees to a fatal clearing in the wood *au clair de lune fatale*, where he meets Nina Foch, and attacks and kills her. Did he rape her first? Or afterward? Did he flee, potent for killing, impotent even for kissing? Children don't know. The adult can think of these myths as fantasies of impotence, following the King Kong tradition which requires that the monster must always carry off the heroine but then afterward he doesn't know what to do with her, except to spend the whole content of his powder keg of love in the salvos of his sighs. The child, that child who looks like me sometimes, sits there suffering a delicious torture and sees nothing but the beautiful, white lifeless body of Nina Foch. No, not Nina Foch, no, because Nina is also a wolf, a wolf-woman, a she-wolf, CaNina Fox, a vulpine actress, just as the delectable, tiny, easy-to-fondle Simone Simon is the leopard-lady who stalks silently around the heated pool in the gymnasium/gynaeceum, and savagely slashes her rival's bathrobe on the edge of the swimming pool and makes the swinging doors echo her invisible presence walking past the lockers and up the stairs, where I fixed her forever: black and savage and utterly catlike: with fire blazing from her eyes all the better to seduce Kent Smith and foaming at the mouth, a mouth that is entirely full of fangs and bestial breath all the better to kiss Kent Smith and with her well-manicured claws all the better to caress, caressing, scratching, digging into, tearing to pieces and rending apart the enamored soul and aroused body of poor Kent Smith who never went down the spiral staircase, and it's a crying shame and a shying crime against nature that this lovely gamine Simone should feel such feline urges, as it is also a dreadful misfortune that the poor little Mexican girl in *The Leopard Man* (1943), besides being so poor, has to go out in the dark night of the border on an errand and when she is almost safely back home, after wandering terrified and all alone through the deserted streets of Tijuana, followed by those stealthy footsteps which get closer and closer and she walks faster and faster and faster and then she breaks into a run and runs and runs and arrives at her house and knocks and knocks and nobody opens, like in a nightmare, and the stalking footsteps turn into a black and overwhelmingly evil presence, and the Beast '43 destroys her in front of the closed door, with no sense of justice at all as the poor are more mortal than the rich, and the traces of this hideous crime are left on the door, the shy blood of the innocent little girl trickling down the uneven hinges while the Beast runs off treacherously through the film night, his black evil camouflaged by the somber sets and the subtitles, and when I went to the Actualidades on July 21, 1944, there were eight or ten people sitting in separate parts of the hall, but little by little, without us noticing it, we began to move together in a group and by the middle of the film we were a tight cluster of bulging eyes and clenched fists and shattered nerves, rooted to the spot and united by the delights of the ready-made terror of the movies, like when I saw *The Thing* in the Radiocine on January 3, 1947, and the same thing happened, except that it was a different kind of terror that I felt, that we felt, that the group of us felt as we huddled together in the stalls, a terror which I know now is not just atavistic but a real, almost political terror, and which starts right at the beginning when the aviators and actors and audience, all of us together, are so reckless as to try and measure the object that had fallen from the sky and buried itself in the ice, remaining there for all to see in the fish tank, behind the polar glass, and all of us were standing around it, around its edges, and they saw, we saw, *I* saw, that it was round, that it looked like a platter, a scary saucer, that it was, yes, you've guessed it: *a ship from outer space*. THEM!

What a relief it is still daylight outside.

XIII

We had been drinking. We still were. Only that Cué had gone to the can a while ago, but there were six empty glasses of his already lined up on the counter and a seventh that was half empty coolly awaiting his comeback. What would Mayito Trinidad say? Trinidad Torregrosa *el brujo*, the African witch doctor, the Cuban sorcerer, Mayito! I had gone to his place one day with Jesse Fernández, to the first floor of the *solar* he lived in, to take some photos of him for *Life* and write a story on him for *Carteles*, and he had brought out The Shells to perform a secret ceremony for me, casting the white shells like dice in the dark, in his room with the blinds drawn at midday and a little candle on the floor to light the cowries in the Afro-Cuban version of an Orphic mystery, and I remember the three pieces of personal advice he gave me then as clearly as I remember the seven shells rattling in his African long bony hand and then rolling over the Spanish tiles of the floor—the secrets of the tribe as he called them. Three. Warnings more than secrets. *Tres*. 3. *Periodista,* he said (that is, journalist: in Cuba nobody can be a writer: That's not a *profession!* the librarian at the National Library told me one day when I was filling in my card to take out a book and I wrote the twice four-lettered word *escritor* in the space where they ask for your profession), you're a journalist so don't let anybody write with your pen (I always write with a typewriter) nor on your *maquinita* in that case, he said. Never *nunca jamás!* Never let anybody comb his hair with your comb. And never leave a glass half empty and come back for it later. The three threats of Trinidad. However, there at the counter was his glass half empty or half full and Arsenio Cué wasn't around to keep an eye on it. The only sorcery he believes in is the magic of numbers, his *numeritos,* adding them together and getting the final figure, a magic trick he was performing only a moment ago, just before he went to the john, adding the numbers of one thousand nine hundred and sixty-six once again and getting twenty-two as he sometimes does and then adding and adding again and again and getting the final solution, or the Definitive Quantity as he also calls it, which was seven—and there were seven letters in his name! I couldn't resist telling him that I had never before seen a name that stretched as far as twenty-two letters on some occasions and contracted to seven on others, that this wasn't a name but an accordion. He answered me by going to the *juan.*

He had been talking. We still were and we ordered a sixth round because the conversation had gotten around once more, of its own accordion, to what Cué called *El Tema,* and which was neither sex nor music nor even his incomplete Pandects this time. I believe we arrived there on the Gulf Stream of Consciousness, going around and around the subject of words without ever getting to the question, the one and only question, *my* question. But it was Cué who landed first, insisting that I follow him ashore.

—What would I be then? Just one more average reader? A translator, another traitor?

He interrupted me with a flashing signal, like a lighthouse of speech.

—Don't let's go into details, my God, and still less don't start quoting names. Leave that to Salvador Bueno, to Invert Andersen, to Chansez or his blind surrogates like Seemore Fantoms. But I, Arsenio Cué, consider that all Cuban writers, but *all* (and he said the *l*'s in all with a trill, his tongue sticky with rum) with the possible exception of yourself and if I say that to you it's not because you're sitting in front of me, as you well know, but because (I'm not sitting behind you, I said) because I had a vague feeling that that's how it is. (I said thank you.) You're welcome. But wait a minute, like a parenthesis or better yet a musical term, with a half-note rest. All the rest of your generation are no better than secondhand readers of Faulkner and Hemingway and Dos Passos or, if they use just intonation, lip-readers of poor Scott and Salinger and Styron, to tune in on writers under S. (Under-S-timated writers? I asked, but he didn't hear me.) There are also aweful readers of Borges and others who read Sartre but don't understand him and who read and don't understand Nabokov or even have any feeling for him, he said. —If you'd rather I talked about other generations you could read Hemingway and Faulkner where I read, I mean said Faulkner and Hemingway and you could throw in Huxley for good measure and Mann and Lawrence the Hetero, for excess, and to build once more this tower of Isaac Babel which is a national metaphor, to set up shop in a *quincalla*, you could then add Hermann Hesse to the list, and Guiraldes to boot (he pronounced Güiraldes without the diaeresis, so it sounded: girlsalltheys) and Pío Baroja and Azorín and Unamuno and Ortega and maybe even Gorky! Though I may be landing now in the no-writer's-land of the last republican generation. Who else is there? A handful of names like . . .

—But you said you weren't going to mention any names.

—So I did. But that was in another context and besides my word is dead. He didn't smile. In fact he didn't even stop. —As for your contemporaries, there is René Jordán, I suppose. Or would be if he stopped making an idiot of himself with those frivolous film reviews and forgot about Fief's Avenue and the *Nude Jerker*. Aside from that there is this Montenegro fellow: his *Men Without Woman* would be O.K. if his prose wasn't so underdeveloped; then there are two or three short stories of Novás Calvo, who is a great translator.

—Lino? Excuse me! Have you ever read his version of *The Old Man and the Sea*? There are at least three serious mistranslations on the first page alone and it's a very short page. Man, did I feel sorry for him, so I didn't look for more. I hate disappointments but just out of curiosity I looked at the last page. I found that he managed to transform the African lions in the memory of Santiago into *sea* lions! *Morsas,* which is not a morsel but a mouthful of shit!

—If you'll let me finish. You're acting like a minority whip, *coño!* I know all that and I also remember that in the book on pirates by Gosse which he translated he thought the word vessels meant glasses, not ships, so that now for the Spanish reader there are two hundred glasses at the bar of Algiers harbor waiting for the Barbary pirates.

—The most vicious bout of drinking in naval history. What do pirates toast with, Bloody *Maria*?

—Enough's enough. Don't forget that he's your forerunner in the use of the vernacular. When I said translator I meant it ironically, meaning that as a writer he is a very good translator of Faulkner and Hemingway into Spanish.

—Into Cuban.

—All right, into Cuban then. Following an order that one might call disorder and early sorrow, apart from Lino and Montenegro and bits of Carrión, frankly I can't think of anybody else. Piñera? I don't want to talk about the theater. For obvious reasons, which are always the most obnoxious.

—And Alejo? I said, carried away by the literary game and gossip.

—Carpentier?

—Is there another Alejo?

—Yes, Antonio Alejo, a painter who is also a friend.

—There is also Georges Carpentier, the violet or orchid or

rose of the ring. Yes, I mean Alejo Carpentier.

—He is the last of the French, who wrote in Spanish in retaliation against Heredia (he pronounced it Herediá). A trophy.

I laughed.

—You're laughing. Just like a Cuban. People here always have to turn anything that's true into a joke. To extract truth with laughing gas.

He fell silent. Then he swallowed his daiquiri in one gulp, a period to what he had said. Can you drink a period? Only with alphabet soup, maybe. I decided to tie up the end and the beginning, to make the conversation happy.

—What are you going to do then?

—I don't know. But don't you bother yourself about that. Something will turn up. I can do anything. Anything but writing.

—What I meant was what are you going to do for a living?

—That's another question. For the moment I am living, to take a leaf out of your dictionary, off a physical and economic phenomenon called pecuniary inertia. But get this straight, my money will last me past countdown and long after blastoff, as long as my pocket and I can stand up to the pressure of three G-notes, notwithstanding the period of metal fatigue which is particularly severe in the case of silver. But I'll resist the journey through vacuum if I then change all my money into nickels, because it's a well-known fact that nickel is heat-resistant. If all systems go, then I'll have to tighten my Van Allen belt.

I smiled. The drinks had restored Cué to his dialectal origins.

—I know where you want to get to, he said. —You want to know where I'm heading for.

—Not only in your career.

—You can mean it in any sense you want. I know. But I'm going to give you one more quotation. Remember (he was telling me, not asking): *"Ce qu'il y a de tragique dans la Mort, c'est qu'elle transforme notre vie en destin."*

—It's well known, I said with Cunning. In situations like this I always manage not to be alone.

—Actually, Silvestre, there's no such thing as a career. All there is is inertia. Many inertias or a single repeated inertia.

Inertia and propaganda plus, in some cases, a percentage. That's life. Death isn't a destiny, but it makes a destiny of our lives. *C'est a dire, en las diez de última,* when it's all added up, it is a destiny. Is it not so?

I nodded with my head, which was lolling to one side. From alcohol, not emphasis.

—*En las diez de última.* Or when it comes to the last ten. O wisdom of the folk! Continuing with these methylated maieutics I could ask you whether death or Death, to use these great Words a la Malraux, is not some kind of destiny?

He paused and said please *viejito* repeat it to the waiter. Or the boss.

—It's curious how a photo transforms reality at the precise moment that it freezes it.

It was at the end of the sentence, as though he was speaking German, that I realized what he was talking about, because I followed his eyes fast and was able to splice up his speech by drawing a zigzag line between his eyesight and a photomural at the back of the room. He, Eve's novelty, Fall. Vale of all Vanity. The valley of Viñales.

—Please note that there is a balcony in the foreground. Also note that the term foreground is a convention of Códac *e gli altri.* But now, precisely at this moment, balcony and palms and hills and distant clouds and the sky in the background are one and the same. A single reality. A photographic reality that refers to the reality of Viñales. Another reality. An unreality. Or to use a term that you cherish, a metareality. Don't you see how a photo can become a metaphysical happening?

I didn't say anything but pondered over his pandects (cont'd) and over the popularity of the word metaphysics. I thought that all we need is for Códac to come in and sit down and nod his head approvingly. Códac whom Bustro called Cádóc. Let Bustro come instead of Códac. Let Him come, for He must come if only to make our silence pregnant. Will there be a limbo for jokers? Or will He be in Bustroferno? If not, where is He? In heaven? In those particles of dust that fix, like Códac's chemicals, the blue of the sky, yet still a prisoner of earthly gravity? Or would he be beyond Roche's Limit, where a console coming from earth would break into a thousand pieces. But Bustrófedon is not a console. What about his con's soul? The soul of a con man would break into a thousand peaces beyond Roche's Limit? Would Bustrófedon become a ball of soulid gas rolling and smouldering around in that siberial, sidereal cold? I think a great deal. (Not now, but on other occasions.) I have thought a great deal about the province of souls, by which I mean the demesne of spirits and ghosts in the blue yonder. Ghostronomy. Would I be able to resoulve the enigma by modern physics and astronomy? It isn't the first time that physics has been food for metaphysics—cf., Aristhotels, the alchimeraests, Raymond Lullaby, Talehard du Jardin—but the phenomenon doesn't cease to astonish me; if anything, the reverse. (The non emone h P.) I knew where this province of Ultimate Tulip could be found, this Nether-never-land, this Lethe, from an article about astrophysics in *Carteles*, which talked about the velocity of light and relativity and made mention of a zone near the earth, a gaseous magma where light achieves extraordinary speeds well above its normal level: its last frontier, absolute speed, metaphysic's absolute, discovered by the physicists. (*C'est a dire*, the materialists.) This article and a fact that has almost no importance coincided in Cué's automobile a while ago. I was riding beside him and thinking about the article and I saw a bubble being formed in the glass on the windshield (we were doing about eighty and because Cué had said something then or a little earlier about going at the speed of a tortoise compared with the speed of sound I had said that for somebody traveling at the speed of light we were standing still and the idea appealed to him) and I looked at the bubble and then thought about light traveling at speeds greater than itself, then I thought that the molecules traveling at such a speed would think that their colleagues of the slow light ray were going at a tortoise's pace, then I thought that perhaps there were other even greater speeds than these speeds of light and that contrasted with those these molecules would be traveling at zero velocity, and thinking this way, in telescopical Chinese boxes, I felt such a vertigo that I might have been falling into the void at a greater speed than the idea of falling. It was then, precisely at that moment (which I will never forget and to make sure that I didn't I took these notes when I went home), that I saw the bubble in the glass. I don't know if you know, you who live on the other side of the page, that the glass panes in automobiles, the windshield pane at least, is made of two hyaline sheets separated by an invisible strip of plastic. The three sheets are then forced together by a pressure ten times greater than that reckoned as the safety limit for the final plate of glass. On one side, then, of this apparently and effectively homogeneous surface a little air had gotten in—a puff, a breath, the thousandth part of a sigh—and it had turned into a bubble before my eyes. I thought, for the love of Craft, of H.P. and his anterior anthropoids and of the gaseous magma and once again of the speeds of light. Couldn't the ether be peopled with ghosts, bubbles of a man's last breath in the great bubble of the cipher? Wouldn't it be on funereal bubbles such as these that the molecules of light would ride? It seems there is as much food for thought here as there is lack of substance for belief. Final hypothesis: the magma must be composed of the last breath of souls while the void, the cosmic ether, not so long ago called cipher, must accommodate all the former spirits, which had been shot into its confines through a sort of metaphysical Roche's Limit. Would our Bustrófedon, Bourtrophedon, the Nostrofedon be there, in the comic ether? In the serious half of the hypothesis, in the hypo or spectrum (good word, that), in the grave spectrum I see the gaseous remains of Julius Caesar Cué looking for the invisible nose of She, of Cleopatrayesha, of Plato, that essential spirit, presiding over another symposium, not of ghosts but of Socratic air bubbles, of a Joan of Arc made of pale smoke burning in an ignis that would be less than fatuous, of Shakespeare unBowbblerized but wrapped up in a pomp of rhetoric named *The Globe*, Cervantes minus his airy arm or subtle limb, as Góngora would say, Góngora who is sitting gaseously beside him and both of them plus Lope surround the weightless hand of Velázquez who is trying, with the aid of black light, to paint the passionate stardust of Quevedo, and farther off, much farther off, almost this side of the limit, who is that I see? It is not a plane it is not a ghost-bird it is Superbustrofedon! traveling on his own starlight and telling me, in my ear, my telescopic ear, my soundscope: Come on, when are you going to come over here and he makes all kinds of obscene gestures and whispers in his ultrasonic voice, There's so much to see here, it's better than the aleph, almost better than the movies, and I'm just about to jump, balancing as I am on the diving board of time, when I hear the earthly voice of Cué bringing me back alive to the present.

—Isn't that the case?

—The thing that bothers you about photos is their being still. They don't move.

He made a muffled sound. What does a sound look like in its muffler? Idiocy of the folk. Muffled noises. Empty vessels make muffled sounds. Sounds to all deaf. Deaf words falling on silk purposes. Till deaf do us part. The early bird catches the first post. You can lead a horse to the water but you can't make him think. (*Though you can make him sink.*) Too many cocks spoil the brothel. We need a revolution among proverbs, for God's sake. Proverbs a la lanterne. Anyone who says a proverb should be shot. Ten sayings that shook the workers. Marx, Marx-Mao, Mao-Mao. It's a Mao's world. Soldiers, from the height of this sentence twenty centuries and Big Brother are watching you. Wiscondom of the folk. A phantom is hunting Europe, it is the phantom of Stalin. Crime, how many liberties have been taken in thy name. One must tend socialist man, as one would tend a tree. Ready. Aim. Timmmmmbeeerrrr! A call of duty is a beast forever. Isn't it true? Isn't it true? Isn't it? True.

—ISN'T IT TRUE? I was speaking about life, not about photography, shit!

Somebody was hissing at us from the far end of the bar.

—Shut your fucking mouth, Cué shouted.

—Shutvestre Moutherfucker at your service, sir, I said, playing the Cid Conciliador, loud but not loud enough.

—I was speaking about life, *viejo*.

—Yes, I know, but you shouldn't shout like that, *mon viux*.

An unmistakable sign of alcoholissimo. Galvanized French spoken here. Volta turns on his batteries and out comes alcohol. How many amperes has ma mere? Sixte Ampere. French scientist of Spanish stock & exchange. The name was originally written Ampérez. His grandfather, Grampere, emigrated to France crossing the Pyrenees on the back of an elephant in search of Liberty Valence (I, chloride ion in HCL eq. Nacl. =

Nacional) and died in Paris. He died poor. He died in Pairs. Pompée funebre and attendant gogo circucisms. Ohm y soit qui mal y pense. I honestly think I'm going to be sick. Let foreigners invent! Unamuno said as he watched the Ampersand family crossing the Basque country. Encyclopaedia Tyrannica.

—It's impossible to speak in this country.

—You weren't speaking, you were shouting.

—Shit, it's not the form that matters, but the content. Or so they say.

—Hadn't we agreed that you weren't going to talk about politics.

He smiled. He laughed. He became serious again. One two three. He was silent for a moment. The aftereffect of hissing? That's why snakes are deaf.

—Look, they've just given me the solution.

I looked, but I didn't see any solution. I saw a *mojito* and seven daiquiri glasses. Six empty and one full.

—I can see two solutions.

—No, Cué said, —there's only one.

—It's just that you're seeing single. Anti-alcoholism.

—There's only one solution. To my problems. The one and only.

—What is it then?

He came surfing on alcohol waves to whisper in my ear:

—I'm going to the Sierra.

—It's very early for the late-night and very late for the early-morning. It won't be open.

—To the *sierras* not to the Sierra, *madre!*

—The John Huston film?

—No, damn you, to the Sierra Maestra! I rise up in arms. I'm going to join the *guerrilleros*.

—What!

—I'm going to join Fffidel.

—Brother, you're drunk.

—No, I'm being serious. Sure, I'm drunk. Pancho Villa was drunk all the time and look at him. *Please* do me a favor, don't turn around to see if Pancho Villa is coming in or not. I mean it seriously. I'm going to the Sierra.

He was ready to leave. I grabbed his sleeve.

—Wait a minute. We have to pay the check first.

He shook his arm free impatiently.

—I'll be right back. I'm going to the can first.

—Are you crazy? It's like the Foreign Legion.

—What? The john?

—Not the john, dammit. Going to the Sierra, going off to fight. It's like joining the Foreign Legion.

—Nashional. The Nashional Leshion.

—If you carry on like that you'll end up like Ronald Colman. First you make a Beau Geste and then you start thinking you're Othello and finally you die in the play and you die in the movies and you die in real life and so you're dead, stone dead, dead dead.

"Profoundly dead, fundamentally dead, deadly dead. Dead. Deadfinitely, Terry, terribly, interminably dead." He was imitating Nicolás Guillén's Congolese voice. So I started imitating him too: Shall I be Guillén Banguila, Guillén Kasongo, Nicolás Mayombe, Nicolás Guillén de Castro?

—"What an enigma along the waters!"

—Neither an enigma, nor hydromancy nor a hydra nor a sphinx. What Nicolás should do is to go to the registry office.

—What will my name be in that case? Roger Casement? What will my name be, Cassius? Acacia?

—What an enema between two waters. Talking of waters, I have to go and pass them on my way to the pisshouse or shithouse. Both words *can* and should be applicable. Also the word can.

—You are *excusado*.

He began once more to make the descent of the north face of the stool he was sitting on, only he didn't finish the climb. He turned toward me and emitted a long sharp hiss and I thought he was ordering another drink, but then I saw he had raised his index finger horizontally to his vertical lips. Or vice versa?

—Ssssss. 33–33.

—Another cabala?

Now he will tell me that one and one makes two and also eleven and that eleven times two is twenty-two and three times eleven is thirty-three and thirty-three and thirty-three makes sixty-six, which is a perfect number. Arseniostradamus. But the noise continued insistently.

—Ssss. 33–33. A stool pigeon. SIM.

I looked around, I couldn't see anybody. PerseCuétion mania. Yes, there was a waiter who had changed out of his uniform into civvies and had gone out into the street, toward the canals.

—It's a Venetian *cameriere*.

—He's a 33–33. In disguise. They're devilishly clever. Classes with the Gestapo and the Berliner Ensemble and all. They're masters of duplicity and disguisity. It's incredibly.

I laughed.

—No, old boy. It'd better be a cabala. There's nobody from the SIM out there.

—SSS. Hide your face.

—SS more likely. *Schutzstaffel.*

—Hide your face.

—How? I'd rather camouflage myself. I'm an ideal chameleon.

—Leave it to me. I'm the king of disguises and pseudonyms. Actor at large. You know that if I was Stendhal they'd be reading me in 1966? It's my lucky year.

What had gone wrong? Now he was in the midst of explaining how the year one thousand nine hundred and sixty-six was—but, *coño,* he's been a damn long time in the men's room. I'm going, I went to look for him. He was looking at himself in the mirror, a thing he does at the slightest provocation. I once even caught him looking at himself in a glass. *My* glass. It's a good thing that mirrors are public, like toilets. This Narcissus would use up all the quicksilver. I told him so. He replied by quoting Socrates who, like Martí, had something to say about everything. He said that he, Socrates, said that you had to look at yourself in the mirror. If everything's O.K., then you're reassured. If it's not, you can always fix it. What if it's incurable, like in my case? Socrates doesn't know. Nor does Cué. As to myself, search me. That's what I'm doing. Ready to piss. Narcissus Cué is concentrating on his vertical river. But, he says, I'll tell you something: I look at myself in the mirror not to check whether I'm O.K. or not, but only to check if I am. If I'm still here. That there's nobody else in my skin. Take good care of your skin, I tell him, it's your frontispiece, vulgo facade. If I'm still here. Yes, I'm still here. Is it an echo, an eChué, an eCué, Ekué? Hyaline cherry pits with a mercurial echo: I am/I am not/I am/I am not/I am. You are here, I tell him. Yes, I'm here, he says, I'm here. But do I exist? In any case I know that it was I who is vomiting and he points to a corner of the bathroom. But was it I who will vomit, and he points again. I take a look and then I look him up and down. Is it/was it/will he? In any case, he looks impeccable. Implacable, Bustrófedon would say if he was able to look at himself in the mirror. And what about Dracula? How does the Divine Cunt D know that he is, that he is alive, that he exists? Vampires can't see themselves in the mirror. How did old Bela manage to part his hair in the middle? As I reflect on these matters I feel nauseated. Can I be sick? Cué says yes, I can, anyone can as long as he has something to sick up. Even the can can. I go to one of the deodorized cubicles which, as they always do, gives the lie to its name. I urinated once on the ice in the Floridita, a famous bar in Old Havana. Hemingway slept (off a hangover) here. Now the Negro who cleans the bar of the toilets, or is it the bar's toilets? the negro who cleans the toilebaret there at the Floridita tells me the block of ice is there so there won't be a bad smell, because urine ferments with the heat which he called *la* calor instead of *el* calor. A Hemingwayan, he makes the masculine feminine. I leave my traces in the ice. I look at the yellow and ocher and white toilet bowl which looks like a guitar but is really an Aeolian harp. It sounds when the winds blow. I am not sick. I put my finger down my throat. I can't be sick, I pull my finger out. Could it be that I don't have anything to vomit with? Obviously a Sartrean nausea. Metaphysical, metapissical. I go out. I look at myself in the mirror. Is it me who is looking at me out of the mirror? Or is it my alter ego? Walter Ego. Wallace in Wanderlust? Or is it Malice in Underworld. What would Alice Faye make of these faces I'm making? Alice in Yonderland. Alice in underlandia. Aliceing in Vomitland.

—You know what's happening to you? I ask Arsenio Cuévering, who is wanting to leave the bathroom and can't find the right hole.

—What?

—You're tired of growing and growing and getting smaller and smaller and of going up and down and running all over the place, and wherever you go there are all these rabbits giving you orders.

—What rabbits?

He starts looking between my feet.

—Rabbits. The rabbits that talk and consult their watches and organize everything and run everything. The rabbits of the (c)age we live in.

—It's too early for delirium tremens and too late for the gods, Silvestre, *coño!* Stop fooling around.

—No, I'm serious, I really mean it.

—And how do you know this?

—Alice told me.

—Adela.

—No, Alice. This is another girl.

But Buster Kuéton is almost a genius at having the last word. He points at the door, which he has finally found without any assistance from me. There is a heart carved on the wood. With a little arrow and initials (G/M) and so on.

—It's an ad for General Motors, I say, trying to get my shot in first.

—No, he says, shooting straight from the hips. —For love has scratched initials in/ The place of excrement.

XIV

Should I speak to him now or wait till later? Perhaps he would forget his new-found enthusiasm for a guerrillahood. Or had he forgotten it already? Neurosis. Realization of erroneous projects. Addling machine. Shit! he probably will go to the Sierra, Cué's one heck of a neurotic. I let him pay the cheCué. Are we going to the Sierra now? I go outside and the sea, the basin, is another mirror. He'll have to stop looking at himself, or he'll fall in. On the dock there's a kid throwing flat stones into the smooth water and they hit the surface, skid, jump, hit it again two or three times and finally break the mirror and disappear through the other side, forever. On the wharf a fisherman who has no shadow in that light which Leonardo would call *universale* was pulling fish out of a launch. He pulled out an enormous ugly fish, a sea monster. A big hunk of fish that would be stinking in a while. What could it be? Cué was leaving the bar. He was talking to himself.

—What's wrong?

—What am I? A jester? A poor player.

A pool player?

—What's wrong?

—Nothing, it's just that we're out of cash, as Casshius said. We haven't a dollar or a nickel or a dime. Not a penny. Goddammit.

—What?

—We're ruined. *Kaputt.* Broke. *La pasta è finita.* They've bled us dry. I had a row with the barman. He wants to make money hand over fist.

—Didn't you lose it by bending your elbow? Orthopedic metaphors cancel each other.

—Do you have any money?

—Not much.

—As usual.

—As usual.

—Don't worry about it. You've got a bout of the poor man's inertia. That will soon change.

—What are you? A sooth sayer?

—*Que será, será, 'sta sera.* To be sung by Doris Day tonight. Or is it Doris Knight today?

I walk toward the wharf dwarfed by curiosity.

—Arsenio, what's this fish called?

—How the fuck should I know? You think I'm a naturalist? A Naturalist without Plata. William Henry Cué, alias Arsenio Hudson.

—What kind of fish is that? I ask the fisherman.

—That's no fish, Cué says. —It's a catch. Fish are like people, they change their name when they die. You're Silvestre, you die, and before you know it, you're a corpse.

The fisherman stares at us both. Could he be Mike Mascarenhas?

—It's a sturgeon, he says.

—If it's a surgeon, it could do with some spastic sturgery, Cué says.

The fisherman looks at him. No, it's not Mike: he's not violent nor is he fishing for sharks. Nor is this lagoon the Pacific.

—Don't pay any attention to him, I say to the fisherman. —He's drunk.

—No, I'm not drunk. I'm a drunkard. I saw it in the mirror darkly.

The fisherman turns back to his hooks, harpoons, lines and rods. Cué looks closely at the fish.

—I know what it is! It's the Beast. Let's turn it over and see if it's got 666 written on it. In forpile, I mean profile, it looks like the beast.

I support him by an arm so he doesn't lose his balance and fall into the water or among the fishes.

—What do you make of it, Silvestre?

—What do you make that I'd make of it? I say, imitating Cantinflas.

—Don't you think that this 666 is the remedy for venereal diseases. The magic silver bullet. The stake in the breast of the beast that sleeps by day.

—*Vamos, amigo,* you are drunko! I said, still putting on my Moviecan accent.

—I'm as drunk as . . .

—Panchovilla.

—No, as drunk as your Muxical namesaké, Silvestre Revueltas, and look what he composed.

—Hear, you mean, not look.

—Hear, look, play "Sensemayá."

He started humming, drumming on the wooden deck boards with his foot. Senses-may-I La Cuélebra. Nonsensemaja.

—You could do with Eribó's accompaniment, I said.

—We'd make a late lamentable duo. Even doing a solo I'm lamentable.

True. But I didn't say so. I can be discreet at times. He stopped dancing, to my relief.

—Don't you think, Silvestre, honestly, that if you knew that your destiny was to be this fish dead forever, for all eternity, you'd change, you'd give up and you'd try to be something else altogether?

—John Dory Gray got hooked on his own portrait, I said and immediately realized how tactless I'd been. That's the story of my life: tactless one moment, a model of discretion the next swing of the pendulum. It's in my nature, the Scorpion and the Proofrog, the joker is Wilde, et cet.

He made a half turn and stalked off. It looked like we are leaving. Would this swamp, this puddle, this imitation roadstead be our Finisterre? But no. He walked off to the far end of the *dock*. He was talking to the boy with the st-o-o-o-nes. They were very close to each other and Cué was fondling him or whispering in his ear, for a joke. Pedagogy. Demagogy. Dictators and mothers and public figures always put on this act. Cué was capable of embracing a shark, as long as there were witnesses around. He'd even fuck a sea monster, given the right audience. They were almost invisible. Night was falling at thirty-two feet per second. Light, twilight, street lights. I looked toward Havana. There was something like a rainbow in the sky. No, they were clouds, tassels of cloud that the sun was still tinting. I couldn't see the sea from the dock, only this green, blue, gray mud-colored mirror that was getting blacker by the minute. The city, however, seemed to be illuminated by a light that wasn't artificial and didn't come from the sun, but which seemed to belong to itself, to emanate from it, as though Havana was a source of light, a radiating mirage, almost a promise against the night that was threatening to surround us. Cué waved to me and I went over. He showed me a stone and said that *she* had given it to him and it was then that I realized that it wasn't a boy who had been throwing stones into the sea, but a girl wearing shorts, a little girl who now walked away looking back smiling, almost winking at Cué, who was thanking her in a syrupy voice, and I heard somebody calling through the dark come here Angelita. I was glad and sorry at the same time without knowing why and then immediately I knew. I don't like boys, but little girls are something else. I would have liked to talk to her, to warm my hands by her light. Now she was walking away with another shadow by her side. Her father, I suppose.

—Look, there's some writing on the stone.

I couldn't see properly. I'm shortsighted. People who read too much never see clearly in twilight.

—I can't see a thing.

—You're going blind, *coño*. Soon you'll only be able to see movies in your memory. I stared at him. —Sorry, kid, I'm sorry, he said, putting on a pained look. He put an arm around me.—I won't kiss you because you're not my type.

What a bugger!

—You're the worst kind of *peorcito,* I said.

He laughed. He recognized this familiar Cuban quotation. The key to twilight. Presidente Grau San Martin had used it: *amigos* my dear true friends to be Cuban means to be a friend, etcetera, that was how he had described his political rival in a speech. *De lo peorcito*. Grau was talking about Batista of course. Will El Hombre kill more people than time?

We walk among the palm trees and I point to Havana, with its lights, land of promise on the historical horizon, its limestone skyscrapers looking like ivory towers. San Cristóbal *la blanca*. It should be called Casablanca and not that city in Morocco nor the little fishing village on the other side of the port. I pointed this out to Cué.

—They are whitewashed sepulchers, Silvestre. It's not the New Jerusalem, kiddo, it's Somorrah. Or if you prefer, Godom. I'm not convinced, so I say:

—But I love it. It's a snow-white city, a delectably salty sleeping beauty.

—No, you don't love it. It's your city now. But it isn't white or red, it's pink. It's a lukewarm city, a city of lukewarm people. And you're lukewarm yourself, Silvestre. You're neither hot nor cold. I knew you were incapable of love, I know now that you can't hate either. You're just a writer. A spectator, a tepid soul. There's nothing I'd like more than to puke you up, but I can't because I've already puked up everything I had in me. Besides, what the hell, I couldn't do that to a friend.

—Think of the things of the spirit as well. Now I'm Payanini, with his magic instrument, a payola or loote.

—Is nothing sacred to you?

—Remember that *sin* means without in Spanish.

—Have you no convictions, then? No honor?

"The best lack all convictions," I quoted and he didn't even give me time to finish.

—The Beast lacks all convictions while the words/ Are full of passive immunity. Do you like The Second Coming?

—Yes, I said, naïvely thinking he was talking about Yeats and forgetting he once said Yeats had to wait till he was fifty to have his second coming. —It's a great poem. Things fall apart, the center cannot hold . . .

—I prefer the third.

—Third what?

—The Third Coming. The third time I come.

He went off atarun, metaphorically speaking, toward the car. In my village, when I was a kid, they used to say at moments like this, wildly indecent, Mare Metaphor is loosed upon the world. Rhetoric of the nation?

XV

The wind sprang up and our mauve-colored pleasing dome became magenta violet purple navy blue and black when Arturio Gordon Cué switched on his lights and cut the air in front of us up into dark bands that bent when they hit the propinquous park and gardens and the speedy houses across the street, and these ultraviolet curbs rounded down, rebounded and ran alongside the car until they fell silently making night behind our backs. As we were driving east the sunset no longer existed except as a slightly paler blue trembling halo above us and as I looked back Lotswively I saw a moribund pallor straddling the horizon and the equally black barrier of clouds that were so twilighted before and now made of graphite not only because the sun had in fact sunk into the sea but because we were traveling, accelerating toward the city and under the trees of the Biltmore avenue. We left the Santa Fe highway to the west at fifty, sixty, seventy-five as Cué's foot was hungering to turn the road into an abyss of speed—no: already it had become an acceleration, a free fall. He continued to hurtle at full tilt down his horizontal precipice.

—D'you know what you're doing? I asked.

—Yes, going back to town.

—No, *mi viejo*, I don't mean it like that. You're trying to turn the road into a Moebius strip.

—Kindly explain yourself. You know I didn't graduate from high school.

—But you know what a Moebius strip is.

—On and off I do.

—Then you know that what you want is not to follow the road into Havana, but to go into the fourth dimension, that what you'd want to want is for the street to continue till instead of being a circle it becomes an orbit in time, and your car is then a humming-top of time, Brick Bradford.

—That's what is known as total culture. From Moebius strip to comic strips.

I scarcely caught a glimpse of Santo Tomás de Villanueva, which had turned from a catholic university (what a tautology!) into a blurred white and gray and green stain on the night-ground.

—Hey, watch out. You'll kill somebody.

—Or something, namely boredom or the stillness of the night.

—You're driving like a maniac.

—And what's so bad about that? I'll tell you, my crime is that I'm not a falcon. Do you know how hawks make love? They copulate at a dizzying altitude and let themselves fall, beak against beak, flying into union, caught up in an intolerable ecstasy (was it a recital he was giving?). The hawk or falcon, after copulation, rises again, swift, arrogant and alone. To become a peregrine falcon now and my trade to be the Faulknery of love!

—You're drunk.

—Drunk with vertigo.

—You're drunk like any other drunken slob and please quit looking for poet's liquor license. You're not Edgar Allan Cué.

He changed his tone.

—No, I'm not. I'm not pretending to be either. But if I am drunk, let me tell you I drive better when I'm drunk.

He could be telling the truth because he slowed down right in time for the double lights of the Náutico to switch from red to green as though turned by our inertia.

I smiled at him.

—That's what's known as sympathetic action.

Cué nodded.

—Today you are riding the tandem of physical delirium, he said.

Now he braked easily to allow some dogs to cross the avenue led by three men in red uniforms who held the leashes firmly in their hands.

—Greyhounds for the dog tracks. Now don't you go telling me I'm like them, please, running after a March hare.

—It would be a lousy image, because it's too obvious.

—Besides, you mustn't forget the things of the spirit. Nobody's going to lay bets on me.

—Except your ventriloquist.

—He's a poor chess player or, as you say, a pool player. And I don't need to tell you that chess is the opposite of a game of chance. Nobody puts bets on Botwinnik because there's nobody to challenge him.

—If Capablanca could take him on, by means of a medium, I'd take all bets against myself.

I smiled as I thought of this eschatological possible game of chess and I remembered my ancestor, that ancient artificer who was something better than a scientific chess player because he was an intuitive thinker, an incurable womanizer, always a happy player: a winsome winner and a loser who was a chess bank because he laughed when he lost and never cared for training and was incapable of cheating: the opposite of Maeltzel's invention, he didn't play scientifically nor was he a chess machine: but an artist who kept his chess next to his heart, a chest player, a jazz player, a guru, the Zen master of grand chess, who like the Horse Dealer gave immortal and masterly lessons to the worst and most disreputable disciples.

"I remember the case of a friend of mine, an enthusiast who had little talent, who used to play in his club in the evenings. Among his opponents there was one who beat him regularly, and it got to the point where he was really troubled by this. One day he called on me, told me what had happened and asked me for help. I answered that he should study the books and see how quickly things would change. He told me: 'Fine; I'll do just such a move.' He told me the opening the other player had used and the particular thing about his opponent's development that bothered him. I showed him how he could avoid getting into that humiliating position and drew his attention to certain general elements in the game; but above all I insisted that he study the books and proceed in agreement with the ideas that they expounded. . . . A few days later I met him looking very pleased with life. As soon as he saw me he told me: 'I followed your advice and it went very well. Yesterday I played the man I told you about two times and he beat me only twice.' " That was the way the Master would talk in his Last Lessons. I wouldn't send him out to buy horses, but I knew that there was some relation between his lessons and the lessons of the master of Zen in the art of archery and if I knew that Death wanted to play a game of chess for my life, I would ask her one favor: that Capablanca should be my champion. That wise chessire with the luminous name-grin is the guardian angel, and the real reason that the one good film of that mediocre director Vsevolod whom the movie morons call the Great Pudovkini, his only encounter with the right path, is called *The Chess Player*, and that Capablanca should be his protagonist and saving grace like the black knight who leaps finally from his light hands and falls on the white cape of the snow is something more and something less than a symbol.

He took the roundabout of the Yacht Club gracefully and turned into Fifth Avenue again, passing almost under the pine trees, the two of us blinded, dazzled, riddled with lights from the radiating vertigo of Corny Island and the electric honky-tonk of bars and street lamps and the luminous speed of headlights coming in the opposite direction. When we had gone around the darkened roundabout of the Country Club, I saw that Cué was concentrating on the wheel once more. It was a vice of his. You're hooked on space, I told him but he wasn't listening. Or hadn't I actually said it? We crossed the avenue and the night sheathed us in an envelope of speed and smells. It was a pleasant vice. He spoke without looking at me, focusing on the street or his double drunkenness. Treble.

—Do you remember Bustrófedon's games with letters?

—The palindromes? I don't forget them, I hope I never do.

Nor his jokes, I thought softly. Wherever he made a pun a pain was hidden.

—Don't you find it significant that he never hit on the best of them, the one that is the easiest and the most difficult and at the same time the most terrifying, *Yo soy*?

I spelled it out, I read it back to front, yos oY, I'm I, and said:

—No, not especially. Why?

—I do, he said.

The city had become a quantum night. The bulb of a street lamp slipping swiftly past yellowing and making visible a ticker tape of storefronts or a sidewalk with people waiting for the bus or pale, speckled trees that left off being trunk and branches and leaves and disappeared in a dark facade, was also a single blue-white light, struggling overhead to light up still more space and only managing to deform things and people with a sick unreality, and at times it was a fugitive window, of chrysolite, where you could see a family interior which because it was so alien seemed always peaceable and happy.

—Bustrófedon, who was my friend as much as yours (I was on the point of saying, No kidding!) had one failing, aside from his vulgarity. Like on that memorable night (*coño,* how it bothered him: looking back in rage is the name of the game) and this particular fault was that he thought about words, all the time, as though they had always been written and nobody but he had ever said them and then for him they weren't words but letters and anagrams and games with signs. My problem is sounds. At least that's the only profession I've really learned.

He fell silent dramatically as he often did and I examined his profile, until his trembling lips, faintly outlined by the amber light of the panel, relayed to me that he was going to go on speaking.

—Say a sentence.

—What for?

—Please.

An insistent gesture came with his petition.

—O.K., I said and I felt a little ridiculous: caught in a sound trap as though I was testing an illusory microphone and I was even tempted to say testing one two three, but instead I said: —Let's see. I was silent again and finally said: —Mama is not a palindrome but Madam is.

Homage to Departed, held in contempt these days.

A familiar and at the same time unknown noise came from Cué's lips.

—Simadam tub emordnilap a ton siam am.

—What the heck does that mean? I asked him, smiling.

—What you've just said but inverting the sound.

I laughed with a trace of admiration—which is no mean feat.

—It's a trick I learned during recording sessions.

—How do you do it?

—It's very easy, like writing back to front. All you have to do is spend hours and hours recording shit, programs with incredible dialogues that are almost unsayable or at least inaudible conversations made of silence, rustic comedies or urban tragedies with characters that are about as probable as Little Red Riding Hood and whom you have to impersonate with a superhuman naïveté and do it knowing that, because your voice has the bad luck to be what they call euphonic, you'll never be allowed to play the wolf, wasting your time as though it was something you could use all over again, like one of the tritons in the fountain at the entrance to the tunnel spouting water.

I told him to do it again. Encore, Cué, encuére.

—What do you think of it?

—I think it's great.

—No, I don't mean that, he said, rejecting my flattery as though I was a fan asking him for an autograph. —I mean how does it sound to you?

—To me? I don't know.

—Listen again, and he unreeled several other sentences.

I couldn't describe what I felt.

—Doesn't it sound like Russian?

—Possibly.

—Nais surekild noustit n seod?

—I don't know. It's more like ancient Greek.

—How the fuck do you know what that sounds like?

—It's not a secret language, if you don't mind me saying so. I mean I've got friends who study philosophy and they speak it—with a *habanero* accent, I was going to add, but I could see he wasn't in a mood for jokes.

—I'm telling you it sounds like Russian. I've got a good ear. You should listen to a complete recording, but it would only need a bit of the track to convince you that Russian is only Cuban in reverse. Isn't it weird, like really strange?

No. What astonishes me now is not what astonished me then. What amazed me at the time was that there was no trace in his voice of what we had been drinking. Nor in his driving. I was even more surprised by his reference to time and the tritons. But I was so fascinated by his verbal acrobatics that I completely failed to notice that it was the only time I'd ever heard Arsenio Cué talk about time as though it were something vaguely precious.

XVI

We drove into Havana along Calzada. The lights on 12th were with us and we are passing in front of the Lyceum like a Buddhist arrow—zen! instead of zoom! I can't see the Trotcha, with its meandering gardens and the ancient deluxe bathhouses (which were located, my god, at the end of the century, in a remote *hacienda* outside the city walls called, because it was off limits, *Vedado:* a point for our Le Cuérbusier, who calls music melting architecture), just a lousy labyrinth of ruins today and the former colonial theater next door which is a hotel now, less than a hotel: a decayed pension that has gone down in the world: ruins which won't find me unmoved because I can never forget them, ever. The traffic stopped us on Paseo.

—Are you serious?

—About what?

—Do you seriously mean it when you say that Russian is Cuban spelled backward?

—Not spelled, *read* backward. Yes, I am. Perfectly serious.

—My god! I shouted. —We are glasses, communicating vessels. That fits right in with Bustrófedon's theory that the Cyrillic alphabet (what did he call it? Cyrillic/cilyric) is the Roman alphabet in reverse, that you can read Russian in the mirror.

—Bustrófedon was always joking.

—You know that jokes don't exist. Everything that gets said is said seriously.

—Or everything one says is a joke. Life was an absolute joke for him. Or Him, if you prefer. Nothing human was divine for him.

—In other words nothing was serious for him. By the same token, there are no jokes. Aristotelian logic.

He started off again, first sketching an exclamation mark with his lips. Jimmydeancué.

—Shit, *mi viejo,* he said. —Nobody would miss you if I drove you off in this time machine to live with the sophists.

—Look who's talking! All you have to do is to stop your *quadriga,* your Quatre Chevaux, and get out and kill a steer and pull out its liver to make the future present and find out whether we're going to Sardis or the sea. (He smiled.) But I'm going to suggest we form a new presocratic duo. We could easily be Damon and Pythias.

—Who's who?

—You choose.

—I don't see you giving your life for me.

—And what else is yours truly doing when he's sitting in the suicide seat?

He laughed, but he didn't take his foot off the accelerator.

—Besides, I'm more than willing to take your place wherever you want.

He didn't hear or he didn't want to hear. Words are not enough for the Pythagorean listener. It needs figures. I'd have to show him some prime numbers. A pity. I could have spoken to him just now. Well, I'll talk to myself instead. To masturdebate. In the idiom of a mastur race. Thus masturspake Zarathrusta. Make a solution of pollution. The solution of a sage is to pollute a page. Or a pageboy. Bring a boy to the boil. Bugger the little boys to come unto me. It is harder for a camel to enter a needle's eye than to have its prick up your neighbor's asseye. Don't shit till you see the white of their oneyes. In the country of the oneyed, the blind man is king. A la lanterne rouge with all proverbes. Red Light District. Was it the whores who invented the traffic signal? No, because the inventor has a statue in Paris. It comes in *The Sun Also Rises*. The sun always comes. About the only thing which either comes and/or rises in the novel. The Sun Only Rises. Poor Jake Barnes. He'd be luckier on the moon. Luckier or cockier? There's less pull there. Or would he waste all his moonshots in blanks of love? The sylphilis of Chopin. According to the theory of the master (guru) of ceremonies every man has an exact number of shots in his locker, no matter how or when or where you spend them. If you fired fifty in your youth you'll have fifty less for your old age. How you aim is your problem. Don't (dis)charge until you see the red light. Chicko, chico, you're preoccupied with sex. I've never seen a single human being who wasn't preoccupied with sex. Come again, who said that? Aldoux Huxley. Ah, I knew it didn't sound like your subject. Essays were never your strong point. A weakness of yours. A weakness for *ensayos*, *essais*, essays and French *lettres*. To Aldous Husley they are exsayssive. Is he dead? No, he's alive. Old writers never die: they just go Chrome Yellow. Shit, there's that old man of the sea with his trident and his tritons. hings happen in threesT. He always turns up in Cuban literature. Like the Eiffel Tower in Paris. I see him/I don't see him/I see him. What a beautiful row of arches. R of retches. Artches or reches or just pure baroque puke. I'm the Masturbanger of Venusberg with a baruque peruke. Art makes me sick. Sick. Arch. Artch! Aagggh! if you feel sick. A closed mouth tells no flies. Lies. There are no flies on me. Flies don't lie by night. *Mosquitoes* then. Good-bye Neptune. In El Carmelo there are people eating dinner and the Auditorium lights were not dimmer, on the contrary, it was lit up, hiccup, sick-up. Like you're going to be. Sss. $33.33 Gestapo? No! 33 rpms? No, I meant that music begins when words die. Heine. Hein Hitlere. All die. All dust. Aldust Huxley. Ad lib. Adliberace. All die die all. Dial Hitler. Heil Heine! When the word dies. It's a concerto. Bachaldiviv? Krauts sonata. Kreutzer sonata. It's a concerto not a sonata! A concert. There's a Konzert and Enna Filippi will be going to battle with her harp, waltzing plus que lente. A cuntcert then. Cut that sex out! Ouch! It hurts. Shit, it's Ravel, a famous asexual. He only wrote boleros, you know. Though I don't know what he was up (or down) to in Antibes. Remember that Ida Rubinstein danced on a table. Big deal. Idadown? *Ida* means to go in Spanish. So what? Just because you go it doesn't mean you come. Harping in the dark. Ina? Inna? In her? No, Edna asking for More by Salzedo, making harpwaves in the Seltzedo water, celestial lyre-player (liar-plier) who on the syrinx (rhymes with sphinx, like in sphinxter) makes it a celesta, an Arp. Arp? Is that how it's spelled? Then it should be Hans Harp. What are women who play the harp called? Harpies. Enna making her celestial sounds material: Marxing the Harp. Or is it the eruction of Mount Edna? It could be Kleiber. Erich Klavier. Eines Wohltemperirte Kleiber. Eine Kleiber Nachtmusik. Ein feste. Stop festering around, Silver. Ein feste Brandenburg. No good. Komm Susser Todd-AO. No good either. Could it be Celibidache, Chelibidaque, celodese, celousy. Cellofabitch, Coelovideo. Celiberethoving, eroicating, changing the third (drei) movement, Cuévidache accelerating, because (he says that) there's a dusty score (an old score to settle, let the dust settle) in Salzedoburg which demonstrates (to demons trate, where demons fear to trate) that Ardebol and Kleiver and even Sylvie & Bruno Walter were so immerdsed in each other that Adolfas Gitler (for Adolferers Only) was quite right to prevent Walter by any means from playing Beethoven or Reichearsing, ffaisant des repetitions eroically or erotically amusicking themselves, n-no there's nothing like French the Frenchman said, as that *chivato,* portrait of the informer as a young man, the kid who's going to die as the melomane wants in the concert hall, as squealer-dealer, Bully the Fink, listens to the music from the terrace where he's hiding as he reads *Implosion ex Cathedra* written to fffastidiare il souvenire d'un grand'uomo and to be read (Jazz a l'homme or Ella Cossa) in the time it takes Celibidet to play the Aeolica symphony number three because they had both taken a course in rapid reading. Rabidreaders. Accelerated readers. Gli scelerati. Or reader becomes rider. So we went back down the Avenue, down the Evenue of the Presidents. The impudence of office. They are all Fucker Wolffs and when they're fucked off they are replaced by *Vice* Presidents. Agnewsticism.

She was walking along the sidewalk when I saw her. Boccato di castroati. I told Cué. Latins are lady-lovers.

—Who? he said. —Alma Mahler Gropius Werfel?

—Vesper Maries. Spermary. Spermaceti. Sperm whale.

—Whale? I mean where?

—Starboard, sir. Ahoy! Ahoy! Thar she blows me!

Captain Cuérageous looked.

—Holy mackerel! Am I blind drunk? I don't see one of them, I see two.

—There are two of them. Excuse my infralanguage, but I only know the one on the outside. She's a friend of Códac.

—Fiend not friend. *Sacré maquereau.*

—I mean the one on the outside, *viejo*. Metalanguage for you. And mindyourlanguage.

—*Coño!* That's some sight.

—Some spectacles you should say.

—Thanks to Ben Franklyn Delano. A whore in each lens. Bifocal lenses for the opposite sex. *Contraria contrariis curantur.*

—Biconvex lenses. Bisexual lentils. *Similia similibus curantur.*

—Do you *really* know her?

—Yes, *viejo*. Códac introduced me.

—You don't introduce women like these, you make love at first sight. A touching sight. Contact lenses.

They were turning the corner. It was her, whatchama callit? There was no miss taking her. With a friend of course. *Le amiche*. The well-knit longliness. The tits of loveliness. A tribe of tribades. You say trilogy, titralogy, and even pentalogy for someone who dares to go as far as five. Would you say sexology for six works? What about two? Biology. Freud says that primitive women, like children, can be persuaded to enjoy any kind of sexual experience. He didn't say they were underdeveloped. He didn't know them biblically or otherwise. But this one is overdeveloped. Was she persuaded into it or was it the work of Mother Nature? There's no such thing as nature. Everything is history. Hystery. Hysteria is a concentric chaos. History, I mean. Freud also said that one might indulge in the most extreme forms of oral kissing, but that one would hesitate to use the toothbrush of one's beloved. (Or *la plume de ma tante*?) Julieta? What is it, Romy darling? Have you been using my Prophy-lactic again? Bleaghh! Sigismondo was wrong. I'm ready to go deeper than any toothbrush. Where brushes fear to sweep. Shit, they're turning down 15th. They are turning the corner of 15th Street, excuse me, Bertrand. Where Russells fear to think. Turn Cué turn, fuck you, fuCué.

—They'se gone.

He winced at my infralanguage, the radio-pedant, but, still looking like Cuéptain Ahab hunting Morbid Dyke, he immediately pulled the wheel hard over and the convertible turned, tacked about, with all aboard, including this binnacle or log, the log of Gog and Magog, magloglog, and it sailed into the narrow straits of the side street. Magellan Cué. Cuégellan. Macuéllan. Magalena! That's who it is. TechniCué. Mnmotechnics. Technical memory. Arsenio Sebastian Cuébot lowered his sails, lay to and anchored on the other corner, to starboard. Depth, five fathoms, three fathoms, two bosoms, mark twin! Lower the boats. Harpoon at the ready.

—Magellena's her name. Magalena.

—Leave it to me!

Shit, I'll have to stay on board. Call me Ishmale. He opened the hatch and using the pilot light looked at himself in the rear-view mirror. He slicked his hair down. He has an obsession with his hair. This kid hasn't learned anything from Yul Brynner. He disembarked. Alone. Prince Valiant. Prince Radiant. With his singing sword, a sweet-voiced myth. He plunged into the Jungle.

—Bring 'em back alive, Frank Buckué!

I looked in the mirror and saw him walk off down the left-hand quayside, Cué's side and certainly not the gayside, as I saw them coming toward him in the mirror road. He's getting warmer. Nine eight seven sex five four three two one bang! Collision of the sexes. A cross-sexion. A coalision. When works collide. When words collogue. A collusion. A monologue, as he's doing all the talking. What the fuck will he say? The tale of Cuésimodo and Esmeralda. Call me Emeralda. Enchanteused to meet you. Cuésimodo tries to kiss Esmeralda's hand—and everything else as well. Sorry, nothing doing. Boy, are you homely. I was born that way. My teepest sympathy. But you're more homely than Ulysses' host, what's his name, Polyphoetus, if you'll excuse me saying so. He accepts her cuéndolences. Quésimodo racking his brains and pondering and walking up and down the quéys, roués, ballbards and aVenus of his mind thinking how can he get Emeraldita laid. Thinking in the rain. A light bulb for a whalo. That's it! He would sell fake gargoyles, postcards and other junk as souvenirs of the cathedral of Notre Mom. A procursor. He'll get rich, like almost all the pioneers, any five-year-old child knows that! Bring a five-year-old boy then. He leaves his little culture's nest high up in the Gothic rooftops and goes to Pigalle. He hires the most beautiful woman he meets and takes her to dinner at the Tour de Nesle, the best restaurant of the age (thirteenth century, a terrible century: all the men who were born then are dead), and he orders one or two miniatures by artists of the school of Fondantbleu (say cheese) who are historically known to be the best. People will see him the next day titillating the tits of somewhore or more in the morning tablet. Edited by Téophraste Renaudotty. Cuésimodo begins to be on everybody's lips. Le Tout Paris—and all the other touts too—call him *tú*. The rest call him Cuési. They go cuézy over him. Some of them call him Mody, Americanizing his name. The same people who say the Bastill when they spend a night in jail (another Americanism) or une drink d'hydrohoney and dance the country dances, well ahead of their times. Quel horreur le Franglais. It would take a Holy Roman Umpire to separate them. It's the fault of all those Plantagenets with their goings and comings. Les anglais a la lanterne! We shall take care of thee lateh, Joan of Arc. Cuésimodo repeats his journey with another girl of his choice. Today he goes to the Equus Insanus, une taberna. Quel horreur le Franlatin. It's all the fault of the Ecclesia Romana. Quod scripsi scripsi, Rabelaisius. Vae vatis. Carmen et error. Facsimiles are reproduced on every parchment. Esmeralda who, like almost everybody in the medieval world, is unable to read (that's why we have to wait five centuries before there is a daily press in Paris) begins to see, like almost everybody else in the medieval world, the very small paintings, esp. a portrait, on ivory, vellum or the like. Cuésimodo with Carmen and also with Error. Cuésimodo with La Belle Dame and with Mercy. What's he got, this Cuésimodo? she begins (at about the same time as she begins looking at the miniatures) asking herself. Then follow the journeys aux Champs, à la avenue de la Grande Armée, à Saint Germain des

Pres and he's the talk of the town. In this town of talk. Esmeralda is more than intrigued and decided to take a closer look at Cuésimodo. Horror. Even closer. Karma et horror. Closer and closer. Esmeralda has this habit when she is talking to a man of buttonholing him and unbuttoning his shirt. It's actually a nervous trick: Cuésimodo is one of the giants of real life and of poetry. Esmeralda's getting warmer. She begins to play with his buttons. But Cuésimodo is no longer interested in this mulatto girl who's trying to pass herself off as a gypsy. Why? Because there are all those other girls, who are much better dressed and, besides, quel metier! Medievilly speaking, he buttons up his codpiece anew. What the fuck will he say to them? It's impossible that they'll recognize him in the dark. By his barky baritone of course. "Oh Rose & Mary I love you!" Fuck his barbitone voice. The cunnilinguage of the heart. They walk. They walk and talk. Walkie-talkies. The talkies. What a technique. Experience rather. They are coming talking. Trumpets off, clarions off. Strumpets on. And here come the Earwickers, the ear vicaries. Here they are. I open the door and get out. Luckily there's not much light. I feel a bit like Quasimodo. Uneasy like Queasy. I'll plug in my erogenous tone. Perfect mimicry. I'm a dumb show-off. Latins are loudy lovers.

—Good evening.

Arsenio introduced us. They're old friends. We're old friends. Truly friends over the years and the tide of pubic affairs or private parts, to say Cuban is to say amigo and the bird sings even though the branch is breaking and never mind the downpour it's only Cuban water falling amigos todos woman is king, queen I mean. No, I mean king. Silvestre, Beba and Magalena. Magalena and Beba, Silvestre Inshort. Delighted. I'm soo pleazed to meat you. It's a pleazure. Noo, I'll meazure you now and pleazure you later. Giggles. I'm going down well. Was it me that said that? Yes, because Cuérteous Cué magallantly opens the sound-doors of his convertible to bring to you ladies the emotion and romance of a new episode—*Tarsanio's on the air!* from the unconscious depths of the jungle in the heart of Darkest Africa boccato di missioneri a cry is heard that defoliates the virgin forest Tanmangakué! It is Zartan, Tarzan's elder brother's pet bugger and zoodomite. Listenhoney. Who's talking? You don't think baby-blue that we're going to get in just like that without a roof over our heads. It's not Magalena. I'm not going in that. Exposed to the bad weather. Don't you see we've just come out of the beauty parlor. It's the other one who's talking. What the hell's her name? Don't jog me. Don't hustle me, gentlemen. I've got a godawful memory. Beba! Which not only means baby, but also to drink in Cubanned. Drink Coca Phony, the refreshing menopause. Come alike! Drink Fantasy! Señorita, no paella can be fun/ without a sausage in a bun. Radio Suaritos or commercials considered as pubiscity and advertenticing. A sexage and a pun. On all fours, I mean in four hours, señora, we will *fly* you from Havana to New York, by Nacheeonal Earlines. Are your hands clean, señorita? Then use Revlon nail polish and see the difference. Men about town, if you want a ready-maid go somewhere else. If you want a good hand job go to Casa Pérez, the shirt house. Magalena is talking, Magalena who's rounded my Cape Horn making the round tour of Dante's InCuérno and sits down in the back seat. Next to me. Me for you and you for me. Formecation. I sail through the straits of Magellana and founder on a breast, I think. Or are there two of them? Feminine fashions tend to homo . . . Don't get me wrong. To homogenize, I mean, it's my tongue that gets me wrong, to make one of what nature intended to be two. There are two breasts, two buttocks and every fashion tries to make them look like one. Cué pressed a knobble, a knipple, a *knob*. We are sitting two a breast in the Verdun theater and over the sound of the roof sliding back into place we can even hear background music. He also turned on Daniel Amfitheatrophy. Or is it Bakueleinikoff? Or perhaps Erichué Wolfgang Corngold? He's turned on that sonofabitch of a radio. "Technique is condensed experience." Evaporated silk. Indirect music that predisposes you to love. "Dear car owner" (the voice interrupting the music purring like a cat in perpetual heat could almost be Cué's), "please inscribe a knob on your radio panel with my name." The air carries the words away but melady lingers on. "And now, in the romantic voice of Cuba Venegas and by courtesy of Casino socks, Piloto & Vera's bolero, 'Nostalgic Meeting.' It's a Puchito record." Puchito! What a name! Puke-ito. Cuba Venegas. The romantic voice of the queen of the bolero. La puta nacional, folk's whore, that's what she is.

Socks in the cocksino. Shit. Neuralgic meeting by Vera and his co-piloto, by Pilot and his co-vera, by Piloto and Viera, Plotov & Beria, the stakhanovites of the bolero. Arslongo Cuébrevis fastens the top and drives off with all on board toward the night of love, madness and death. Would you like to hear the sad Tristory of Isolde? Don't forget to tune in to the next episoda.

That's how they talk on Cuban radio and the episolde is only another selected item from my two years before the mast (urban), the adventures of Long John Silver and how he met Robinson Cuésoe on the Island of Lesbos. Caco Phony.

Cué missed his cue going down 17th not because he's superstitious but because he prefers 21st, for reasons that are purely numerical and besides it's personal. So we return to the avenue and make for the sea. The red light stopped us on Línea and I saw Magalena's beautiful face turn from cinnamon to cinder thanks to the mean tungsten light. It was then I noticed her birthmark, a pale shadow cutting across her nostrils and on her cheeks. I thought she noticed me looking so I said quickly:

—Códac introduced us one evening.

—That's what he said, and she pointed her finger at Cué, its long nail painted with what would have been red nail polish if the lapis lazuli, chalcedony or chrysoprase (it needs words like these to correspond to its infernal color) bulb of that brilliantly lit public enemy of lovelight hadn't been shining over us.

—Arsenio's the name. Arsenio Cué.

Ferocious barbarhythms, translated of course from the American. He also says *afluente* instead of *próspero, moron* for *idiota, me luce* instead of *me parece, chance* for *oportunidad, controlar* instead of *revisar* and things like that. Qué horror el Espanglish. Doctor Esperanglish, I consume. We'll take good care of you one day, Lyno Novás.

—Ah, the other one said, the one who's called Beba. —It's true. You's the actor on TV. I've often seen you on it.

She was a woman not a girl and she must have had some ancestor from Africa who had disappeared in the crossing of other tropical rivers. One of those mulattos who aren't mulattos, but so cleverly mixed that only a Cuban or a Brazilian or maybe Faulkner would be able to detect it. She had long black hair that had been done up a moment ago and big brown eyes with plenty of eye shadow and a mouth which was not so much sensual as what people here call depraved. Wisdom of the elite. As though forms, aside from being sketched in by light and having dimensions and a position in space, could also adopt moral concepts. An ethics for Leonardo. A touch of the brush is a moral problem. The face is the mirror of the soul. Lombroso's prog-nose. O tempera, O mores. Venus vide, da Vici.

Etcethics. She must have a stunning figure but now all I could see of her was a sculptor's bust, her head in the shadows. I saw Cué looking at himself in the mirror. Or rather, looking in the mirror. He was spying on Magalena in the rear-view mirror. Supposing he offers me a swap, what then? Or is he planning a chicken switch? I'll tell him to go fuck his mother and get out. Or should I stay and say O.K. cunt me in. In any case I'd gain by changing. Shit, I don't like oldies. Gerontophobia. Is a woman old at twenty-five? You must be out of your mind, you pervert. A sensualist, a sexualist, that's what you are. I don't want to deprave you of life but you'll end up like Humbert Humbert started off. Or like Hunger Humbert. Or like Humble Humbert by Humperdinck. Hansel & Gretel. First with Gretel and then fuck with. You Humble Pervert. Shit! Better a eunuch. Eugene Eunusco. I'll go work for Unesco. Just a moment. Have you no honor? No country? No loyalty to royalty—royalty to loyalty? Magalena's no chicken, nor's the other so old as all that. One at a time. A chick in the hand. Don't covet thy neighbor's whore. Let's take another peep at her. She's not at all bad. Why the fuck should she be? Who saw her first? I or me? Nineteen and thirty-six, twenty-four, thirty-eight. The Cabala? No, statistics. Cuban bodice. Cuban boy. Cuban body. Body by Fisher. MagaleNash Ramper, exhibited on La Rampa. The name of the agency is Amber Motors. Sepia Motors. General Motels. Window wenching. Fordnicating. Statitstics. Venus video. Vice. Latin's a lousey lover. Cacofunny.

—What?

—Where are you? Up in the clows someplace, honeychile?

—Come down from that cloud and get back to where you once belong (the good-natured clavier of Johann Sebastian Cuéch). It's a song to re-member.

—Excuse me, ma'am. I didn't hear you, I apologized.

—Silvestre, *viejo,* for heaven's sake. Nobody's going to call a lady madam in my car.

—I beg your pardon, I said to Beba mock Apollogetically.

—No, said Arsenio, —in my car you don't!

They laughed. This ace knows how to be a joker. I'm inkorrigible, but dirigible as well. Blimp!

I'll make a big effort and now that I've ascended to the skies I'll descend to the humble cabins, even if they do belong to Uncle Tom. We have to go down to the populace, if they're feminine. To eat the milk of human kindness. *In medias res* in Carnation.

—What'd you say, Beba?

That's my voice you just heard. It doesn't sound like a eunuch's. I'm no Castrato. Pepin the Short maybe, though I have a good voice for imitating other voices: this time it's an amiable and attentive and popular voice. Populacrity.

—What do you do, baby?

—I'm an aesthete.

—What! they both said. They were a duo. A capella.

—I'm looking at you (they looked at me) and that's my occupation. A thing of beauty is a job forever.

Giggles. Laughter by Cué.

—But how charming!

—No, *niño,* I mean what do you do for a living. Agtor, are you an agtor?

—I am a w—

Cué like another librarian came between us.

—He's a journalist. For *Carteles.* Do you remember Alfredo Telmo Quílez and the joke about No lampoons? But no, you're much too young to remember that.

Smiles all round.

—Charmin'.

—You're very kine to us, Beba said. —But you can buy the magazine on the street, it's not ancient history.

Not so bad. A trace of humor. A trace is better than nothing.

—But we also sees it in the beauty pallor, don't we, Beba?

—That's a woman's privilege, Cué said. —We are forbidden to enter so sacred a place as your *zenana.*

—We can only imagine what the mysteries of the Bona Dea are.

Cué gave me a look that meant damned Latinist. But he said,

—We have to read it at the barber's.

—Or at the dentist's, I said.

He looked at me in the mirror, with grateful eyes. It was my sentimental education. Call me Moreau not moron.

—And you, what do you do there? Magalena asked.

—I work incognito.

I felt Cué's look fall on me with more force than the combined decibel power of Magalena's and Beba's shocked What! I decided to ignore Cué. I'm a rebel without a pause.

—He's joking. It's because he's being modest, Cué said.

—Modest Moussorgsky, at your service. And, of coursze, at the czar's czervice.

I got the feeling they weren't listening. I took no notice of Cué.

—This man here, Cué said, —is one of the first journalists of Cuba and when I say first I don't mean that he interviewed Columbus when he landed, even if he does have the face of an Indian.

They laughed. One point for the radio.

—And talking about Columbus, Cué said, —where shall we go to in our caravelle?

—Should be pronounced care-a-belle, I said, meaning Magalena. Smiles. They've no idea. So they tell Cué. You choose and we'll sing or dance or what you will. Exwhyzedetera.

—How about a club, bar or cabaret?

—That's no go by me, Beba said.

—She won't go, Cué said.

—And we always go everywhere together, Magalena said.

—Where would our Siamese sisters like to go then?

I thought I heard a note in Cué's voice that sounded more weary than wary. Bad news. Panic in the bourse. Bursa plus inflation equals bursitis. A slump to follow.

—I don't know, Beba said. —You decide.

Bworse. We were in the Circus Maximus of always. "Take a woman, caress her, ask her what she wants and you'll have a vicious circle"—Ionescué. "Unable to separate the end from the beginning. Happy animals"—Alcmeon of Cuétona. "Would that all the women in the world had a single head (maidenhead)"—Cuéligula. He was talking again.

—O.K. then, how about a clean badly lit place like el Johnny's?

—El Yoni. That's not bad, don'tcha think, Beba?

Beba thought about it. She looked at us: first one then the other, and then she played a game of profiles: she sat there looking at Cué's profile while showing me the implacable outline of her own face. Pretty mouth. A sober man's Eve Gardener. Ava to the inebriated. She opened her mouth. Then said to Cué, He's real cute, talking about Cuéte in that affected, affectionate, popular third person we use in Cuba, in Havana. Folk winsom. He look like a movie star. She closed her mouth. You should never have opened it, Beba Gardner. Only in the dark of a movie house, Cué said. He was talking about his beauty. She smiled. What beauty. (Beba's I mean.) Cué turned around again to take another look and as a traffic signal stopped us (conventional time interrupting the natural solution of our space continuum) on the Malecón he asked Magalena:

—Don't we know each other from somewhere?

—I offen see you on TV and lissen to you and all.

—Haven't we seen each other before? In the flesh.

—Could be. In Códac's house or on La Rampa.

—Not before that?

—Before what? I thought I noticed a trace of suspicion in her coolness.

—When you were much younger. Three or four years ago, you must have been fourteen or fifteen.

—Don't remember, honest.

Beauty didn't remember. Honest. Better. Beba's interruption was good too. O.K., young feller, you'd better sort it out in your head or wherever, which one you like best, that's for you to decide, baby. You of course, honey, Cué said, I don't want to offend anybody present, but you're unique. It's just that I thought I knew her when she was a lolittle girl, but I don't thank heavens for little girls, only for little women. Cross my heart, for you are my vagina pectoris. O.K., said Beba, that makes things different, Ise soore glad to hear it. Magalena laughed. Cué laughed. I thought it my duty to imitate them, but first I asked myself if Beba knew whether Cué kept his heart on the right or on the left. Nobody answered me, I didn't even answer myself. So do we go or don't we? Cué said and Beba said yes and Magalena jumped up and down excitedly giving me a promising look. Mentally I rubbed my hands. A difficult exercise, believe me. Arsenio Cué gave me an unpromising look. Spiritually I clenched my fist. Latins are loser lovers.

—Silver Starr.

His voice also sounded promising, but there was a suggestion of a doubt or a question placed on top of it like an accent.

—Yeah?

—Sheriff Silver Starr, we're running outa gas.

He was putting on a Texan accent. Now he was a marshal in the West. Or a deputa sheriff.

—Gas? You mean no gasoline?

—Horses all right. I mean the silver, Starr. Long o' women but a little this side of short on moola or mazuma. Remember? A nasty by-product of work. We need some fidutia, pronto!

—I have some, I've already told you. About five pesos.

—Are you loco? That won't get us not even to the frontera.

—Where can we get some more?

—Banks closed now. Only banks left are river banks, because park bancos are called benches in English. Holdup impossible.

—What about Códac?

—No good bum. Next.

—The Teevee Channel?

—Nothing doing. They've got plenty o' nuttin for me.

—I mean your loan shark.

—Nope. He's a sharky with a pnife, and a wife. Not on talking terms.

I laughed. (In English, that is. Ha-ha instead of ja-ja.)

—Johnny White, then?

—Outa town. Left on a posse. He's a hideputy sheriff now.

—And Rine?

He fell silent. He nodded approval.

—Righto! Good ol' Rine. It's a cinch. Thanks, Chief. You're a genius.

He turned left and then right and returned finally to the Malecón going in the opposite direction—and it takes me longer to write what he did than he took doing it. The girls on board, picked up and thrown about by the centrifugal and centripetal forces, by the coriolis effect and maybe by the tides, as well as the pull of the moon, that has such an influence on women, were getting seasick and went to the captain to protest.

—Hey, what ya doin'? D'ya wanna kill us or what?

—We'd better get out if he's gonna go on like that, Beba.

Arsenio slowed down.

—Aside from that, Beba said, —would ya quit talking English without subtitles.

We laughed. Arsenio reached out a hand toward Beba and it disappeared into the dark flesh. Beba looked really beautiful, especially now she was only half pretending to be angry.

—It's just I'd forgotten an urgent message I had to give a friend. I've just remembered it. Duty calls.

—You can say that again.

—Beauty calls.

Beba and Magalena laughed. They understood that at least.

—Besides, Beba honey (Cué plugged in his romantic radio voice, the one we, his friends, that is, call Oh what a lovely noise) think of the spiritual side of It. I was talking to Silvestre here about how much I love you, and how my natural shyness doesn't let me express my passion for you. I told him, Silvestre Here, that I'd made up a poem for you in my head, but that I couldn't let it gush from my innocent lips for fear of the pitiless criticism that this professional critic right behind me might unleash not to mention how other people might react (and Magalena, who picked up the Cue, immediately said, It's O.K. by me, because I ain't said anything and besides I really like potry). It wasn't for you, beautiful lady, but for others yet unborn but who will be, I hope, someday. I also said to my distinguished friend and fellow traveler here that my heart does a hundred a minute for you and that I am only hoping that it will beat in unison with yours. That was the true and real cause of my distracted driving which must have been so upsetting for you aside from being bad for this excellent automobile. No pun intended.

Beba was enchanted or at least chanting:

—But how charmin' he is!

—Let's hear you recite, Prince Charming, please, I said.

—Yes, please, Arsenio Cué, Magalena said enthusiasthmatic.

—C'mon, please, Beba said.

—I beg you, recite it. I've always been prone to catch Poets, anyway.

Cué raised a hand over the steering. The one he had lost somewhere in Beba country. Deeply moved by the sound of La Muzique Cuntcrete, he started on a Cuéamble.

—Beba, love of my life, I'll always have you here, in my breast, next to my wallet, because of these forgettable words which fill me with unspeakable feeling. Pause plus passionate pianissimo. Introduction. Theme. To Beba (a bubbling and trembling of the *b*'s on Arsenio Cué's culpable lips, a single version of the two Richards Burtons) to whom I belong in body and (conjunction indicating suspense) soul (with emotional emphasis) this poem which comes from my heart and other parts. Private properties. A clash of symballs, please, night percuéssionist. Love in the place of increment. Blank verses filled to the brim to buttertoast to my beloved. Muffled drums. Stock exchanges. Perfect pitch. (The beardless Aezra Poundquake profile rises and his tremulous voice fills the car. You'd have to hear Arsenio Cué and see the face of the ladies in waiting. The Greatest Show on Hearse.)

WOULD YOU WERE CALLED BABEL AND NOT BEBA MARTÍNEZ

O
Oh
Oh, if only you'd say it,
If with your lips you'd say it
Contraria contrariis curantur,
What seems so easy to say for us who are allopathic.
If you'd say it, Lesbia, with your accent,
O fortunatos nimium, sua si bona norint, Agricolas.
Like Horace.
(Or was it Virgil
Publius?)
Or just a little
Mehr Licht
That is so easy
That anybody in a dark moment
Might go and say it.
(Even Goethe.)
If you'd just say it, Beba,
I say, if you'd just say it,
Beba,
Say it,
With Bathos, Baby, not bathe in it:
Thalassa! Thalassa!
With Xenophon in the Grecian mode

Or with Valéry always begun again,
Pronouncing clear and true the final a—ah
A flat a
And with a grave accent on it.
Or if only
Even with
Saint
John
Perse
You'd say it
Ananabase.
If you'd say it
Thus conscience doth make cowards of us all.
With murmuring syllables
like Sir Laurence and Sir John,
Laurence Olivier, Gielgud et al.
Or with the somber gestures of a talking version of Asta
Nielsen with Vitaphone.
If you'd say it on Friday,
Crucified Lesbia on my sheets,
With love:
Eli, Eli, lama sabacthani!
If you'd say it, Lesbia or Beba,
Oh, Baby
(Or better: Lesby Baby, Oh Beba)
If you'd say it
La chair est triste, hélas, et j'a lu tous les livres!
Even if you were lying and all you knew of livres
was their covers and their spines,
Not the volumes
And not even some forgotten title:
A la Recherche du Temps etcetera
Or Remembrance of Things Past Translation
(How good it would be,
how good it
would be,
Beba, si tu pronçais *lèvres* au lieu de livres!
Beba, if you said lips instead of books!
Then you would not be you

And I not I
And still less you,
I or I,
You:
We would be Saint Augustine and Saint Anselm
Or maybe Augustine and Anselme
Or, simply, Augustín Tant Lara and his carnal Anselma.
Or if you'd just say viande in lieu of chaire,
Though you said it like a martini-quaise,
I would be a happy Nappo
A lion to your carnal, feeble, edible, josephinetude.)
If you'd say it, Bebita,
Eppur (or E pur) si muove,
As Galileo once said in excuse
to those who reproached the astute astronomer
Having married an old ugly whore,
An adulterer who happened to be poor.
If you'd say it, Beba,
Lesbeba,
Although you pronounced it wrong:
If you transformed with your mobile tongue,
animated as though it had a soul of its own,
The little Greek, the less Latin and the no Aramaic into living tongues
Or if you repeated forty-four thousand times
and still many more times
Or even 144
Because the former figure,
The forty-four
thousand, in words, is for the boy in the back and the latter figure
in written numbers is for a hidden destiny,
that's still hidden: it's not yet my destiny,
If you'd repeat with my lama
(Lagrán Rampa)
Or with just a modest gurú,
If you'd learn from him to say, murmú-
ring:
Om-ma-ni Pad-me-Hum,

With no result,
Of course.
Or if you'd make a mudrá for me
with your middle finger upright,
and your ring finger and the other, index it's called,
the two, the four, all the rest
on their sides prostrated there.
If you'd grant me just this favor,
I would be myself no longer,
because I'd be the bardo
not just a bard—man.
But that's too complicated
and much too hardo.
If you could only say
a simple, single phrase.
If you could say it,
If you could say it and I with you
And with us the whole half world
Le demi-monde
The mali mir
That catch-phrase which reads:
Ieto miesto svobodno!
Svobodnó!
Oh, would you were called not beba, but Babel Martínez!
Oh.
O.

Arsenius Cuétullus fell silent, and the silence continued to fall and reverberate in the car as the Mercury turned into a Pegaso. I almost applauded. What stopped me was the tone of dismay in Babel's voice. Or Lesbia's. Or rather the speed with which Beba bounced back, per caputt Cué pedes Cué:

—But baby Martine ain't my name.

—Isn't it, Cué said very seriously.

—No, and I don' like that nickname Annabel.

—Babel.

—Whatever it is.

Magalena speaking:

—Besides it was just too weird. I swear to God I didn't understand a word of it.

What is to be done? Even if we had really been talking Russian and not mirror-Russian, Lenin couldn't have told us what to do next, still less Chernyshevsky. Henry Ford came to our rescue instead. Cué stepped on the accelerator right down to the floor—or rather to Chez Rine or Rine's or Ca'Rine. Dom Pyni.

XVII

—How!

—Yatta-heh!

—Dungawa!

—Ahallani chá!

—Good evening, *señoritas,* Cué said to them, getting in and sitting at the wheel. —Excuse me if I call you *señoritas* but I don't know you yet.

Adrenaling, O-Read corpuscles, O. Reaction Marx-negative. Humors, traces of.

—Was Rine in?

—Yep.

He was doing an imitation of Gary Cooper as he drove off pulling down the brim of an imaginary stetson. He was the White Knight, the savior. Savior Cué.

—*Un año sin verde,* I said gravely, copycatting Katy Jurado's country countralto in *High Noon.*

—See low say, said Gary Cuéper in Texican. The wild West dubbed in Spanish, for the audience's benefit. Self-criticism. Autocritica. He drove on and we rode together.

—What did Rine say?

—Opened his mouth.

—Was it large?

—Uge.

—A big boy now, eh?

—Henormous, said Cué.

—A rinesaurus, Bustrófedon would say.

—Who's this Rine? Beba asked.

—One of nature's marvels, Cué said.

—One of history's.

—But is he a man or a woman or what?

—A what, I said.

—He's a dwarf who is also a friend, Cué said.

—A friendly neighborhood Lealliputian.

—A dwarf? Magalena asked. —He's not that journalist who's a friend of Códac?

—Yep.

—That's who it is, I said.

—He's no dwarf. He's the same as you or me.

—*Was,* you mean.

—Whaddya mean?

—He wasn't sanforized, Cué said.

—Say dat again?

—Dat again.

—Oh, c'mon!

—He's gone and shrunk himself, darling, I said. —He ate some mushrooms. . . .

—Anatomic mushrooms, Cué cut in.

—Hallucinatory mushrooms, and before you could say Edward G. Robinson he went psss and deflated. He's a midget now.

—The mightiest midget on earth.

—You're putting us on! Magalena said. —You don't expect us to swallow that, do you?

—If we've swallowed it I don't see why you shouldn't, Cué said.

—Women are no better than men, I said.

—And none the worse for that, Cué said.

—That's what I say, I said. —Some of my best lady friends are women.

They laughed. At last. We laughed.

—Seriously, who is he? Beba asked.

—He's a friend of ours who's an inventor, Cué said. —Seriously.

—He used to be called Phryne, but he got old and his Ph

dropped off so he couldn't phiss phroperly and the why turned into an eye. Lack of calcium.

—So now he's just Rine though his last name is Leal.

—But that doesn't stop him from being a great inventor, I said cutting in on Cué to stop the game going semantic.

—A phabulous hinventor! Cué said with radiophonic emphasis.

—Oh, come on! said Magalena. —There aren't any inventors in Cuba.

—Not many but they do exist, I said.

—It was necessary to invent them, Cué said.

—Everything here comes from someplace else, Magalena said.

—Quel heurror! Cué said. —Women who have no faith in their country, may their children all be steel born.

—All that's needed, I said, —is for you to say, Bwana, white man he invent all thing good. Mistah Kuétz, he dead?

—No, Silbwana! What we need here is a soupçon of nationalism, Cué said, tuning in his built-in, shit-full public address system. —Look at the Japanese (he pointed to the street). They are no longer to be seen. They have disappeared over the horizon of history. But they'll come back.

—Besides, I said, —Rhine is a foreigner.

—Really? Beba asked. —Where from?

Snobbery is stronger than the spirit: it blows where it laysteth.

—Actually he doesn't have a country, Cué said. —He's a foreigner everywhere.

—Yes, I said. —He was born in a United Fruit Company ship chartered by Guatemala that was sailing at fourteen international nautical miles per diem under a Liberian flag when.

—His father was an Andorran naturalized in San Marino and his mother was Lithuanian but traveling under a Pakistani passport.

—Boy oh boy, that's too complicated for me, Magalena said.

—That's what an inventor's life is like, I said.

—Genius is an infinite capacity for enduring everything, Cué said.

—Except the unendurable.

—Take no notice of them, baby, Beba said. —They're pulling your leg.

Where'd I heard that phrase before? It must be a historic quote. Wisdom of the cliquetoris. To the unhappy few.

—Seriously, Cué said and suddenly his voice was serious, —he's an inventor of genius. It's possible nothing like it has been seen since the wheel.

Beba and Magalena laughed noisily, to show they understood. Only they got it by the wrong side of the wheel. By its axle. Axes. Sexa. The wheel of wives? Immoral coils? Or was it the Ananga-Ringa-roses?

—I'm talking seriously, Cué said.

—Seriously he's talking seriously, I said.

—A great inventor. Extra. Ordinary.

—But what does he invent?

—Everything that hasn't been invented yet.

—He doesn't invent anything else because he would consider it pointless. Also edgeless.

—Someday he'll get his due, Cué said, —and mothers will name their boys and girls after him.

—Like Catulle Mendes, for example.

—Or Newton Medicinelli, who was my physics teacher in another red-incarnation.

—Or Virgilio Piñera.

—And La Estrella, ci-devant Rodríguez.

—What about Erasmito Torres? He's in the Mazorra asylum now.

—He a doctor?

—No, a patient. But he'll come out with true firsthand evidence on insanity. Titled *Mazorrae Encomium*.

—I don't doubt it. In the end, parodying Grau, there'll be rines for everyone. It will be a common name.

—Oh, c'mon! What this Rine invented?

—Don't worry, we'll make you a catalog.

Cué kept on driving while he pretended to read a long list like a herald unrolling an invisible parchment. His Cuétalog.

—For example, Rine invented dehydrated water, an invention which solves in one cast of science that will never abolish thirst, the increasingly urgent problem of Arabia. An invention for the UN. There they'll give him his deserts.

—Such a simple sample.

—All you need to do is to drop some pills of water in your djellaba pocket and drive down the desert.

—Or up. Then you have to put your camel into first gear.

—You drive and drive and drive and you don't find any oasis or oleoduct or even a wandering camera unit. Put an end to that stuffy nonsense. You pull out your pill, drop it in a glass, dissolve it in water and presto Chango! you have a glass of water. In two seconds flat. Will drink two Bedouins. Or Lawrence and his dune bugger, if you please. An end to imperialist whitemail, in any case.

They weren't amused. They hadn't understood. What did they want? Real inventions or maybe more wheels? We went on. In incomprehension like this Christianity, Communism and even Cubism were born. All we need is to find our Apaullinaris. Our Saulution.

—He went on to perfect the distilled water pill. It is guaranteed germproof. No more Veni VD vici!

—Meanwhile he invents other inventions. The headless and bladeless knife, fr. xmpl. Not a pointless invention, believe me.

—Or the windproof candle.

—A brilliant idea.

—Luminous! Simple too.

—How simple?

—Every candle has the words Don't light! printed on it in red ink.

—At first he thought of dyeing them red and writing Dynamite on them in black letters, but the idea seemed too flamboyant. Besides there'll always be the risk of suicides or wayward miners.

—Juvenile delinquents.

—Miners, not minors, you mongol aide!

—What about terrorists?

—What about horrorists?

Like Queen Vicaria they weren't amused.

—Another invention of genius was his urban condom.

A few scattered giggles.

—You cover the city with a huge sheath of inflated nylon.

—That invention belongs to what will someday be known as the Pneumatic Period in this man's oeuvre.

—It will protect cities in the desert or the tropics from the sun, and northern cities from the wind and storms and cold.

—But not from pollution, I said. —An American wet dream?

—Also, Cué went on, —you'll be able to control the rain by zones, because the sheath will have zippers that will open up certain sections and allow the water that has accumulated above them to fall. All the weather stations will have to do is say, Today it will rain in the borough of El Vedado and environs, for example, and then signal to Zipper Code: Showers over El Vedado and environs, please.

Disappointment among the women. But there's no stopping us now. Rine, ride, ricci.

—Another invention of this epic epoch is the rubber road for cars with wheels made of concrete or asphalt, according to taste. An accidental discovery to end all accidents.

—Think how much drivers in the future will save on tires.

—This invention has of course one fault. Small but bothersome. The roads may burst. All that's needed then is an announcement over the radio. Radio Reloj announces: All traffic detoured from Fifth Avenue, which has had a flat. Drivers are requested to go down Third or Seventh, while the road is being blown up. Bleep bleep bleep. More inventions for you in exactly one minute.

They didn't say a word.

—There's also his invention of rolling cities. Instead of you traveling to them it's they that come to the traveler. One goes to the Terminal . . .

—One? Supposing two go?

—It makes no difference. There'll be equality. The polis is for the hoi pollute. Polite. Polloi. These two people will stand, then, like a single man on the platform. When is Matanzas City coming? he asks a ticket inspector. Matanzas City should arrive any minute now, according to the schedule. One hears another voice behind, When does Camagüey get in? Oh, there's been a slight delay in Camagüey. (*Over the loudspeakers*) Attention! Passengers to Pinar de Río! The city of Pinar de Río is just arriving at platform number three. Attention! Passengers for

Pinar de Río please hurry! Some passengers pick up their baggage and step off the platform onto the city. All *abroad!*

Nothing nothing nothing.

—There are other less ambitious little inventions.

—Poor but honest.

—Like the car which doesn't need gas. It's worked by gravity. All you need to do is to build roads that slope downward. Shell will discover that its pearl is only a cultured one.

Nothing but nothing.

—Also in the field of public constructions the masterly rolling sidewalks should be mentioned.

—With three-speed gears.

—There are three endless rolling sidewalks and the first one goes at the speed of people in a hurry (this can be adjusted to the character, economy and geography of the different cities), the middle speed for people who are just strolling or who want to arrive late for an appointment or for tourists, and finally the inside sidewalk, which goes very slowly, for people who want to go window-shopping, or talk with friends, or pay compliments to a girl in a window.

—This inside walk will sometimes have benches for the old and for invalids and war veterans. You are also obliged to give up your seats to pregnant women. Or both.

Nothing but nothing but nothing.

—Or his erasable magnetic film.

—Or the music typewriter.

—Just imagine what use Mozart could have made of it.

—There will be stereostenographers, tachymelos or melographers. Perhaps they could even do some typedancing.

—Tchaikovsky would have been able to sit a male secretary on his knee and at the same time score his Sexth Symphony.

—Better still is the new system of writing music which will make us all musically literate.

—It is such a revolutionary invention that it has already been officially banned in all the conservatories. There's an agreement signed in Geneva to prevent its use. The same thing happened with his sexophone, which offsprang from the rape of a virginal by some viola d'amore.

—It is simplicity itself, like everything Rine does: Simple

Fidelis! You simply write on the score (and you don't need ruled paper either) Tararara tararari or Um-pa-pa-pa or Nini nini nini, depending on the character of the music. You make notes in the margin: nadagio/ calento/ con frio/ all egro/ nosale/ maestoso paffuto/ trompetuoso. This is the only concession to the traditional notation. Pom-pom-pom-pöom, Pa-pa-pa-paaá, for example, will be the opening of Beethoven's Fifth Symphony, which Rine has already transcribed completely in his system. The sol-fa notation, of course, will be called the Humming Way.

Our nadaing that art in nadity nada by thy name. A last attempt. A lost intent.

—His latest invention, the Definitive, the ultimate counter-weapon, is an anti-A -H or -Cobalt bomb.

—These bombs, little darlings, split the atom. Rine's anti-bomb puts it together again.

—As the bomb is dropped an automatic device fires off the anti-bomb which integrates at the same speed and with equal intensity as the other disintegrates, so that the enemy bomb ends up by being reduced to a piece of scrap uranium falling out of the sky. It can damage a building, make a pothole in the road, or kill a mockingbird.

—Like a tile falling off a roof.

—You will read in the papers the next day: War News. Yesterday a crow was hit by an atomic bomb dropped by the enemy of our heroic motherland. He was killed but not scared. These heartless criminals will soon pay for their misdeeds. Our army continues to execute victoriously its strategic retreat. General Confusion, from Hindquarters.

—Buggle, blow Booze and Soda.

But total silence ensued us. It felt like an ad for Rolls-Royce because I could hear my heart ticking on the dashboard. Nobody said a word. Except Arsenio Cué, who bellowed as he made a sharp turn to avoid running down a fat man. The heavy pedestrian suddenly became light with fright and made the sidewalk or unmade the street with a flying leap and balanced on the curb, doing a hop, skip and jump, spinning around and somersaulting like a night-ropewalker. I heard a cascade of laughter, a single long torrent of laughter, more Cubane than urbane. Our she-fellow-travelers were cracking up and splitting their sides and pointing amazedly or amusedly at the near-miss—or rather mister. They went on laughing for several blocks. Cuésullus sulked: nothing's more silly than a silly laugh.

We wanted to sail them into Johnny's or Yonis, you can say it either way in Havanaise, between their gales of laughter and the hot wind outside—without much success. Now, once inside, cooled off by the bitter chill or killed off by the bitter cool of the air-conditioning sipping an alexander, a daiquiri, a manhattan and a cuba libre, a drink for each, we tried grinding them in our fun machine. For them, it was quite clear, the result was more pus than fun or more fuss than pun. But we went on with joking and choking, washing our dirty jokes in public. What the hell for? Maybe because Arsenio and I were getting high on it. Or because there was still a wake of alcohol in our resentful blood vessels. Or else it just made us happy this facility, the facile felicity, this phalluscity with which we'd carried them off, kiddingnapping them: the ease of this Rape of the Sapphines, our elephantine levity, the Eliphas Levitation we'd accomplished, plus my idea that tumescence is the opposite of the Fall. At least I think that's what I was thinking. I don't know if Arsenio Cué felt it or not but right now we both decided at the same time, with tacit tactless tactics, to be Gallagher and Shean for them, Gallastello/Abbottshean Gallaurel and Costardy & Shabbot and Haurelello/Cabbott Shardy and Custer pie for them—it was our Custard Last Stanceley. Bugle, blow Booth and Sadist. We began with a Bu(stro)ffoonery, of course, preposthumous but never too late for this master, the Maestrophodon, my Maelstromedon, the Ground Maestro.

—Do you know the story of the time when Silvestre Here was found naked in a park?

A good beginning. Female interest in nudity for its own sake, not for mine. Lewd of the rings. Envy of the pen. Castrati complot. Latins are ludic loafers.

—Please, Cué, couldn't you tell us something else. My voice had a false blush in it.

Their Cuériosity aroused.

—Tell us, Cué.

The thing is the play.

—Please tell us.

—O.K.

—Please, Cué, don't.

—Eribó and Here (giggles) Bustrófedon (giggles) and Eribó and I were in this park . . .

—Cué!

—Here and Eribó (giggles) were . . .

—If you're going to tell it you might at least tell it properly. Eribó wasn't there.

—How can I tell a naked truth properly? (Giggles) We were Here and . . . You're quite right (giggles), Eribó wasn't.

—You know that's not possible.

—No, it's Eribó who wasn't possible. (Petty laughter) Bustrófedon and Here and . . . was Bustrófedon there?

Boustrofelon. Trespissing is cuntsidered a phallony.

—I don't know.

—It's your story not mine.

—No, it's your story.

—It's yours.

—It's yours!

—It's mine but it's about you, so it's your story.

—It's both our story.

—O.K., then, it's both our story. The story goes like this. (Giggles) This fellow (little giggles) and I and I think Códac too. No, Códac wasn't there. But Eribó was. Was Eribó there?

—No, Eribó wasn't there.

—No. Then Eribó wasn't there. So there we were, Here (giggles) and Códac . . .

—Códac wasn't there either.

—Wasn't he?

—No, he wasn't.

—O.K. then, it's better if you tell the story, since you know it better than I do.

—Thanks. I've got an inflatable memory. There we were (S-laughter), this fellow and Bustrófedon and I, all fours of us . . .

—You only said three.

—Three?

—Yes. Three. You and me and Bustrófedon.

—So that makes two of us, because Bustrófedon wasn't there.

—He wasn't there?

—No, I can't remember him and I've got a log for a memory. Do you remember if he was there?

—No, I don't know. I wasn't there myself, remember.

—That's true. O.K. then, so here we are (laughter) here we were (laughter) there we were in the park (laughter) Códac and I . . . Was I there? (Laughter on Tenth Avenue)

—You're the Memorandum, don't you remember? Mr. Memory. Mamory Blame.

—Yes, of course I was there. There we were. No, of course I wasn't. I should have been there, wasn't I? If I wasn't there where am I? Help! To the rescue. To the risqué! I'm lost bare-assed in the park! Ataja! Achtung! Au-secours! Al-ladro! Astop-thief!

We both laugh. It's always us two who do the laughing. They didn't even realize that this version by Bustrófedon of the Surprise Symphony was the story that never got begun. We then went on to invent other games. Who for? For anyone who doesn't like it hot, three tips of metaphysical Horse Feathers marilynaded with inedible dungus. Athlete's food.

—Would you like me to sing you a song?

This was a gambit Bustrófedon had stolen from a dodgy reverend and which Arsenio Cué had perfected to infinity, while making it his own. Petty L'Arseny. I will now be his erect fall guy, his bent straight man, his fool pigeon, and as Magalena or Beba or Bebalonia both said Ugh! meaning enough's enough or you're being a drag, I began right away. *Señoras y señores.* Ladies and gentlemen. *Tenemos mucho gusto en presentar.* We are glad to introduce, to insert (Cué made an obscene sign with his finger: his mudrá), to present, *por primera y única vez,* once and only, *al Gran!* the Great! Arsenio Cué! Arsenic Ui! Music. A rine of applause, please. Music and song. A gong is borne. A great internationally renowned singer. He sang in Covent Garden. In the vegetable market, of coursage. Belittled by Eliza. He sang in Carnegie Hall. Right there in the lobby. He also did some scales at the Scala, since then known as La Schola for Scandals. A hunique occasion. They will never repeat it. . . .

Our passengers gave a repeat performance of the noise they'd made which sounded like something they'd eaten. It was a belch that hit us under the belt, straight from the gut strings of boredom and tedium. Too much metaphysical duck soup. I ushered in the performance with a patriotic element, borrowed from that tenor who whenever he got the bird or a frog in his throat or both covered it up by croaking, Viva Cuba libre!

—A tribute to a great Cuban artist.

Cué gargled tunefully. Mimi Doremy. I approached him, lapel salt shaker in hand.

—Are you going to sing, sing?

—By General Consent, I'm going to say Three Words.

—That's a fine title, I said.

—It's not the title, Cué said.

—Is it another song?

—No. It's the same song.

—What's its name?

—I was crossing the Khyber Pass when I fell over a dead ass. I didn't fall upon my foot Nevertheless (that's my right foot's middle name, the other foot's called Nevermore) but passed right over that gassed ass.

—Isn't that rather a long name for a song?

—It's not the name of the song. Nor is it rather a long name. It's a very long name.

—So it's not the name of the song?

—No. It's the name of the title.

—What's the title then?

—I don't remember. But I can tell you the name.

—What's the name?

—Victoria Regina.

—That's the song. I know it. Delightful!

—No, it's not the song. She's just a friend. We are not a music.

—A friend? So you've dedicated it to her? To Rectoria Vagina?

—No, she's just a friend of the song.

—A fan.

—No, she's a woman. Though being a woman she's liable to use one.

—Use what?

—A fan.

—That's short for fanatic.

—Then she's not a fanatic. As a matter of fact she's a bit skeptical herself and if you want to know who she is and not what she isn't, all I can say is that she's a friend of the song.

—So what's the song then?

—The one I'm going to say.

—What are you going to say?

—Three Words.

—That *is* the song!

—No, that's the title. The song is what comes under the title.

—What comes under the title?

—The subtitle.

—And under that?

—The sub-subtitle.

—But then, you Sonofabitch, what's the song?

—The name is Cué, if you please. I'm not a Russian. So don't call me Cui. Czar Cué. One against five.

—WHAT IS THE SONG?

Here

or

there

—That's just another title.

—No. It's the song.

—The song? But it's only three words.

—Three Words, but exactly!

—*Coño,* but you didn't even sing it!

—I never said I was going to sing this song. *Coño*? I don't think I even heard of it. I said I was going to *say* Three Words, not sing them.

—In any case, it's a beautiful composition.

—That isn't the composition. The composition is something else.

We braked. They hadn't laughed. They hadn't budged an inch. They hadn't even protested yet, not loudly in any case. They were dead to being—and also to nothingness. Sartre would have made nothing of them. Or being. Or perhaps Ness. Infemmey thy game is human. Thy name is woeman. Thy game is omen. A bygame for tribs. It's all over. Over. And out. For the time beings.

The game was over but only for us. It hadn't ever begun for

them and only Arsenio Cué and I were playing. The nympths with eyes blind to the night stared at the night of the bar. Woman! Arsenio said. If He hadn't existed it would have been necessary to invent God to create her. (Or to fabricate Adam, which spelled backward means nothing. At least in Spanish. *Adán = Náda*. It was my voice I heard, half in earnest, half in jest, adding now: Bugger, blow Blues and Soda.) But Arsenio, as always, had the last word. Softly he said:

—Women: Sphincters without secrets!

XVIII

I think it was at this point that we began wondering tacitly (in the style of Tacitus, Bustrófedon always said when alive) whether it was worth making them laugh. What were we? Clowns, 1st and 2nd gravediggers when we weren't laughing or human beings, common and garded persons, people? Wouldn't it be easier to make love to them? This was, doubtless, what they expected. Cué, who was more resolute or less aloof, began with his Murmur for the Left Hand in one corner and I said to Magalena why don't we go off someplace. Where? Commonplace.

—Outside. Alone. By the silvery moon.

The moon wasn't alight but all you need to turn it on is a cliché.

—What if she miss me?

—Then I'll Mrs. you.

The criminal always returns to the scene of his.

—I mean, she'll get mad at me.

—Do you have to ask her permission?

—Permission? No, not now. But what about later?

—Later you'll be old enough to hold your own.

—I mean later now. She'll start talking and making comments and giving me hell.

—So what?

—Whaddya mean so what? She keeps me.

I'd guessed as much though I didn't say it.

—I'm staying with her and her husband.

—You don't have to explain why you can't.

—I'm not explaining, Ise just telling you so you know why I can't.

—You've got a life to live.

It was truism versus altruism.

—Don't let them live your life for you.

Love versus self-love.

—Don't put off till tomorrow what you can enjoy today.

Horace Cué's argument wins. Even in the battle of the sexes vanity is the one forbidden weapon. She looked like she was cuénvinced by my Cuban carpe diem or at least she looked like she was chewing it over, which was more than a good beginning and with the same pretense of thinking over, or a continuation of it, she gave a sidelong look at Beba Beneficencia. We were in the lead. Old Pindar and me.

—O.K., let's go then.

We got out. Above us the red blue and green letters that spelled out Johnny's Dream flashed on and off. Exotic colors. Neonlithic Age. I almost fell over during one of the dark phases of the sign, but my fear of ridicule more than my sense of balance turned it into a dance step.

—I was dazzled, I said, explaining myself. I'm always explaining myself. Verbally, that is.

—It's real dark down there.

—That's what I don't like about clubs.

She was taken aback.

—You don't?

—No. I don't like dancing either. What's so great about dancing? All it is is music. A man and a woman. Holding each other tight. In the dark.

She didn't say a word.

—You should have said and what's so bad about that? I explained.

—I don' see what's so bad about it. But don' get me wrong, I don' go in for dancin' neither.

—No, just ask me: What's so bad about that?

—What's so bad about that?

—The music.

It's no good. She didn't even smile.

—It's just an old joke of Abbott & Costello.

—Who's that.

—The American ambassador. It's a double-barreled name. Like Ortega y Gasset.

—No kidding.

Pervert. Seducing little girls. Little minds. Prévert.

—No. That's just another joke. They are two comedians in American movies.

—I don' know them.

—They used to be famous when I was a kid. Abbott & Costello meet the Invisible Man, Abbott & Costello meet Frankenstein, Abbott Costello meet *their* Mummy. They *were* very funny.

She attempted a vague gesture and vaguely it faded out.

—You must have been very young.

—Yeah. Quite likely I'd not been born.

—Would you had never been born. I mean, you would have been born later then.

—Yes. Around 1940.

—Don't you know when you were born?

—More or less.

—And you're not afraid?

—Why should I?

—Wait until Cué hears about it. No special reason. At least you know you were born.

—Ise here, ain't I?

—Circumsized evidence. If you and I were together in bed, it would be conclusive. Coitus ergo sum.

Of course she didn't get what I meant. I don't even think she was listening. I didn't even have time to be surprised by my high dive. That's what happens to a timid soul on a springboard.

—Latin. It means that when you're making love you know you exist.

Sonofabitch. Sexus Propertius.

—Like you imagine. You're here. Now. Walking. With me. In the heat of the moon.

If you go on like that you'll end up saying, You Jane, me Tarzan. Antilanguage.

—Youse confusin' me. You muddle everything up.

—You're soveryright. But exackly.

—You do go on so. Like nonstop.

—You bet your sweet etcetera you're right. You'd beat Descartes at his own game.

—Yes, I know Descartes's game well.

I must have jumped. As big a jump as the one Arsenio Cué gave one day in the Mambo Club, this whorehouse, one day, one night rather, a night full of whores and a table piled high with handbags, and music on wings alas!—Alas de Casino, a singer who was all the rage then, and fuck would have it that one of the girls was in love with his voice, and as she couldn't have aural intercourse she did nothing but put on his *five* records again and again, until even I knew by heart not only how one record ended but how the next was going to begin, strung together like a single endless song. Cué began pedantically as ever, talking with another whore, a real cute one, a doll, and told her I was called Exilophon and that his name was Cyruscué and that I'd come to fight by his side in the War of the Sexes, our Analbasis, and there was a whore sadly sitting by herself at another table: she was about thirty: a bit old for the trade (yes, in the Mambo Club une femme de trente ans was an old bawd, you ballsy Balzac) and she lowered her eyes on Cué looking sweetly at him and asked, Against Darius Codomannus? and she launched into a 1,000-word dissertation on the Anabasis till it almost seemed like the retreat of the 10,000 whores to a broadwalk by the sea she knew it so well and it turned out she had been a high-school graduate who through accidents of history (she'd changed her name to Alicia, but she told us her real name which was Virginia Hubris or Ubría) and sailing through economic straits had landed up on this whoredom a short while back, the opposite of the others who had started off as putas when they were still puber—and you can bet that Arsenio Toynbee Cué, better known as Darius Cuédomannus, left his little bonbon half dressed in her silver-paper wrapper and this very elephantine pedant, Arsenic Babbitt, spent that night studying under Virginia Lubricious, mistress of clapsickal and medicevil hysteros. What had he learned from her? Veni VD vice? I returned from my jump. (Sal de salto.) Less than two seconds had passed. Theory of relativity extended to include memory.

—It's French. Ecarté. Like vingt et un. I can play 'em both. Beba taught me. She taught me polker too.

Jeux Descartes. If wise men played bridge the way women play poker. Polker. Poke wisdom. *Cogitus interruptus*.

—Yes. It's the same game.

I decided to change the subject. Or rather, to return to the previous subject. Cycling. Marrying Mircué Eliade with a bicycle. A twindem. My twindom for a hussy!

—Don't you like to dance?

—Would you believe no?

—Really! You have the face for it.

Shit, that's racism. Physiognomancy. It would serve me right if she said you dance with your feet not your face. Chiropsody.

—Honest? When I was a girl I was just crazy about dancing. Not anymore, am not kidding.

—You were kidding then.

She laughed. At last a real laugh.

—Youse sure funny.

—Who do you mean?

—You and that friend of yours, wasisname, Cué.

—But you didn't laugh till now.

—I mean funny peculiar. Youse weird. You say real strange things. Both of you say the same strange things. Youse like twins, youse somethin' else. Whew! And you talk and talk and talk. Whaddya talk so much for?

Could she be a literary critic in disguise? Mary Magarthy Maga McCarthy.

—So maybe you're right.

—Sure Ise right.

I must have made some kind of face because she added:

—But youse not so bad by yousself.

Better. Was it a compliment?

—Thanks.

—Youse welcome.

I saw she was looking hard at me, and in the half light her eyes looked, almost *felt*, like they were burning bright.

—I like you.

—Yeah?

—Yes, really.

She looked at me and planted herself opposite me looking in my eyes and she raised her shoulders and neck and face and opened her mouth and I was thinking that women feel love felinely. Where did she get this expression from? Nobody told me because there wasn't anybody to tell me. We were alone and I took her hand, but she removed hers and scratched mine as she did so without meaning to or knowing she'd done it.

—Let's go down there.

She pointed to the darkness of the shore behind us. Was she that susceptible to light? Photophobia. I couldn't see a thing! Nyctalopia. On the other side of the river the lights of the Malecón were shining. We walked. I saw a shooting star fall into the sea behind La Chorrera. I took an invisible hand. It grasped mine firmly, digging its retractile nails into my flesh. I turned her around and kissed her and I felt her breath on mine, with its carnal taste, warmer than the night, warmer than the summer and it was a gust, a dawn breeze, another river and she filled, flooded the wasteland with her kisses her scent her love moans her wild smell, her domestic perfume (because I got some vague whiff of cheap Chanel, false Nini Ricci, I'm not sure, I'm not a scent scholar) and she kissed me firmly, hard, rough, on my mouth, her tongue pressed my lips open and she bit my lips outside and in, and my mucous membrane, my tongue, my gums, as though seeking something, my soul maybe and she tightened her fingers which had now become claws around my neck—and I remembered Simone Simon I don't know why, yes I do know why, out there in the dark, and I gave her back kiss for kiss tooth for tooth till our kisses became one long single kiss and I kissed her neck dracularly and she said, she moaned yes yes yes and I opened her blouse and she wasn't wearing any undergarment or bra, or what the French call a *soutien-gorge*, a throat support, a soutien-George, Georges, though who was supporting whom or what I don't know and as I was surrounded by her nipples her nibbles her kisses her caresses her expert hands her nails drawn in now as they searched for a love breech, a beach head, I thought, I had the idea that she was dreaming she was a flying trapeze artiste without a net, in no Mayden-Form Bra, last night and I laughed inside myself while outside myself I was taking my tongue for a tour over her naked breasts (I was beside myself) around the world in two hemispheres and I went back along the same route, slowly along her neck toward my home in her mouth and I wetkissed her again the very moment she had found her road, her inner path and

She slipped away from me suddenly. She looked behind me and I thought it was someone coming and I believed she could see in the dark and I wondered if she had a dappled skin or spots or stripes and I told myself she had become black all over again and as she went on staring fixedly, I thought it must be Beba. No, it wasn't Beba. It was nobody. Nobody was coming. Personne. Nessuno. Nadie.

—What's the matter?

She was still looking behind me, and I turned around quickly, and there was nobody behind me, nothing, just the night, the darkness, the shadows. I felt afraid or cold at least—yet it was hot, very hot on the banks of the river.

—Anything wrong?

She was in a trance, hypnotized by something I couldn't see, that I didn't see, will never see. Were there Martians on the banks? Were they coming by boat? Shit, not even a Martian could see in this darkness. I could hardly even see the white of her eyes. I shook her invisible shoulders. But she didn't come out of her trance. I thought of slapping her. Gently. It's easy to slap women. Besides that's the way they always come out of a trance. In films. Grabbed her shoulders instead.

—What's bitten you?

She pulled herself free and slipped and fell at the same time over some dark shadowy object that bulked behind or to one side of us. A pile of earth from the works on the tunnel. Earth and maybe some mud too. The river was very near. I could hear the water beating against her breath, an image that has no logic to it, but what do you expect? Nothing had any logic at that moment. At times like this logic slinks out through some pores in the skin. Like cold sweat. I helped her to her feet and could see she was still not looking at me. It's amazing the number of things you can see in the dark when you're right in it. She wasn't looking at me, no, but she no longer had that look of someone lost seeking for nobody in nothingness.

—What was it?

She looked at me. What could it be?

—What's up?

—Nothing.

She began sobbing, hiding her face. She didn't need to, the dark made a good handkerchief. Perhaps she wasn't hiding her eyes because she was upset but against an outside danger. I let go of her hands.

—What is it?

She closed her eyes and bit her lips and her whole face became a somber grimace in the night. Shit. I've got lynx's eyeglasses. Better still, an owl's. I'm the barn owl of the sowl.

—What the fuck's wrong?

Do obscenities have magic in them? They certainly conjured up something, because she began speaking in torrents, the words pouring out uncontrollably, beating Cué and me at our own game, because she spoke with a vehement internal violence, stammering over the words.

—I don't want to. No, no. I don' wanna go. I can't go back.

—Where to? Where don't you want to go back to? To Johnny's?

—To Beba's place, I don' wanna go back with her, she beats me and shuts me up and she don' lemme speak to anyone, but nobody. Please don' lemme go. I don' wanna go back, she shuts me up in a dark room and she don' give me water nor food nor nuttin' and she beats me when she opens the door or she opens the door and catches me lookin' outa the window and she ties me to the foot of the bed and beats me real hard and I go whole weeks not eatin', can't you see how thin I am. no. no. Ise not goin', shit, Ise not goin' back to her. she's nuttin' but a bitch. she treats me like shit and she lets him shit on me too and they don' mean anythin' to me that I should put up with this shit and I don' wanna I don' wanna Ise not goin' ta. oh no. Ise not goin' back. Ise stayin' right here with you. ya goin' ta lemme stay with you, right. Ise not goin' back. don' let them make me go back nomore.

She looked at me her eyes bulging and she slipped away from me and started running, straight for the river, I think. I caught up with her and held her hard. I'm not strong, I'm fat more like, so that I was breathing hard as I held her, but she wasn't very strong either. She calmed down, she seemed to pull herself together and started looking over my shoulder again, which is not difficult, looking for something precise and concrete. She found it. In the dark.

—*Them!* she said. Fuck, it's the Martians. But it was only Cué and Beba. Only one of them was a Martian. Just Beba. Shouting what's goin' on here? Why didn't she add, *Moia sestra*? Elizabeba Russell.

—Nothing.

—Somethin' wrong?

—No, I said. —We were just walking around here and it was dark and Magalena slipped over. Nothing serious.

She came closer and looked at her/at us/ at her. Another nightbeast. Her look could go right through you on the darkest night. One hundred percent Gorgon. Flash Gorgon.

—I'll bet she was puttin' on some act for you. She gets these dramatic spells.

Shit. Dramatic spells. What a way to talk! Hunique wisdom.

—No, I didn't say nuttin'. Swear to God. We weren't even talkin'. Ask him.

What's this shit? Me, a witness? Fuck. What next? Anything you say may be taken down. Or up. Your ass.

—What's going on here?

Cué. Cuérry Mason. I knew his voice, counseling voice, consoling voice.

—Nothing. It's just that Magalena tripped and fell.

—A quoi bon la force si la vaseline suffit, Cué said.

They didn't answer, it was almost as if they didn't exist, silent in the dark. ShaCuéspeare had turned tragedy into comedy, resolutely.

—Good signiors, keep up your bright swords, for the dew of the night and the river will rust them. Hold your hands, both of you of my inclining, and the rest: were it my Cue to fight . . . and we'll all go back to the castle.

Shitspeare. We returned to the club. Johnny's Dream! Who the fuck are you kidding? A nightmare without air-conditioning. As she slipped past me she said (aside) please, don' let her take me off, be good to me and she went over to Beba Martínez or whatever the shit her name is. They went straight to the ladies' and I took exception to tell Cué everything.

—Good night, bitter prince, he said. —Now cracks a noble mind. I'm sorry for you. You lucky fucker you. You've gone got yourself fixed up with a real nut. As to the other one, she's her aunt. Even if you don't believe it, I do because it's easier that she's her aunt than anything else. Common and guarded people are always more simple than you think, baroque only comes with culture. Why would she say she's her aunt if she ain't? Her aunt, then, told me all about her when you'd both gone away. She was worried about you when she saw you get out. The little girl's a raving lunatic, she's attacked people and all. She's been under treatment. Intensive treatment. Electric shocks and all. Not in Mazorra, fortunately. In the Galigarcía clinic. The cabinet of Doctor Galigarcía, as you call it. She's been shut up there a couple of times. She escaped from home and did everything she told you about or at least I think she's just told you outside. Revelations, brother, real-life experience. Great for a writer, but a prize drag, if you've got to live with it. I know.

—I'm telling you she's not her aunt. The fuck she is. She's a ferocious lesbian, that's what, and she virtually kidnapped her.

Kidnapped! Shit! Should I call the vice squad?

—So what's Magalena then? Our Lady of Sorrows? The Black Virgin? I'll say she is, of course she is. They all are. But that, as your buddy Eribó says when he thinks he's impersonating Arturo de Córdova, *Eso no tiene la menor importancia.* Who do you think we are? Judges of morals? Or just two angry men? Aren't you always saying that morals is a common contract imposed by the majority stockholders? Chiaro, seguro, of course, bien sur, natürlich, the aunt or so-called aunt as you'd call her, or whatever kind of aunt she is, is a dyke or whatever she wants to be when she's in her room or in bed for half an hour or one hour or two al max, but she's also a human being and the rest of the time she's just like you or me, just a person, and she, she told me the troubles she'd had with her niece, or adopted daughter or whatever she is. I don't believe she was lying. I know what people are like.

My God. They'd turned him into a shocked shell of himself while I'd been outside. The invasion of the body-snatchers had already begun and they had placed a gigantic has-been pod beside him and the man who was talking to me now was only a replica of Arsenio Cué, a zombi, a doppelgänger from Mars. An Arsenio Cuépy. I told him so and he laughed.

—Seriously, I said. —Because this is serious. You ought to look at your belly button. You are Cué's robot.

He laughed.

—If I was a robot I'd still have a belly button.

—Right then, you'd have some mole or birthmark or the scar of some wound. But they'd be on the other side of your body.

—So I'm not a doppelgänger then. I'm my mirror image. Eucoinesra. Arsenio Cué in mirrorese. Or in Basic Basque.

—I'm telling you, I'm not joking, this chick's got problems.

—Of course she has, but you're not a psychiatrist. And if you decide to become one don't come running to me for help. Psychiatry leads to disaster.

—Ionesco says that about arithmetic.

—It's the same thing. Psychiatry, arithmetic and literature all lead to disaster.

—Drink leads to disaster. Cars lead to disaster. Roads lead to disaster. Sidewalks lead to disaster. Boxcars lead to disaster. 707 jets lead to disaster. Sex leads to disaster. Women lead to disaster. Little boys lead to disaster. So do little girls. Ass leads to disasster. Chastity leads to disaster. Origen leads to disaster. Original sin leads to disaster. Translations lead to disaster. Virtue leads to disaster. Monks and nuns lead to disaster. Christianity leads to disaster. The devil leads to disaster. Buddhism leads to disaster. Hash leads to disaster. So does LSD. So does £SD. LSdesaster. Dollars lead to disaster. Even a bent dime leads to disaster. Movies lead to disaster. Dreams lead to disaster. Radio leads to disaster (he made a gesture that meant, you don't need to tell me that) and water leads to disaster and even coffee with cream leads to disaster. 7-Up and root beer and rye whiskey lead to disaster. So do gin and bloody mary and cuba libres. Drink leads to disaster. Everything leads to disaster.

—I know what I'm saying. There's no way of getting into the forbidden garden, still less of eating the tree of good and.

—Eating a tree?

—The fruit of the tree, you fucking Russell! Do you want me to recite it to you, to complete the quote (I made signs to say that I didn't, but it was too late) "Of all the trees of the garden you may eat, but of the tree of knowledge of good and evil you may not eat . . ."?

—Then the best thing to do is not to move at all. To be a stone.

—I'm talking to you about something concrete and real and imminent and, above all, about something which is dangerous. I know a thousand times more about life than you do. Leave the chick alone, forget her. Let her aunt or whatever she is look after her. That's her job. Yours is something else. Whatever it is.

—Shh, she's coming back.

They came back all dolled up. Magalena, I mean, because Beba had never been dolled down. Magalena looked like another woman. Or the same, the same as herself, identical to what she was before eternally. Mallarmena.

—Please excuse us but we's gotta get a move on, the aunt or Beba Martínez or Babel said in her multilingo. —It's getting even so later.

What rhetoric. Gimme the gist of it ma'am the gift to is the key o' it the code. The Cuéode. Who said of course and called for the check which he paid with Rine's money of course. We drove back to Havana and to wherever the beeootiful señoritas would like us gay cabalerros to drop them Cué said still keeping armorous blanks in his Arsenal and the aunt said where we met up with both of you earlier this twilight (of the gals?) we live very closed and he said fine and shooting straight from the solar plexus he Arsyvarsy told the aunt good real looked she, woman a her of inch every and finally he asked her with finality to ring him up sometime and he gave her his fucking phone number repeating it like a jingle till aunty mome had it by heart and by ear and she said she wasn't promising anything but she would repeat the call and we'd got to Avenida de los Presidentes and we left them there on the corner of 15th and said good-bye all of us, very friendly, and Magalena got out without even squeezing my hand or slipping a billet not so doux between my fingers or telling me her phone number. Not so much as a scratch except on the record of my memory. That's life. Some people have all the luck. Some guardian angel looks after them so they never find themselves in Dracula's castle and they never read too many chivalric romances, because as everybody knows reading the adventures of Glancealot & Gallahead or of the dashing White Night always leads to disaster. What you have to do is to go on your way, all quiet and good, to the movies—at least the real women you find there lead you to nowhere more dangerous than a seat in the stalls. They're just usherettes. Although in Switzerland there's this White Russian, several times an exile, who has the idea that even usherettes can lead to disaster. Venus. VD. Vice. What's to be done then? Stay with Kim Novak? But doesn't masturbation lead to disaster too? At least that's what they told me when I was a kid, that I'd get TB, that it softened the brain, that it exhausted your vital fluids. *Coño!* Life is a disaster area.

XIX

—We could do with some air, Cué said and he slowed down to switch the top down then we tore down 12th and across Linea. Back along the demesnes and terrains of Moebius, vulgo Malecón up and down, topologically.

—We could do with Bustrófedon, I said.

—You still going on about your freak and the dead and the "great men who are no longer with us"? You've been ghost-writing too hard, that's what. Or perhaps ghost-reading too much.

—Do you know what they are, ghosts?

He gave me a look like he wanted to send me to hell or to tell me to stuff it up and then added a gesture of complete helplessness. I'm a helpless case.

—Ghosts or apparitions are the departed who come back or who just can't let death do us part. Don't you think it's fantastic? Dead people who can't pass away. Immortals, in other words. When I say fantastic, please listen, I mean extraordinary, majestic, monumental, in a lovecrafty way.

—I get your meaning O.K. but, please, you listen to me. I think I've told you before that a dead man is no longer a person for me, or a human being, it's just a corpse, a stiff, a thing.

Worse than a thing, it's just a bit of gray trash that's no good for anything but rotting and getting more and more hideous every moment.

The conversation was making him nervous for some reason.

—Why don't you go bury Bustrófedon? He's beginning to stink.

—Do you know how much it costs to bury a great man when he dies?

He didn't get what I meant. I recited a list that I knew.

3 boards of cedar wood	$3.00
5 lbs. of yellow wax	1.00
3 lbs. of gilded nails	0.45
2 packets of wire nails	0.40
2 cartons of candles	0.15
Coffinmaker's fee	2.00
Total	$7.00

—Seven pesos?

—Seven pesos reales or seven gold dollars perhaps. You must also include a fee for the sexton or the gravediggers. Altogether ten or eleven pesos.

—Is that what it cost to bury Bustrófedon?

—No, that's what it cost to bury Martí. Sad, isn't it?

He didn't answer. I'm not a Martían. Neither of us was. I used to have a great admiration for Martí, but then there was all that stupid fuss about him, everyone trying to make a saint of him and every politico saying he was his son and sole heir, that I got sick of the sound of the word Martían. I liked the word Martian —or even Marxian—or even, heaven help me, Maritain!— better. But it's true that it's sad, it's sad that it's true, it's true that it's sad that it's true that he's dead, dead like Bustrófedon, and this is the thing about death, that it makes all the dead into a single long shadow. This figure of speech is called eternity. While life separates us, divides us, individualizes us, death reunites us and makes us into one long dead man. Shit, I'll end up as the Pascal of poverty. Poorscal. I took advantage of him turning around, I don't know why, by the Farola de Neptuno, to put off till another day my questions, my question, *the* question. Don't put off till tomorrow what you can do yesterday. *Carpe diem irae. Todo es posponer*. Life proposes, God disposes and man postposes. Silvestre Postcal. *Mierda seca.*

—O.K., I said, —after this excursion into nothingness, after this season (translating from French, if you'll permit me and I don't think you can stop me), this vacation in hell, after this descent into the Maelstrom, after all this transculturation, osmosis or contaminatio, as you'd put it, I'm going to enjoy some less disturbing, more innocent nightmares.

—It's very late for the movies and very early to be saying adieu.

—I said I was going to enjoy some harmless nightmares, not to have any unquiet dreams. I'm going home to get some sleep, to curl up, to snuggle down: I'm heading back to La Mama, I'm making a journey from imago to cocoon and straight into mommy's shroud. Nightmeres. It's safer by Wombbound. Leave the driving to you. It's always good to travel backward. As a wise man said through the mouth of a queen, you can remember more this way, because you remember both the past and the future. As for me, I like remembering more than I like humble pie.

—I beg to remain. The night is still young, as another wise man says through Rine's mouth. Or as Marx says, the air is like wine tonight. There is still plenty to be seen, thank God and Mazda. The latter, as you know, is *not* the Assyrian divinity of light. Suppose we get something to eat?

—I'm not hungry.

—The dish invents the appetite, as Trimalchio would say. We still have our credit account with First National Rine. The gift of Don Rine or Donation Rine. Or even better, the Rine Leal Memorial Foundation Phallowship. We've got enough left for a royal banquet, a feast fit for Falstaff's friend. A cena chameleonis.

—I really don't feel like eating. Not tonight.

—You just keep me company then. Forget us this night our early bed. Have a glass of Lethe with a slice of lemon, ice and sugar. Milk of amnesia, that's its name. Then I'll drive you to your door. To sleep till day be morrow.

—Danke. It's very considerate of you. For a moment I

thought you would just leave me at the entrance of the metro, subway, tube or subte or whatever it's called in those civilized countries where they travel in them. In other words, where the cold belongs to rich and poor alike.

—Stay a little longer.

—I can't. I must go home.

—You're not going to write all this down, are you?

—Come on. I haven't written a thing for ages.

—Remind me to buy you a Nussbaum wristband at the five and ten as soon as they open tomorrow morning. The leaflet says that it's the best remedy against writer's cramp.

—You jerk. Who showed you the clipping?

—You did. Silvestre Primero, the man who was first to arrive, I-named-it-before-Adam, the Disc-Overer who saw Cuba (Venegas) before Christoforibot, the first man on the moon, the master who teaches you everything before he's even learned it, the One and Only, Top Banana, Plotinus's one, Adam, Nonpareil, the Ancient of Days, Ichi-ban, Numbero Uno, Unamuno. Salve, I, El Dos, Yang to your Yin, Eng to your Chan, the Disciple, the Plural, Number Two, Second Fiddle, Dos Passos, the 2, salute thee, I who am about to die. But I don't want to do it alone. Let's continue to be, as the enlightened Códac once said, the twins, Marcandtwain, Eribó's *ñáñigo* version of the Gemini, two friends and come with me please.

What do you expect? I'm susceptible to flattery. Besides, Cué, as always, wasn't slowing down for anybody. I wasn't going to jump out. So once more we became Cuéstor & Pollee, the heavily twined.

—O.K., I'm coming with you. As long as you promise to go slower.

—Da, little father. How many versts an hour?

He slowed down to a walking pace and I was able to ride back to El Vedado in Cué's buggy. I pointed to the horizon.

—A perfect Universal Pictures backdrop for my scene with Créole Dubois not so long ago.

There was a storm on the horizon. I asked him to park so we could see it better. It was worth the trouble and cost us nothing. Being free it would have delighted Rine, even though he's afraid of the elements. There were fifty, a hundred lightning flashes a minute, but we couldn't hear any thunder, except for a muffled rumbling every so often, when no cars were passing. A distant kettledrum beaten with *baguettes d'éponge*, Hector Berlioz Cué said. (I laughed, but I didn't tell him why.) The lightning flew from the sea to the sky and back again, in balls of fire, arrows of quicksilver, white streaks in a blinding network of blue-white branches and from time to time the whole sky was lit up for two or three seconds and then went black again but immediately a single flare ran parallel to the horizon till it dropped or drowned in the sea making a bubble of light in the waters, which were completely calm and received the lightnings with the same indifference as they reflected the harbor lights on this side. Now on the left another storm served as a mirror to sea and sky. I saw yet another storm, then another and another. There were five different electric storms along the horizon, lightning weaving a neon tapestry in the dark.

—A splendid celebration of some forgotten Fourth of July, Cué said.

—It's the Wave of the East.

—What?

—It's called the Wave of the East.

—So thunderstorms have names now, like hurricanes? Adamania is loosed upon the world. Soon they'll have a name for each cloud and every wave.

I laughed.

—No. It's a meteor formed above the eastern provinces which runs all along the coast to disappear in the Gulf Stream.

—Where the hell do you get all this information from?

—Don't you read the papers?

—Only the headlines. I've got an illiterate or a shortsighted man inside me. Or maybe it's a woman as you and Códac say.

—An article came out a short time back on these "electrical phenomena," signed by Carlos Millás, engineer and captain of corvette, director of the Navy Observatory.

—Naval brass.

We went on looking at the storms for a while watching them turn the sky and sea into a myorama version of the cabinet of Dr. Frankenstein.

—What does it make you think of?

—That it's coming from the same place as us.

—From Johnny's Dream?

—No, you dope, from Oriente province.

—His captainship the engineer Millás wasn't referring to our Orient but to that more abstract one on the compass rose of farts, vulgo winds, and which you can find exactly over on the right ear of the Aeolus printed on the maps.

He drove off and we slid forward at the speed of an early astronomer. An astronomyer.

—I imagine, Cué said, —that in earlier times they used to think it was hell coming up for air. What would you say about that, Ancient Mariner?

—They had Vulcan or Hephaistos and an Olympic forge to account for and even Jupiter with his multiple ire.

—Not so far back as *that!* History's your time-Malecón. In the Middle Ages, I mean.

—Haven't you read in the books that these were the Dark Ages? They didn't even allow themselves the luxury of using lightning lighting. Coal miners in a tunnel at midnight, that's what they were. Seriously, I imagine they explained it by saying it was another form of the wrath of God. But after all, it couldn't have been much of a problem for them. Don't forget, the Middle Ages didn't get as far as the Tropics.

—How about the Indians?

—We Redskin people love prairies of earth and heaven. We no care about pyrotechnics of the great spirit.

—*Pyrotechnics* of the great spirit. An Indian talking like that! Aren't you ashamed of yourself?

—Me Cherokee. Big chief me give poetic licenses.

—Were they very cultured?

—Haven't you heard of the contraries?

—No. Who were they? A tribe?

—A caste within the tribe. A prairie-Samurai. Warriors who because of their bravery in combat and their nimbleness with arms and their skill at riding horses were able to break the laws of the tribe in time of peace.

—What's the moral?

—It's very interesting. Seriously. The contraries were famous tricksters who fucked everything up because they always did the opposite of what was expected of them. They didn't greet anybody, not even another contrary. They knew what they could depend on. For example, there's the story of an old woman who was cold and went to a contrary to get a skin from him to keep herself warm. The contrary didn't even answer her, although it is obligatory to answer your elders. The old woman returned to her tent cursing these new times in which nobody had any respect for anythin', with traditions dying out and young Indians wearing their hair short. What are us Indians headed for anyway? If only Chief Rutting Bull were alive! He wouldn't let things like this happen. After many a summer died the baldheaded eagle and that very morning when the old woman got up she found a human skin in front of her tent. Feeling duped and disappointed, she laid her complaint before the council of the elders. The elders assembled and judged that a punishment was called for. For the old woman! In consideration of her age, she was only given a reprimand. You old woman (they said, I imagine, the Indian equivalent of these words), the blame is yours and only yours. Don't you know, Krazy Kow, that you mustn't ask anything of a contrary? On you and your family the curse of the soul of this poor corpse will fall.

—That's an Indian gift for you.

—Indian justice, rather.

—*Contradictoria contradictorii curantur*. Does Perry Mason know this case?

—It's in his Indian files. Mason is a contrary. So is Philip Marlowe. So is Sherlock Holmes. There's no great literary character who isn't. Don Quixote is a perfect example of an early contrary.

—What about you and me?

I thought of telling him to be more modest.

—We aren't literary characters.

—What about when you write down our night deeds?

—Even then we won't be. I'll be a scribe, just another annotator, God's stenographer but never your Creator.

—That's not what I'm asking you. What I want to know is will we or won't we be contraries?

—We won't know till the final episode.

—Is Haulden Coldfield a contrary?

—Of colts.

—And Jake Barnes?

—Sometimes. Colonel Cantwell is a good contrary. Hemingway too.

—That's what you say.

—I interviewed him once and he told me he had Chickasaw blood. Or Ojibway, was it?

—Did they have contraries in those tribes too?

—It's quite possible. Everything is possible on the wide open prairies of the West.

—What about the tightly shut patios of the past? Was Gargantua a contrary?

—No, nor was Pantagruel. But Rabelais was.

—And Julian Sorel?

Did I hear an oral row of dots between the conjunction and the name, a suggestion of doubt, a dashing bridge of necessity and fear at the same time, a daring modulation in his voice? Even if I hadn't heard it Cué's mouth compensated with a hyphenated smile.

—No, he's not one. Sorel is French and as you've seen for yourself the French try as hard as possible to be ractionalists to the point of madness. They are deliberately anti-contrary. Even Jarry wasn't a contrary. There hasn't been one since Baudelaire. Breton, who tried so hard to become one, is about as far from being a contrary as he could be. He's a pseudo contrary. Beyle might have been one, if he'd been born in England, like his friend Lord Byron.

—How about Alphonse Allais?

—*Sí* Allais: this gift-wrapped palindrome is for him.

—Only because you like it.

—Who invented the game?

—O.K., so you did. But don't quit the game with your bat and glove and balls.

I smiled. Was it a smile of humble origins?

—Was Shelley one?

—No, but his wife Mary definitely was. She was the doctor Frankenstein of Frenkenstein.

—Is Eribó a contrary?

—You won't become one yourself just by jumping to and fro like that. You'll only be an epileptic inquisitor.

He smiled. He knew. I'd given him my oracle, with an Rx printed on it.

—I wouldn't say so. Eribó is presumptuous, and self-sufficient.

—And Ascyltos?

If he was jumping I could go one higher.

—He was a contrary. So was Encolpius. Giton too. But not Trimalchio.

—Julius Caesar?

—Yes, of Corse he was. Aside from that, he was a modern man. If he were here today he'd be able to talk with us without much trouble. He would even be able to learn Spanish. I wonder what Spanish would sound like spoken with a Latin accent.

The archaic smile of early Greek sculpture appeared clearly chiseled on his lips. The fact that it was night and he was in profile added to the effect.

—And Caligula?

—He was perhaps the greatest of all.

We turned into Paseo and drove up past those natural terraces that history had turned into a park, and which always make me think I'm in its twin, Avenida de los Presidentes, and we drove down again along 23rd Street heading for La Rampa, where we turned into M and down M till we turned off at the Havana Hilton, and went up 25th and into L Street to go into 21st, crossing 23rd Street under auspicious traffic signals.

—Look, Cué said, —talking about the king of Rome.

I thought that Caius Caesar was strolling along La Rampa in his golden caligae. He was another modern man: witness Hitler and Stalin. He would have liked La Rampa and would hardly have been out of place there. Less out of place at any rate than that horse he made consul. But they were neither Caesar nor Incitator.

—There goes the S. S. Ribot, Cué said, —keeling over because of a heavy payload of alcohol and goatskins.

—You mean the Saint-Exupéry of are drums?

—*Oui, monsieur*.

I took a good look unimpeded by Cué's intrusive profile.

—That's not Eribó.

—Isn't it?

He braked and took another look.

—You're right. It's not. Shit, but it's like him. As you can see, everybody has his doppelgänger or, as you'd say, his ribot from Mars. Magalena had a point: everything here's foreign made.

—I didn't see the likeness.

—That means that even the concept of a double is relative. Everything is points of view.

I resolved to make a start and artificially provoke revelations, since I was so adept at producing them spontaneously.

—Tell me something. Did you sleep with Vivian?

—Vivien Leigh?

—I'm talking seriously.

—D'you mean to say that that noble first avatar of Blanche Dubois isn't serious?

—Seriously I'm talking seriously.

—Could you mean, Vivian Smith-Corona y Alvarez del Real, by any chance?

—Yes.

He seized the moment to turn back along 21st and bear toward the Nacional with all sails unfurled. Captain Kuédd. Was it a way of not answering me? We cruised into the green gardens of the hotel, a live lush lobby.

—Where do you want to eat?

—You're forgetting I don't want to eat.

—How about the Monseñor.

—I'll go where you go. Consider me your spiritual bodyguard. He made a deep bow.

—O.K. Let's go to Club 21. I'll leave the car here. It's always good to have a friend to cast an eye on your horses.

An eye with a cast in it, I thought. We drove into the parking lot and left the car under a lamp. Cué went back to get the key. He glanced up at the sky.

—Do you think it's going to rain, dear Gally Leo?

—I doubt it. The storm is still over the sea.

—Great. I guess that reading the reports from the front is better training for a soldier than a battlefield. Vamoose.

—Nothing's been written about our heavens.

He looked at me with his head cocked on one side and his eyebrows wrinkling ironically. Cuépernicus.

—I was talking about the Cuban sky, I said.

He paid at the gate.

—Hasn't Ramón come by?

—Ramón who?

—The one and only Ramón, Ramón García.

—The thing is I'm called Ramón too. Ramón Suárez, at your service.

—I'm so sorry. Isn't the other Ramón here?

—He's out on duty. Did you want him for something?

A message to García, I thought and almost said.

—I just wanted to say hello. Tell him Arsenio Cué was asking for him.

—Cué. Fine, sir. I'll tell him tomorrow or I'll pass it on to him if I don't see him.

—It's not important. Just hello.

—I'll see he gets it.

—Thanks. Bye.

—You're welcome. Good-bye, sir.

Versailles. If *le Nacional m'était conté*. We are walking under the palms and I stopped to look at the nymph that holds a cup of everlasting water in the hotel fountain, naked, barefoot, balancing on tiptoe, surrounded by night but lit up by a flood-lamp that tried to throw a light of scandal on a drunkenness both blatant and private, almost an intimate act of narcissism, like the girl who looks at herself naked in the bathroom mirror and is surprised by the watchful, meddling eye of a Peeping Tom. It was an obscene lighting effect. Sin & lumière.

—Pretty, eh? She gets high on water. Be thankful, Silvestre, that Pygmalion and Condillac aren't on the prowl. She's nuts, like all women. Besides, she's too clean for my liking. *She's spoiling her flavor*.

Why does he have to put on this English accent which only succeeds in being Jamaican singsong?

—I know a couple who aren't crazy.

—More power to you. But keep your station. I'm speaking to you as a friend.

Who the fuck asked for his advice? Señorita Lonelyhearts.

—It's a watering Lily, he said as my eyes wrapped the wet wench scopophillically. I never told him that I had one eye closed while I was panning around the fountain.

Arsenio greeted the cripple who sold gardenias in front of the Casino del Capri and bought a flower off him and exchanged a few words, which I didn't hear because I wasn't interested.

—Do you wear gardenias in your buttonhole?

—I don't even have a lapel on my jacket.

—Then what are you going to do with the flower?

—I'm just helping a poor invalid.

—Of the wars of the roses? More flower to you.

—I'd do no less for Jake Barnes or Captain Ahab. Besides, a chorus girl is bound to deflower me sooner or later.

Sooner. Out of the silk hat of the night a rabbit jumped. A bunny rabbit. She was the spitting image of the hydromaniac nymph.

—Cué, my darling! What a pleasure to see you!

—The pleasure is yours. Dildo-it-yourself. Let me present you with this flower. sIrene, Flowers to the flowerlet. Lastly let me introduce you to my friend here. Silvestre Goodknight, Irenita Atineri.

—Howdy, marm.

—How gallant you are. Ooh what a lovely name! Dee-light-ed. She stripped her lips to teasingly show off her lovely teeth.

—I'm a night gallant, said Cué.

—The pleasure is mine, belladonna.

—He's cute too, isn't he. You're both alike.

—You mean you don't know who's who and who's Cué?

She laughed. She came from a different circle than Magalena and Beba.

—But I love you both the same.

—But one at a time, Cué said.

She went off to a round of kisses and ciaos and come and see me at Las Vegas one of these days. One of these nights, Cué said and turned to me:

—What did I tell you? A deadly night show.

—You know the topography of your inferno.

—La Rampa it's called in Spanish. Sorrry, I mean in Cuban. At the door of Club 21, I confessed.

—I can't get this chick out of my head.

—Irenita?

I gave him one of his topical looks.

—You mean the statue then? That's nympholepsy, *mi viejo*.

—Don't fuck around.

—Flowero is a man, so's homomorphism then.

—I'm referring to Magalena, you jerk. I can't stop thinking about her. She's bewitched me. She's a witch. Fata Magana. Magan le Fay.

Cué stopped in his tracks and held onto one of the pillars of the marquee, as though the steps were a wellhead.

—Come again.

His tone of voice surprised me too.

—She is a witch. Maga Lenay.

—Say that again, please. The name and the title, nothing else.

—Maga Lenay.

—I got it!

He jumped backward and struck his forehead with the palm of his hand. I think he's got it. By Tod he'd Gott it!

—What's happening?

Nothing nothing at all he said and went into the restaurant.

XX

Arsenio Cué ordered roast chicken, french fries and apple sauce plus a green salad. I ordered a hamburger with mashed potatoes and a glass of milk. Hold the may please. He was almost bad-mannered, talking about the chicken as he ate it. I felt I was repeating myself, that I was back once more in Barlovento.

—I would suspect, he said, —that there is some relation between board and bed, that food and fuck share the same fetishes. When I was young or younger rather, when I was adolescent (he said ad-do-l-es-cent, lengthening his syllables to indicate the passage of time), some years ago, I really went for the breast of chicken and always ordered it. A girl friend told me one day that men always go for the white meat and women like the legs. It seems she tested this theory every day at dinnertime. If they served chicken in the boardinghouse.

—Who eats the wings, neck and gizzard, then?

Me, who else? I always let myself be gone with the winds of conversation.

—I don't know. I suppose that's the poor man's chicken.

—I've got a better hypothesis. Let me suggest a possible triad. Steve Canyon, Count Dracula and Oscar Wilde. In that order.

—The gizzard of Ozcar.

He laughed and wrinkled his brow, the same ironical grimace as before. He's the daring young face on the flying trapeze.

—I thought the woman was right, if she thought she was. I also thought that my friend (I won't tell you her name because you know her well), who was very poetic or at least pretended to be, had certainly just been reading Virginia Woolf. But today I look back in hunger on that conversation because I find now I prefer the leg to the breast.

—I'm a leg man myself. Have we become effeminate?

—I fear something worse: the sudden rout of the theory before the brute fact of the praxis.

It was my turn to laugh and I did so with simple pleasure. The exterminating angel couldn't have had a sense of humor. Neither this nor any other angel, archangel, throne, cherubim or seraphim. Humor always leads to the fall.

—You know, now that you mention leg of chicken, the thing I look at most in a woman is her legs. Not only that but I had a dream a short while back where I was at a particularly oneirific banquet and they served me Cyd Charisse's legs with boiled potatoes.

—What do you think the boiled potatoes means?

—I don't know. But there's a certain method in your hidden blond friend's mad idea. (He looked at me with a start when I said blond and then smiled. I was just on the point of saying, Elementary my dear Cuatson when I went on:) I used to like breast best and that was the time when Jane Russell and Kathryn Grayson were in style, in me, that is, and a little later, Marilyn Monroe and Jayne Mansfield and Sabbrina!

—Have you dreamed of any of them lately? If so, pass me the dreamer, please.

—We're all living on borrowed dreams.

I stopped in middream and made a show of being interested in dessert. I fancied a flan followed by coffee. Cué said strawberry shortcake and coffee. Dessert became desert. Not because he ordered a strawberry shortcut, but because I imitated Stanislavski's method of dramatic pauses, which I'd copied from him et alias. It was then that the waiter thought of asking if the gentleman would like a liquor afterward. I said no.

—Do you have any cointreaury?

—Come again?

—Do you have any Cointreau?

—Yessir. Do you want a glass?

—No, bring me some Cointreau.

—That's what I said.

—No, you asked me, you didn't say anything. And you asked me if I wanted a glass. But you didn't say a glass of what.

—You already said you wanted a quntrow.

—She must be a friend of mine.

—Who's she?

—Forget it. It's a joke and besides it's personal. Bring me a Benedictine, but not a monk, *please,* I want a *glass* of Benedictine. The liqueur.

I didn't laugh. He didn't give me time. He didn't even give me time to remember what we were talking about.

—Is Jay Gatsby a contrary?

I gave a reflex answer.

—No, nor's Dick Diver or Monroe Starr. Nor's Scott Fitzgerald. On the contrary, they're very predictable. Same with Faulkner. It's curious but the only real contraries in his books are Negroes, though only the proud Negroes, like Joe Christmas and Lucas Beauchamp, and maybe one or two of the poor whites, or the carpetbaggers called arrivistes in la Nouvelle Orléans. But not Sartoris or the other aristocrats; they're too rigid.

—How about Ahab? Was he or wasn't he?

—No. And Billy Budd still less.

—The only contraries in American literature are the half-castes. Or people who behave like half-castes.

—I don't know how you came to this conclusion. It can't be anything I said. What do you mean by "behave like half-castes"?

It's a strange mixture of behaviorism and race prejudice.

—Oh, Silvestre, come on, we were talking about literature not sociology. Besides, it was you who said that Hemingway was a contrary because he was half Indian.

—I didn't say that! I didn't even say Hemingway was half Indian or half back. All I said was that he told me in an interview that he had Indian blood. How could anybody be half Indian? D'you mean that one half was white and had a beard and wore spectacles and the other half was clean shaven, dark-skinned and had eagle eyes? That Mr. Ernest was white and wore a hat and a tweed jacket while Chief Heming Way went about with a feather headdress and smoked a peace pipe when he wasn't waving a tomahawk?

I'm the Perry Mason of the underdeveloped and of waiters and especially of underdeveloped waiters. Cué made a very professional gesture of despair.

—Wassa matta?

—Dost thou come here to dine? Show me what thou'lt do! Eat a crocodile? Or Lobster Quadrille?

—No, Kronprinz Omlette, this is not the Gesta Danorum. But let me tell you this, the notion of the contrary comes from a treatise on sociology.

—So? Weren't we talking about literature?

I couldn't agree with him and say I found sociology as interesting as Bustrófedon right now must find the concept of being, or confide in him that perhaps we were giving back contrariety to the Indians.

—Not talking about, *playing with* literature.

—And what's so bad about that?

—Literature, of course.

—That's better. For a moment I was afraid you were going to say the game. Shall we go on?

—Why not? I could go on to tell you that Melville was a formidable contrary and so was Mark Twain, but that Huck Finn isn't, nor is Tom Sawyer. Maybe Huck's father was, if we knew more about him. As for Jim, he's always a slave. An anti-contrary, that is. That's why Tom and Huck aren't contraries, because they would have exploded at the slightest contact with Jim.

—Permit me to do a Somersault Maugham. Isn't this a concept from post-Einsteinian physics, amigo?

—Yes. It comes from Edward Fortune Teller. Why do you ask?

—Oh, nothing special. *Obrigado.* Let the gig go on.

—Guess who's the most contrary of the contrary Americans?

—I don't dare, in case there's an explosion.

—Ezra Pound.

—Who'd have guessed it?

I looked at him. I made a sail, a vessel, a glass with my hands, lifted it, them, to my mouth, I blew out and then breathed in. Red Indian ritual.

—What are you doing?

—Does my breath bother you?

—No.

—Do I have bad breath?

I threw vapor of human water toward his face like when someone goes near a mirror.

—No. It's O.K. Did I look like it wasn't?

—No. It's just me. I thought Hali Tossis was paying me a visit. He's the Greek shipping tycoon who launched a thousand vessels, all because Curtis made Helen immoral with a kisser.

—Your breath's the same as mine, it smells of food and drink and too much talk. Besides, don't forget you're downwind.

—Some people have halitosis in every quadrant.

—And even in profile sometimes.

We both laughed.

—Shall we play another round?

—It's better than dominoes.

—At least you don't have to wear an undershirt to play. Like your father does.

—He doesn't play dominoes. Or any game.

—He a puritan?

—No. He's Departyed.

He laughed because he knew it was a joke. Like the time I swore on my father's ashes, meaning the ones in his ashtray, of my father, who isn't dead and doesn't smoke or drink or play games. He abstemious? No, he's Cuban though a founding father of the Party. A teetotalitarian.

—Do you wear an undershirt, Arsenio?

—Me? No, *qué va!* How about you?

—No, I don't either. Or long shorts.

—Glad to hear it. Shall we go on?

—You cut, I'll deal.

—You deal, I'll Cué. Quo vadis Cuévedo? Quevedo, the poet who declared lust to dust? Francisco Gómez de Quevedo y Villegas, don Paco who is only sensible ashes now in Newville of the Infantes, Don Poco, was he or wasn't he?

—Quevedo lives!

—Only in memory.

—In literature too. But your question was answered, *avant la lettre,* like so many others, by Borges, who says that Quevedo is no writer but literature. He's no gentleman either or even man, he's humanity. He's the history of Spain in his time. Nor is he a contrary because history itself was contrary then.

—So Cervantes is no contrary.

—*No señor.*

—What about Lope?

—Don Félix Lope de Vega y Carpio, the Phoenix of Wits, the fucking priest who wrote 1,800 *comedias?*

—*Sí señor.*

—Lope was less a contrary than anyone. He's a too frequent Phoelix rising from his own arson. Creator of the Carpio Diem, he was the opposite of Shakespeare.

—What about Marlowe?

—Our wholy father who is in Hellen.

—Are you a contrary?

—Just a figure of speech.

—Who? You or the contrary?

—I mean my way of speaking.

—Be careful. Ways of speaking are also styles of writing. You'll end up by spiking Spunnish. Or using blank pages for graffiti, or having an origami on paper. *Vade rhetor.*

—Do you think that rhetoric is to blame for bad literature? It would be like blaming physics for the fact that we all fall down.

He please-turn-overed the page of conversation with his hand in rapid flight.

—Who d'you know who's a contrary? I mean you personally.

—You.

—I'm talking seriously.

—So am I.

—So you are one?

—I'm talking seriously.

—So am I.

—You are, you really *are* a contrary.

—So are you.

—I'm speaking seriously.

—So am I. You even have what's needed to make an early contrary, according to you.

—Really?

Vanity. It leads to the perdition even of those who are already missing. O Solomon!

—Yes, really. You're Indian. Or half Indian. I'm sorry, I mean you have Indian blood.

—And Negro and Chinese and possibly even white.

He laughed. He shook his head as he was laughing. Is it possible to do that?

—You're a Mayan. Look at yourself in the mirror.

—No, because then I won't be a Mayan but an Aztecué or an Incué.

He didn't laugh. He should have, but he looked more serious than a cigar-store Indian.

—Listen. You've proved my point right now. You don't even need to spill Indian blood. Only a contrary would or could behave like that.

—No kidding?

Something was bugging him.

—Really?

—Why don't you write a book on Character Assassination Considered as One of the Fine Arts?

—One thing I do know, neither you nor I are contraries. We're eyedentical, as your friend Irenita said.

—The same person? A binity then. Two persons and one single true contradiction.

I threw my napkin on the table, without meaning anything by it. But there are gestures that force one's hand and when the napkin fell on the tablecloth, white on white, we both knew that

I'd thrown the towel in the ring. Riot win the glen. Write in the long. El thin Ringo wet. The match was over, naturally.

—When shall we have a return bout?

—What, after beating you like that, over fifteen rounds?

—Think of it as a technical K.O., O.K.?

—O.K., schmelling Gut. Tomorrow. Another time. *Mañana.* Tomorrow and tomorrow and tomorrow. Next season in Hell. The twentieth of Maybe.

—Why not now? That way I'll learn.

Good, Arsenio Gatsby, better known in the ring as the Great Cué, you've asked for it.

—I'd rather the other way around and *you* teach *me.* I have another game, Arsenio. And it's one you know much better than me.

—Let's hear it.

—First I'm going to tell you the dream. Do you remember? We were talking about dreams.

—About breasts, I thought.

—Breasts and dreams.

—A good title for Thomas Woolf. Of breasts and dreams.

—Let's talk about another kind of literature, the metaliterature of dreams.

I stopped in my tracks. You know that situation when one really stops short in a conversation, unable to go on talking, when your words and acts freeze at the same moment, when the voice is silent and one's movements stand still?

—Please, if you don't mind, let me tell you the dream that this cryptic girl friend of mine had, a girl friend who's as secret as yours and almost as obvious. It should interest you. It's very similar to yours, this dream.

—To mine? You were the one who told a dream.

—I'm talking about the one you told me this evening.

—This evening?

—On the Malecón. On that Malecón which winds around Maceo Park more than once at a time.

He remembered. He resented my reminding him of it.

—It's a biblical dream a la page. As you'd say.

—So's this one. My friend, *our* friend, told me this dream.

The girl friend's dream

She was sleeping. She dreamed. She remembers that it was night in the night of her dream. She knows she is dreaming but the dream of the dream belongs to another dreamer. It's black in the dream, very black. She wakes from the dream within the dream and sees that everything in her reality-dream is black. She gets frightened. She wants to turn on the light but she can't reach the switch. If only her arm would grow longer. But that never happens except in dreams and she is awake. Or is she? Her arm grows and grows and crosses the room (she can feel it, she thinks she can see it outlined in darker black against the blackness of the dream-reality) but slowly, very slow, s,l,o,w,l,y, while her arm is traveling toward the light, in the direction of the light switch, someone, a voice in the dream, is counting backward, from nine downward, and just as he or it is reaching zero her hand touches the light switch and there is an incredible white-white light, a light of a terrible and terrifying whiteness. There is no noise but she fears or rather knows that there has been an explosion. She gets up terrified and finds that her arms are her arms once more. Perhaps the arm which grew was another dream within the dream. But she is frightened. Without knowing why, she goes to the balcony. The sight from there is horrifying. The whole of Havana, which is like saying the whole world, is on fire. The buildings are in ruins, everywhere there is destruction. The light from the fires, from the explosion (she is convinced now that there has been an apocalyptic blast: she remembers she had thought of that phrase in her dream) lights up the scene as though it were broad daylight. A rider appears from out of the ruins. It is a white woman on a gray horse. She gallops toward the building with the balcony, which by some strange miracle is still intact, the balcony, that is, hanging between the ironwork that has turned to ashes, and the rider stops under the balcony and looks up and smiles. She is naked and has long hair. Could she be Lady Godiva? No, that's not who she is. That rider, that pale woman is Marilyn Monroe. (She wakes up.)

—What d'you make of it?

—You're the one who interprets dreams and searches for confessions and tries to heal the insane. Not me.

—But it is interesting.

—You could be right.

—What's even more interesting is that our friend, my friend, has had the dream again and other times it's she who's riding the horse, which is always a gray horse.

He didn't say a word.

—There are many things in this dream, Arsenio Cué, just as there are in that dream Lydia Cabrera told us both, do you remember it?, the day you'd gone to her house in your new car and she gave you a cowrie shell to wear as a good luck charm which you passed on to me later, because you didn't believe in that old Negro magic, and Lydia told us that some years back she'd had a dream in which the sun rose red on the horizon and the whole of the sky and the earth was bathed in blood and the sun had Batista's face and a few days later the coup of the tenth of March took place. That's what this dream makes me think of too, that it could be a warning.

He was still silent.

—There are many things in dreams, Arsenio Cué.

—There are more things in heaven and earth, Silvestre, than are dreamt of in your phoenixophy.

Did I smile? I seem to remember I did.

—What are you getting at?

My smile vanished. Cué was ashen, his skin clung to his skull and looked like wax. He was a death's head. He reminded me of a dead fish.

—Me?

—Yes. You.

—In the dream, you mean?

—I don't know. That's for you to say. It's some time ago, some hours back, that I felt you, saw you trying to say something to me. The words had almost formed on your lips. Now you suddenly ask me, using the pseudo-Eribó as a pretext, something, I believe, about Vivian.

—It wasn't me who saw an Eribó when there was none.

—Nor was it you who had that dream.

—No. It wasn't me. I've told you so.

There was a sudden confusion in the dining room and people left their tables and the stools at the bar and ran to the door. Cué shouted something and headed in the same direction. I got up asking him what was going on what.

—Nothing! Fuck! Take a look. You're a great astronomer.

I looked. It was raining. It was the storm in the form of a torrential downpour. Niagara falls on Cué. *Niágara undoso. Templad Milira.* Pluck my lyre. Who was Milyre? An Heredia swan song? A Canadian girliefriend of Humberedia? *Templad mi lira/ Dádmela que siento/* The torrent falls on the last syllable. A wet rhyme.

—It's not my fault. I'm not the Gunga Din of God.

—I should have put the top up, dammit!

—They'll see to that in the parking lot.

—The fuck they will if I don't go myself. You're so damned naïve.

But he went back all the same and sat down to drink his coffee, quite calmly.

—Aren't you going?

—Hell no! It must be Bartlett's Depth in the car by now. I'll go when it lets up. (He looked at the street.) If it lets up. In any case it looks like we're stuck here for a while.

I sat down too. After all, it wasn't my car.

—Forget about the water, he said. —And listen to me. Or don't you want to listen?

He told me everything. Or almost everything. His story is on page forty-seven. He got as far as the fatal shots. He paused.

—But did he miss?

—No, he didn't. He got me. As a matter of fact I died that day. What you're looking at is only my ghost. Shit, wait a minute!

He ordered another coffee. A cigar. Do you want one? Two cigars. A Romeo here and a Juliet there. Generous was his middle name. A. Generouso Cué. Going through a spendthrift thrust in memories and in cigars. The end of the story came in the end.

I saw another mighty angel coming down from heaven, wrapped in a cloud, and he called out with a loud voice like a lion roaring. I couldn't hear what he said. The voice that spoke to me from heaven spoke to me again and said something else that was as cloudy as his head in the clouds. The heaven brightened and first I saw in the center an extinguished sun, and then, in the same part of heaven, a lamp, two lamps, three lamps—and then, a single lamp that was a conical tube hanging from a white ceiling. The angel had a pistol book in his hand. Could he be Saint Anton? But it wasn't a pistol book, or even a book, or a little scroll, it was simply a long pistol that he waggled in front of my face. I thought it had to be a book because every time I hear the word pistol, I reach for my book.

Hunger does strange things to you. I even listened to what he was saying.

—Go on.

Go? Where to? To the dining room? To bed with the water nymph? Back to the street and hunger? Because it was he and not He who was speaking.

—Go on, go on, he repeated. —You're a very good actor. You should have been a comedian and not a writer.

I wanted to tell him (hunger does things like that to you, you know) writers make the best actors, because they write their own dialogue, but I was unable to say a word. —Go on, Go on, said this man with his sudden whims and his steady income. His voice seemed to have a note of fear in it. But it wasn't fear.

—Go on. Get up. I've got a job for you.

I got up. With some difficulty but I got up, by myself. Unaided.

—Uppity-up! That's better.

All this time I was unable to speak. I looked at the angel and silently gave him thanks for not having let me eat the little book. Then I spoke to the man with my voice.

—When?

—When what?

—When do I begin my work?

—Oh. He laughed. —You're quite right. Come to the studios tomorrow.

I shook off the dust which those who fall and rise again always imagine they have on them, Lazarus' syndrome, and I went out. Before I left I looked at the angel for the last time and gave him thanks once more. He knew why. I felt sorry that I hadn't eaten the little book. However bitter it was, it would have tasted of ambrosia to me—or marzipan.

—What do you make of it?

—If it's true it's incredible.

—Every word of it.

—Shi-i-i-t!

—I'm going to let you keep your obscenities and other folk rhetoric to yourself. I won't tell you the rest.

—But what about the bullets? Why aren't you dead? How did you manage to recover from your wounds?

—None of his bullets hit me. I could tell you that he was a bad shot but he wasn't. The bullets were blanks. The perfect host only wanted to frighten me in passing, for a joke. Some time later he explained all that to me, he supported me, then made me a supporting actor, and finally gave me the lead. He told me then that he had wanted to teach me a lesson that day, but that it was actually he who had been taught one, because of the shock I'd given him. D'you see? It's Poetic Justice. Don't forget that I introduced myself as bard or troubadour at the court of King Candolle.

—What about your apparent death?

—Possibly it was hunger. Or fear. Or maybe I just imagined it.

I couldn't make out if he had imagined it then or now.

—Or a combination of the three.

—And Magalena? Is it the same girl? Are you sure?

—Why do your questions always come in threes?

—Everything happens in trees, Tarzan would say.

—It's got to be the same one. A little older, a bit more worn by the blows of life, her sort of life, not mean but mad now and with that mark across her nose. That was what put me off the track.

—She told me it was cancer.

—Cancer? Don't give me that shit. It's a symptom of hysteria.

—It could also be lupus vulgaris or perhaps even the erythematous exanthematic variety.

—Fucking wolf! The sound of it gives me the creeps. But whichever it is, it put me off the track though I was watching her closely tonight.

—I was watching *you* and thought you liked her. I was afraid you'd decide to swap. I didn't go for the aunt or pseudo-aunt at all however good-looking she may have been.

—Me? Like her? When have you seen me go for a darkie?

—It's always possible. She's a beauty.

—She was out of this world when I first saw her and I didn't go for her. She couldn't have been more than fifteen then.

—Thank heavens!

He ordered another coffee. Was he thinking of staying up all night? Why don't you drink tea? I asked, raising my voice. But did I raise the question? They make it very strong here and it tastes bad. Chesterton says that tea, like everything else from the Orient, is poisonous when it's made too strong. Could he have meant Oriente? I asked him. He smiled, but didn't say a word. I was sure I'd loaded the dice this time. But Arsenio Cué was more interested in his tragic poker strip than any other game in the world. Right now anyway.

—When I told you I'd spare you the obscenities I didn't mean any description of the marvels of the opposite sex, but the reverse. Some of them can't be told anywhere. On that day of disgrace time stopped. It did for me, at least. Afterward I fell from grace and into a pit deeper than the well of my dream or hallucination. The things, the things I had to do, Silvestre, to arrive! If I arrived anywhere at all. You couldn't imagine it. That's why I'm not telling you. Besides, it's you who'd vomit, I'm not going to at this stage, not with this charming chicken chow inside me. I'm speaking like that because our Friedrichmeister Nietzsche says you can't talk about things that are really important except cynically or in baby talk, and I'm no good at babbling.

Besides his voluntary cynicism there was a lot of instinctive self-pity. He was feeling sorry for himself, for Arsenio Cué or for euC oinesrA, as he called his alter ego—ego altered. Enuc

O'Raise. I arse on cue. One is a cure. I waited for him to go on, but he fell silent.

—What about Vivian?

He pulled out his dark glasses and put them on.

—Forget about your sunofabitch glasses for there's no sun. It isn't even a clean well-lighted place. Look.

The table was full of ashes and I thought it was from his cigar and that he hadn't noticed it. But a black speck came flying that I mistook first for an eye-fly, and then for a butterfly, some kind of insect, and it landed on my sleeve. I brushed it away with a finger and it fell to pieces. It was a bit of soot and I was surprised because I'd never seen soot fall in the night. It must be because factories don't work nights. There are some that work night and day. The sugar mills and the Puentes Grandes paper factory, for example. More flakes of soot came flying and landed on my suit and shirt and on the table and then a flurry of them swirled around the floor like a black snowfall.

—I thought it was a butternightfly.

—In my pueblo they call them *tataguas*.

—In mine too. Here they're called moths. Where I live they say they bring bad luck.

—In Samas they say the opposite, that they are a sign of good luck.

—It all depends on what happens after.

—Maybe.

He didn't like this skepticism among believers. I picked up a flake and it almost glittered, black in my hand between the pale lines of Life and Death and Fate, it swirled around the Mount of Venus for a moment and then flew away and settled on the ground.

—It's soot.

—Flakes of almost pure carbon. If it crystallized it would be called a diamond.

Cué made a clicking sound with his tongue, lips and mouth.

—And if my granny had wheels she'd be a Model-T Ford. Come on! he said, taking off his dark glasses and putting them on again. —It's just that all that wind and water have bust the chimney and sent the smoke and soot back into the kitchen.

His common sense astonished me. Of course he was right. I'd

never even thought of the kitchen, or of a broken chimney or the torrential downpour that had occurred in another hemisphere: of associating the soot with its maker. Even more practical, Pragmaticué called the waiter and pointed to the table telling him to clean it and close the kitchen door, please.

—They have good service, he said, —at Club 21.

I remembered that there was also a parrot of pragmatism inside him: an announcer of TV commercials.

—My hands are dirty, he said and got up and went to the inhouse. I went too and I don't think it was a coincidence.

XXI

I went too and I don't think it was a coincidence they had drawn a realistic top hat to indicate the right door. (There are wrong doors: morality in architecture: on the facade: over the entrance: *lasciate ogni ambiguitá voi ch'entrate:* there are no epicene ways to the jack.) A top hat. (To the gents.) A silk hat. (Silkroi was here.) Was Killjoy here? I asked Cué over the swinging doors behind which he was going through the sounds of pissing: Which came first, the water closet or the saloon? The answer-question to the other question which was my answer came like a shit. Wyatt Earpsenio Cué whipped out a couple of pistols.

—So you think you're a gentleman! Ain't I psychic?

Was he a southpaw? Dunno, but dey doan call me Wildbilly Hitchyourcock for nuttin.

—Mind your p's, chiaro amiCuo. I fired my sex-shooter thrice and every time I got him with those quick, sharp, dumb bullets of mine:

—Pray tell me, which is worse: to think you're a caballero or a cabalist? Or am I talking in cablese?

I saw him come out with his hands up and I thought he was giving himself up. But no, it was only a prefatory movement prior to going to wash his hands. He looked at himself in the mirror and parted his hair again. Parting is such sweet sorrow. He wasn't a southpaw in real life, only in the mirror.

—How about you, have you no faith?

—Oh, sure. I believe in many things, almost everything. But not in numbers.

—That's because you can't add.

He was right. He's right: I can hardly add.

—But didn't you say that mathematics was a lottery?

—Mathematics yes but not arithmatics. There was a magic of numbers before Pythagoras and his theorem, long before the Egyptians, that's for sure.

—So you believe in the precious stones in Lady Luck's kidneys, also called hedonic calculi. I believe in other things.

He looked in the mirror, passing a hand over his cheekbones which had been given a hard edge by the night he was leading, over his pale cheeks and his cleft chin. He recognized himself.

—Is this the face—

What did I say? A line of three, a lane of trees, Helena Trois. Who lunched a thousand shits.

—of the man who went into the youngle at twenty-two and didn't come out rich? I'm the living contradiction of Uncle Ben, not the one of the long-grained riches but Willy Loman's brother Ben.

—Trovato. Of the famous writing duetto Simone Evero e Ben Trovato.

—*You* know what I mean. You know I've lived dangerously.

—You still do.

—Yes, I live dangerously.

Arsenietzsche Kué. The poor man's Nietzsche. A niche for the boor.

—I'm saying that you live dangerously, just by being alive. *We* live dangerously, Arsenio Lupino. We are alive so we're all in danger.

—Of dying. You mean we're all going to die.

—Of living. I mean we the living have to live, as you say, howforever we can.

He looked at me and pointed to the mirror with his index finger and I didn't know if it was his south or north index.

—A contradictory. Of movies, literature or real life? Or do we have to wait for the final epicoda, like in those old Monogramed serials? Unmasked or Evilly the Kid Strikes Back?

He turned an imaginary crankshaft.

—You do believe in film.

—I was born with a silver screen in my mouth. I'm not a convert.

He pretended to write some invisible letters on the mirror.

—What about writing?

—I always use a typewriter.

He went through an exaggerated mime of someone typing. It was bad typecasting.

—Do you believe in words or in the Word?

—I believe in word benders.

—So you believe in our Honi Father Hugo who art in heavyside?

—Nerval heard of him.

—But you believe in literature, right?

—Shouldn't I?

—Do you or don't you?

—Sure I do. I've always believed in the written word, I always will.

—Don't forget that two of the men who've had most influence on history never wrote a line, or even read one.

I looked at him in the mirror.

—Come on, Cué, we know all that. Your duo's two names and one mystic mythic misfit. Christ crossed with Socrates. Christocrates. When you say literature, *caro,* I always understand Literature by it. Another history, in other words. But taking you at phrase value I can ask you, where would they be, The One and the other, without Plato and Paul?

A man of about thirty-three came in like some kind of answer.

—*Que sais-je? C'est a toi de me dire, mon vieux,* said Cué.

He looked at us as he pissed, puzzled, as though he thought we were talking Greek or Aramaic. Could he be a late-night prophet? Or a latter-day Platonist? Plotinus with physical needs?

—*Moi? Je n'ai rien a te dire. C'étais moi qui a posé la question.*

The man plugged his leak and turned to us. I saw he hadn't finished yet. He held up his hands. Suddenly he spoke and he said the one thing in the world that could most astonish us—if anything could astonish us this side of paradise.

—*Il faut vous casser la langue. A vous deux!*

Shit to Nemesis. To defatecate. He was French. A drunk Frenchman. *Chauvin rouge*. Cué recovered before I did and fell on him saying, *a quién, coño, a quién,* and then as though he was dubbing for himself, *a qui vieux con a qui dis-moi,* and he grabbed him by the shoulders and pushed him against the pissoirs, the old man (because he's suddenly grown old in the washroom) was uttering some astonished borborygms *mais monsieur mais voyons* and gesticulating like he was drowning in shallow waters. It was then that I decided to intervene. I gripped Cué under the arms. He looked like he was still drunk and the poor Frenchman who'd had his tongue or arm twisted so much he no longer spoke the language of Descartes but a langue de defecate made a getaway from our obtuse triangle, scrambled to the door with the top hat in a faux pas or two and vanished. I think that the three ends of his tie were still hanging. I said so and Arsenio Cué and I we thought they'd take us straight from the head to the headsman. We were killing ourselves laughing.

He wasn't there when we left. I thought Cué had gone after him, but he'd only looked out through the glass doors.

—It's still raining, shit.

Then he laughed and said *le cabron est disparu sous la pluie.* He went away singing in the rain. Banished. We laughed. When we got back to the table he asked me over his shoulder, Orson Welles style, which he did so well, truculent like a freshly shaved Arkadin:

—What do you make of it, my *anuttara samyak sambodhi*?

Cuétama Bugger meant his death and rebirth: his metaphysical resurrection. We're all very cultured in Cuba, if Cuba means me and my friends. Aside from the dangerous French, we also have a lot of useful English, some Castilian Spanish and a few phrases of Sanskrit thrown in. I begged that there shouldn't be a Bodhidharma among the customers. I also looked at him—a phoenix—and yawned sleepily.

—You are not yet risen from your own fame.

—That's what you think.

I took the plunge but he pushed me.

—Did you or didn't you sleep with Vivian?

—Y-yes.

—Now will you please take off your damn glasses. You don't need a mask. Nobody knows you here, man.

It was true. We were alone in the diner. There were two or three customers at the bar with their backs to us, and the singer and her accompianist, but they weren't performing. Were they rained out?

—Was she a virgin?

—Oh, come on, I can't remember details like that. Besides, it was some time ago.

—Yes and it was in another country and besides the wench is dead for you at least and now you go about and poison wells. Marlowe. The other Marlowe.

—Webster.

—We know what you're like, we even know when you're going to start quoting. We can see it coming.

—I wasn't going to say that.

He was genuinely embarrassed. I didn't think it was because of Vivian or anybody whose name wasn't Arsenio Cué or its anagram. Ane (sic) roué. He almost looked like he was about to imitate Quilty and say, "Ah, that hurts atrociously, my dear fellow. I pray you desist." Arsenio Quelty. The theater of Cuélty. A man with Cuélities.

—Did you sleep with her before Eribó?

—I don't know. When did Eribó sleep with her?

—He didn't.

—Then I *have* to have slept with her before he did.

—You know what I'm trying to say.

—I know what you're saying. What I've just heard.

—Were you the first person she's slept with?

—I didn't ask her. I never ask that kind of question.

—*Hombre,* come on, you're an old hand.

—Roué. It's more elegant.

—Turn it off for a minute, will you? Were you the first person Vivian slept with?

—It's possible. But I really don't know. She's studied ballet since she was a kid. Besides, we were both drunk.

—So she was lying to Ribot then?

—It's possible. If it's true what he says. Right, so she told him a lie, the cunt. Women always tell lies. They all do.

What followed, what he said next, was so astonishing that if I hadn't heard it myself I would have thought it was a lie. *Pour épater le blasé.*

—"*Allzulange war im Weibe ein Sklave und ein Tyrann verstecke.* (It wasn't just the quotation that was surprising but the German pronunciation he must have picked up from some actor. Cuérd Jurgens.) *Oder, besten Falles, Kuhe.*" *Friedrich Nietzsche, im Also Sprach Zarathustra.* (I was going to tell him, *No me jodas!*) That's a truth without a fig leaf. For ages in woman a tyrant and a slave have been concealed, that at best she is a cow. Xackly. Cows, bitches, creatures without souls. An inferior species. Kuhen.

—Not all of them. Your mother isn't a cow.

—Silvestre, *por favor,* what kind of predictable opinion or proverb or good sense are you giving me? I'm not going to take offense if you say she is one. You didn't know my mother. But I am going to get offended if you go on with this, with this stupid inquisition. Sure I slept with Vivian, what do you think? Sure I was the first person she slept with. Sure she was lying to Eribó.

—That night, the night I introduced you to Ribot, had you already slept with her?

—Sure. I think so. *Sí señor.* I had.

—When you were engaged to Sibila?

—That's enough! You know damn well I was never engaged to Sibila, that I've never been anybody's fiancé, that I detest this word as much as I hate the relationship, that I was going out with her same as you were going out with Vivian that evening. If I had better luck than you, don't go blaming me.

Is that what it was? Was I jealous? Was she my memory puzzle that love would solve?

—So you made a fool of me that night when I said she would go to bed and you came up with your theory of the ever-virgin typewriter?

—But, my God, so you believed that? It wasn't an adult's dose. It was meant for bongo players so as not to tell the truth to a poor fellow like Eribó.

—The truth being that you'd already slept with her.

—*No señor.* The truth being that she was using him. That she wanted to make me jealous. That she'd *never* sleep with him because he's a mulatto, and, what's worse, because he's poor. Don't you know that Vivian Smith-Corona comes from one of the best families?

Poor Arseny Country Cuéb, do you also come from a good family?

—And that's that. End of scene. Curtain.

He got up. He ordered the check.

—The only thing that bugs you is that you've been made a fool of. Please consider this sentence as an epilogue.

Was he right? I like this thesis that I'm afraid of looking like a fool better than the hypothesis of being in love with Vivian Smith. But I wasn't going to let Arsenio make the last phrase.

—Sit down, please.

—I'm not saying one word more.

—You're going to listen to me. It's me who's doing the talking now. *I* am going to have the last word.

—You must be joking.

He sat down. He paid the check, put a cigarette in his black-and-silver holder and lit it. He was going to chain-smoke all night now, until the room, the restaurant, the universe was filled with smoke. Cuértains of. How should I begin? It was the thing I'd been meaning to tell him all that night, all that day, for days. The moment of truth had come. I know Cué. All he wanted was to play verbal chess with me. Crossedwords.

—O.K., let's go. I'm waiting. You pitch. I don't want any spitballs.

What did I say? Baseball, that's living chess.

—I'm going to tell you the name of the woman of the dream. She's called Laura.

I was expecting him to hit the ceiling. I'd been expecting it for weeks, I'd been expecting it all day, all through the evening and the early part of the night. I no longer expected it. He didn't even jump up. But I had something you don't: his face opposite me.

—It was she who dreamed that dream.

—So?

I felt like a fool, more than ever.

—It was her dream.

—You've already said it. What else?

I fell silent. I tried looking for something better than the usual pat sayings and catchphrases. A phrase to catch. Words and sentences scattered here and there. It wasn't either baseball or chess, it was a seesaw puzzle. Crisscrosswords.

—I've known her for days. A month or two, rather. We've been going out. Together, that is. I think, I believe, no: *I'm going to marry her*.

—Who?

He knew quite well who. But I decided to keep to his rules. Doublecrosswords.

—Laura.

He made as though he didn't understand.

—Laura, Laura Elena, Laura Elena Día.

—Never heard of her.

—Laura Día.

—Díaz.

—Right, Díaz.

—Then why say Día?

Was I blushing? How could I tell? One thing Cué wasn't now is my mirror.

—You know where you can stuff it. Giving me a diction lesson this time of night.

—Elocution, you mean. Your problem is articulation, delivery.

—Stuff it.

—Am I bugging you?

—Me? Why should I be bugged? Quite the opposite, I feel great, tired but in great shape. Like a man who has no secrets. The only thing that bothers me is seeing you sit there like that.

—What do you want me to do? It's raining.

—I mean I tell you I'm thinking of marrying Laura and you just go on sitting there like that.

—I don't see why I should sit in any special way just because you say you're thinking of marrying. What about this pose? Or should I sit in profile?

—What about the name? Doesn't it ring a bell?

—It's an ordinary name. There must be at least ten Laura Díazes ringing bells in the telephone directory.

—But this one is *the* Laura Díaz.

—Of courts, your betrothed.

—Stop fucking around.

—O.K., your fiancée then. Or is it financée?

—Listen, Arsenio, please, I'm sitting here so I can talk with you and you don't bat an eyelid. Why?

—*Primo,* it was me who *dragged* you here and now I'm almost sorry I did it.

Was it the truth? At least it was true he'd insisted.

—*Secundo,* you tell me you're getting married. That you're *thinking* of getting married. I'm the first to congratulate you. At least I think I'm the first. With luck, I'll go to the wedding. I'll buy you a present. Something for the ménage. What more do you want? I'll be a witness if you like. Or your best man, if the wedding's in a church and as long as it's not in San Juan de Letrán, which I loathe, you know why: it doesn't have a bell tower and they play a record with the sound of bells over loudspeakers: a radio church. Honestly, I've done all I could. The rest, *mi viejo,* is up to you.

Was I smiling? I smiled. I laughed.

—Great, so there's nothing I can do.

—There is. You can introduce me to your bride.

—Go fuck yourself.

I looked over his shoulder. A sequence shot. People moving. The rain had let up. Patrons were coming into the restaurant. Or leaving. A waiter was sprinkling sawdust in front of the door.

One night in nineteen thirty-seven my father took me to the movies and we went past the town café, El Suizo, with its swinging doors and its marble-topped tables and a huge picture of naked odalisques over the bar, by courtesany of *Polar Beer the Beer Everybody Drinks and Everybody Can Be Wrong!* and a promised lapland of ice cream behind the counter, and meringues like sleeping beauties locked in a glass case and Pandora boxes of colored corn candies everywhere. That night on the doorstep we saw a funny stripe of wet sawdust. Funny because it hadn't rained in months. The stream reached the end of the veranda and trickled between the excited onlookers. In that café of the Far Eastern Province an action-packed Western had taken place. A man had gone mad and challenged a rival to a duel. They had been comrades and now they were enemies and there was a hatred between them that you only find between foes who have formerly been friends. "I'll kill you wherever I find you," one of them had said. The other man, more cautious or less experienced, trained in secret. The first man met him earlier that night sitting at the bar, drinking a pale rum. He swung a door open and from where he was standing, almost in the street, shouted, "Turn around, Cholo, I'm going to kill you." He fired. The man called Cholo felt a blow in the chest and fell against the zinc counter, pulling out his revolver at the same time. He fired. His rival fell with a bullet through his head. The bullet that had been aimed at Cholo (by pure chance) lodged itself in the silver glasses case he kept (by pure habit) in the inside pocket of his coat, on the left, above the heart. The sawdust hygienically or piously concealed the spilled vengeful blood of the challenger, now dead. We went on our way. We got to the theater. My father was distressed, I was excited. We saw an old film which had just opened starring Ken Maynard. The Rattler serial. The aesthetic moral behind this bloodstained fable is that Maynard dressed in black, daring and adroit, the black-minded Rattler, and the pale, beautiful girl are real people, are alive. But Cholo and his rival, who were friends of my father, the blood on the floor, the spectacular and absurd duel are shrouded in clouds of dreams and memory. Someday I will write this story down. But first I have told it like it is, to Arsenio Cué.

—Sounds like Borges, he said. —Let's call it the Theme of the Good Guy and the Heavy.

He hadn't understood. He couldn't understand. He couldn't see that it wasn't a moral tale, that I'd told it for its own sake, to communicate a minute memory, that it was an exercise in nostalgia. The past didn't make me bitter. I wasn't an angry young man. But he couldn't understand. Period.

—What was Cholo drinking?

—How the fuck should I know? I said.

—It wasn't a liqueur?

—I tell you I don't know.

He called the waiter.

—Sir?

—A couple of glasses of what Cholo drinks.

—What?

I looked at him. It was another waiter.

—Two liqueurs.

—Quantrow, benedicteen, marybreezer?

Was it another waiter?

—You choose, I'll sip.

He went off. Yes, it was another. Where'd he come from? Did they have a waiter factory at the back? Or had he been pulled out of the top hat?

—What was the dead man called?

—I don't remember.

I corrected myself.

—I never knew. I think.

The waiter returned with two little glasses of a liquor that the French Heredia would have described as *couleur d'ambre*. Cool it, *hombre*.

—Here's to your health and Cholo's better marxmanship, Cué said, lifting his glass. I wasn't amused, but I thought perhaps he was beginning to understand and I felt tempted to accept the toast.

—To friendship, I said and downed the glass in one gulp. But he became silent. Gulp a glass darkly. In a blackamood. Direobscure he. I hunted for money with a small display, as if wanting to pay the bill now that it was too late, and at the bottom of my pocket I found a new vision of bills—or a vision of new bills. Could he see surprise written all over my face? I pulled out the bills, all of them. There were three old crumpled peso bills, so blackened by loving handling that Martí almost looked like Maceo, plus two other bills, the kind Cué would have called billets doux. Billing and Cuéing. They were two white slips of paper folded double and I thought immediately that Magalena had left me a note. But what was the other slip of paper? Some advice from Beba? A note from Babel? A message from García? I unfolded them. Shit.

—What is it? Cué asked.

—Nothing, I said, meaning something else.

—You don't have to tell me if you don't want to.

I threw them on the table. He read them. He threw them back on the table. I picked them up, made a ball of them and threw them in the ashtray.

—Shit, I said.

—*Ah, qué memoria la tuya,* Cué said, parodying El Indio Bedoya in the stolen burros scene. —*Debe de ser el air-conditioningado.*

I picked the slips up again, and smoothed them out on the marble tabletop. I suppose that Arsenio isn't the last of the Muxicans and that there are still people left in the world with cuériosity.

DO NOT PRINT

Silvestre, Rine's translation is terrible to put it mildly. If I said it less mildly it would be wildly. Please could you make another version for me using Rine's text as source material. I also enclose the English original so you can see how Rine constructs his metaphrase, as you'd call it. Make haste not love. Remember we don't have a story this week and we'll have no alternative but to use something by Cardoso, that poor man's Chekhov, or by Pita, which is pitiful. (They'll pay Rine for the translation whatever happens. What's got into him that he is now using that incredible pseudonym of Rolando R. Pérez?)

GCI

PS. Don't forget to write me an introductory note in time. Remember what happened last week. The Ed was foaming Fab (that's our friendly neighborhoodetergent) at the mouth. Address it to Wangüemert.

BOX

12 Bodoni Bold—

Short Storytellers of U.S. . . .

William Campbell, no kin to the famous manufacturers of canned soups, was born in 1919 in Bourbon County, Kentucky, and has worked in a great variety of jobs before discovering his vocation as a writer. Currently he lives in New Orleans and is a professor of Spanish literature in the University of Baton Rouge, Louisiana. He has published three very successful novels (*All-Ice Alice, The Cod Came COD* and *Map of the South by a Federal Spy*) and has had stories and articles in the main literary quarterlies of the United States of North America. He was also a roving reporter for *Sports Spectator* at the 2nd Havana Rally held here recently. He has drawn on his experience in Havana in this stunning story which was published a short while ago in *Beau Sabreur*. The autobiographical device of the story becomes a literary joke of the finest vintage when one learns that Campbell is a conformed bachelor and sworn teetotaler and that he has not yet reach forty. This short story with its long name will have, then, a double or treble interest for a Cuban audience and *Carteles* takes great pleasure in offering it to its readers in its first Spanish translation. Now we leave the one in the hands of the other—and vice virtua.

—Shit, I said.

—Can't you take the note around tomorrow?

—I'll have to get up at dawn.

—At least you've done the translation.

—Hopefully.

—What d'you mean hopefully?

—All I did was to take Rine's translation and put the adjectives that were in front of the nouns after them.

—And vice version.

I only smiled. I picked up the slips of paper from the table, crumpled them in a ball again and threw them into a corner.

—Down with them.

—That's up to you, Cué said.

I pulled out one of the bills and laid it on the table.

—What's that? Cué asked.

—A peso.

—I know that, you bum. What are you trying to do with it?

—Paying for the drinks.

He laughed his phony actor's laugh.

—You're still a poetical prisoner.

—How do you mean?

—Didn't you hear what the waiter said?

—No.

—You've just been drinking free hemlock. It's on the house.

—I didn't hear him.

—Either you were dreaming memories or thinking of Rine's treason, or tradition or translation and how he managed to keep to the letter of the lawyal.

—It's stopped raining, I answered. We got up leaving.

XXII

Ain't gonna rain nomore tonite.

It isn't going to rain any more tonight.

—The passing of time's proved Brillat-Savarin right, Cué said, walking talking waving his arms. —It's more important today to discover a new recipe than a new star. (Pointing to the cosmos) There are so many stars *already*.

The sky had cleared and we walked under its leisure dome toward the Nacional.

—I should have brought my bailing pump. I invite you to take a ride in my boat, *caro*.

Swin' low, sweet Charon. I didn't answer. Everything was dark and silent. Even the drunken doll was dark and still. Shrunk not drunk. Cué didn't say anything either and our footsteps sounded more like footprints. In the skies there was a silence that lasted for light-minutes. When we got to the car, before we got to it because the light in the parking lot was still on, we saw that someone had put up the top and closed the windows.

—Well done, Cué said as he got in. —We're haigh and dry. A sober boat.

I sat in my seat, suicide as usual. We started up and he stopped at the gate, got out and woke the night watchman to give him a tip. He wouldn't take it. It was the other Ramón still. The friends of my friends are my friends too, he said. Cué thanked him and wished him good night. Tiltomorro. Habla Versalles. We drove off. He dropped me off five minutes later although El Nacional is only four blocks away from my home.

The shortest line between two points is the curve of the Malecón for Arsenio Einstein Cué. Torporlogy.

—I'm dead tired, he told me as he yawned and stretched. —Stone dead.

—Still stone gathers all moss.

—As *your* Marx says, *Better rusty than missing.*

—Consider him the Marx Bros. Companion to Soulitude. From here own you are on your on.

—You're forgetting the Old Man, old boy.

—The Old Man and the Seer?

—*Le vieux* M, the one who said that *le vrai néant ne se peut ni sentir ni penser.* Still less communicate.

—What a con man! He's the Great Cuntradictory, that's who.

He pulled on the hand brake and half turned to me, moved by inertia. Cué was alive and living in outer space and neither gravity nor friction nor the coriolis force could lessen his momentum *de la verdad.*

—You're in a state of herror, he Cuéoted.

I remembered Ingrid Bergamo, poor girl, who thought that Bustrófedon, poor son of a bitch, said good when he said you are miss taking. Ingrid Moe, bald, with Irenita Curly, the one we saw last night permanently waving good-bye and saying which twin has the Toni (not knowing that one was "Tony") together with Edith Cabell, doubly poor with her starry eyes and her hairdos a la page: they formed a threesome that could easily be taken for Curly, Larry, Moe. The Three Stooges. Poor dolls. Poor guys. All of them. All of oz. We two, we are poor too. Two hard-boiled eggos. Why wasn't Bustrófedon with us to make it three? The Three Mocksteers. It's better that He isn't. He wouldn't understand. There are no signs. Only sounds and, perhaps, furies.

—Really! You were talking about Sartre, the Saint Augustine of the Third Millennium, your Third Coming, weren't you?

—No, no. I'm not even talking about myself. I'm talking about you, *chico.* Groucho, I mean. Or rather, Harpooned Marx.

—Wordswordsworth.

—You're about to make the first really irreparable mistake in your life. You've had it coming to you. The other mistakes will all come under their own weight.

—Net or gross?

—I'm talking about gravity. With gravity. I'm being serious. Perfectly, terribly serious.

—Deadly serious. With a net, then. But Arsenio, *viejo,* who's going to take us seriously when we're so high-phalluting?

—We'll take ourselves seriously then. We're aerialists more than materialists. Can you imagine a trapeze artiste, in midair, doing a double or trouble summersault, asking himself: Am I serious? or Why am I doing these useless acrobathics instead of something serious? It's not possible. He'd fall. And he'd make the other fellows fall with him.

—Same with errors. Newton's Fig Law. Apples, like doubting trappists, tend to fall.

—O.K., but don't say I haven't tried to warn you. If you get married your life's as good as over. I mean, the life you lead now, you know. It's another destiny, a double death.

—I know quite well what you mean.

I can be Silvestre Innuendo when I want to. He looked at me squinting waving his arms making his mouth into an I.

—I'm just advising you. Without interest.

No percentage either: the rest is missionary silence. Lost in the junkle. Send Stanley Laurels. Dr. Dyingstone, I exhume.

—It's your mistake, not mine, he said. My Miss Take. Missed ache. Mistquote. Mixed Cué. Shall I miss Cué? Miscue. My missed cue. A cue line. Cuénard.

—I could tell you what Clark Gable said at the banquet or symposium on board, where they wouldn't admit the ghost of Jean Harlow because it's Plotinum blond, and Gable decided to go off with her and sail out on a low boat to China, saying, to quote the condemned man as they put the rope round his neck, "I'll never forget this lesson." I tell you: I'll take it, I'll swallow your advice in bed before breakfast and I'll lie on my right side.

He let go of the brake. I got out.

—I'll bet your wife, or *Cuéntame tu Viuda,* as we say in Spanish. Spellbound. B,o,u,n,d.

—I thought you were talking seriously.

—I'm jestingly in earnest.

In Ernest. Seriousian. The Doring Jungray in the frying trapiscis. Sometimes called Orsini Cué. Free falling as. He let go of the brake. I got out.

—Abyssinia.

I walked around to the other side of the car, almost sliding against it. As I reached his side he said, John Sebastian Cavotte, *que le vent du bonheur te souffle au cul* and please end well your trip around the underworld, and sleep well, bitter prince, and marry then, sweet wag, which was a prophetic Queote. For the benefit of my dying tongue he added:

—*Muchas gracias por el culo, Sir Caca.*

So I shouted back the blessure's mine, lord Shit-land! E. M. Forster was wrong, he thought that London was the swinging world and the Thames the Seven Seasons and saw his friends as the hole of humanity. Who would betray his fatherland or his motherland (Sumatriarchy is the father cuntry of us humaliars) to keep a friend, when he knows he can betray his friends and still preserve them like candid fruits, in a humanidor? Arsenio DelMonte and also Silvestre Libbys. But why shouldn't I say it truly *amigos* Havana is a cigar and not the capital of Cuéba. Call us Ismailiya. Small isle. The Assassinners. Sevener Elevener. Imam/Mami. Like Boustrophedon I decided to join the Silent Majority. Mymajority.

He let go of the brake. I got out.

—When you know who is the veiled contradictory, drop me a tarot card, he shouted over the cuécuécué of the engine revving up. —Write to me poste restante. That's my last resting place. And the echo of the narrow street split up his Cue-bid: —Marry Charistmas and Harpy New Yeats!

In the silence that the car left behind he climbed the steps with their dated palms in flower on either side and crossed the dark corridor alone and in silence fearing neither werewolf nor panther-woman and he took the elevator in silence and switched on the light in the car and turned it off again so I could go up in the dark and in silence he went into my apartment and in silence I took off my shirt and my shoes in silence and in silence I went to the *escusado* and pissed and I took out my smile in still more silence and in silence and secrecy he put the bridge in a vessel and in silence I hid this false truth high up behind the medicine cabinet and I went to the kitchen in silence and swallowed water in silence three glasses three in silence and he was still thirsty and I went off in silence with my stomach swollen and I massaged myself gently all over the Hemingsphere of his belly and in silence I goes out to the balcony but all I saw was the bay windows of the funeral parlor lit up in silence and the ad saying *Funeraria* of silence *Caballeros* where in silence they also underwake *señoritas* in silence and in silence I drew the blinds in silence and I went back in silence to my room and stripped myself naked in silence and I opened the window in silence and the silence of the last night came in through it in silence and also what they call dead of night that silent phrase and in silence I heard water dripping silently from the balcony above which was also silent and in silence I smoked my universal peace pipe and like Mortaldi-Bach I saw how silently the dead Havana rose in spiritual silence in something more than nothing in smoke of silence through the silent lighted hole of my port window which I looked at and looked in and looked through till it became round and disappeared, in complete silence, and I looked out there beyond the other side of the heaviside at the great dark prairies of the heavens and farther than that and farther than farther and farther still toward where there becomes here and all directions are the same and there is no place or a place which is no place with no up or down or east or west, ever-ever land, and I could see with these eyes of mine that the worms will eat, wicked wisdom of the West, I saw, the stars again, a few of them: seven grains of sand on a beach: a beach which is itself a grain of sand on another beach: a beach which is a grain of sand on another beach which is a grain of sand on agnother beach, just a tiny beach, the beach of a roadstead or pond or puddle that forms one of the infinite seas that swim in a bubble of a phenomenal ocean where there are no longer any stars because the stars have lost their name: the nulliverse, and wondering if Bustrófedon's sentity was expanding multiversally, the non-signs of his specter now on the rosy shift, moving like a Doppelgänger in my memory and thinking how a light year also converts space into a limited time while it makes time into infinite space, a velocity, a Pascalian ver*your mother should have told you* *yesterday not to lean over this bottomless well you will ask her again tonight repeatedly why it has no bottom and she'll repeat again because it comes out on the other side of the world and again you'll want to know and what is there on the other side of the world your other mother will be telling you always a bottomless well*tigo which waswillbe more terrifying even than the idea of the Martians infiltrating my own body, carrying the vampire in my blood vessels or nursing in my body an unknown microbe, which was the fear that in reality there are no Marxians or Martíans or any UFOs, that there is simply nothing or perhaps only nothingness, and in a state of terror in hemisfear afraid of staying awake more than of sleeping and vice universa, I fell asleep and I slept the whole night and the whole of the next day as well and a good bit of the next night since it was already sunrise, when I woke up in a state of error and everything was silent and I was the creature of the sleeping blackgoon and I took off my glasses and my pipe out of my mouth and brushed the ash off my lipstray and he let go of the brake, I got out and I went once more down the long vertical corridor in a state of coma and I said, then it was then was it, a word, I think, a girl's name (I didn't understand it: Clue's Ravel at Dawn) or perhaps something about women being actually the men of Wo, a queendome by the sea, and I went back to where I was sleeping dreamiendo soñing of the sea lions on page a hundred and a one in the Spannish varsion: *Morsas:* re-Morsas: Sea morsels. *Tradittori.*

Eleventh session

I had an awful quarrel with my husband because I woke him up crying. I was crying, he was sleeping. I didn't want to wake him up, but he woke up. He'd been sleeping for some time but I hadn't been able to get to sleep, because I was thinking about a little girl from my village who was very poor. You remember the girl who was a cook in Ricardo's parents' house, don't you? I can't quite remember if it was her or her sister or someone who looked a lot like her. The thing is that this little girl was very poor, but *really* poor, and she was an orphan too. She'd been adopted by the baker and she used to sleep in his store and worked very hard and she was the same age as me, but she was so skinny and so shy she walked all hunched up and timid to the point she'd speak to nobody except me and another girl who used to play with us too. Well, this girl used to work in the bakery and at night she slept in the store and the baker who'd adopted her slept with his wife in one of the rooms of the house. The baker had just got married and it was his wife who'd adopted the girl before she was married and one night there was a big uproar in the bakery because the wife woke up and heard a noise and went into the store and found that the baker had climbed into the cot where my little friend was sleeping. He was stark naked and had grabbed hold of her and pulled up the slip she wore in bed and he was trying to rape her or else he had raped her. The thing is he'd threatened to kill her if she said a word but to make sure she didn't scream he'd stuffed a roll in her mouth and that's when his wife came in and caught him. The whole village rushed out and they wanted to lynch him and two of the local police took him away and the man went off crying and his wife and daughter went with him (because the other little girl who used to play with us was the baker's daughter, he was a widower and he had this child ten years ago and she used to sleep in the other room in the house) and they went along shouting things at him and his daughter said, "You ain't my daddy anymore" and the woman insulted him and yelled at him that he deserved to be hanged. They gave him something like ten years in jail and then the woman and the daughter moved to another village and the little girl, my friend, that is, was taken in by another family and I used to go over there to play with her, it was about ten blocks away from my house, but in the same village. For a long time the kids used to make fun of her and even the grownups would say she'd let the man touch her and fool around with her and rape her (they didn't say rape but other things that meant the same, you know what I mean) and she used to cry and cry and I would shout insults at these kids and throw stones at them and I told my little friend that they were all liars, that they were just saying it to make a joke and she would cry and cry and say, "It's not a joke," and it wasn't, so every time I saw her she was more and more withdrawn. Finally we left and came to Havana.

I told my husband this story. I told it to him many times, but he always contradicts me, and says that he thinks this all happened to me and not to my friend. All I know, doctor, is that I don't know anymore if it happened to me or to my friend or whether I made it up all by myself. But I'm sure I didn't invent it. But there are times when I think that I am really my little friend.

EPILOGUE

fresh air I love fresh air thats why Im here I love perfumes thats what he thinks he makes faces at me faces faces faces Im going crazy with all his facemaking I love sweet perfumes thats what he thinks that Im going to kiss his putrid ass theres nothing better than fresh air the fresh air of nature I love the sun and sweet perfumes he makes faces faces faces and then he shove the seat of his dirty pants up my nose with so much water around us they have to shove their stinking ass-prints in your nose yessir people are like that filth and immoral Im with the Germans the ape punishes you the ape human flesh whats he grabbing my hand for Im sure hes gonna eat it hes gonna cook it and then hell eat it this ape he follows me around just follows me and follows tell me your moral principles Im protestant I protest against you all youre just savages powder of snakes of crocodiles of toads and you go crazycrazycrazy tell me your morals your moral principles your religion why dont you tell me Im not a witch or a sorceress or a santera all my family are protestants and they protest youre getting me mixedup now why are you trying to stick your law on me your dirty law you get race mixedup religion mixedup you mixup everything moral principles of catholics not ñañigos or spiritualist the air dont belong to you this aint your house you shove your nose in everything this stink is rotting my eardrums and the bells and the sane cells of my brain I cant go on like this anymore you push and push and push here comes the ape now with his knife hes shoving it in hes rummaging in my belly and pulling my guts out he wants to see what color they are for sure cant go no further